The Natural Order

The Natural Order: Book I

R.J. Vickers

Cover art by Amber Elizabeth Lamoureaux
Cover design by Maduranga

www.RJVickers.com
For orders, please email: **r.j.vickers@comcast.net**

ISBN: 1986157342
ISBN-13: 978-1986157346

This book is dedicated to Lindy and Kayla,
who never lost faith.

Chapter 1

Professor Merridy

Tristan Fairholm stood before his brother's grave, the shadow of the disciplinary officer stretched across the moss by his feet. He had been in juvie for three months, and his parents hadn't been to see him in all that time. They hadn't even let him attend Marcus's funeral. Of course not—they thought Tristan had crashed the car on purpose. They thought he had murdered his brother.

Tristan fingered the broken watch in his pocket. Marcus had given it to him just days before his death, a beautiful gold wristband with a few gears that had rusted through. Tristan loved to fix things—bikes, old clocks, splintered furniture—anything he could get his hands on. It made up for everything he couldn't fix. His parents' divorce. Marcus's weak heart. And now the ragged, rusting hole his brother had left behind.

But Tristan hadn't been allowed near any proper tools since his arrest. The watch remained broken.

Footsteps crunched in the bark behind Tristan, and the officer's shadow receded. He was probably off to smoke another of his foul-smelling cigars. Without looking over his shoulder, Tristan knew he was alone for the first time in three months.

I could run for it.

The thought crossed his mind like a spark, unbidden, but he hurriedly stomped it out. He didn't want to be a fugitive. He just wanted his family back.

The late afternoon shadows lengthened as Tristan stood there, hands in the pockets of his orange slacks, until the gravestone was half bathed in golden light and half in icy blue shadow. He didn't turn when he heard footsteps shuffling towards him, but it was not the officer. Instead, an unfamiliar woman spoke.

"You must be Tristan Fairholm." Her smooth voice was clipped.

Tristan grunted noncommittally. Were there any other bright orange delinquents wandering about the graveyard?

The woman took a step closer. "Your brother's death was not an accident."

"Who are you?" Tristan shot back. When he'd continued to insist on the earthquake story in court, he'd been hauled off for several rounds of questioning—once with an actress trying to convince him she could spring him free if he told the truth—to see if he was mentally unstable or just a very convincing liar. This woman had to be another questioner.

Tristan was still staring defiantly at the headstone when

something shifted at his feet. He blinked. Was it a mouse? No, something green was poking from the moss, and as he watched it began to grow taller. It was the stem of a plant, which shot higher and unfurled leaves in a matter of seconds, finally slowing when it reached Tristan's knee. He stumbled back a pace and shook his head to clear it as a drooping bud began to swell at the highest tip of the plant. An instant later the bud burst into bloom.

Tristan whirled to face the woman. "What's going on?"

She was tall and young, with narrow glasses and brown hair pulled back in a bun. "I can give you answers," she said with a thin-lipped smile. "My colleagues and I know exactly what happened. We know more than most. If you want to share in our knowledge, take a leap of faith and come with me."

"What happened that night? Why did I kill my brother?" His voice cracked on the last word.

"There are some who would say the death was necessary." The woman removed her glasses and polished them on her sleeve. "But a tragedy nonetheless. I beg your pardon—my name is Darla Merridy."

Tristan and Darla Merridy stared at one another in silence. Tristan knew she was examining the scars that gutted the left side of his face; even with a fringe of dark hair drawn low over one eye, the disfigurement was plain. Ever since the crash, Tristan had been treated with revulsion and fear; all but the most sympathetic detention officers shrank from the sight of his scars.

At last Darla Merridy slid her glasses back into place

and said once again, "Come with me."

Tristan cast a final glance at Marcus's name and turned to follow her down the path. He was learning to obey orders without question.

Even when they broke from the evening shade of the pines, Tristan could not see where the disciplinary officer had gone. Ten steps down, they left the graveyard behind and came to the curb where the officer had been parked. His car was no longer there. A moment later a taxi pulled up beside Darla Merridy. When she stepped back, waiting for Tristan to climb in first, he just stared at the taxi.

"Where the hell are we going?"

Darla Merridy's mouth tightened. "The airport. All will be explained presently."

Tristan stuffed his hands into his pockets. "You're taking me to an asylum, aren't you?" He had been terrified of this. If someone had decided he was insane, his life was over. He'd never be let free.

"No." Her eyes softened. "I promise you will never go anywhere near an asylum. Your records show that you are an intelligent, responsible young man who does not deserve to be locked away. Your criminal record will not accompany you to your new home."

Tristan swallowed. "Are we going far?"

She nodded.

He would never get a chance to see his parents. There were a lot of impolite things Tristan wanted to say to Merridy, but he didn't want to make trouble. If he had learned anything in the past three months, it was that a great deal of his future depended on this woman's first impression of him. So he closed his mouth and slid into the taxi seat.

"Jamestown Airport, please," Merridy said, joining Tristan in the back and slamming the door shut.

"I'd hate to be rude, ma'am," the driver said, turning to frown at Tristan, "but I'm not usually in the business of shuttling criminals about. Not helping him run away, are you?"

"Of course not." Merridy leaned forward and handed the driver a wad of cash through the plastic divider window. "There will be no trouble from us. Please, we have a schedule to keep."

The driver cleared his throat. "That seems perfectly reasonable," he muttered.

They drove for a long time, the sun setting as they passed beyond the city limits.

As the city fell behind, Tristan was left numb with emptiness. He had nothing outside of North Dakota—no friends, no relatives, no cities he would recognize. "Can I say goodbye to my parents?"

"You would impose yourself on them?" Merridy asked sharply. She sighed. "I apologize. That was unkind."

But it was true. Tristan sank lower in his seat, wishing he could be alone.

It was a relief when the terminal loomed ahead of them. The taxi driver seemed equally relieved to be free of Tristan; he pocketed Merridy's cash without a word.

Though the sun had vanished, Merridy bypassed the

doors into the brightly-lit terminal, instead leading Tristan around a dark corner and onto the tarmac. Something didn't seem right; surely the disciplinary officer would have warned him if he was about to be carted off to another state. And for what—tighter security? Compared with the other kids in juvie, Tristan was barely worth taking note of. What if Merridy was kidnapping him? No, that couldn't be right. How had she known his name?

Tristan hurried to catch up to Merridy, who was hard to make out in her black dress. Though it wasn't cold, he gave an involuntary shiver.

As they rounded another corner, Tristan saw a small plane, devoid of any company logo, standing in a pool of light near the parking lot fence. A ladder descended from an open door behind the cockpit.

"This is ours," Merridy said. Slowing, she let Tristan lead the way to the steps.

"Who's in there?" he demanded softly, trying to make out faces in the scratched-up windows.

"Young men and women just like yourself." Merridy put a hand on Tristan's shoulder and nudged him forward. "They, too, are getting a new chance at life outside bars."

Tristan swallowed and raked his hair more firmly into place over the scarred left side of his face. The broken watch was heavy in his pocket as he climbed the stairs into the plane.

He hadn't known what to expect from his fellow criminals, but he could tell from a look that they were just like the ones he'd taken pains to avoid at the detention center. A dozen pairs of eyes glared at him, hostile and arrogant.

"This is Tristan Fairholm." Merridy put a hand on his shoulder and nudged him forward. "Make him feel at home."

As she knelt to fold away the ladder, Tristan stumbled down the aisle, making for a pair of empty seats. He sank into the window seat, wishing Merridy had given him something to wear besides his bright orange jumpsuit. Only two others were still in their prison garb. Inadvertently he caught the eye of a beautiful red-head across the aisle; she gave him a sneer that turned his stomach.

Tristan looked quickly away and studied the heads of the two boys in front of him. One was still in his jumpsuit, and he had black hair that had been dyed an odd, pale yellow on top; the other's was a messy brown. As Tristan buckled his seatbelt, the boy with messy brown hair turned and grinned at him.

Then the small plane roared to life and surged into the air. Tristan leaned back and watched the dark sky beyond the window, unexpectedly excited—he didn't know where they were flying, but it had to be better than juvie.

Hours later, the plane descended through clouds and touched down near the faint speckling of lights that marked a small town.

"I have one final girl to collect," Merridy said, getting to her feet. "This should not take long, as she was warned of my arrival." Her tone grew icy. "Unlike you, Evangeline

Rosewell is not a criminal. You must treat her with the utmost respect. Also—Eli, Ryan, and Tristan, your street clothes are at the back of the plane."

"Have the damn clothes been there all along?" the boy in front of Tristan grumbled.

The messy-haired boy who had grinned at Tristan jumped to his feet and let his seatmate out. "Hey!" he said brightly, sticking out a hand. "You're Tristan Fairholm, right? Why'd Professor Merridy take so long to get you? We figured you were extra dangerous or something."

Tristan snorted. "Well, I'm not." He didn't shake the boy's hand.

"I'm Rusty Lennox, by the way. That's Eli." He nodded at the boy who'd gone in search of the new clothes.

"Catch," Eli called from the back of the small plane, tossing a bundle at Tristan's head. He already had his jumpsuit zipped down to the waist and his arms through the sleeves of a cleanly-pressed white shirt. Trying not to glance in the direction of the beautiful red-head, Tristan struggled into the new clothes and finally kicked his garish jumpsuit under the seat. The fabric felt stiff and grainy after the sagging orange uniform.

"Makes you feel like a person again, doesn't it?" Rusty asked with a lopsided smile.

Tristan just nodded. Meanwhile, Eli stomped vigorously on his bedraggled jumpsuit before resuming his seat.

Leaning forward, Tristan asked in a low voice, "Where are we going, then? Has she told you guys?"

Rusty shook his head. "Some sort of school, I think, though she won't say where. But it doesn't matter, does it? I'm just excited we're going somewhere new!"

"Right," Tristan said dubiously.

Not ten minutes later, Professor Merridy returned with Evangeline Rosewell, who was hovering so close to the teacher that her face was at first lost in shadow. Tristan sat up straighter, and when he finally saw Evangeline's pale, nervous face, he felt a surge of protectiveness. The look in her pretty, downcast eyes reminded him of Marcus returning to school after his first seizure. Clutching a ratty backpack to her chest, she looked completely lost.

At a nudge from Merridy, Evangeline shuffled down the aisle to the empty seat beside Tristan, where she sat stiffly and turned away from him.

"This is everyone," Merridy said. "You will be spending the rest of the school year together, so I recommend you become acquainted. From this point onward, you may forget what happened in your past. You are equals here—each of you has been hand-picked for this school."

Glancing left at the sneering red-haired girl, Tristan shook his head. 'Hand-picked' was not the word he would have used to describe the group. And what on earth were they doing? This couldn't be a routine relocation, or anything the juvie court would have arranged.

Instead of answering the unspoken questions on the face of every student, Merridy returned to her seat just in time for the plane engine to grumble to life. Tristan crossed his arms, still unaccustomed to the stiff fabric of the new shirt, and watched Evangeline out of the corner of his eye as the plane turned onto a badly-lit runway and again took to the air.

Soon Evangeline's ragged brown hair blurred to darkness, and Tristan was again reliving the final hours of Marcus's life.

It had been a strange night. Tristan and his brother had been alone when the house started shaking, and they had fled as the roof began to crumble. But not even their next-door neighbors had reported feeling the earthquake. Tristan and Marcus had tried to escape to their mother's home in the next town over, but they never made it.

Again Tristan heard the sirens, and that awful, flat voice that had haunted his dreams—*he's dead*. The two simple words had ended everything.

The plane gave a jolt, wrenching Tristan from his thoughts. Feeling nauseous, he glanced at Evangeline, who was frowning determinedly at the back of Rusty's head.

For a long time neither one spoke, and Tristan began to doze off once again. But that was dangerous. He didn't want to think about Marcus, not here, not with so many strangers around him. Desperate for a distraction, he finally turned to Evangeline.

"So you're Evangeline, right?" As if he could have forgotten. The expression she turned on him was just as achingly vulnerable as before. He wanted to comfort her, but he could not find the words. Fumbling for something appropriate to say, he settled on, "Can I call you Evvie?"

"No." Her mouth hardening, she turned even more firmly away from him.

"I'm Tristan." He endeavored to keep his voice pleasant. "It's nice to meet you."

"Stop talking to me," Evangeline said crossly. "I'm trying to sleep."

"No, you're just sitting there," Tristan said at once. "Are you trying to meditate, or something?" A second later he regretted the jibe.

"Be quiet," she snapped.

Tristan swallowed hard, trying to smother his temper, and his ears popped.

"You know what?" Evangeline said after a pause, fixing Tristan with a hard look. "I don't like boys with long hair." She flicked a strand of her own straight-cropped hair behind one ear. "You look like a slob with your hair all over your face like that."

"Well, I think Evangeline is a stupid name." Without knowing why, he turned and brushed his hair off his face so Evangeline could get a good look at the scars. "Do you like me better this way? Is that what you want?"

Evangeline gasped and jerked away from Tristan, nearly tumbling off her seat.

Tristan let his hair fall back into place, an ugly smile crumpling his face.

Now the roar of the plane sounded like the wailing drone of sirens—breathing hard, Tristan fumbled with his seatbelt and jumped to his feet. He kicked Evangeline's backpack to the side and stalked to the back of the plane, where there was a single empty seat next to a sharp-faced girl.

"Mind if I sit here?" Tristan asked in a choked voice.

The girl turned, revealing a scattering of freckles across her nose and dark eyes to match her long, black hair. "Sure. I'm Leila Swanson, by the way." She scrutinized Tristan for a while, her gaze curious rather than hostile. "Don't judge yourself by what the orphan girl thinks of you," she said bitterly. "People like her—well, they don't think we're even people. If she'd been to Juvie, she'd know."

"I suppose," Tristan muttered, slumping into the seat beside her.

Leila must have caught sight of his scars, because she leaned suddenly forward. "What happened to you?"

Tristan pressed his hair firmly down. "Nothing."

Leila stared at him, one eyebrow raised in disdain.

"You know what?" Tristan said coldly. "I don't even know why I'm talking to you. You're no better than Evangeline."

"Thanks," Leila said sarcastically.

Feeling claustrophobic, Tristan stared at the seat in front of him until his eyes began to drift closed.

In the foggy darkness, Marcus swam into view, eyes wide and soulless. He touched Tristan's arm with fingers icy as death. *I trust you.* A flash of red light, and Marcus screamed.

My fault, all my fault.

"Tristan?" Someone was shaking his arm.

He flinched, his eyes flying open. It was Leila.

"You all right?" There was no trace of sarcasm in her voice.

Tristan clenched his fists. "Talk to me, would you?" he whispered. He was frightened. "Just keep talking."

Eventually Leila nodded and said, "Do you remember the story of Beauty and the Beast?"

Tristan didn't reply; he knew that she was referring to him as the Beast, but he couldn't bring himself to care.

"Once upon a time…" Leila's voice lowered to a murmur as she began the story. It was soothing, and the words gave Tristan something to focus on. In Leila's version, the prince challenged a soldier to a fight and lost, whereupon he limped home and locked himself in his palace, hideously scarred and too ashamed to show his face.

"I thought he was put under a spell," Tristan said.

"This is a *retelling*, you dolt," Leila said. "I'm glad you're listening."

"Of course I'm not."

Leila continued her story. The hum of the engine turned her words into something melodic, and Tristan half-closed his eyes as he listened. When she finally finished with, "And they lived happily ever after," Tristan sat up again and rubbed his eyes.

"Lucky Beast," he grumbled. "But it was a good story."

Leila was watching him with a peculiar expression. "Could I see—?" she ventured.

"No," Tristan snapped. He took a deep breath.

"Thank you, though."

Chapter 2

The Lair

By the time the plane began its descent, Tristan's eyes were dry and splintery. He had been playing hangman with Leila for the past several hours, his guesses growing wilder with each round.

"Thank god," Tristan said when the plane sank into the low cover of clouds. "I thought we'd keep going all the way to China." He massaged his aching head and turned to watch the wisps of cloud flitting past.

"Where do you think we are, anyway?" Leila pressed her forehead against the window.

He just shrugged. A moment later, he noticed dark shapes whipping by the wing, their forms indistinguishable in the mist. It wasn't until the plane jolted and then roared to a halt that Tristan recognized the shapes for enormous bushy pines.

They had landed.

Ahead of them, Merridy got to her feet to address them once again. "Please be sure to—to—"

She had to cover a yawn with her hand; the momentary weakness made her look much younger and less severe.

"Please bring all of your belongings with you. You will not want to return to the plane. The school is still a good distance from here."

Unbuckling his seatbelt, Tristan leaned over Leila to peer outside. He could see nothing but heavy gray fog and the ghostly outlines of trees.

"There's nothing to see," Leila said. "I can barely make out the runway."

As Tristan descended the ladder from the plane, a chill breeze raked through him. Shivering, he joined Leila and the other students milling around on the runway.

The last person to appear through the hatch was a white-haired, round-faced man who had to be the pilot. When he turned to face the students, he was beaming.

"So nice to meet you at last," he said cheerfully. He would have looked like Santa Clause if he grew a beard and put on a few pounds. "My name is Gerard Quinsley, and I'm part of the school's faculty. That is, if we ever manage to get there."

Chuckling, he sidled over to Merridy.

"Well, that was a boring flight, eh, Darla? I always hate flying over clouds. But the headmaster seemed to think it was for the best…"

"Gerard!" Merridy said sharply, cutting the pilot off midsentence. "Enough."

Winking at the students, Quinsley turned and began

leading the way down the airstrip.

As Tristan and Leila started forward, the kid who'd spoken to him earlier turned once more.

"Hey!" Rusty said brightly. Tristan noticed that one of his front teeth was cracked so it looked like a fang.

"What are you talking to us for?" Leila's tone was unnecessarily cold.

Rusty shrugged. "I think Eli was getting annoyed at me."

"So you thought you'd come bother someone else?" Leila said. She didn't complain when Rusty fell into step beside her, though.

Tristan rubbed his eyes and turned up his collar; the air seemed to be growing colder already.

"Maybe we're gonna walk to the school," Rusty said.

Tristan groaned.

"We're still in the airport, stupid," Leila said. "And I don't know why you'd want to walk anywhere."

"It's like an adventure," Rusty said. Taking a running start, he leaped over a patch of grass between the airstrip and a dirt path.

"Through a dumb airport," Leila said, rolling her eyes.

Tristan glanced back at the two students behind him. "I don't think this is an airport." As far as he could tell, this was no more than a lone patch of concrete in the middle of a forest.

One of the kids behind him was the red-haired beauty, and when she caught his eye she glared at him again. Lowering his voice, he said, "Who's that?"

Rusty looked over his shoulder and made a face. "That's Cassidy McKenna. She's not very friendly."

"Most of them aren't," Leila said, exasperated. "What were you doing before Tristan got here, playing musical chairs?"

Rusty didn't answer. Now Quinsley was leading the way down a narrow dirt trail, the mist growing colder and wetter with each step. When the icy air nibbled its way into Tristan's skin, he tucked his chin into the collar of his shirt.

"What d'you think this school's gonna be like?" Rusty asked, his spirits not marred by the cold or the unsettling silence. "Seems awfully secretive, doesn't it?"

Though Leila was still scowling at Rusty, she seemed to decide after a moment that his question wasn't too stupid for her to answer. "We're all criminals, remember?" she said. "Except Evangeline, of course. The school had to be somewhere remote, because we're not supposed to be allowed back into regular society yet."

"Yeah, but how come this place wants a bunch of kids like us?"

Leila shook her head. "No idea."

The three of them were quiet for a moment. When Rusty bounded forward to rejoin the kid with the oddly dyed hair, Tristan fell back, pressing his hair more firmly over his face. It was incredible to think that he'd left the detention center only hours ago—this eerie, ancient forest seemed worlds away from that reality. Maybe he could just pretend that he was someone new, that Marcus would be waiting for him back with his parents…

Again craving distraction, Tristan hurried to rejoin the group ahead of him. "You're the one with all the knives, aren't you?" Leila was saying to Eli. "I can't believe Professor Merridy found them all."

Eli grinned ruefully. "She got every last one."

Leila turned and whispered to Tristan, "Professor Merridy searched a few of us before you got here—she was confiscating weapons and drugs and electronics."

Tristan narrowed his eyes.

"It was a bit creepy, actually," she said. "It was like she knew exactly who to search—everyone she called out was hiding something, and the others say they weren't."

"Were you hiding anything?" Tristan asked. There was something very odd about this whole thing, something ominous.

"I had a knife." She must have seen something in Tristan's expression, because she snorted. "Really, Tristan, I'm not a serial killer."

Eventually they reached the smooth stone beach of a lake, its surface shrouded so heavily in mist that it appeared ethereal. Tristan's hopes that there might be a warm boat waiting for them were quickly dashed when the white-haired Quinsley emerged from the forest and began shepherding them along the shore. Their progress raised a clamor as they slipped and stumbled over the damp stones. Moments later, the mist had closed around Tristan and Leila again.

In the silence, odd thoughts and unformed illusions nagged at Tristan. Though he tried to suppress the idea, he couldn't help but imagine that this was some sort of border between life and death, a lake where the dead passed into the next world. He was almost convinced he saw pale bodies floating beneath the water, reedy and emaciated.

A long time passed, the darkness growing deeper and deeper. The slap-slap of waves was hypnotizing.

Suddenly he caught sight of a ghostly white figure floating towards him on the water. It was standing motionless, its arms raised, almost translucent beneath a cloak of mist.

For a moment Tristan couldn't breathe. The last of his warmth drained away…

Something caught his foot and he stumbled forward, grabbing Leila's shoulder to steady himself. He shuddered as he wrenched free of the spell. "Sorry," he said hoarsely, straightening. Now that he looked properly, he realized that the ghost was just one of the girls from the plane, standing motionless in a canoe that she must have stolen from the shore.

"Who's that?" Leila asked sharply.

"No idea." His voice sounded too loud. Now that he thought about it, Tristan was surprised that he hadn't noticed her before. The girl was pale and wraithlike, with wispy white hair, and her large eyes were striking as the only color in her face. She didn't seem to realize that Tristan was watching her—instead, she stared at the fog overhead with a curious sort of fascination. A moment later, she vanished once more into the gloom.

Not long after, the fog lifted slightly to reveal a tall,

grassy slope rising from the lake's edge. Without waiting for the others, Merridy turned away from the lake and started up the hill.

Glancing around the group, Tristan realized that the strange girl was missing. She was probably still floating somewhere on the lake.

"You go ahead," he said. "I'll catch up."

Leila started to protest, but Rusty grabbed her sleeve and dragged her forward.

Quinsley jogged past Tristan to join Merridy. "I could've sworn I saw a boat drifting off across the lake," he said, frowning. "But I must've imagined it."

Merridy's eyes narrowed. "You should have been keeping a better watch on the students. They were supposed to stay away from the water."

Quinsley's reply was too quiet for Tristan to hear.

As Quinsley and Merridy guided the students away from the lake, Tristan dropped to his knees by the water's edge to wait for the wraithlike girl.

The mist was tinged with black now, signaling the approach of nightfall. It swirled in spirals over the lake, creeping closer and closer to the shore. Tristan could barely see beyond the small circle of rocks and water where he was perched, and when the students' excited voices faded in the distance, the silence swelled around him.

He was utterly alone.

In the stillness, he felt Marcus's loss more keenly than ever. If he just reached beneath the icy water, he thought he could drag his brother back to him. It was here that Marcus had come to rest, surely, not in that dusty old graveyard. Tristan pressed his palms to the damp rocks and hunched forward, remembering Marcus's beautiful, solemn face and his dark curls pressed against the car window. Tears burned his eyes, but he made no motion to wipe them away. They traced hot lines down his cheeks, quickly going cold. Marcus was gone, gone forever, gone where he would never come back.

Tristan didn't notice the approaching boat until it scraped gently against the rocks. The strange girl was still standing at its prow, eyes closed and arms extended like wings, her face glowing moonlike above the water.

Tristan jumped to his feet and scrubbed at his eyes.

At the sound, the girl's striking turquoise eyes flew open. There was no revulsion or scorn in her gaze, merely surprise.

Tristan sniffed and wiped at his nose. "What's your name?" he asked awkwardly.

"Amber."

"Do you need help with your boat?" Tristan bent to take hold of the line bolted to the prow, trying to hide the evidence of his tears from her unblinking stare.

Amber said nothing, though she let her arms fall to her side. As a swell of water sent the canoe scraping farther up the shore, she stepped gracefully onto the rocks. The boat did not shift with her weight, as though she truly was a ghost. Tristan brushed his hand against her wrist in the pretext of helping steady her, just to reassure himself that she was solid.

After a moment, Amber turned and stared back at the water. "You waited for me," she said faintly. It was almost a question.

"I guess."

When Amber stepped back from the water's edge, looking wistfully at the fog, Tristan reached down and dragged the canoe out of the water. He gritted his teeth, and with a reluctant groan the canoe slid forward onto the beach. At least he wasn't crying any longer.

"Thank you," Amber said, wonder in her voice. "That was very generous of you."

"Why did you go across the lake?" Tristan asked. "You weren't supposed to."

He began walking towards the hill; after a moment Amber came ambling along behind him.

"I wanted to leave. The current is very strong—I tried to fight it, but it led me here." Amber brushed her wispy hair from her face.

"You were trying to run away?" Tristan said. "You would die out there!" He glanced back at the empty canoe and frowned. "Besides, how were you supposed to go against a current with no oars?"

"There are other ways."

Tristan blinked. "Well, let's hurry and see if we can catch up to the others. The fog looks like it's getting worse, and I don't want to get lost."

Though Amber made no reply, she started moving slightly faster.

When they finally reached the top of the hill, Tristan

was clutching at his side and panting; he sighed with relief when he saw a circle of dark shapes just ahead. Beyond the small group, a carved wooden arch marked the start of a clearing that vanished into the fog.

"Thank goodness," Merridy said somewhat breathlessly when she saw Tristan and Amber. "I cannot believe we nearly lost you." As Tristan and Amber joined the circle, Merridy gave Quinsley a disapproving glare.

"It's all right," Tristan said, glancing at Amber. Her gaze was still distant, fixed on a point above the trees. She didn't seem to notice when Tristan left her side and rejoined Leila.

"Hey, Tristan," Leila said, her tone exasperated but grateful. "Thanks for not *completely* abandoning me."

Tristan blinked in surprise. "What's wrong? Weren't you with Rusty?" He shoved his numb hands into his pockets.

"No, of course not," Leila said coldly. "Rusty wanted to make friends with *Zeke*."

"Well, sorry I left," Tristan whispered as Merridy began talking again. "Amber decided to take a canoe, and she needed help with it."

When Merridy turned to reprimand Quinsley, he interrupted her.

"Come on, Darla." Quinsley was stamping the ground and rubbing his hand together. "We're all here now, and that's the only thing that matters. Let's talk inside, where it's warm and we can see properly."

Merridy pursed her lips. "Indeed. The other professors

should be waiting."

"Oh, thank god," Leila said. "I can't feel my toes."

Already the warmth Tristan had gained jogging up the hill was gone, leaving his hands stiff and useless. He hoped that the school wasn't as drafty as the location suggested.

"However," Merridy continued, narrowing her eyes, "you will each need to relinquish the majority of your belongings before you are allowed down to your beds."

"What's the matter with you?" protested a short-necked, hulking boy Tristan thought was called Damian. "Haven't you stolen enough of our stuff already?"

Tristan didn't even own the clothes he was wearing, so he hardly cared. He just wanted to get out of the cold.

Ignoring Damian, Quinsley stomped around to the front of the group and began hustling the students forward. As they drew near, Tristan realized that the arch was made up of hundreds of carved, stylized creatures, reminiscent of a totem pole.

Past the arch, the school buildings loomed—they were hulking structures in the style of old Native American longhouses, encircling a clearing that seemed in danger of disappearing into the fog.

Just after she passed beneath the arch, Merridy turned left and drew back the doors of the nearest longhouse. Tristan hoped there was a fire inside. Past the creaking doors, though, the structure was completely empty. The longhouse smelled musty and sweet, like an old barn, and there was nothing inside apart from a flight of stairs gouged into the dirt floor.

Without pausing, Merridy continued onto the stairs and started down, her figure disappearing almost at once into the darkness.

With a skeptical glance at Leila, Tristan put a hand to the dirt wall of the stairs and followed. Even at the top he could barely see where to place his feet; three steps down, he could see nothing at all. He trailed his fingers along the packed dirt, searching with the toe of his shoes before trusting his weight to the next step.

Then the outline of Leila's head disappeared altogether. "Leila?" he muttered. "You still there?"

There was no reply.

Swallowing hard, Tristan looked back up the stairs. He was completely alone in the darkness. Grasping for purchase on the dirt wall, he hurried down the next few steps.

Suddenly everything changed.

The stairway filled all at once with blinding light. Tristan stumbled and clutched at the wall, but even that was wrong—the cold dirt had become smooth stone. Warm air rose around him, lacing its way through his frigid shirt, and he shivered as the cold began to relinquish its grip.

He couldn't believe what had just happened. He had passed through—what, solid air?—and ended up somewhere warm and bright and completely unreal.

Leila was just ahead of him on the stairs, staring at him as though he'd just dropped out of the sky. Blinking in surprise, Tristan looked back up the stairs. One step above where he stood, the stairwell was blocked with a curtain of black streamers. Stranger still, the light ended abruptly just beyond the streamers. Not a single beam of light passed through—if Tristan hadn't just walked through the space, he would have sworn it was a solid wall.

"What the hell was that?" Leila asked in a hushed voice.

Tristan shook his head. Whatever had happened, it was so strange, so *unnatural,* that he couldn't begin to comprehend it.

Looking down the stairs, he noticed for the first time where he was.

The stairs ahead were carved from white marble, and at their base, the steps widened before giving way to a gleaming marble floor.

Gripping the bronze rail with one hand, Tristan walked carefully to the foot of the stairs. From here he could see the full room spread out before him. It looked like an enormous ballroom, its tall ceiling radiant with light from five chandeliers that dripped candles like dew-encrusted flowers. The center of the floor was marked by a many-pointed star, each tip cut from stone of a different color. Directly across from where Tristan stood, the marble floor rose two steps up to form a sort of platform cut into the wall.

"I didn't realize we'd come down so far," Leila said in awe.

Tristan, still wide-eyed in shock, couldn't think of a reply.

Merridy and Quinsley were both standing at the edge

of the platform, in front of a cluster of chairs and tables set for dinner. As Quinsley shrugged off his coat and slung it over the back of a chair, Merridy's face softened into a smile.

"Welcome," she said, "to the Lair."

Chapter 3

Professor Brikkens' Show

Eventually the students were all seated at the round tables on the platform—Tristan and Leila joined a pair of unfamiliar girls, while Rusty sat with Eli and Trey.

As the students glanced around expectantly, Damian voiced what everyone was thinking. "Where's the food?" he asked loudly. "We're starving."

Quinsley smiled indulgently. "We'll eat soon enough. Abilene Gracewright prepared the feast tonight, since I was off fetching you lot. I hope she's a decent cook."

"Yes, but when are we going to eat?"

"As soon as—ah, here they are," Quinsley said.

On the far side of the ballroom, a pair of enormous double doors swung open, admitting a group of five professors. Their leader was tall, thin, and dark-haired, with a narrow face and sunken eyes. As he strode forward, his gaze flicked between the students, glaring at each in turn.

No one spoke while the professors filed onto the

platform and stood in a circle around their large table; beside them, Merridy looked frightened and very small.

"Sit down," the leader snapped at the other teachers, who hastened to obey him. One man was rather large, while another was pale and dour and looked something like a vampire. The tall man remained standing.

"I am Professor Drakewell. I am the head of this school, and I do not tolerate laziness or rulebreaking." He looked directly at Damian as he said this. "I detest childishness, so I expect you to behave as adults while you are here. You have been given a remarkable opportunity to remake your lives, something many of your inmates would have died for. If you do not show the proper gratitude, your professors will—enforce it."

Professor Drakewell lifted a chain on his neck to reveal a sort of pendant, which he tapped with a thin finger.

"There are three rules here—first, do not stray off the marble floors."

Tristan was not alone in glancing down at the polished stone underfoot.

"Second, do not consider wasting my time."

Again he fingered the pendant.

"And third, obey all further rules as given by your professors."

When Professor Drakewell dropped his hand from the chain at his neck, the pendant glinted in the light from the chandelier—Tristan realized it was a tiny hourglass filled with black liquid. Then Professor Drakewell took his seat at the teachers' table, leaving the ballroom quiet and uneasy.

"Ahem," Merridy began, her voice squeaking slightly. When she tried again, her voice was steadier. "Let me introduce your professors. This is Professor Grindlethorn." She gestured to a stocky, hook-nosed man across the table from her.

The large, cheerful man was Professor Brikkens; the vampire was Professor Alldusk; and the other two, a tiny woman and a bald man, were Professors Gracewright and Delair.

Finally Merridy was finished with introductions. Once she was seated, Quinsley leaned forward and rapped his knife on the rim of his wineglass.

"Abilene Gracewright, bring us our dinner!"

Tiny Professor Gracewright jumped to her feet and scurried to a door on the side of the platform, through which she reappeared a moment later pushing a cart laden with food. When the door swung closed behind her, the aroma of spiced chicken wafted through the ballroom.

As she passed around bowls and platters of food so large that they barely fit on the tables, the students began muttering once again.

"This is fancy," Tristan overheard Rusty saying from the next table over. Rusty was examining his fork, turning it over and over to look at the design.

Leila shook her head at Rusty. "I'll admit, he's right," she said. "It's not just the forks, though. It's the whole place—this ballroom looks like it belongs in a palace, which is even more impressive considering we're underground."

Tristan nodded and looked up at the high tiered

ceiling. "I wonder how they got so much money."

Leila just shrugged, and a moment later their food arrived. There were mashed potatoes mounded beside a gravy boat, chicken wings in a creamy sauce, ravioli with mushrooms, and sourdough rolls in a basket.

"Finally," Leila said, moaning with relief. She dragged the potatoes towards her plate and spooned them on, drenching them so vigorously with gravy that she splashed Tristan's arm. Tristan grabbed a roll, still warm, and tore off a piece with his teeth. Inside the brittle crust, the bread was soft and airy.

The feast went on until late into the night, rounded off with a towering chocolate cake that could have fed Tristan's entire high school.

Drakewell got to his feet as Professor Gracewright came around collecting plates. "Gerard, you will escort these students to the bunkroom. See that they obey you."

He turned and strode across the ballroom.

"Lovely," Quinsley said, chuckling, as the doors swung closed behind the headmaster. "I'm the jack of all trades around here, I suppose. I fly planes, I cook, I herd students all over the woods—"

"Badly, I might add," Merridy said, some of her sternness gone now that the headmaster was away. "Losing two out of fifteen students must have been quite a feat."

A few of the students laughed at this, and Tristan smiled drowsily.

"I suppose I'd better show you kids where you're sleeping," Quinsley said.

His chair screeched against the marble as he pushed himself away from the table.

"I don't want any of you passing out here; I'd hate to carry you down three flights of stairs." He was looking at Evvie, whose eyes had drifted closed. Her chin was resting on her fist, but she looked in danger of falling into her plate. When the tall girl at her table nudged her awake, Evvie gave a start, and Tristan felt a renewed surge of protectiveness.

Past the tall ballroom doors, Quinsley led the students down a marble hallway to a set of stairs leading deeper into the earth. The walls were lined with glowing orbs that cast a bright shine onto the marble, though there was something distinctly odd about the lights.

"You know what?" Leila whispered in his ear, making Tristan jump. "If this is a fairytale palace, it's one of those creepy places where everyone who comes through the doors is cursed."

"That would explain that weird thing we passed through on the stairs," Tristan said, still staring at the lights.

As they continued farther and farther down, Tristan lost track of how many stairs he'd descended. At one point, Leila grabbed his wrist and pointed to a dark tunnel leading away from the well-lit marble hall. "That's the doorway leading to hell," she whispered. She turned to grin at Rusty.

Shaking his head in amusement, Tristan squinted down the tunnel. The passage gaped wide, like an endless black hole.

A moment later, Quinsley stopped in front of a door

on the right side of the hall. "This is where you'll be sleeping," he said, pushing open the door. "The bathroom is a bit further along this hall."

As the students filed into the room, Quinsley looked around and shook his head. "Well, this doesn't look like it was very well planned."

There were eight bunk beds pushed up against the walls of the square room, with an enormous space in the middle. Along the wall closest to the door, Tristan could see a haphazard grouping of desks, wardrobes, and drawers.

Quinsley shrugged. "Girls on the right and boys on the left, I guess," he said skeptically. "When you're ready to go to sleep, blow on the lamps to turn them off."

He turned and left, closing the doors behind him.

For a moment everyone just stood and stared at each other. Zeke was the first to move—he headed for the closest top bunk on the right. When Damian took the right side as well, Tristan, Leila, and Rusty chose bunks to the left.

Amber joined them, along with the two girls from dinner—Cailyn and Hayley—followed by Eli and Trey. Tristan felt a twinge of disappointment when Evvie followed Cassidy McKenna to the right. He wondered why such a vast underground palace did not have space for a separate boys' and girls' bedroom, but with a glance at two of the hulking, mean-looking boys on Zeke's side, he decided it might be better this way.

Kicking off his shoes, Tristan climbed the ladder to the top bunk. There was a pair of navy-blue pajamas folded on top of the quilt, but he threw them to the end of the bed and curled up, fully clothed, on top of the quilt.

Overwhelmed with exhaustion, he slept dreamlessly.

When Tristan came gradually back into consciousness, he rubbed his eyes, wondering why his room was so dark. Usually the sun streamed through his window. As he stretched, his feet collided with the rail of his bunk bed, and everything came back to him—the graveyard, the misty lake, and the strange underground school. He opened his eyes to the marble ceiling, which was lit dimly by the glowing orbs on the wall.

"Morning, sleepyhead," Leila said cheerfully as Tristan swung his legs over the side of the bunk.

He just groaned.

"Those are your new clothes," she said, gesturing at a pile near his feet.

With a yawn, Tristan picked up the clothes—dark jeans, a light blue shirt, and black jacket—and made his way for the bathroom.

Rusty was in the boys' bathroom when Tristan kicked open the door, enthusiastically drying his hair with a scrappy towel.

"Hey, Tristan! These showers are awesome—they've got the greatest—"

He broke off, his grin fading.

Tristan cursed. Rusty had seen his scars.

"What happened to you?" Rusty asked nervously.

"Nothing, okay?" Tristan had a strong urge to hit

Rusty; instead he stomped over to the toilet stall furthest from the sinks and slammed the door.

"I won't say anything," Rusty called. "Don't be mad at me."

"Just shut up."

It was a while before Tristan convinced himself to go looking for the other students. Inside the ballroom, he avoided Rusty's eyes and hurried to join Leila. He was dismayed when Rusty came to sit at their table a moment later.

"What's up with you?" Leila asked, raising an eyebrow at Rusty.

He grinned. "I want to hear more about those demons in the tunnels."

Leila snorted.

Just then, Quinsley came around serving breakfast. "Morning," he said when he reached their table. Twirling his spatula, he dropped pancakes onto Tristan's and Leila's plates. "I'm glad you kids didn't kill each other last night."

"Very funny," Leila said. "Hey, would you mind if I helped out in the kitchen sometimes?"

Quinsley started laughing. "You've just arrived! Wait until your classes start. I'd love the help, though."

Tristan and Leila were the last ones to finish eating; when at last Quinsley came to clear their plates, the heavyset teacher—Professor Brikkens—lumbered to his feet. Today he was wearing a pair of tiny round glasses that were nearly buried in the extra flesh on his face.

"Hello, kids," Brikkens said, smiling like a satisfied cat.

His bald patch was rimmed by short gray hair that stuck straight out. "I've got you for the first hour."

Brikkens' double chin wobbled as he spoke, and Tristan cringed, slightly repulsed by the man.

Hayley Christiansen raised her hand. "Miss Merridy? What do you teach?"

"*Professor* Merridy," she corrected sharply. "I will be taking your environmental studies class."

Hayley frowned at the rebuke and began polishing her glass so fiercely that her napkin looked in danger of fraying.

"Well," Brikkens said. "If you would follow me this-a-way, I'll show you my classroom."

Brikkens' classroom was on the same level as the ballroom, just past the stairway. Pushing the door open, Brikkens waited, bouncing on the balls of his feet, for the students to file in.

Tristan's first thought was that the sunlight looked odd and pale on the walls. Then he remembered they were far underground—looking up, he realized that the tall domed ceiling was ringed by a circle of lights that gave off the same white radiance as the sun.

The room itself was round, with relief patterns carved into the white marble walls, creating the impression that the floor was encircled by pillars. Instead of desks, there was a single round table in the center of the room, surrounded by sixteen chairs. The room was so large that the table barely took up half of its space.

As they took their seats, Rusty tilted his head back and gaped at the domed ceiling. "This place is awesome!"

This made Tristan grin briefly. "You also thought walking through that miserable fog was awesome."

Once Brikkens had settled himself fussily into his tall armchair, he rapped his knuckles on the table. "This class is going to explore the intricacies of—"

A loud thump interrupted Brikkens. Damian had slammed his elbows on the table. "I just want to know what's going on here, *Professor* Brikkens." Damian glared at the other students as though looking for support. "No one's bothered to let us know why we're here, or even where 'here' is. I'm getting damn tired of it."

A few others nodded warily.

"Oh, dear," Brikkens said. Pushing his tiny glasses further into his face, he folded his arms. "I'm afraid I don't have the authority to tell you that. If Professor Drakewell didn't see fit to explain—"

"Well, then tell us what you're teaching, *Professor*," Zeke said. He leaned back in his chair and put his feet up on the table. Even wearing his newly-pressed uniform, he managed to look handsome and unconcerned.

"I can do that," Brikkens said, brightening considerably. "My friends, I'll be teaching you how to use magic."

A dead silence fell.

For a long moment Brikkens' words didn't register in Tristan's thoughts.

Then Zeke started laughing, the table shaking under his feet; Eli and Damian joined in, the sound echoing around the curved walls.

"I bet this is an asylum," Leila muttered. "They couldn't think of anything else to do with us, so they've sent us somewhere we'll be forgotten."

Tristan nodded blankly.

As the laughter died down, Brikkens chuckled uncertainly. "I assure you, this is no joke. You are here—at this school—to learn magic."

"God, I can't believe this," Damian said. "We're not insane—what are you playing at?"

With a great effort, Brikkens resettled his bulk in the padded armchair. "My dear boy, why would I lie to you?"

Smirking, Zeke folded his hands behind his head. "In that case, let's see some magic. It'll be entertaining, right? To see you fail."

Brikkens seemed to have missed the end of what Zeke said. "Well, kids, it's not that easy." He began patting at his immense maroon vest as though searching for something in one of its countless pockets.

"Magic," he began in a ponderous tone, "has nothing to do with waving a wand—or a staff—and saying the correct words. It's much more complicated and discriminating than that. Commanding magical power— that is, the energy harnessed from destruction—requires great mental skill."

"Yeah, and a special room with trapdoors," Zeke said. He had closed his eyes.

Tristan wanted to hit Rusty for looking so foolishly expectant.

"No, my friend," Brikkens said. He withdrew his hand

from a pocket, fingers fisted around something small. "There is no trickery involved. Magic, you see, is all about balance. Indeed. Balance and order, both mental and physical."

He opened his hand and showed the students what he had found. "Here we are."

Tristan had to sit up straight to see what Brikkens was holding—resting in his palm was a small golden orb about the size of a marble, unremarkable apart from the fact that it appeared to be molded from solid gold.

"Any guesses as to what this might be?"

"Something magical, no doubt," Zeke drawled, his eyes still closed.

"Ah, yes. Very good, Mr. Elwood." Brikkens smoothed his vest over his stomach. "Now, where was I?"

The tall girl next to Cassidy McKenna sat forward eagerly. "You were talking about balance, sir."

Cassidy pinched her. "Shut up, Stacy." The tall girl winced.

Oblivious to this, Brikkens nodded. "Wonderful. Magic is called such because it is derived from thin air and therefore does not follow the distinct laws of science. Magic, in its purest form, is the creation of something from nothing. That is where balance comes into play—you see, the source of magic is found in its equal but opposite force: the reduction of something to nothing. Indeed. Magic is powered by destruction."

"What's that thing in your hand?" asked Cailyn Tyler, her blonde ringlets bobbing.

"So glad you asked, my dear, so glad you asked." Brikkens opened his fist again and let the marble glow warmly in the light that streamed from the ceiling. "This is pure magic. When something is destroyed, it releases a vapor of undiluted magic. If you collect that vapor, it congeals to form an orb such as this."

"And what's that supposed to do?" Cassidy asked derisively.

"Anything at all. Only a small amount of magic is stored in this orb, so it only works for small-scale spells. What would you like to see, my dear girl?"

"Grow a tree," Eli suggested dully.

Brikkens' face fell. "I cannot do that. Not here, at least."

"Wonderful," Eli said coldly. "You're not even a decent fraud."

"No, no, growing a tree is not an impossible task." Brikkens smoothed his ugly vest. "However, magic cannot entirely disobey the laws of nature. To grow a tree, I must first have a seed."

Crossing his arms over his chest, Tristan slouched back in his chair. A flower flickered in his memory, and it was a moment before he remembered it as the flower that had grown on Marcus's grave, seemingly from nowhere. He had passed it off as a trick of the light.

Brikkens dug through his pockets again and drew out an ordinary penny. With great ceremony, he set the penny on the table and waved his hands over it.

"Maybe we'll learn to do magic shows," Leila

whispered in Tristan's ear. "My god, can you imagine us pulling rabbits out of hats for the rest of our lives?"

Tristan had a sudden vision of himself wearing a magician's colorful suit and top-hat; he groaned.

"This should work nicely," Brikkens said, still flourishing his hands over the penny. A moment later the gold marble appeared once more in his palm, and he blew on it. Then he flipped his palm over and let the marble fall.

For a split second the marble just dropped, exactly like it should; before it hit the table, though, it slowed and began to blur strangely.

Tristan sat up straighter in his chair. As he watched in surprise, the marble dissolved and floated apart to form a dense little cloud of gold smoke. The smoke drifted lazily down to settle on the penny like a cloak, where it hovered for a moment before disappearing.

Nothing happened.

The room remained silent, waiting.

Then, slowly, the penny began to wobble like jelly. Tristan thought he could see Lincoln's face expanding slightly before the picture turned to liquid—the penny gushed lazily across the table like melting wax. A second later there was nothing but a copper-and-zinc blob where the penny had been.

"It's going to ruin the table," Hayley said into the silence. For some reason she sounded indignant.

Tristan didn't know what he had just seen. There had been no sleight of hand, he was almost sure, because Brikkens hadn't moved during the demonstration. In that case, what had happened? He frowned at the molten blob that had moments ago been a penny, trying to puzzle out a rational explanation. None came to mind.

"Wow," Rusty said, his voice hushed. "How did you do that?"

"That, my dear boy, was magic." With one finger, Brikkens worried at the glob of metal until it peeled away from the wood. Then he passed the melted penny around the circle of students.

When Cassidy handed the penny to Zeke, he finally took his feet off the table and leaned forward for a closer look. Casually he drew a knife from his belt and plunged its tip into the hardened puddle of metal. The blade struck with a dull metallic thud—the melted penny was real.

"Well, it's not a complete farce," Zeke said, tucking his knife away.

Rusty frowned. "I thought Merridy took everyone's weapons," he said to no one in particular.

"Yeah, and there's no way at all to find a new knife." Zeke flipped the penny to Damian.

As the penny finished going around the classroom, Brikkens reached into his pocket again and produced a whole handful of marbles, which he set onto the table with a series of metallic thuds. "I should clarify—with these orbs, I will only be able to influence processes that already happen in nature."

Then he began taking suggestions from the students of further 'magic' to perform. Cailyn was the first to shyly suggest he turn the ceiling purple; after that everyone started calling out ideas.

During the next hour, Brikkens grew himself a remarkable black moustache, turned Zeke's shirt a shocking shade of pink, froze a rubber band from Hayley's hair so it shattered when he threw it on the table, and created a dense round cloud of vapor over the table which began to spin in a miniature funnel.

By the end, Tristan's head was beginning to ache. His carefully devised explanations grew thinner and thinner with each demonstration.

Finally Brikkens released them to their next lesson; Zeke's face fell when his shirt resumed its usual blue. Everyone sat motionless at first, stunned, while the cloud of vapor continued to spin lazily over the table.

Rusty was the first to move, though he was so dazed that he fell out of his chair when he tried to stand. He hit the tiles with a thud, breaking the startled silence, and the students began shuffling their things together.

Rusty sat on the ground for a moment, cursing and rubbing at his elbow.

"Do you reckon it's real?" Tristan asked Leila as they ambled through the door.

"I really don't know." She bit her lip, watching Rusty struggle to his feet. "Like I said before, there's definitely something wrong with this place."

Tristan nodded fervently.

Chapter 4

An Affinity for Magic

None of the other lessons that day came close to surpassing Brikkens' magic show.

Professor Grindlethorn—the short, hook-nosed teacher—took their next lesson. Grindlethorn had a brown beard cropped close to his face and serious, beady eyes that missed nothing. His classroom was narrow and dark, and from his brusque introduction Tristan gathered that he would be teaching medicine.

"The school's hospital is the next room down this hall," he said, his voice deep and gravelly. "If you ever need medical assistance, you will come to me."

It wasn't long before Grindlethorn released the class, handing each student an enormous gray textbook. Tristan groaned and heaved the textbook into his bag.

Their next lesson was on the lowest level of the school, a flight of stairs below the bunkroom. The narrow passageway and classroom were much dimmer and less airy than the rest of the school, though they were carved from the same white stone. A dark tunnel gaped open directly across from the classroom door, and Tristan hugged his arms over his chest as he walked by. After what they had seen that morning, it seemed that anything could be lurking down there.

This teacher, Professor Delair, was bald apart from a long white moustache. Despite his apparent age, he looked hale and strong. As he handed around copies of a purple textbook entitled *Discrete Elementals*, he said, "We will be studying the fundamentals of earth, air, fire, and water—the foundation of all magical processes."

Tristan nodded vaguely, massaging his temples; by this point he wouldn't be surprised if a teacher announced that they would tame dragons or learn to fly.

Delair continued speaking as though he'd said nothing unusual. "Classes won't be meeting every day, but if you fail to appear on the day of a lesson, you will receive no less than one hour of punishment."

"What do you mean, punishment?" Damian asked.

Delair explained that misbehavior would earn students hours of punishment, which they would have to work off with the teacher of their choice.

"And if we don't work it off?" This was from Zeke.

Delair's moustache twitched. "We thought of that," he said. "You will have until each Friday at midnight to work off your weekly punishments. If you fail to do so, you won't eat until you complete the hours."

At that, Delair stood. "Homework—read the introduction of the textbook. There will be a quiz next time we meet."

Oblivious to the groans from many of the students, he turned and left the room, disappearing into the dark tunnel across the hall.

"I was hoping for more magic," Rusty said as they retraced their path up to the ballroom. It was lunchtime.

"I'm glad it's over," Tristan said, adding the *Discrete Elementals* book to his bag.

"But aren't you excited? I didn't think it was gonna be like this. Aren't you glad we're not in juvie?"

"That doesn't mean we have to be excited," Leila said darkly.

Several teachers were already in the ballroom when Tristan, Leila, and Rusty arrived. There was Brikkens, eating heartily from two overflowing plates; Grindlethorn sat to his left, sipping from a steaming mug.

Merridy got to her feet and stopped Leila before she could take a seat. "The other students are on their way down to the bunkroom," she said. "As I mentioned upon our arrival, you must relinquish all of your personal items. Each of you may choose one belonging to keep, and the rest must go. Your peers are currently sorting through their things."

Tristan had forgotten about this; clearly Leila had too, because she dashed off, leaving her book bag at Tristan's feet.

"I don't have anything," Tristan said.

Rusty reached in a pocket and drew out a small woodcarving. "This is all I'm keeping," he told Merridy.

"I've been carrying it around ever since you told us that we'd have to get rid of our stuff."

Merridy gave them both a thin-lipped smile and let them take seats on the dining platform.

"Can I see that?" Tristan asked, eyeing the carving.

Rusty opened his fist and showed him what looked like a fairy girl kneeling in prayer. As Rusty ran his fingers along the tips of her tiny wings, his eyes grew sad. "A friend made it for me." After a moment he blinked and stuffed the carving back into his pocket. "Well, this'll be different." Tristan couldn't tell if his enthusiasm was faked.

As the students began returning to the ballroom, most looking disgruntled or downright angry, Quinsley came around with grilled cheese and tomato soup. Both were hot and delicious and soothed Tristan's headache.

"I thought you didn't have anything valuable other than your knives," Rusty said to Leila, who was sitting in an irritated silence.

Leila snorted. "Slitting people's throats isn't the only thing I enjoy doing."

Tristan hoped she was joking, but her expression made it hard to tell.

Professor Gracewright's class was immediately following lunch. She led the students up the grand staircase to the clearing above the school, passing again through the insubstantial barrier on the stairs. The sudden darkness and drop in temperature was just as unerring as before.

Outside, the clearing was still shrouded in damp mist.

Tristan could barely see the outlines of trees beyond the native longhouses.

"This is my classroom," Gracewright said, gesturing around the clearing. Her sunhat wobbled dangerously. "I will be teaching botany, so our classes will deal with everything around us. However, for days like today, we have a greenhouse and an indoor garden to shelter in."

The greenhouse only materialized when they drew near; from afar its glass walls had looked like wood panels. It had to be an illusion of some sort.

Instead of making for the greenhouse, Gracewright turned left and pushed open the door to one of the longhouses. When she vanished through the dark entrance, Tristan realized that it was guarded by another one of the strange barriers. He held his breath as he stepped into the black emptiness.

Once through this barrier, Tristan could see that the floor of the longhouse was nothing but packed dirt, with patches of grass covering most of it. Flowers, vines, and small trees clustering along the walls gave it the appearance of a well-tended garden.

Four large purple blankets were spread across the grass—following Gracewright's example, the students settled onto the blankets and looked around.

"We'll begin the semester by identifying basic varieties of useful plants," Gracewright said.

They got to work right away, examining the lawn they were sitting on until each student could pick out five different species of grass.

They were given two new textbooks at the end of the lesson, each as heavy and tedious-looking as the ones from their morning classes. One appeared to be a standard textbook entitled *Encyclopedia of Botany*. The other one, unfortunately, was called *Beyond the Basics: Magical and Medicinal Herbs*.

When Gracewright dismissed the class, she handed each student a drawstring bag filled with herbs to identify before the next day's lesson.

"Can't we just do something normal?" Tristan complained as they trudged back towards the stairs. "I'm getting sick of all this crazy talk about magic."

Leila nodded pensively. "I know what you mean. It's a bit too strange to be completely fake, don't you think?"

"What are you talking about?" Rusty stopped in his tracks, surprised. "Didn't you see Brikkens? This stuff is real!"

Tristan sighed. "That's what I'm worried about."

Their next lesson was taught by the vampire, who greeted the students in a tall, echoing chamber two stories below the ballroom. Here the walls were hewn from icy gray stone, entirely at odds with the marble floor. Four long tables were arranged in a square, partially enclosing what looked like a stone-ringed fire pit in the center of the room. There were no seats, so the students clustered around the tall tables with some confusion.

"Good afternoon," the teacher said, once the muttering had subsided. "My name is Brinley Alldusk, and I'll be teaching chemistry."

When he smiled, Tristan was almost surprised that he lacked fangs.

"First of all, I want to make it clear that 'chemistry' is a bit of a misnomer for this class."

"Oh, great," Tristan muttered to Leila. "More bloody magic, no doubt."

Alldusk heard, and his smile widened. "You've got that right," he said. His features softened, and he suddenly looked very friendly. "Tristan, is it?"

Turning back to the other students, he said, "I believe Professor Brikkens showed you the gold orbs?"

Rusty was one of the few who nodded eagerly at this.

"Good. This class will involve the creation of those orbs; in other words, we will be collecting magic and condensing it into a functional form."

As Alldusk strode to the center of the room, Tristan leaned forward, suddenly curious. The gold marbles had fascinated him.

"In order to capture this free-floating magic," Alldusk continued, "we must destroy something and collect the vapors released in conjecture to the destruction."

"Sir?" Hayley Christiansen said. "I don't think I understand…"

"The fire pit," Leila whispered, nodding towards the ground. "We're going to burn things."

Leila was right. While he began to explain, Alldusk bent and unfastened a rusty grate that had been covering the fire pit. The hollow was filled with glowing coals, which Alldusk scooped into a metal bowl.

"Unlike your other teachers," Alldusk said, "I believe you deserve to know exactly how the collection of magic is made possible."

He brought the metal bowl over and set it on the table in front of Eli.

"To release the magical vapor, we burn various materials, and the vapor is given off along with the smoke."

Reaching beneath the table, Alldusk produced a small leather pouch and an empty glass jar.

"The volume of magic given off depends on what is being destroyed. This is where chemistry comes into play." Holding up the pouch, he tipped a small pile of brown powder into his palm. "Certain combinations of plants and minerals create more magic than others when incinerated, and a greater magnitude of destruction produces more magic. Watch carefully—the vapor is subtle, and most of you won't be able to see it."

At this, Alldusk dropped the powder onto the coals. The powder sparked as it hit the embers; Tristan squinted at the air directly above the bowl, waiting for something to happen. After a moment, he thought he saw something like a wisp of pale gold, which drifted up from the bowl in a hazy cloud.

Once the gold cloud had floated away from the trail of smoke, Alldusk turned the empty glass jar over and scooped the gold vapor out of the air.

All was silent, aside from the faint cracking of the embers. Then—

"You didn't catch all of it," Amber Ashton said faintly.

Tristan turned and stared at her. He wasn't the only one; many of the students wore confused frowns, as though they had never seen her before.

Leila shifted impatiently on his left. "What are we supposed to see?" She was still peering at the jar. "You didn't even catch the smoke."

Rusty and several others nodded, while Eli continued to stare at Amber.

"You mean you can't see that gold stuff?" Tristan asked, surprised. Now that it was in the jar, the magic vapor was growing brighter and more substantial than before.

Alldusk smiled. "As I said, it is rare for a student to spot the magic immediately. Raise your hands if you can see it."

Tristan put his hand up slowly, and was amazed to find that Amber was the only other student to raise her hand. Meeting her eyes, he shrugged.

"Excellent," Alldusk said. He nodded at them both. "Both of you appear to have an affinity for magic. And well spotted, miss…"

Amber didn't supply her name, so Alldusk cleared his throat and continued.

"You're quite right that some of the vapor slipped away. Unfortunately, we don't have a more efficient way of collecting the vapors. We could use larger jars, of course, but they are extremely impractical."

"What are you talking about?" Rusty asked. "What happened?"

Alldusk moved over to the next table and held the jar

up for Rusty to have a closer look. "It should begin appearing to the rest of you as it grows thicker," he said. "Watch carefully."

The gold was deeper now—more concentrated, Tristan realized—and it was swirling towards the bottom of the jar in a lazy spiral.

While Rusty continued to frown at the jar, eyes screwed up in concentration, Alldusk made his way around the room to give everyone a closer look. When the jar came back around to Eli, he jumped and drew back.

"I see it!" He gave the jar a look of wary scrutiny, eyebrows arching. "There's something spinning in there."

Across the room, Cassidy had struck a haughty, bored pose, though her eyes kept flicking back to the jar of gold mist. Meanwhile, Zeke followed the circling vapor with the lazy unconcern of a cat tracking a string. Damian and most of the other students continued to frown in confusion.

When the gold was almost dense enough to be solid, glowing brighter than ever, Rusty let out his breath.

"Oh, *there* it is," he said, rocking back on his heels. "There's definitely something there."

"What is it?" Leila hissed in Tristan's ear. "Why can't I see anything?"

"Look near the bottom," Tristan said quietly. "Right in the middle—if you squint at it, can you see anything moving?"

Leila shook her head.

Holding the jar by its lid, Alldusk crossed to their desk and held it in front of Leila.

"There's a bright gold streak there," Tristan said. Leaning over Leila's shoulder, he put his finger on the jar. "Right...there."

Leila breathed a sigh of relief. "There it is. Thank goodness."

"Not to worry," Alldusk said. "No one knows why some people have an easier time spotting the vapor than others; when I was learning, it took me weeks before I was able to see anything. Good work, everyone."

He set the jar on a dark wood shelf, where it joined a line of similar jars.

"For those of you who are able to see the orb beginning to form, the vapor will continue spinning for many more hours. By our next lesson, there will be a golden ball of pure magic sitting at the base of the jar."

As the students began gathering their books to leave, Alldusk said, "For homework, you should practice *observing*. Everything has an aura; those of you who had difficulty seeing the magic vapor would do well to begin searching for auras wherever you go. This will make your future work in my class much easier."

Tristan made to follow Leila from the room, but Alldusk said, "Tristan. Would you and the young lady stay a moment?"

When Tristan touched Amber's shoulder to keep her from leaving, she gave him a startled look. "This is Amber Ashton, Professor."

Alldusk nodded. "Good to meet you, Amber." He waited until the last of the students had cleared the room before saying, "I will be speaking to the headmaster about you two. Professor Drakewell was interested to learn who had a special talent with magic."

Alldusk looked from Tristan to Amber, his expression becoming grave.

"There is a special…job at this school that one of you may be asked to fill someday. Professor Drakewell will wish to discuss this with you at some point."

At this they were dismissed.

Tristan fell into step beside Amber as they made their way to the next class. "Can you see auras around everything?" he asked.

She glanced at him. "Yours is pale green, like new aspen leaves."

Tristan blinked in surprise. He didn't know what to say to this, so they continued to their next class in silence.

After that, the only class remaining was Professor Merridy's. Her lesson came with yet another textbook, *Earth Science and Environmental Studies*, and a convoluted explanation that had something to do with plate tectonics. Tristan couldn't concentrate, his thoughts still on Alldusk's lesson.

He was startled from his daze when Leila hit Zeke very hard with her new textbook.

"Ow!" Zeke howled. "Damn it, Leila, I'll—"

"Enough!" Merridy called.

Tristan blinked at Leila. It appeared that Zeke had been digging surreptitiously through Leila's bag; when she had noticed, she had slammed her textbook onto his head to make him stop.

"Leila, please, this is not a detention center," Merridy said, her eyes narrowing behind her glasses. "Zeke, are you quite all right?"

Zeke got to his feet, massaging his head. "I'll survive," he said sourly, aiming a kick at Leila's ankle.

"An hour of punishment for you, Leila," Merridy snapped. "And you too, Zeke. Class dismissed."

After dinner, Tristan piled up his textbooks and stared at them for a while, exhausted just thinking about how much homework he had. When Leila curled up on her pillow and started working doggedly through a set of notes on the *Discrete Elementals* introduction, Rusty and Eli went around the room complaining loudly.

"Will you idiots shut up?" Damian finally shouted across the room.

Leila slammed her textbook shut. "This is hopeless. I can't concentrate."

Rusty quieted, looking guilty. Tristan still hadn't opened his first textbook.

At Hayley's suggestion, everyone abandoned their books and began rearranging the bunkroom so it looked less like a junkyard. After a heated debate, Tristan and Damian came to the decision that the room should be divided in half by the assorted furniture that was currently pushed against the far wall. Damian and his friends would take the right side, while Tristan and the others claimed the left.

While Cassidy and Zeke stood to the side, making scathing comments instead of helping move furniture, the other students from both groups worked together to create the makeshift wall. Tristan had a bad feeling about the bunkroom division—he was afraid that his side and Damian's side would never quite be friendly after this.

To the left of the wall, Tristan, Leila, and Rusty were joined by most of the kids that Tristan had spoken to: Eli and Trey, Hayley and Cailyn, and Amber.

Damian, Zeke, and Cassidy—the three who seemed intent on antagonizing Tristan and his new friends—were joined by a tall girl Tristan thought was called Stacy Walden, along with two boys he didn't know.

After standing near the door for a long time, biting her lip and shifting from foot to foot, Evangeline chose a bunk on Tristan's side of the room. He had difficulty hiding his triumph at that.

Eventually Tristan showered and went to bed, warm and content and with none of his homework done. He fell asleep quickly…

…and slipped into a nightmare. The darkness resolved into a flash of brilliant light, the sudden illumination of a curve in the highway…why hadn't he turned? The wheel was cold in his grasp, and everything was sluggish…a terrified scream and a thud, and Marcus was splayed beside him on the seat, hair limp and damp with sweat. Tristan's eyes burned.

See what you've done, the darkness hissed.

Tristan threw his arms over his head, cheeks wet with

tears, and tried to stifle the vision. *Go away. Leave me alone. I hate you.*

There was a hand on his shoulder, shaking him, and he knew it wasn't part of the dream because the hand was warm. Swallowing fiercely, he forced his eyes open.

Leila stood on the corner of Rusty's bed, bending over him. "Are you all right?" she whispered. "You were talking in your sleep."

Tristan realized that his eyes were wet—he really had been crying. Embarrassed, he threw his covers over his head. "I'm fine," he said, his voice muffled. In the silence that followed, he knew Leila was still watching him. "Thank you," he whispered at last.

Leila squeezed his shoulder gently and then retreated.

After that he was afraid to sleep. He rolled onto his stomach and stared at the single ball of light that glowed dimly beside the door. It was the only way he could keep from falling back into darkness.

When Leila's breathing had slowed once again, Tristan shrugged off his covers and climbed down the ladder. He could lie still no longer; his bed felt like a pool of cement that was slowly hardening around him. Maybe a cool drink would settle his nerves.

The hallway was wreathed in shadows. The glowing orbs had been dimmed until each one held only a tiny spot of light. Curling his toes against the cold stone, Tristan tiptoed forward—

He froze. He'd just seen something strange—beneath the nearest orb was a thin silver line that glowed in the darkness, long and scaly like an eel. In fact, it *was* an eel, the outline etched deep into the wall. Eyes widening, Tristan crept closer. The silver eel seemed almost to be moving, swimming sinuously through a field of silver stars, its eye fixed on a fleeing wolf. As his gaze moved along the wall, he saw that the wolf bounded after its howling pack, which had escaped to the shelter of a forest.

From afar, Tristan thought he heard the echo of a wolf's howl winding through the tunnels of the Lair. His breath caught in his throat.

Whirling, Tristan was faced with even more glowing silver; the opposite wall was thronged with monsters, horned and fork-tongued and bloodthirsty. Forgetting his drink of water, he turned and ran back to the safety of the bunkroom.

Huddling under his bedclothes, Tristan could not close his eyes. Was he going crazy? Nothing made sense. Of course there was no such thing as magic. The teachers were just testing who would lose their grasp on sanity the quickest, and Tristan's so-called 'affinity for magic' meant he would be the first to go.

He wouldn't let them poison his mind. He had to remember what was true, to sort out the facts from the distortions.

I won't go mad. Tristan's feet were still icy, but his palms itched with sweat.

This isn't real. I won't go mad.

Chapter 5

Zeke's Reward

In the morning Tristan was exhausted. As soon as his classmates began to stir, he stumbled to the boys' bathroom and stood in the shower for ages, as though he could wash away the memory of his nightmares.

None of the other boys were up yet. When Tristan had finished his shower and pulled on his clothes, he stood in front of the mirror and studied his reflection, pulling his hair back from his face to examine the scars.

Even months after the crash, his face had hardly improved. The gashes across his left cheek and through his eyebrow were healing badly—the scars were red and mottled, his skin coming together in raised contours as though something evil was trying to take root there.

With a grimace, Tristan dragged his hair violently back into place.

On his way up to the ballroom, he paused and stared at the patch of wall where he'd seen the outline of the eel the night before. Not a trace remained; had he dreamed it all?

In their medicine class that day, Professor Grindlethorn called forward Finley Glenn, who was one of the boys Tristan hadn't known the day before, to participate in a demonstration. Finley Glenn, squat and bespectacled, looked very confused when his name was called. His jacket was inside out.

"Glenn. Have you ever experienced a major injury?"

Finley bobbed his head and almost walked into a desk.

"When I was twelve, I fractured my radius and tore the ligaments. I still have the scar." He folded up the cuff of his left sleeve and showed Grindlethorn his wrist.

A thrill of excitement ran through Tristan—could Grindlethorn heal the scars on his face?

"Shoddy work," Grindlethorn said. "With proper care, this scar should have disappeared entirely."

He scratched at his beard, frown deepening, and then turned to the other students. "In my class, you will learn to heal without using modern medicine. Our work will partly involve magic, though we will also cover basic care techniques that have largely been forgotten these days."

Grindlethorn continued to grip Finley's wrist with his stout fingers. "The bone is still weak," he muttered. "Try eating less for a few weeks, Glenn. With so much fat around the bone, strengthening its structure will prove challenging."

Finley turned bright red and tugged his arm away from Grindlethorn's probing fingers.

Tristan's excitement faded. He wasn't going to ask anyone to heal his scars if it meant public humiliation.

That night, after struggling through two days' worth of homework, Tristan was so exhausted that he slept dreamlessly. He saw Leila watching him carefully at breakfast the next morning, so he smiled and said, "I'm fine."

When they climbed the stairs for botany after lunch, the students were awarded their first real view of the school's surroundings. At first Tristan didn't know what was happening when he found himself at the back of a holdup on the stairs; there was a great deal of shoving and cursing, and Zeke shouted, "Move it, spotty!" at Leila.

She didn't seem to hear him. She and Eli had frozen in the doorway, staring at something just out of sight; shoving past Damian and Cassidy, Tristan edged his way to the top of the stairs…and stopped.

The mist had lifted, and in its absence their world had grown a hundred times larger. What had appeared to be an endless pine forest enveloping the school was nothing more than a tree-filled valley, beyond which loomed craggy, glacier-draped mountains. The midday sunlight glinted off every peak, smoothing out their crevices in a blinding sheen of white.

For a heartbeat Tristan thought he could see the aura of the mountains, a faint turquoise shimmer that swirled and flared in the wind. When he blinked, the color vanished, and he shook his head in irritation. His mind was playing tricks on him again.

"That's something," Leila said quietly.

Rusty blundered into Leila from behind. "Whoops— sorry, Leila, I didn't see you."

She rolled her eyes.

"There you are," an amused voice remarked. Turning, Tristan saw Gracewright making her way towards the students, her face lost in the shadows of her wide-brimmed sunhat. "It's a real beauty, isn't it?" Today her wispy white hair shone almost silver in the sun. "After a time you forget how it is to live anywhere else."

When Gracewright stopped in front of round-faced Hayley Christiansen and stubby little Finley Glenn, she was beaming. "Well, I can see you kids won't be much use in a sit-down lesson today," she said. "I hope you have your textbooks—we're going to do a bit of a scavenger hunt."

From a pocket in her heavy leather apron, Gracewright produced a stack of papers, which she handed to Finley. "Pass those around," she prompted Finley, who had been squinting at the top of the stack. "You'll each receive a list of important magical and medicinal plants; each specimen on this list can be found within a mile of this school. Whoever manages to find the most plants from this list will be excused from tonight's homework."

Tristan took a sheet of paper and frowned down at the list. There were two columns running down the page—one was headed "Magical Specimens," the other "Medicinal Plants." He sighed.

"I don't recognize any of these," Leila said. "Look— spotted jewelweed? Hooked crowfoot? Gnome plant? These sound ridiculous."

Rusty laughed. "*Gnome* plant? What's that supposed to be?"

Tristan scowled and let his copy of *Beyond the Basics: Magical and Medicinal Herbs* fall open to the center. "Is it magical or medicinal?" he asked.

"Magical," Rusty said. "But maybe it's in the *Encyclopedia of Botany*, too. That'll mean it's real."

Tristan flipped to the index of his textbook while Rusty started thumbing through his *Encyclopedia*.

"Of course it's real," Leila said impatiently. "How are we supposed to hunt for it otherwise? We just need a picture."

"You know what I meant," Rusty said. "Aha—I found it!"

Tristan looked up from his own book as Rusty read aloud the passage he'd found.

"'Gnome Plant, or *Hemitomes congestum*, is a small, extremely rare flower limited to the northwest coastal region of North America.'"

Leila snorted. "That's really helpful. What does the other book say, Tristan?"

After a moment, he found the right page. "It says, 'Apart from its high-volume production of congealed magic,'—I think that means those golden orbs—'the gnome plant may also be used to slow or cease magical reactions.'" The passage continued for the remainder of the page, though Tristan didn't understand a word of it.

Tristan slammed the book shut. "Why don't we start with something less rare?" He scanned the list of plants again. "Wild ginger, for instance—that's something I've heard of before."

Once Tristan, Leila, and Rusty had studied the picture of the wild ginger plant until Tristan was sure he could recognize the dark, heart-shaped leaves, they set off into the trees, heading in three different directions.

"How do you think we're supposed to tell the difference between magical and normal plants?" Tristan asked Rusty, scanning the ground.

It was not Rusty who answered. "You have to look at their auras," said a soft female voice.

Tristan whirled. Amber was kneeling beside a tree and easing a small plant from the soil, its roots intact. She looked up briefly, blinked at Tristan, and returned her gaze to the earth. "The radiance of any object's aura indicates the strength of its magic. Plants with a higher concentration of magic will glow brighter."

"Thank you?" Tristan said, somewhat bewildered.

Amber straightened, clutching the plant in her pale fingers. "When you learn to see auras, the world gives you its secrets." Tilting her head, she turned away. A moment later she was gone.

When Amber was out of sight, Tristan dropped to the ground where she'd knelt, trying to see which plant she'd unearthed. There were several tiny leaves hugging the base of the pine, along with a clump of moss—though none of the leaves belonged to the wild ginger plant, Tristan plucked a bit of each plant just to be safe.

By the end of the hour, everyone began straggling

back—Rusty first, empty-handed and covered in mud; followed by petite Cailyn Tyler, clutching an armful of pine boughs and long grasses; and then Leila, who looked as though she'd actually managed to find a clump of wild ginger.

"What'd you find?" Leila demanded of Tristan, eyeing his handful of leaves.

"No idea."

When Zeke and Amber finally returned, Gracewright told the students to sit in a circle in the clearing. "Come up here, one at a time, and we'll see what you have," she said. "You first, Miss Ashton."

"There's no chance we're getting out of homework," Tristan grumbled, noting the odd variety of plants that Amber laid out before Professor Gracewright.

"Excellent work," Gracewright said, checking each plant off her list as Amber laid them on the grass before her. "That's over half of the specimens I assigned—quite impressive." She smiled at Amber. "Mr. Elwood, you're next."

When Zeke deposited his plants on the grass, Gracewright started laughing. "You don't know a thing about botany, young man," she said, "but you've spotted the loophole."

Still chuckling to herself, Gracewright turned to the other students. "You may have guessed this already, but your assignment wasn't terribly specific. Half of the species on these lists won't grow around here." She shook her head in amusement. "Luckily we have our greenhouse for the less adaptable specimens, which Mr. Elwood here managed to break into. Homework—sketch each of the plants that you didn't manage to find. Mr. Elwood and Miss Ashton are both exempt from this—well done, you two."

Zeke smirked at Leila.

"What?" Rusty protested loudly. "How's that fair?"

Tristan shared his indignation. Was Gracewright trying to encourage them to be criminals?

Gracewright turned to Rusty. "One of the first things you should know about magic is that it can't be restricted by human laws or ethical codes. The only rules that matter are those of nature and magic. If you have something to show me, Mr. Lennox, I'd be happy to look. Otherwise, class dismissed."

Rusty scowled. "Clovers look a lot like wild ginger, okay?" he said, frowning at Gracewright.

"No, they really don't," Leila said.

"Is she actually going to let Zeke get away with that?" Tristan muttered, dropping his armful of plants.

Shaking her head, Leila threw a dark look at Zeke. "Hasn't Juvie taught you anything? Life isn't fair."

"Duh." Tristan ground the moss he'd collected to bits with one toe. "I just didn't think our teachers would encourage that sort of thing."

"How come you were in Juvie, anyway?" Rusty asked, distracted.

Tristan pressed his hair unhappily over his face. "I don't want to talk about it."

"Why don't you tell us what you were arrested for,

Rusty?" Leila suggested. "And what happened to your tooth?"

Rusty poked his chipped front tooth with his tongue. "I'm turning into a vampire," he said happily. "I'll start sneaking around and drinking your blood in a couple of days."

Laughing, Tristan abandoned his pile of wilting plants and hurried to catch up with him and Leila. "You're mental! What really happened?"

Rusty's smile vanished. "Don't joke about that," he said, his face somehow dangerous despite the scruffy hair.

"Sorry," Tristan said quickly. "But were you in a fight or something?"

The threatening look on Rusty's face passed as quickly as it had appeared. "I wish it was that exciting." His grin was back. "Naw, some guy pushed me down the stairs when he heard I was leaving that godawful detention center in Texas."

"What were you there for?" Leila asked again. She paused at the entrance to the Lair, waiting for Eli and Trey to draw ahead of them. "What did you do?"

Rusty shrugged. "Not much, as far as I can tell. I got wasted at some party and passed out, and when I woke up I was lying in the middle of some old field with beer cans all over. There was a barn and a farmhouse nearby, and they were both on fire." Rusty shook his head and stuck a foot warily through the magical barrier. Once Tristan and Leila had joined him, he continued. "That's when the police started showing up. No one believed me when I said I didn't know what happened, so I got arrested for bloody arson."

This made Tristan feel guiltier than before. Leila and Rusty were probably assuming he'd been arrested on similar charges, not for something like manslaughter.

Leila noticed his sudden frown. "What's up with you?"

"I'm just annoyed about Zeke," he lied.

"It's not fair at all!" Rusty said, eagerly resuming the subject. "We should tell one of the teachers. Drakewell would have to do something about it, wouldn't he?"

"Yeah, right," Leila said. "Give it up, Rusty."

Everyone began settling in quickly enough. Tristan soon learned that the only thing the teachers gave out as readily as homework was punishment; the only student who spent more time working off hours than Zeke was Leila. Though it was easy enough to find enjoyable work to complete, the punishments cut into their already limited study time.

After working off her first several hours of punishment in the kitchen, where she quickly took a liking to Gerard Quinsley, Leila never went to any other teacher. When Rusty asked her if she ever got bored of it, she said, "Gerry knows lots of good stories. Besides, I like cooking."

Tristan received his first hour of punishment later that first week, when he forgot Grindlethorn's medicine assignment in the bunkroom and had to run back to grab it. He approached Merridy to work it off; to his dismay, she appeared just as anxious and unfriendly as usual. He found himself wishing he'd gone to Alldusk instead.

"You could help grade these pre-tests, I suppose," Merridy said distractedly when Tristan arrived in her office. She handed him a pile of quizzes from the day before. "As I said in class, they were merely intended to determine how I should structure the course."

Tristan took a seat in the corner of her tiny office, perched on a spindly chair. "Professor?" He smoothed his hair over his scars. "You haven't given me an answer key."

Merridy sighed. "Sorry, Tristan." She drew a page from her top drawer and handed it to him.

Flipping through the stack of quizzes, Tristan found his own to grade first. The test had been complicated—Merridy had asked them about the geology of natural disasters; the movement of odd weather patterns; and the maintenance of fragile ecosystems. Tristan had done terribly. Unwilling to calculate his failing score, he merely made a slash through each incorrect answer.

"Thank you so much for your help," Merridy said an hour later, taking the finished papers from Tristan. "In the future, I would suggest finding another teacher to assist—I have quite a lot to deal with just now, and I cannot make time for this on a regular basis."

"Sorry, Professor," Tristan said. Bobbing his head at her, he left.

The following week, Tristan worked off hours with Professor Alldusk, helping bottle dried herbs and scrub accumulated soot from the walls of the chemistry classroom.

After making a bad first impression on the students,

Professor Drakewell seemed determined to intimidate and unnerve them still further. The headmaster had a disconcerting habit of roaming the halls of the Lair, appearing from the shadows where people least expected him and doling out punishments to any student who couldn't come up with a good excuse for being there. Professor Drakewell was anything but stingy about giving out hours. By the end of the first week, everyone knew how Finley—surprisingly brilliant in class but slow at everything else—had blundered into Drakewell's office and earned himself ten hours to work off.

Tristan wasn't about to tell Leila or Rusty this, but he had the uncomfortable feeling that Drakewell was watching him more carefully than anyone else. The headmaster ran across Tristan in the hallways more often than could be considered strictly accidental.

If anything, though, Merridy seemed more frightened of Drakewell than any of the students were. On their second Monday of classes, Merridy's sixth period class was interrupted by the sudden appearance of the headmaster in their midst.

"Though the overall tides are governed by the moon," Merridy was saying, "there are many smaller forces that can trigger much more dramatic phenomena. For instance, underwater earthquakes or tremors may lead to the formation of tsunamis, while the meeting of two separate currents will often create whirlpools or, on a larger scale, maelstroms. Whether we discuss—"

Merridy broke off, eyes widening behind her glasses.

Tristan turned in his seat to see what had scared her—
Drakewell had materialized at the back of the room,
sneering at Merridy from beside a pillar.

"I hope I have not interrupted anything important," he
said mockingly. "Would you please join me in the hallway
for a minute?" Drakewell tapped the black hourglass at his
neck.

Tristan could have sworn the headmaster had been
invisible a moment ago—the pillar wasn't wide enough nor
the shadows deep enough to hide his tall form.

Merridy opened her mouth and closed it again; with a
nervous glance at the front row of students, she hurried
towards the door. When Drakewell drew the classroom
door shut, the room was left in utter silence. Tristan
glanced at Leila, but she shook her head and put a finger to
her lips. No one moved.

Merridy returned a full ten minutes later, white-faced
and flustered. "Where was I?" she said, glancing towards
the door and fidgeting with a pile of notes on her desk.

"What's the matter, professor?" Zeke teased. "Can't
keep your eyes off Drakewell? Darla and...what's his first
name, anyway?"

For that, Merridy gave him an hour of punishment.

After class, Rusty was the first to jump up from his
seat.

"What're up to?" Tristan said, elbowing Rusty.

Rusty shrugged. "Just wondering where Drakewell had
gone. There's gotta be something he's always doing, right? I
mean, he's never in his office, and he isn't at dinner much

either. So where does he keep hiding?"

"Maybe he's just invisible most of the time," Tristan said shortly.

"I doubt that," Leila said, though she surely realized Tristan had been joking. "Maybe he has some job here that the other teachers are afraid to do. Remember what Gracewright said about magic? It doesn't follow moral codes—maybe Drakewell is torturing people, or—"

"Let's not talk about it," Tristan interrupted. For the first time since the crash, he was almost happy. He didn't want to ruin that by thinking about Drakewell.

"I wonder what we'd be doing if we were still home," Rusty said one Thursday night two weeks after they'd arrived. No one was asleep yet, though the bunkroom lights had been extinguished. Leila often told stories once the lights were out, but tonight she was in the kitchen.

"You mean if you were still locked up?" Tristan said darkly.

"Whatever. I wasn't in jail for long," Rusty said. "I mean if we were really home. What would be happening right now?"

Tristan bit his tongue, glad it was dark. "Nothing good," he muttered.

"Are you gonna tell us how you got those scars?" Rusty asked.

"We all know your face is messed up," said Eli from the next bunk over. "You don't have to keep hiding it."

"Shut it," Tristan snapped, throwing the covers over

his head.

"I'm glad we're here," Rusty said quickly, saving Tristan. "It's all so exciting, don't you think? Plus, I'm sure this is way more valuable than regular school."

"But what is *this*?" Eli said. "I don't see the point of what we're doing. Why study magic if we can't use it?"

"I'm sure we'll get to that later," Rusty insisted. "I bet..."

"You know what we would be doing, if we were home?" Leila said from the doorway.

Tristan pulled the covers off his head.

"We would be starting our sophomore year of high school," Leila said. "Everything would be the same—the history classes and math classes, the new textbooks and new teachers. But when you walk through those familiar hallways, you realize that everything has changed. The other students realize it, too—they notice your scars and your broken teeth. They avert their eyes, and they whisper behind your back. 'That's the criminal,' they say. Even your friends ignore you. Did you ever have friends? Suddenly you can't recall."

No one spoke. Leila tiptoed over to her bed; Tristan heard a soft rustling as she pulled on her pajamas in the dark.

"You want to scream at them," she whispered. "'It was an accident!' Instead you keep silent. There is nothing left for you but silence."

That night the nightmares were worse than usual.

He dreamed he was attacking Marcus, flailing desperately at him, trying to break him. Everything was growing hazy, and his fists seemed to connect only with damp air. Finally the haze cleared, and Tristan looked down to see Marcus lying at his feet, his body crumpled. With a jolt, he wrenched himself away from the scene, though Marcus's dead body wouldn't fade.

He was struggling to wake, chest slicked with sweat, when he felt Leila's hand on his shoulder.

Groaning, Tristan rolled over to look at her. "Was I shouting again?" he whispered.

Leila nodded.

With a sigh, Tristan closed his eyes. He heard a creak of bedsprings as Leila stepped down from Rusty's bed.

"Wait!" he whispered suddenly. "You have to see something." There was something he needed to know, something that would assuage a small part of his fears.

Leila waited for him at the foot of the ladder and followed him into the hallway.

"What is it?"

Tristan beckoned her forward. It took a moment for his eyes to adjust to the dim light; then the hallway came alive with brilliant silver figures, bright as stars against the stone. If anything, the shifting silver designs were more vivid than ever.

"Can you see that?" he asked, pointing at the figure of a bear splashing through a river.

Leila looked at Tristan's finger and then squinted at the wall. "It's too dark. What am I supposed to be looking at?"

Tristan's hopes plummeted. "There. Do you see anything at all?" He traced his finger around the outline of the bear, from its perked ears to its shaggy hind feet. At least the shape didn't appear to be moving.

Now Leila was looking at Tristan instead of the wall. "It just looks like gray marble. Is there supposed to be anything special about it?"

"Right," Tristan said gloomily. "Forget about it."

Chapter 6

The Lemon Tree

Before long they had settled into a routine, where auras and fire and golden orbs became commonplace. In the daytime, Tristan came to a point where he could accept magic to a certain extent, and the headaches ceased. At night, though, his inevitable madness was never far from his thoughts.

The classes themselves were quickly becoming more exciting; while the other students grew more confident at seeing bottled magic, Tristan was already becoming adept at collecting magical vapors and recognizing the brightest auras in nature.

Alldusk's chemistry classes were the most entertaining by far. As Tristan had guessed, Professor Alldusk was generous, quick to smile, and—best of all—rarely gave punishments. He explained that although the strongest magic was often collected while burning the subtlest plants or minerals, colorful flames and explosions were useful as well.

"This school is situated above a number of mineral deposits," Alldusk said. "We therefore have ready access to any number of chemicals that would otherwise be too rare for everyday use in creating magical vapor."

One day Alldusk asked Tristan to stand by and help him bottle vapors while he proceeded to burn lithium chloride, copper sulfate, and a number of other chemicals. The resulting flames burned blue, red, green, and purple.

The next week, Alldusk spent the lesson making explosions with different chemicals—Cailyn Tyler hung back, covering her ears and wincing at each deafening bang, while the other students crowded forward to get a better look. Every thunderous reaction rocketed off the stone walls, echoing around the tall chamber, until Grindlethorn showed up halfway through the lesson and told Alldusk to keep it down.

"I'll go to the headmaster if I hear another explosion," Grindlethorn said, waving away the cloud of smoke that billowed towards the doorway.

"Beg pardon," Alldusk said. "I assumed the stone walls would muffle the noise."

"Well, they don't," Grindlethorn said irritably. "If you want to blow things up, go down to Delair's mine. As long as you're on *my* floor, I'd like a bit of peace."

Grindlethorn stalked away, slamming the classroom door behind him.

Alldusk shrugged, smiling. "Maybe we should see about soundproofing this room," he said.

Tristan and Rusty laughed.

When Tristan and the other students made their way down to Delair's first-floor classroom the next day, Tristan paused beside the dark tunnel, wondering if it really was a mine. Delair couldn't be expected to show up for more than three class days a week, though when he did he punished anyone who was absent. When he was in class, Delair often brought rare rocks and colorful crystal formations to show off—he was much more interested in these rocks than in his subject, which he claimed was purely theoretical anyway.

"Most books on magic assert that power can be collected from any of the elements," Delair said. "Unfortunately, we currently only know how to produce magical vapor from the elements of earth and fire. If magicians were once able to use air and water as well, that knowledge is long since forgotten."

Out of the corner of his eye, Tristan noticed Amber shaking her head.

Even Grindlethorn's medicine classes were far more interesting than Tristan had expected. The majority of Gracewright's herbs were used in Grindlethorn's classes; usually the students spent the hour crushing plants to make poultices and copying down endless uses for each new herb they procured. Grindlethorn also had a habit of calling impromptu class sessions whenever a student came to him for medical attention—after Cassidy and later Cailyn were put through this embarrassing ordeal, Tristan decided he wouldn't go to the hospital room unless he was dying.

Easily the most disappointing class proved to be their

magic lessons with Professor Brikkens. After the magic show on the first day of school, Tristan had expected more of the same; instead, Brikkens usually spent the period lecturing the students on the dangers of magic. His rambling, roundabout way of talking quickly grew exasperating—since his was the first class of the day, Tristan and many of his fellows often spent the hour with their heads pillowed on their arms, drifting off to sleep. Only Rusty attended the class as enthusiastically as ever.

It came as a surprise, then, when Brikkens announced that he would be giving everyone a chance to try magic.

At the unexpected announcement, Tristan lifted his head from the desk and blinked up at Brikkens, whose bulk was spilling over the arms of his sturdy chair.

"Ah, Mr. Fairholm," Brikkens said happily. Pushing his glasses farther up his stubby nose, he leaned forward and peered at Tristan.

"Yeah?" Tristan said sleepily. He sat up straighter, smoothing his hair over his face.

"Brinley Alldusk tells me that you're rather good at detecting auras. Is this true?"

Tristan shrugged.

"Well, come forward," Brikkens urged. "You will be the first to attempt a rudimentary spell, because out of everyone here, you are the most likely to succeed."

Tristan was sure that Amber knew more than him, though he decided not to correct Brikkens. Instead he rose and crossed the room to stand behind the professor. No one was napping now—Leila eyed Tristan with doubtful curiosity, while Zeke sat forward in his chair and smirked.

Brikkens dug into a pocket of the hideous maroon vest he always wore. Then he grabbed Tristan by the wrist and pressed one of the golden marbles into his hand. Tristan looked in surprise at the marble, cold and metallic against his palm; he had expected something a little more unusual, given that it was spun from pure magic.

"Now what?" Tristan said. "How am I supposed to use it?" He tried not to look around the room—half of the students wanted him to fail spectacularly, while the others anticipated no better.

Brikkens cleared his throat. "Well, the key to magic is concentration. To manipulate the power of this orb, you must isolate a single thought from within the complexity of your mind, and use this command to direct the magic. Allow any unnecessary thoughts to intrude, and the spell will be broken—hence, the magic will drain away with no results. Or, if you're unlucky, the spell could go awry."

Swallowing, Tristan closed his hand around the icy marble.

"Well, now, let's see what you can do," Brikkens said enthusiastically. "The amount of magic stored in a single orb isn't enough to do any real harm, so give us a show, my boy!"

That was it? Had the professor given better instructions the week before, when Tristan had been dozing off? Why hadn't he paid better attention?

Tristan took a steadying breath and looked around the room, hoping for inspiration. The curving walls shone white and empty, as blank as his thoughts, but as he turned his gaze to the ceiling, he remembered their first day of class. Brikkens had changed the color of the domed ceiling...but first, Eli had suggested he grow a tree.

Cradling the marble in the palm of his right hand, Tristan dug in his pockets with his left. After a moment he unearthed a handful of debris from botany; mixed into the dirt and pebbles were a few likely-looking seeds. He dropped the whole handful onto the clean marble floor behind his back.

Now what? The students were beginning to lose interest. When Brikkens had done his magic show, he'd blown on the marbles before dropping them, so Tristan did the same, just to be safe. Then he closed his eyes and tried to marshal his thoughts.

Slowly he managed to dull his awareness, until his mind was empty aside from the single desire. *Grow*, he thought, trying to be stern. *I don't know what kind of plant you are, but you're getting plenty of sunlight and water and...*

The marble began to change in his hand, growing warmer and warmer, while at the same time becoming less substantial. Tristan opened his eyes just to see that it was still there, and his concentration shattered. The marble hadn't moved, though it was starting to cool already. He was losing hold of the spell.

Okay, Tristan continued, ignoring the thrill of anticipation that ran through him. He squeezed his eyes shut once again. *This time you're actually going to grow.* He pictured a seed unfurling its leaves, easing its root into the earth, stretching a stalk towards the sky....

The marble was getting hot again, until it was like holding a naked flame. *Now grow.* He turned his hand over and let the weightless magic vapor slide away.

Shoulders tingling in excitement, Tristan opened his eyes and looked across the polished round table. Damian and Zeke were sniggering, and Eli had turned to mutter something to Trey. Leila shrugged and mouthed, *it's all right.*

All at once, the room grew silent. Zeke sat up straighter in his chair, and Hayley's round eyes widened until her eyebrows disappeared beneath her bangs. Tristan didn't know what they were looking at. Could they see his scars? He pressed his hair into place again.

Then something nudged Tristan in the back of the knee. He jumped and whirled around—there was something shooting up from the ground.

His seeds were growing.

Shocked, Tristan stumbled away from the cluster of plants. The tallest was a pale, delicate tree that shivered as it grew, sending out leaves and new branches that uncurled faster than a lizard's tongue. There was another plant blossoming to its rear, a tangled dark bush with thorns. As the bush crept its way up the tree's thickening trunk, it budded and then erupted in scarlet blooms.

When the tree unfolded like an umbrella beneath the domed ceiling, Tristan's spine tingled with power. In that instant he could feel magic coursing through his veins and hovering in the air, just beyond his grasp. This magic wasn't frightening or confusing—no, it was subtle and potent and *good.*

Professor Brikkens began applauding, leaning his weight so heavily on one arm of his chair that the whole chair looked in danger of falling over. "Bravo, my friend! Really excellent! What a surprise!"

After a moment of bewildered silence, most of the class joined in Brikkens' applause. Rusty grinned and said something to Leila, who scowled.

"I never expected you to succeed, Mr. Fairholm," Brikkens said. "You clearly have a remarkable—"

He stopped short, hands frozen in mid-gesture. The plants hadn't finished changing—the roses shuddered, and a moment later Tristan realized that the petals were withering. The flowers crumpled in on themselves until the petals began dropping to the ground, brown and dead. After sending out one last branch, the tree seemed to droop, its leaves drifting down to join the rose petals on the floor.

"What's happening?" Rusty asked, his voice loud in the stunned silence.

"Unless Mr. Fairholm intended to kill his lovely new plants," Brikkens said, "I would assume this comes from a gap in concentration. That's only to be expected; I don't know anyone who has performed such a large-scale spell within a year of learning the method. My dear boy, you have a remarkable gift."

Slightly disappointed, Tristan slunk back to his seat. From here he had a better view of the tree—the tops of its dying branches had sagged over the trunk, casting an odd shadow across the dried rosebush.

"But how come that tree died?" Rusty said anxiously. Tristan heard a thud—Leila had kicked him under the table.

"Well!" Brikkens adjusted his glasses. "Mr. Lennox, you have just given me a splendid idea. I want each of you to come up here and try reviving the tree. It won't require a great deal of magic; come up here, dear boy, you can begin."

Looking startled, Rusty joined Brikkens at the front of the room.

"So, er…" He took the marble from Brikkens and turned to stare at the tree, fists on his hips. With a furtive glance at Tristan, Rusty blew on the marble, closed his eyes, and then let the ball drop. As soon as the marble left Rusty's hand, Tristan knew the spell wouldn't work. The marble fell just like a lump of metal, where it hit the ground with a heavy thud and rolled to the foot of Brikkens' chair.

"Ah, well," Brikkens said cheerfully. "Next!"

Leila was also unsuccessful; when she returned to her seat, she nudged Tristan in the side and whispered, "How did you do that?"

"No idea." Tristan realized he was grinning, so he reached for his pencil, trying to straighten his face. "I just concentrated on what I wanted—it's like Brikkens said."

Leila was scowling at him, so he sighed and muttered, "Okay, he did a really bad job explaining it. I've just had a lot of practice controlling my thoughts lately."

Brikkens called up every student without success, until he reached Amber, seated directly to his left.

"Well, we're already out of time," Brikkens said, "but you might as well give it a shot, Miss Ashton."

Tristan sat up straight as Amber made her way uncertainly to the front of the room.

When she took her place in front of the class, eyes downcast, Amber smoothed a wisp of pale hair out of her face and studied her marble. After a moment her brilliant eyes grew clouded, and she poured the magic from her hand like water. As the golden vapor drifted towards the tree, something began happening almost at once.

The leaves on the ground swirled as though caught in a breeze, while the remaining dead leaves dropped from the branches. As soon as the dry leaves fell away, they were replaced by green tendrils that bulged and unfurled into glossy new leaves. The tree shot out another branch and began to grow bigger than ever, stretching up towards the high domed ceiling until it was fully twice as tall as Amber. Cloudy white flower buds sprang to life, hugging each branch like a robe of brilliant moss. A second breeze coursed through the branches, and as the petals swirled away in a honeyed rain, small yellow fruits swelled in their place.

Suddenly the floor creaked hideously, and the marble heaved—there was a deafening CRACK and the tiles split in two.

"Earthquake!" Brikkens shouted, surging to his feet.

As the marble floor splintered, the tiles pulling apart, something thick and brown shoved its way through the crack. It took Tristan a moment to recognize the wooden thing as a massive root.

Brikkens paled at the sight of his beautiful floor being ripped apart. He opened and closed his mouth like a fish, struggling for words.

Tristan looked back at the tree and saw that its branches were now drooping with lemons, the sweet smell wafting through the room. Smiling absently, Amber plucked one of the lemons and brought it to Tristan.

"Thanks—what's this for?"

Amber shrugged. "They're your lemons."

"But…but…" Brikkens sputtered. "My room…my classroom!" His face turned from white to crimson. "Miss Ashton. Mr. Fairholm," he wheezed. "Ten hours' punishment for you both. If you had enough control over magic to grow that tree, you should have known better than to ruin my pretty floor!"

Tristan glanced at Amber in annoyance—this was by far the longest punishment he'd ever received. Amber didn't seem to realize what Brikkens had said, or perhaps she didn't care, because she was still gazing happily at her lemon tree.

Though they were already late in leaving for Grindlethorn's second period class, Tristan and Rusty stayed behind to help Leila gather an armful of lemons for Quinsley.

"That was completely unfair," Leila said as they walked down the hall towards the kitchen. "Brikkens didn't give you any instructions, so he can't punish you for wrecking his floor! If he had any decency, he'd blame himself."

"It does seem kind of unfair," Rusty said consolingly. "You could always work off the hours with Gracewright, though—she hardly makes you do anything."

"It's not that," Tristan fumed. "Do you realize how much *time* that is? It's three hours a night if I'm going to be done by Friday, and that's on top of homework and classes! I won't be able to sleep!"

Leila paused to readjust her armful of lemons. "That's the problem with this place. No matter how nice the teachers are, they all follow Drakewell's orders."

"You've gotta admit, though, we're being treated awfully well," Rusty said fairly. "We're learning a ton, and I've never eaten so much good food in my life."

Tristan shrugged. "We just need a bit more security," he said, following Leila into the kitchen. "If we had a different headmaster, I'd ask for two separate bedrooms. I don't like having Damian's crowd so close—they make me nervous."

They had reached the kitchen, so Tristan held the door for Leila. "Hey, Gerry," she called. "Look what Tristan grew!"

Quinsley wiped his hands on his apron and turned to greet them. "Morning, Leila. Aren't you supposed to be in class?" Then he noticed what the three of them were carrying. "Lemons! Good morning, Tristan, Rusty—I haven't gotten a chance to talk with you two in ages! Did you really grow these, Tristan?"

Tristan nodded and dropped his armful of lemons at the edge of the enormous counter. "And if Grindlethorn punishes us for missing class, I'll come back this evening and help you cook them."

Quinsley beamed at him. "All right, now run along. I'll see you all later. Thanks a bunch, Leila!"

As they hurried out of the kitchen, Leila muttered, "I wish we had separate bedrooms too."

"What?"

"It's like you were saying a moment ago—I don't like sharing a room with Zeke and Damian. Last week I stopped by the bunkroom in the middle of dinner, remember, and I ran into Zeke there. He was standing over my bed and cutting a hole in my book-bag with a massive knife."

"And you didn't tell anyone?" Rusty said, wide-eyed.

Leila turned onto the stairs, walking faster now. "Of course not." Tristan and Rusty bounded ahead to catch up. "I pulled out a knife and threatened him—he ran for it."

"So now you're stealing knives, too?" Tristan asked, grinning.

Leila paused just outside the classroom. "I'm always in the kitchen. How hard do you think it is?"

That night they had lemonade for dinner and lemon pie afterwards, and when Tristan had finished eating, he and Amber made their way up to the greenhouse to work off their punishment with Gracewright.

It was a perfectly clear night, the black sky peppered with stars. Tristan lifted his head, the ever-present wind grazing his cheeks, and watched the full moon bobbing along the distant ridge.

"That lemon tree was really beautiful, once you saved it," he said softly, though he wasn't sure Amber was listening. Her eyes were clouded and distant, just like when she'd done the spell earlier that day.

"You're not mad at me?" she asked, surprising him.

Tristan shrugged. "I'll get over it."

He had asked Gracewright at dinner whether she needed help that night, and she'd looked surprisingly relieved by the offer. Now the professor waved to them from the greenhouse door, her glittering silver shawl appearing to float above the ground in the dark.

"I've just been rearranging the greenhouse," she said, "so I'll need your help outside this evening." Pulling the greenhouse door closed behind her, Gracewright crossed the lawn to join Tristan and Amber. "Auras tend to glow brightest under a full moon, so both of you should be able to distinguish magical plants from the regular varieties. I'm hoping to use whatever you find to restock the greenhouse, so be sure you dig up the roots as well."

Tristan glanced at Amber, who nodded dreamily.

"I'm desperately in need of your assistance just now," Gracewright continued, lowering her voice. "If you each put in three hours of good work tonight, I'll give you credit for six. Sound good?"

"Thanks," Tristan said fervently.

Amber had already wandered off into the forest, her dark coat and jeans melting against the black trees—Tristan could only make out her silver hair now, a small moonbeam against the soft forest darkness. He hurried after her.

"Do you think I'll be able to see the plants?" he asked.

"Of course." Amber stopped and put a hand lightly on his shoulder, turning him so he faced a gap between two trees. "You simply need to learn how to look. Concentrate now, just like when you grew the tree."

"But what—"

Amber touched a finger to his lips, stopping his question; then she pulled her hand away and looked down. It was too dark to tell whether she was blushing.

Tristan didn't know what he was supposed to concentrate on, so instead he tried emptying his mind. From far away came the melancholy hooting of an owl; he followed the hollow note until it faded, until the only sound was the wind sighing through the pines. He looked down, running his eyes across the featureless dirt—and stopped, surprised. Ringing the base of the closest pine was a wreath of glowing blue leaves, speckled with white flowers.

"Whoa," Tristan said. He dropped to his knees beside the plant, afraid the glow would fade if he blinked. "So what is this, anyway?"

Amber's lips twitched. "I understand magic, not plants. I have no idea."

Just as he was easing a section of leaves from the earth, Tristan heard voices from the clearing.

"Who's that?" he whispered, pausing with one hand in the dirt. One of the voices definitely sounded like Merridy, and he was certain the other ghostly figures were teachers as well.

Amber was no longer paying Tristan any attention; while she made her way deeper into the forest, Tristan abandoned his plant and hurried back towards the clearing.

The teachers were wending their way towards the greenhouse now, and Tristan recognized dark-haired Alldusk and bald, mustached Delair accompanying Merridy. He followed them around the clearing, hiding just within the trees.

Gracewright emerged from the greenhouse as the other professors joined her, almost glowing in the light that spilled from the open doorway.

"So good of you to come," Gracewright said. "I trust (she lowered her voice and whispered something that sounded like 'Drakewell') doesn't know about this?"

"Of course not," Merridy said brusquely. "Though why *you're* afraid of him, of all people…"

"Fear has nothing to do with this, Darla," Gracewright said, her white hair bobbing as she shook her head fiercely. "I just think we should observe caution, as long—" She pulled the greenhouse door closed behind her, cutting off the end of her sentence.

Cursing under his breath, Tristan ran around to the back of the greenhouse. The trees brushed right up against the glass behind the greenhouse, so he crouched in the shadow of a towering pine and brought his face close to the opaque glass. After trying for a moment to register the confusion of voices, Tristan noticed a small pane of broken glass level with his shoulder. He stood cautiously, trying not to rustle his feet against the dry mulch, and pressed one eye to the edge of the cracked pane.

The greenhouse had been completely torn apart. The long wood table that spanned the room had collapsed, as though someone had chopped it in half with an axe. The ground was strewn with wreckage, both dirt and shards of pottery from the flowerpots that had lined the walls and shredded leaves from the plants that had hung from the ceiling.

The professors were silent and ashen, gazing around the room. Merridy muttered to herself in distress, glancing over her shoulder as though she expected Drakewell to swoop down from the ceiling. When she turned to look at the broken pane behind her, Tristan barely managed to duck out of sight in time.

"You must realize how insecure this school is," Alldusk said gravely. "Perhaps we should look into a few safety measures—keeping the location secret was a good idea, but it only goes so far."

"The caves are entirely protected," said Professor Delair.

Tristan got back to his feet and chanced another look through the broken pane.

"Thank you, Osric," Gracewright said tiredly, "but the caves are the least of our worries. Unless you've run into a colony of trolls or something ridiculous like that, there's no way we could be attacked from underground." She looked unhappily around the greenhouse; even her flyaway hair seemed to droop.

Delair shrugged. "I was merely suggesting that certain

metallic compounds could be arranged to protect this place. Of course, this method needs a great deal of work, and it may—"

"Thank you," Gracewright said more firmly. "Unless you have anything relevant to contribute, you're welcome to return to your coffee. I'm very sorry I disturbed you."

Shaking his head, Delair turned and shuffled to the door.

When Delair was gone, Gracewright sank into a chair whose back had been smashed away and put her head in her hands, looking smaller than ever. "I don't understand," she said sadly. "Nothing was stolen!" She looked up and glanced from Merridy to Alldusk. "Why would someone want to destroy this place?"

"What about the kids?" Merridy asked, looking at Alldusk for support. "Most of them were criminals before they came here."

Alldusk put his hands in the pockets of his black coat and studied Merridy's face. "I don't think it was them," he said at last. "This is their new home—I don't see why they would try to sabotage it."

"You don't know them that well, Brinley," Merridy whispered. "I was the one who met them first, remember? It was different seeing them straight out of detention centers and jails—I doubt you would have recognized most of them."

"I agree with Brinley," Gracewright said. "They're not evil, Darla. Perhaps they were mean at first, but now they're polite and obedient for the most part."

"For the *most* part," Merridy insisted. Her face had gone pale.

Alldusk cleared his throat. "You'll need help putting this back together, I assume?"

"Yes, of course," Gracewright said. "I should have enough supplies for two more weeks of your Chemistry classes, but after that you may have to stick to minerals for a while. Fairholm and Ashton came to work off their punishment earlier tonight, so I've put them to work finding new magical plants."

Alldusk chuckled. "I heard about the lemon tree. I wonder what Drakewell will do about it."

Something brushed lightly against Tristan's shoulder—he jumped back in surprise and tripped. Catching himself on a pine bough, he turned to see what had startled him. It was Amber.

"Don't do that!" Tristan whispered. "Do you want us to get caught?"

Amber said nothing, so Tristan took her elbow and steered her firmly away from the greenhouse. When they were deep enough in the forest that the professors' voices had faded into silence, he stopped and released Amber.

"Sorry I haven't been helping," he said. "Someone smashed up the greenhouse, so the teachers are all upset."

"I know." Amber blinked at Tristan, turquoise eyes reflecting the moonlight. "I was listening."

"You mean you were standing behind me that whole time?" Tristan shook his head, amused in spite of himself. "Please don't do that—it makes me nervous." He had a hard time being angry at Amber, though. The moonlight had transformed her white skin and silvery hair into something magical.

"Can you see the moon's aura?" Amber asked, tilting her head skywards.

Tristan stepped back until he could see the full face of the moon, nestled between pine branches and dark sky. "You mean the white glow? That's just the sun reflecting off its surface."

Amber shook her head. "The true light does not extend so far. That silver light is the moon's aura."

"Why can't anyone else see the magic vapors in chemistry?" Tristan asked carefully.

Amber tilted her head at him, pale eyebrows raised in surprise. "You answered that yourself, only this morning. You told Leila that you have had practice controlling your mind."

Tristan hadn't realized that Amber had been listening. "Does everything have an aura?"

"Everything real."

Tristan didn't bother to ask what she meant by this. He ran a hand along one of the needled pine branches, smoothing the spikes flat until his hand encountered nothing but their waxy spines. "Who do you think attacked the greenhouse?" he asked at last.

Amber gave him a speculative look, hardly blinking. "Magic can easily be used both for creation and for ruin. The greenhouse was wrecked by someone who dislikes magic."

"Was it one of us?"

This time she didn't reply.

After studying Tristan for another moment, Amber turned and began threading her way through the trees. Though she kept her face turned towards the moon, like a flower hungry for sunlight, she stopped every few steps and lifted a plant from the earth. Tristan had no idea which way he'd come, so he trailed behind Amber, squinting at the ground. He found six more glowing magical plants, but eventually he gave up searching and just watched Amber.

By the time the moon had risen directly overhead, casting shadows like the noon sun on a cloudy day, Tristan was sure they'd been outside for three hours at least. "I think we're done," he said softly.

Amber paused, looking startled. Then she nodded, cast a final glance at the moon, and turned back towards the school. She hugged an enormous bundle of plants to her chest.

It seemed like ages before they finally reemerged in the clearing. The lights were still on in the greenhouse—when Tristan knocked, Gracewright came to the door a second later, clutching a broom and wiping dirt from her forehead.

"Thank you, kids, thank you so much," she said, slumping against the doorframe. "You can set those down right here." She waved to the stone step where Tristan stood. "Sorry—the greenhouse is a bit of a mess right now. I'll check you off for six hours. Sleep well." She sounded as though she had a cold; Tristan wondered if she'd been crying. An instant later Gracewright shut the door in his face.

The ballroom was dark and empty when Tristan and Amber descended the steps into the Lair; as they reached the far doors, Tristan slowed. "Do you think we'll forget all of this next year?" he asked quietly.

Amber frowned at him.

"When we leave, I mean. Will we even remember that magic was real?" He'd been thinking about this as they walked through the woods, trying to decide whether he would be relieved or sad to leave this place. He hadn't forgotten the feeling of power that had run through him in Brikkens' class.

This time Amber stopped, though she would not meet his eyes. "The teachers do not intend to let us go," she whispered. "They are growing old here, and so will we."

Chapter 7

The Avalanche

Tristan spent breakfast the next morning telling Leila and Rusty about what he'd seen and overheard in the greenhouse. Even as he related the details of the vandalism, he continued to think about what Amber had said. *The teachers do not intend to let us go*—if she was right, this wasn't a school so much as a prison. Tristan stared grimly into his cereal.

"Do you have any idea who it was?" Leila asked.

Blinking at the soggy granola, Tristan shook his head.

"It could've been Zeke," she said. "That's the sort of thing he would do."

Tristan just shrugged.

After Alldusk's fifth period class, Tristan hung back as the rest of the students filed out of the high, dark-walled chamber.

"No, you go on ahead," he told Leila. "I'll see you in Merridy's class."

She looked skeptical, but after a moment she shrugged

and followed the others down the hall.

"Professor Alldusk?" Tristan said. Alldusk had been kneeling beside the fire pit, his hands cupped around something in the ashes. At Tristan's voice, he started.

"Tristan! I didn't see you there." He clambered to his feet. "What is it?"

Tristan smoothed his hair over his scars. "I was wondering...uh, how long will we be at this school?"

"Well, you get a break over the summer," Alldusk said, frowning.

Heart sinking, Tristan said, "And after that? How many years are we supposed to stay here?"

Alldusk gave him a pitying look. "School officially lasts for four years," he said. "And afterwards..."

Tristan swallowed. Amber had told him the truth. "I have to get to class now," he said, clutching at the strap of his book bag. His knuckles were white. Turning sharply away from Alldusk's sympathetic half-smile, Tristan stalked to the door and thrust it open. The halls no longer felt welcoming—the Lair was cold and dark, a beautiful prison. He took the stairs two at a time to the fourth floor, where he turned left and slouched towards Merridy's room.

"There you are," Merridy said coldly when Tristan threw open the door. "An hour for tardiness."

Tristan didn't even care. Joining Leila and Rusty at the back of the room, he folded his arms on the desk and put his head down, staring blindly at the sanded wood. Leila touched his knee beneath the desk, trying to soothe him; Tristan shook off her hand as though it was a bothersome mosquito.

Maybe this was his punishment, he thought gloomily. He'd deprived his brother of a family, so the school had done the same to him. He would never graduate, never marry, never have kids, never leave this damn school.

A week later, Tristan came up to breakfast to find Merridy and Alldusk missing from the great round teachers' table. Stranger still, Drakewell was filling Merridy's usual seat, glowering at the other teachers and looking extremely out-of-place.

"What's he doing here?" Tristan asked Rusty in an undertone.

Rusty paused, his fork halfway to his mouth. "Beats me." The half-eaten sausage slid off his fork.

Leila turned pointedly away from Rusty. "We should've chosen a table closer to the teachers. Then we would be able to hear what's wrong."

That was a good idea, except the teachers weren't talking. Every one of them looked just as confused by Drakewell's presence as the students. The students were markedly quieter than usual as they ate, barely speaking and taking care to muffle the clank of their silverware against their plates.

Just as breakfast was ending, Alldusk and Merridy came down the stairs into the Lair. Both looked windswept and very upset. Alldusk stalked across the ballroom, Merridy hurrying close behind, until they reached the tables and stopped in front of Drakewell.

"This is unacceptable," Alldusk said harshly, glaring at Drakewell. "You cannot act without permission. I will *not* allow this place to become a dictatorship."

Drakewell sneered at him. "And how do you intend to ensure that?" He glanced around the dining platform. "Perhaps we should continue this conversation elsewhere—where the children cannot overhear."

Tristan dropped his eyes quickly to his emptied plate.

Merridy cleared her throat. "Maybe they should know some of it, I mean…"

"That's true," Alldusk said. "The students have a *right* to know." He slammed his fist on the table for emphasis. Tristan was surprised to see Alldusk so riled—he was usually mild-mannered and reasonable.

Alldusk turned to face the students. "Magic is dangerous," he said carefully, though Tristan could see the anger in his dark eyes. "It can be very destructive if not properly regulated. Now, the purpose of this school may be ethically unacceptable to some, but when we came here we agreed that preserving the natural order was more critical than adhering to any individual's moral code. This—"

"Enough." Every trace of a sneer was gone from Drakewell's face. "Brinley, Darla, come to my office. We need to talk." Eyes flashing, he swept out of the ballroom.

Tristan sat forward in his seat and caught Alldusk's eye; when the ballroom doors swung closed behind Drakewell, the professor crossed to his table.

"What was that about? Where were you and Merridy during breakfast?" Though Tristan spoke in a low voice, the other students turned to listen.

Alldusk sighed. "I wish I could give you a real answer. Don't mention that I said this, but…there was a huge avalanche this morning, not far from this school. It destroyed an entire village."

Merridy put her hand on Alldusk's shoulder; the gesture was almost affectionate. "We should go," she said quietly. "D-Drakewell should not be kept waiting."

Once Merridy and Alldusk had left the ballroom, the room fell silent. After glancing around nervously and fiddling with his vest, Brikkens pushed back his chair with a loud scrape and lumbered to his feet.

"Class began five minutes ago," he said gruffly.

Now Gracewright and Grindlethorn were the only ones still sitting at the large table.

"What's going on?" Damian scowled at the teachers, snatching up his books.

Hayley turned to Gracewright, eyes wide. "Are we in danger?"

It was Grindlethorn who answered. He didn't bother to point out that the Lair was hardly in danger from avalanches, since it was underground; instead he said, "This is not for you to discuss."

"But Alldusk and Merridy—" Rusty began.

"—are young and foolish," Grindlethorn snapped. "Now get to class."

Reluctantly Tristan gathered his things and followed Leila from the ballroom. The teachers had been so close to telling the truth—if Alldusk had just been allowed to finish speaking…

Though the school was buzzing the next week with rumors about the avalanche, none of them sounded remotely plausible. Merridy remained upset with Drakewell—she was distracted through lessons, missed meals, and gave punishments more readily than ever. The weekend came as a relief from the tense, unhappy week.

October arrived the next week, and within a fortnight the valley was smeared with a frosting coat of snow. Rusty had never seen much snow before, so he was skeptical when Eli and Hayley reminisced eagerly about winters where they'd received upwards of two feet in a single dumping.

Gracewright cancelled her lesson after the snowstorm, saying she had a new shipment of vines to repot, so the students spent the hour hurling snowballs at each other. What began as an innocent snowball fight quickly became nasty; Zeke and Damian rolled rocks into their snowballs, and Leila started doing the same, until it looked like they'd been in a fistfight.

When Zeke's snowball gave Leila a bloody nose, Rusty suggested a truce while they went inside to warm up.

Quinsley brought lemon tea to everyone who'd been out in the snow, though Leila was too busy nursing her bloody nose to appreciate it. "I'll get him back someday," she muttered angrily, shaking snow from the end of her black braid.

"Be careful," Rusty said. "Zeke doesn't seem like a very nice person."

"You've noticed?" Tristan said. Turning to Leila, he lowered his voice. "Seriously, though, I don't know what Zeke's capable of doing. Try not to provoke him, okay?"

"Why would I do that?" Leila said sweetly. Twisting in her chair, she glared at Zeke.

Tristan rolled his eyes. Charming and lucky at guessing answers, Zeke was a favorite with most of the teachers—if anything happened, Leila would be the one punished, not Zeke.

"Where's Evvie?" Tristan asked, trying to distract Leila. It worked—Leila turned back to her tea and scowled at him instead of Zeke.

Rusty frowned. "You've gotta call her Evangeline if you want her to like you."

"I don't," Tristan said too quickly. "Evangeline's just such a stuffy name."

"But I thought…"

"Tristan's being ridiculous," Leila said.

The snow lost a lot of its charm when Merridy announced that their first practical exam would take place the next morning. "As I've told you," she said, "this will be a chance to test your proficiency at reading maps and creating shelters."

Damian cursed. "Are you crazy? It's bloody freezing out there!"

Merridy's frown deepened. "The whole point of this class is to learn to survive when faced with adverse conditions. Snow would go under this category, in addition to the related dangers it could cause."

"Like avalanches," Zeke said lazily.

"So you're just going to throw us out there and see if we survive?" Damian said angrily.

Merridy crossed her arms. "It should not prove so difficult. You will each receive a map showing exactly where you will be dropped off, and you only have to walk five miles. If you know your way, you could be finished in less than two hours."

"That's stupid," Damian said. "I'm not going out there."

"Then you can take a zero on the exam," Merridy snapped. "And thirty hours of punishment. The proceedings are perfectly straightforward. You will each be given three days—tomorrow through Friday—to find your way back to the school. Each of you will be provided with a backpack and enough supplies to last a week; however, if you fail to return before Friday evening, you will be picked up."

Finley raised his hand. "Professor? You said this is a test—how will we be graded?"

Merridy gave him an appraising look before answering. "Any student who returns within the allotted time will receive full marks. All others will be given a zero."

"Er, Professor?" Hayley said, her hand in the air. "Do you give extra credit?"

"Is there a prize for getting back first?" Rusty asked, grinning.

"No," Merridy said. "However, the other teachers will be suspending their classes during the three days of the test.

If you make it back before Friday, you will have something of a break until Monday. Cailyn, would you help me pass these out?"

Together Cailyn and Merridy handed around a set of rather ugly brown backpacks, stained and bulging with supplies. When he received his pack, Tristan lifted it onto his desk and pulled at the drawstring, getting to his feet so he could peer inside. There was a great jumble of tools at the top, including a badly-coiled rope and a water bottle.

"Class is dismissed," Merridy said. "I suggest you take the evening to familiarize yourselves with the contents of these sacks."

As the students began to leave, their overstuffed backpacks clattering loudly, Finley's nervous voice rose above the general clamor.

"What if something happens to us?"

"We will be monitoring you. There is a way for us to…pinpoint your location." Merridy's eyes flickered to the pillar at the back of the room. Was she worried about Drakewell? "If you stay in one place for too long—more than an hour, say—someone will come rescue you. We will also check on each of you at nightfall."

"That won't help if you're being chased by a bear," Zeke said under his breath, casting a wicked grin at Leila.

Tristan silently cursed the snow.

"You're being awfully quiet," Leila commented at dinner, frowning at Tristan.

She was right—ever since Merridy had announced their test, Tristan had been arguing furiously with himself.

"Are you worried about the test?"

"Yeah, a little," Tristan said quickly.

In truth, he thought this could be his one chance to escape the school. If he ran away now, he could find a small town with phone service and call his mom. If she wanted him to come back, he would be free. He wouldn't lose his mind. He could be home in a week. And if the detention center hadn't lied, and his mother actually hated him, he would slink back to the Lair.

"The test doesn't sound so bad," Rusty said consolingly.

Tristan nodded vaguely. For some reason the thought of leaving the Lair made him feel hollow and lonely.

"Let's do something fun tonight," Leila said. "We could play cards, or—or help Gerry bake cookies."

As Tristan looked from Leila to Rusty, his stomach knotted. "I'm tired," he said. "I think I'll go to bed early."

That night, as the other students dug through their backpacks and readied themselves for the morning, Tristan just sat beside his supplies, feeling feverish.

"We should try to get back as fast as possible," Leila whispered to Tristan and Rusty. "If we're the first back, we can have a party in the bunkroom—I asked, and Gerry says he would give us whatever food we asked for."

"What about champagne?" Rusty said, grinning.

Eli had overheard. "Why on earth wouldn't we hurry?" he said in a low voice. "Do you think it'll be loads of fun, tramping through the snow and freezing our asses off at night?"

Tristan plucked morosely at the rope in his backpack. His rations were already buried at the bottom of his pack, wrapped in a sour-smelling tarp that he couldn't afford to leave behind.

"Well," Leila said, "if you run across Zeke, throw him in a frozen lake or something."

"Hey!" Zeke shouted from the other side of the bunkroom. "I heard that."

Leila glared briefly at their makeshift barrier before returning her attention to Tristan. She looked upset, as though she knew what he was planning. Avoiding her eyes, Tristan climbed into bed and turned towards the wall, though he was far from sleep.

Tristan started awake the next morning to Zeke's loud voice.

"Hey, ugly."

Tristan sat up, still caught in the grips of a familiar nightmare. It took him a moment to calm down; slowly the shadows receded and he recognized the familiar faces of his friends, who were already moving about below.

At Zeke's voice, Leila had frozen and backed away from the makeshift barrier, shifting on her feet like a cat readying to pounce.

"You scared, little miss grumpy?" Zeke said. He dragged a chair over to the barrier. "I heard you *whimpering* last night. What's wrong?"

Leila's face reddened. "We'll see who's laughing this Friday," she said stiffly. It was unlike her to take offence at Zeke's teasing. "This time you won't be able to cheat."

With a loud scrape, Zeke shoved his chair directly against the barrier; the shabby dresser wobbled dangerously as he stood and stuck his head over the top.

"I'm not worried," he said, grinning. "I hope you're planning to take a shower!" Taking careful aim, he flung his entire water bottle at Leila. The top had been unscrewed—water sloshed over Leila's face, followed by a crash as the metal struck her in the jaw.

Tristan winced sympathetically, but Leila didn't make a sound. Face hardening, she smoothed a wet strand of hair out of her eyes and kicked the water bottle away.

Laughing, Zeke and Damian led their friends out of the bunkroom. With a sympathetic grimace, Eli followed the others up to breakfast.

"Are you gonna be okay?" Rusty asked anxiously. "That was really mean of Zeke."

"You think?" Leila snapped. "Just go eat—I have to dry off."

Tristan didn't leave with Rusty; he just stood quietly and watched Leila. Once they were alone, he said, "I wouldn't retaliate if I were you."

Leila turned to him. "That's not your business," she said coldly. Then she sighed. "What is it you're planning to do?"

Tristan followed her as she stalked to the opposite side of the bunkroom. "Seriously, Leila, you shouldn't—"

"Don't avoid the question," she said. Kneeling, she lifted Zeke's backpack onto his bed and dug through it, eyes narrowed in concentration.

"I'm not doing anything," Tristan said flatly.

Leila drew something from Zeke's backpack; it was his compass. "You're lying," she said. After staring at the compass for a moment, she slammed it against the wall—the plastic cover shattered, littering the floor with small shards. These Leila kicked under the wobbly dresser. Picking up the compass, she tore the needle from its face and shoved both pieces into a drawer.

"Zeke probably didn't know how to use that thing to begin with," Tristan said, though his lips twitched.

Leila flicked her dripping braid over her shoulder and reached for the water bottle sitting beside Cassidy's bed. Unscrewing the top, she upended it into Zeke's backpack. "Better?" she said.

Tristan snorted.

Leila threw Zeke's backpack to the floor where she'd found it, leaving a spreading pool of water on the marble tiles. When she turned back to Tristan, her face softened.

"Don't…"

Her voice trailed off, and she shook her head. Cautiously she lifted a hand and brushed two fingers along Tristan's cheek. Then she turned and hurried from the room.

After breakfast, the students followed Merridy up the stairs to the meadow, talking in excited whispers. Tristan felt very distant from the group, but he tried to smile and nod at whatever Rusty was jabbering on about.

There was a hold-up at the top of the stairs—the students in front had stopped, and Tristan heard them swearing and exclaiming loudly.

"Keep moving." Merridy's clipped tone rose above the other voices. Tristan, Leila, and Rusty had to jostle their way outside, just like the day when they'd first seen the mountains.

This time there was a helicopter sitting in the center of the meadow.

Rusty cursed in surprise, just as Tristan said, "Damn! What *is* this place?"

"*That's* why everyone is so worried about protecting the school," Leila said under her breath. "It's because the teachers are goddamn millionaires, and they have a fortune hidden in the tunnels."

"Will we all fit in this thing?" Hayley asked nervously.

"If we can't," Eli said, "we'll tie you to the tail and just let you hang there."

The front window of the helicopter came unlatched and swung open; Quinsley stuck out his head, grinning at the students. "Is everyone here?"

"How come you're the one flying this thing?" Damian asked indignantly.

"I *am* actually a licensed pilot. I didn't come get you at the start of the year just because I liked doing the extra work." Smile widening at the look on Damian's face, Quinsley pointed at each of the students in turn, counting them. "Perfect. Now, if you'd pop open that hatch, Zeke, we can be off."

Tristan wasn't sure that such a small helicopter could bear the weight of all fifteen students, provided that they fit inside to begin with. Maybe it was supported by magic. He was the last one to climb up the rickety metal ladder into the belly of the helicopter, following Rusty and Leila. Merridy waved to him from the ground—apparently she was staying behind.

Tristan shoved his shoulders against someone's stomach, jostling Rusty and Eli farther into the cramped depths of the helicopter until there was space for him to pull his legs up. When Merridy folded the ladder away and slammed the hatch closed, they were plunged into complete darkness.

After a moment of quiet, the helicopter vibrated and the blade started to spin overhead with a thundering chop-chop-chop. As the nose dipped forward and they lifted off the ground, Tristan's stomach dropped.

Someone's elbow collided painfully with Tristan's ribs—unable to see who the arm belonged to, he leaned over and whispered, "Who is this?"

"Evangeline." The whisper was sharp and unhappy; a second later Evvie jerked her arm away.

Minutes later, the helicopter settled with a jolt, tilting sideways. "Ow!" Tristan cried out—he had slid sideways and smashed his shoulder on something sharp. His voice was drowned out by the yells of his fellow students; just as Tristan managed to right himself, something heavy slammed into him and crushed him against the wall.

"Sorry!" Hayley's voice cried.

Behind Tristan, Zeke cursed loudly—there came a heavy crash and a shriek, and then a shaft of light flooded the blackened space.

"What's—" Rusty shouted, breaking off abruptly as someone's thrashing leg kicked him off balance.

"Aargh!" Arms flailing, Rusty fell backwards and dropped, yelling manically, out of the open hatch.

Leila fell to her knees, staring anxiously after him. Tristan leaned over the doorway and saw Rusty sprawled on the snowy ground. He swayed on his feet, panicked. For a moment he couldn't breathe.

Then Rusty lifted his head and clambered drunkenly to his feet, grinning.

"I'm okay," he said, waving at Tristan. Leila shook her head in disbelief.

Quinsley jumped down from the cockpit, shaking his head. "Honestly," he said. "I leave you kids alone for five minutes, and someone nearly dies." The white-haired cook was smiling, though. "Toss down Rusty's backpack, Leila. He can start the test first, since he's already down here."

Leila rolled her eyes, her face still pale from worry, though she did as Quinsley had asked. The backpack clattered onto the snowy ground, where Rusty picked it up and slung it over one shoulder.

"Good luck," Tristan called, nearly choking on the words. If he succeeded, this would be the last time he saw Rusty.

"It's not fair," Damian said sullenly. He was still lost in the shadows at the back of the helicopter. "He's got an advantage, starting before the rest of us.

Quinsley raised an eyebrow at him. "Didn't you hear

Darla's rules? It's not a race."

"If you can't read the map, a full week's head start won't get you anywhere," Leila said.

Zeke snorted. "You're saying *you* can? I doubt it." He glanced at Damian. "Bet you five bucks she'll call for help before the helicopter has a chance to take off."

Leila's furious retort was cut off by Quinsley slamming the hatch shut, throwing everyone into darkness once again. Tristan grabbed her arm instinctively, afraid she would try to punch Zeke in the dark.

Tristan could feel Leila whirl to face him. "Triss?" she whispered.

"Yeah." He eased his grip on her arm. "Don't do anything stupid."

Tristan was the second one dropped off. As he jumped off the ladder into the snow, he was hit by an icy gust of wind so powerful that it threw him backwards into a snowdrift. He stumbled to his feet and waved at Leila; the propeller slammed him with another blast of air, ripping the goodbye from his lips.

Then he was alone.

For a long time Tristan just stood there, clutching his backpack and his map, taking in his surroundings. He was on a short ledge halfway up the slope of a craggy, towering mountain; how Quinsley had found enough space to land the helicopter, he didn't know. The peak loomed behind him, sparkling like a diamond beneath its sheen of snow, while the slope fell smoothly away just past the ledge. Trees began again about two hundred feet down, tentative at first and then boldly swathing the slope in green, though there was no sign of the school or the lake below that. At the foot of this mountain, another slope rose to a spiny ridge, beyond which he could see more snow-dusted peaks all gleaming in the sun.

Now that he was here, feet already growing numb in his boots, cheeks raw from the fierce wind, he wasn't sure why he'd been so anxious to run away. It would be so much nicer to make a beeline for the Lair, where he would be greeted with a steaming mug of hot cocoa and a warm bed. Besides, his parents probably still hated him. They might be happy to learn that he had gone insane.

Shivering in the violent wind, Tristan unfolded his map and struggled to hold it flat while he got his bearings. The school wasn't marked anywhere, though he could recognize the ledge where he stood, an island amidst a dark wreath of contour lines.

Partway around the mountain, Tristan could make out a ridge that sloped south. Beyond this, the map ended. If he followed the ridge far enough, maybe he could find a way down. At least he would be moving in the right direction.

There was no use waiting any longer, so Tristan folded up the map and tucked it into his pocket. He was going home.

Hunching his shoulders against the wind, Tristan left the ledge and started forging a path through new snowdrifts. There appeared to be a narrow trail curling around the mountain, beginning where the ledge ended and quickly vanishing into the snow. Tristan picked his way along this path, fighting the snow and the wind with each careful footstep.

The sun was dipping low in the sky by the time Tristan caught sight of the ridge he was aiming for. His stomach was hollow and aching—he hadn't found a place safe enough to stop and rummage in his pack for food. When the ridge came into view, he sighed in relief. He had begun to fear he was lost.

Once he reached the end of the path, just below the ridge, Tristan crouched in the snow and dug for his food. The ridge and the mountain slope created something of a shelter, protecting him from the worst of the wind.

The food was at the top of his backpack, so he was able to pull it free without removing his gloves. His first day's rations of an apple and an energy bar looked sadly inadequate, and his stomach grumbled louder than ever as he tore open the plastic wrapper. Next he finished the apple in six bites, hunching forward against the wind. Stomach still growling, he flung the core down the mountainside.

While he'd been walking, though his face had been numb from the wind, his body had flared with the heat of exertion. Now the cold was beginning to seep through his coat and shirt—he shuddered violently for a second, as though realizing this for the first time. Once the tremor subsided, he zipped his backpack closed and jumped to his feet. He was not about to freeze to death.

Tristan scrambled up the short slope to the top of the

ridge, stiff from the cold but revitalized. He was no longer lost; from here the ridge took him nearly to the edge of the map, beyond which he might find real civilization.

The sun was dropping quicker now—as Tristan slogged through the snow, he measured his progress along the ridge against the sun's descent, watching it plummet towards the peaks on his right. The sun seemed determined to win the race, so Tristan trudged faster than ever, his hood falling back in a brutal gust of wind. It shouldn't be so cold, not this early in the season; the wind stripped all the warmth from the air and scraped at his neck like a razor.

Too soon, the sun bobbed against the glowing peaks and vanished, throwing the ridge into the wake of a frigid shadow.

Tristan stopped, shoulders stiff. He had barely come halfway along the ridge. His fingers and toes were numb and aching, the bottoms of his jeans soggy with snow. He couldn't stop here, not with a sheer drop on either side and barely two feet of level ground underfoot.

"Damn it, damn it," he muttered. There was no way he'd reach the end of the ridge quickly enough. He had to make for the bottom of the slope before darkness fell.

Flexing his stiff fingers, he knelt and lowered one foot cautiously over the edge of the ridge. Nudging the snow aside with his toe, he scrabbled his foot against the rocks until he found a solid foothold. He dug his fingers firmly into the snow before lowering his weight onto that foot. In this manner, one tiny movement at a time, Tristan began climbing down from the ridge.

Inch by cautious inch, Tristan crept lower, leaving a deep gouge in the snow where he'd come.

Halfway down, his fingers grew so cold that they wouldn't bend. All at once he began trembling violently, barely keeping his hold on the rocks. He couldn't say whether he shook from cold or fear or exhaustion—biting his tongue, he pressed his body closer to the slope and waited for the new tremor to pass. In the silence, he could hear his breath rasping too loudly in his ears.

CRACK!

A thunderous shot broke the stillness, echoing around the rocks like a giant cracking his knuckles. Tristan stared wildly around for the source—then he saw the snow above him beginning to splinter.

His foot slipped as he tried to scramble away from the shifting ice—

"ARGH!"

He began sliding down the slope, flailing for a handhold, but the rocks were loose and skittered away beneath him. His knee slammed against a boulder, and he picked up speed, yelling wildly, though his voice was drowned in the thunderous rush of snow.

Above him, it seemed that a whole section of the mountain had come loose. Roaring and clamoring down the slope after him came a massive volley of snow, sweeping up everything in its path.

Tristan finally managed to shove his toe into the rocks, slowing his painful fall. He hunched his body against the slope, shuddering and trying to breathe past the icy fear, and then—

WHAM!

The snow and ice hit Tristan, slamming him backwards with the force of a truck. Tristan screamed—he was thrown from his perch and tossed down the ridge, falling blindly, yelling until his throat was raked hoarse. Odd images flashed before his eyes in the flickering blackness—Leila smiling at him, Rusty laughing, Marcus nodding sadly. *I trust you.*

Then Tristan smashed to the ground, one leg wrenched beneath him. The snow pounded him against the rocks, slamming his head and ribs until he gasped for air.

Blackness pooled in his eyes, but he fought it; his mouth was filled with something bitter and grimy, something that pressed his throat closed so he could hardly breathe. He gagged and tried to spit out the filthy snow, but he couldn't even manage that much. He was pinned to the ground, the oppressive weight of the snow growing heavier and heavier by the second. Everything ached; he could hardly find his own arm beneath the crushing mass of snow.

With a tremendous struggle, he managed to shift a single finger. A spasm ran up his arm; everything was so dark, the air growing stale and beginning to wrench at his lungs; he was drowning in the snow, smothered beneath an unbearable weight. He clenched his fist weakly, sending another spasm along his arm. With a grunt of pain, he wrenched the whole arm free of the snow.

Thrusting his fist forward, Tristan smashed a hole through the dense layer of snow—a stream of icy fresh air swirled down to him and he inhaled deeply, shuddering. He turned his face towards the air, trembling, and eased both arms up through the small hole. With an agonizing jolt, he wrenched his body from the depression he'd created and onto the new field of rugged snow.

For a long time Tristan lay perfectly still, struggling to stay conscious. The snow digging into his back was so cold that it numbed his skin through the layers of clothes, which was almost a relief after the agony.

I'm going to move now, Tristan thought firmly. He blinked, hardly aware whether his eyes were open or closed. Either way, everything was shrouded in hazy darkness. It was so easy just lying where he was; his limbs no longer seemed attached to the rest of his body. Giving up would be so easy… Yet Tristan fought the blackness. *I have to get off the ice. If I'm rescued, I won't be able to go home. If I die…*

Who would care?

Tristan was unable to contemplate his own death with anything but an icy calm.

Suddenly he felt hot; why was he wearing a jacket when he could feel a furnace beneath his skin? Shifting in discomfort, Tristan managed to gain control of his arms, though he had the unpleasant sensation that his wrists ended in lumps of rock. He pushed himself to a sitting position and fumbled with the zipper on his jacket. His wooden hands wouldn't grasp the zipper properly, and there was no sensation in his fingers.

Okay, he thought, *now I have to—to find somewhere to sleep.* He would shelter in the trees tonight and continue his trek south in the morning.

Just as he made this decision, every last particle of strength and determination drained from him. What was the point of living, anyway? Tristan could answer that one easily enough—he was afraid of death. But his eyes slid shut against his will and his head dropped forward; gentle as a feather, he settled back onto the snow. He was floating in the darkness, suspended in heavy nothingness, and then it was all gone.

Chapter 8

After the Test

When Tristan woke, he was surrounded by teachers. He lay in a very soft bed; when he tried to turn onto his side, his right leg anchored him in place, heavy and stiff. It was wrapped in bandages, which meant he was in Grindlethorn's hospital room.

"He's waking up," Merridy's voice said. A note of fear had crept into her customarily hard tone. "Someone bring water."

Blinking, Tristan recognized Alldusk, Gracewright, Quinsley, Merridy, and Grindlethorn hovering beside his bed. Quinsley and Grindlethorn were glaring at each other—Tristan had the feeling he'd interrupted an argument. Instinctively he ran a hand through his damp hair so the left side of his face was covered once again.

"How are you feeling?" Quinsley asked, his usually cheerful face grim. He handed Tristan a full glass of water.

Tristan's throat still felt grimy and raw—he took a

deep swallow of the water before he could speak. "I'm fine," he lied.

"Your ankle is badly twisted," Grindlethorn said. "It's a miracle you didn't break anything." Shifting Tristan's blankets to the side, Grindlethorn lifted his foot and showed him the new cast. "The bandaging is sturdy enough that you should be able to walk, but you should be careful until the herbs have fully set. Try and stay off your feet for the next couple days."

Alldusk cleared his throat. "May I have a private word with Tristan?"

"Of course," Quinsley said, cutting across Grindlethorn's protest. "We'll be up in the ballroom. Dinner is probably ready by now."

Merridy gave Alldusk a brisk nod and hurried from the hospital room; Gracewright and Grindlethorn followed, both grumbling to themselves.

Looking uncomfortable, Alldusk crossed to the door and shut it before drawing a chair to the side of Tristan's bed. "I shouldn't be telling you this," he said in a low voice. "However…. If my suspicions are correct, you had best know the truth." Alldusk sighed. "You wanted to leave this school, yes?"

Tristan shrugged, trying not to betray his surprise. How had Alldusk guessed?

"Darla and I were keeping an eye on the students during the test, and I noticed that you decided on a course that led you very deliberately away from the school. No, don't say anything," Alldusk said, cutting off Tristan's denial. "Whether you were trying to run away or not, you should know that it is not safe to leave just now."

"Professor, I—" Tristan was surprised. He had been expecting a reprimand.

Alldusk waved one hand, dismissing Tristan's protest. "I don't know whether you've figured this out yet, but the school is in danger. We're afraid that something is attacking us—the greenhouse was recently wrecked, though you and the other students weren't informed of this."

"Maybe a student did that," Tristan said echoing Merridy's words.

"Maybe," Alldusk said. "However, the greenhouse was locked from the inside, so we're afraid whoever destroyed it used magic to break in."

"And you think someone wanted to stop us from doing—whatever we're doing?" Tristan asked, struggling to sit up. Alldusk took pity on him and propped a pillow behind his back.

"That's a good guess." He sighed. "The idea that someone outside of this school can use magic is a very disturbing thought. And it means that the last thing you'd want to do is run into that person while stranded miles away from the Lair." Shaking his head, he got to his feet. "So you see why we're trying to be careful."

Tristan nodded, grateful that Alldusk hadn't been angry with him. Of course, if the mountains were so dangerous, why had Merridy been allowed to send the students out there alone?

After lying in the hospital bed for some time, Tristan

grew fed up and decided to leave. Though his whole leg jolted in pain, he was able to stand; biting his tongue, he hobbled to the door and limped up the two flights of stairs to the ballroom.

When he reached the doors to the ballroom, Tristan heard raised voices—it sounded as though the teachers were still arguing. He stopped and leaned heavily on the marble wall, listening.

"…telling you this was a bad idea!" Alldusk was saying loudly. "The kids don't know enough; we're practically guaranteeing they'll come back in pieces."

"What are you yelling at me for?" Grindlethorn said curtly. "Darla's the one who gave the test."

"Only because Drakewell forced me to," Merridy said. Her voice was higher than usual. "I tried to argue, but he said he would work the maps instead of me if I refused."

Tristan had no idea what this meant, though it seemed to catch Grindlethorn off guard, because he didn't reply.

After a long silence, Grindlethorn said, "This is the boy's fault, you know."

"That's not—" Alldusk began.

Grindlethorn cut him off. "If he knew he couldn't handle the mountain, he should've stayed put," he said stoutly. "He's just foolish and weak."

Tristan shoved open the ballroom door and limped in. "I'm not weak," he said angrily.

The three teachers looked at him in surprise. Merridy dropped her fork with a clatter.

"There was an avalanche," Tristan continued loudly,

scowling as he struggled across the room. "I was doing just fine until the snow buried me." He was getting tired of the teachers and their lies.

Alldusk gave Grindlethorn a significant look.

"This proves nothing," Grindlethorn insisted, looking surlier than ever. "Fairholm isn't very hardy, that's all."

"It's not my—"

"What about the others?" Merridy whispered, ignoring Tristan. "We know Rusty is fine, but Gerry has yet to see to the others. This argument should wait until Gerry returns."

"I'm sure they'll be fine," Alldusk said gently. "Tristan's test was harder than most." Turning to smile at Tristan, Alldusk said, "Come eat. You must be famished."

Thursday morning was cloudy, though it was much warmer than the previous day. Uneasy at being alone in the bunkroom, Tristan wandered up from the Lair to find that the layer of snow in the clearing had melted. His ankle still throbbed horribly with every step, so he couldn't stray far—he just wanted to get away from the lonely halls of the school. He still couldn't decide whether he was upset that he'd returned.

Past the greenhouse, up a forested incline, Tristan wandered until he came to a tumbling white stream. Though the stream wasn't far from the school, Tristan's ankle was protesting sharply by the time he stumbled to the soggy bank. Cursing, he sat heavily on a rock and stared at the foaming water.

It was quiet in the forest, aside from the merry

churning of the brook—even the usual birdsong was muffled beneath the clouds. The mildewed smell of the mossy river reminded him of the shores of the lake below the school, and of the eerie feeling that lake had given him, as though it belonged in the realm of the dead.

As he traced the water upstream, watching a smooth fold of ripples curl across the dark rocks, Tristan saw something floating around the bend. It looked like an overturned log, bobbing along in the current; then the rest of the thing came into view and Tristan nearly fell off his rock in surprise.

Amber Ashton stood on the narrow log, floating serenely towards him. Somehow the log was fully suspended in the shallow stream.

"Amber!" Tristan called. "What are you doing?" He was afraid she would lose her balance and fall.

"No need to shout," Amber said, stepping carefully onto the bank.

"What the hell are you doing?" Tristan stared at the log as it floated away. "You're supposed to be going back to the Lair, not playing around with magic, or whatever that was."

"I was floating," Amber said, picking a stray twig out of her silvery hair. "Will you come with me?"

"All right, but—how on earth were you doing that?" He struggled to his feet, leaning heavily on a leafless branch. "You haven't been stealing marbles, have you?"

Amber tilted her head sideways. "There are other ways to collect auras," she said. When she turned to look at him, her blue eyes widened in surprise. "You're hurt! What happened to your ankle?"

Tristan shifted his weight. "I twisted it. Don't worry— it's not that bad."

Ignoring this lie, Amber dropped to her knees and took Tristan's ankle in her hands. He sat once more on the rock.

"Where are your things?" he asked. "Weren't you freezing last night?" Amber didn't have a backpack or anything else with her.

"Hmm?" Amber's eyes had clouded over, and she no longer seemed to be paying attention. Tristan didn't bother to repeat his question.

After a moment, Tristan felt something in his ankle tighten painfully. He clenched his hands in fists. Then, to his amazement, the sharp pain eased.

"Crap," he said, rotating his ankle from side to side. Amber looked anxiously up at him, letting her hands drop away from the bandages. "How did you do that?"

Amber let out her breath. "So it worked?"

Grinning, Tristan got to his feet. "You're brilliant, Amber. It doesn't hurt at all."

For a moment Amber just watched him, smiling faintly. Then she said, "Why do we have to return so soon?"

"I'm hungry," Tristan said. "And it's cold out here. You're actually the first one back, so you don't need to hurry, but we should get some lunch."

The ballroom was very quiet with nearly everyone

gone—only Grindlethorn, Brikkens, and Gracewright were eating at the large teachers' table. When Gracewright beckoned Tristan and Amber to join them at their table, Tristan did so reluctantly.

"Ah, my friends!" Brikkens said. He must have forgiven them for the incident with the lemon tree, because there was no hint of coolness in his greeting. "So good to see you, of course. Since you have the next few days to yourselves, would you like to help me arrange a little Halloween party?"

That was the last thing Tristan wanted to do. Gracewright saved him by saying, "Let them eat. You can discuss business later."

Alldusk showed up halfway through lunch, dark circles around his eyes—he slumped into a chair and poured himself a cup of coffee. "Excellent job, Amber. I was worried at first, when you started out in the wrong direction, but…"

"I was exploring," Amber said, eyes wide.

Tristan sat forward in his seat. "How are the others?" he asked quickly. "Are Leila and Rusty safe?"

Alldusk set his mug down rather heavily, sloshing coffee onto the back of his hand. "They're alive," he said, mopping up the coffee with his napkin. "Zeke Elwood will probably make it back by nightfall, and Evangeline Rosewell is heading in the right direction. As to Leila and Rusty…" He sighed. "Rusty seems to be completely lost, and Leila—well, she's badly injured."

"Then why didn't you bring her back?" Tristan

demanded.

Alldusk shook his head grimly. "She refused."

"Well, you damn well should've brought her back anyway!"

"Sit down," Alldusk said gently. Tristan hadn't realized he'd gotten to his feet—fuming, he threw himself back into the chair. "I'm really sorry about this. The whole test has been a bit of a mistake, to be honest."

Grindlethorn cleared his throat. "That's enough from you," he told Alldusk sharply.

Draining the last of his coffee, Alldusk got to his feet. "I should rejoin Darla. See you later, Tristan, Amber." He nodded to each of them and swept off.

Tristan knew why Leila had refused help, of course. She would never let Zeke beat her if she had the choice, though the teachers should've known better than to allow her stubbornness, especially if she was injured.

Just as Alldusk had promised, Zeke arrived in the clearing before dinner, his dark hair bedraggled. Tristan had been sitting near the entrance to the Lair, pretending to do homework as he waited for his friends.

"Where's your girlfriend, Tristan?" Zeke called out as he crossed the lawn. "She's not back yet, is she? What an idiot."

"Leave off on Leila," Tristan said sharply. "She hasn't done anything to you."

Zeke snorted. Dropping his backpack in the middle of the clearing, he strode towards the Lair. "She's a deceptive little bitch, if that's what you think. I'd stay out of it, unless you'd like to find out how weak you are."

When Tristan flew at him, Zeke slammed the door in his face.

Amber reappeared halfway through dinner, cheeks pink from the cold, to join Tristan at one of the smaller tables.

"Someday," Tristan said, "you should tell me where you keep going when you vanish like that."

Amber stirred her pumpkin soup idly, watching Tristan. "I like wandering," she said. "Why did you spend the day sitting outside and staring at the trees?"

"I was waiting for my friends to get back," he said indignantly. The excuse sounded feeble.

Even the teachers were surprised when Evvie appeared at the top of the stairs, disheveled and mud-streaked, before the end of dinner.

"Where is everyone?" she asked as she approached, glancing from Tristan and Amber to Zeke, who sat alone. "I was delayed—isn't everyone back already?"

"No, it's just the four of us," Tristan said. "Come sit with us." He pulled out the chair to his right.

Evvie looked suspicious as she slid into the seat beside Tristan, her mud-speckled clothes giving off the scent of pine smoke and sweat. Her bedraggled hair was lovely.

For a moment Evvie was quiet, filling her plate with lasagna and glancing sullenly at Tristan every few seconds. Then her curiosity overcame her annoyance.

"What's taking people so long? Five miles isn't very far, is it? Like I said, I was delayed. It shouldn't have taken two days to get back." She took a huge bite of the lasagna.

Tristan shook his head. "In case you haven't noticed, some people can't read maps so well." He included himself in this generalization. "I'm pretty sure Zeke found his way back by sheer dumb luck, and Amber just understands more than the rest of us."

Amber reddened slightly at Tristan's praise; she looked as though she was struggling not to smile.

"Don't lie," Zeke said from the other table. "As soon as everyone's back, they'll hear about how you cried for help before the first day was up. You couldn't last one night out there."

"There was an avalanche," Tristan said tersely. "I didn't—"

"Boo, hoo," Zeke said, "so it was a bit cold. I got stuck in the blizzard, same as you, but I'm not dumb enough to lie about a few snowflakes and call them an avalanche."

"What're you talking about?" Tristan said, confused. "The sky was completely clear; there wasn't a blizzard."

"Yeah, right."

At the large table, the teachers were glancing shiftily at one another, perhaps deciding whether to intervene.

"I think you both are telling the truth," Amber said mildly. Tristan and Zeke looked at her in surprise; she was toying with her napkin, eyes down.

"You boys are so immature," Evvie said haughtily. "Where's Professor Merridy?"

"No idea," Tristan said. Merridy was probably monitoring the other students with Alldusk, though he had no idea how or where that was done.

Though Evvie had barely eaten half of her lasagna, she set down her fork and folded her napkin. "I'm going to bed now," she said. "If you boys are going to be loud, don't come in the bunkroom."

"Please tell me you're showering first," Tristan teased.

Evvie gave him a hurt look and stalked away.

After a moment of silence, Tristan decided he was no longer hungry. "You know what?" he muttered to Amber. "I'm getting awfully tired. I think I'll head downstairs as well."

Amber blinked at him and said nothing, so Tristan licked the last of the melted cheese from his spoon and rose. As soon as he left the ballroom, he quickened his pace. Maybe if he just apologized to Evvie...

She wasn't in the bunkroom when he returned, and the lights in the girls' bathroom were off. Where could she be?

Evvie didn't return for hours. Unable to sleep, Tristan read his medicine textbook, the *Practical Guide to Magical Healing*, which Grindlethorn had promised to quiz them over on Monday. The assigned chapter didn't make sense, so he eventually gave up and scanned the index, looking for an explanation of how Amber had fixed his ankle.

Zeke appeared before either Evvie or Amber returned, hair dripping from his shower. Looking bored, he slouched back against the frame of his bed and took a stolen gold marble from his pocket. After examining it for a minute, he began throwing the marble repeatedly at the wall. The marble thunked dully against the stone, over and over...

"Quit doing that," Tristan snapped, slamming his book shut. "I'm trying to sleep."

"No you're not," Zeke said. He threw the marble harder than before.

BANG!

The marble exploded, blowing a hole the size of a basketball in the wall. Bits of stone fell away, crumbling into a dusty heap on Zeke's blankets.

"Nice work," Tristan said. What was up with Zeke?

Scowling, Zeke brushed the marble dust onto the floor. "You'd better not tell the teachers."

"All right," Tristan said. "Just shut up, would you?" Settling back with his face towards the wall, he dragged his pillow over his head. He hoped Leila had found somewhere safe to spend the night.

It was late that night, or perhaps very early morning, when Tristan was startled awake by a hand on his shoulder.

"Who's there?" he hissed into the darkness.

"It's your favorite cook," Quinsley's voice whispered back. "The headmaster wants to see you and Amber right away. Don't bother getting dressed."

Yawning, Tristan slid over the rail of his bed and pulled a sweatshirt over his pajamas. Amber was already standing by the door, and she nodded briefly at him before leading the way into the hall.

Quinsley met them just outside the door, looking surprisingly cheerful for such a miserable time of night.

"What the hell is this about?" Tristan grumbled,

combing his fingers through his hair. "Why couldn't Drakewell wait till morning?"

Quinsley shrugged. "I think the headmaster wants to speak with the pair of you before anyone else gets back. He wanted to talk to you yesterday, but he was busy all day."

Tristan shared a confused look with Amber. Drakewell couldn't be angry at them, could he?

Drakewell was waiting just outside the doors to the ballroom.

"Thank you, Gerard," he said, waving Quinsley away. "Come here, you two."

With another nervous glance at Amber, Tristan followed Drakewell into the ballroom; only the platform with the usual tables was lit, which left the rest of the space cloaked in eerie shadows. Drakewell took a seat at the teachers' table, and Tristan and Amber joined him.

"You two are very quiet," Drakewell commented sourly. "During the day, it's getting you kids to shut up that gives me trouble." Sighing, he put a hand to his black hourglass. "I have heard from two teachers that you both show a surprising aptitude for magic."

Tristan blinked in surprise. Praise was the very last thing he expected from Drakewell.

"As you may have guessed, my duties as headmaster involve more than simply running this school. My position is vital to what we do, and it must be performed by someone with an excellent understanding of magic. When I step down, I—"

The door to the kitchen creaked open, and Quinsley's

head poked around the corner. "Hot chocolate, anyone?"

Drakewell gave a curt nod, and Quinsley brought over a pair of steaming mugs.

"Thank you," Tristan said, cupping his hands around the mug.

"As I was saying," Drakewell continued, "I will be stepping down eventually, and at this point I will need to leave a fully capable headmaster—or headmistress," he said, with a nod at Amber, "—in my place. I will therefore train both of you for this task, provided you prove yourselves worthy."

Tristan took a sip of his foamy hot chocolate. "What if—well, what if we don't want to do what—whatever you're doing?" He tightened his grip on the mug.

Drakewell's hollow eyes narrowed. "I'm afraid this is not your decision, Fairholm. You and Miss Ashton have been chosen for this task, and if you refuse to comply, the consequences will be…unpleasant. Your training will not begin until next year, but in the meantime, I will be watching you closely. Any transgressions from either of you will be punished severely.

"Furthermore, I will now entrust you with a secret. You must never speak a word about this, and must do whatever necessary to stay far away from this place."

Drakewell let the hourglass fall back to his chest and folded his hands on the table.

"There is a room, hidden somewhere in this system of tunnels, that must never be found. Its door, made of wood, can be recognized by the image of a globe on its exterior. If you see this door at any time, you have strayed into forbidden territory. I will know, and I will make you regret ever setting foot in this school. Keep far away from this room, and protect it with your lives."

Tristan swallowed. If anyone else had said this, it would have sounded like a joke. Coming from Drakewell, it was unsettling.

"Do I have your word on this?" Drakewell asked sharply.

"Yes, Professor," Tristan said at once.

Amber nodded, her mouth slightly open.

"You've been very quiet, Ashton. Do you even understand what I said?"

"Oh!" Amber said, sounding hurt. "Of course I understand."

Drakewell got swiftly to his feet. "Good night, then. Speak of this to no one." He strode away from their table and vanished into the shadows before he'd even left the ballroom.

"Let's finish our hot chocolate before we go back to bed," Tristan suggested in a whisper. He was no longer tired; Drakewell's words had startled him awake, though the meaning hadn't quite registered.

"Yes, we should," Amber said. She was gazing into the shadowy depths of the ballroom, watching the place where Drakewell had just vanished. "If Drakewell thinks I'm slow, why does he want my help with his magic?"

"He doesn't think you're slow," Tristan said quickly. "He just...well, he doesn't understand you. You're a hard person to understand."

"I see," Amber said in a very small voice.

"No, I didn't mean it like that!" Tristan said. "It's like you're something magical, and no one else is quite as— special—as you."

Amber's face was growing stonier still.

"Just ignore me," Tristan said, upset with himself. "I'm no good at talking. But I think you're amazing. Come on, let's drink this hot chocolate before it gets cold."

Though she said nothing, Amber joined Tristan in sipping her hot chocolate. They sat in silence until both mugs were drained, and without a word they got to their feet and left the ballroom.

When they reached the bunkroom hallway, Tristan immediately noticed the familiar swirl of silver patterns that he'd overlooked in their rush to join Drakewell.

"Er…Amber?"

She stopped and looked at him, her expression unreadable in the dim light.

Tristan sighed. "I think I'm—uh—going crazy. Sometimes at night I see these strange shapes on the wall, but no one else can see them, and they're gone in the daytime. What's wrong with me?"

This time Tristan could tell that Amber was smiling. "The glow is an aura," she said. "Just as some plants have brighter auras than others, so do some types of rock. The walls are pretty, don't you think? The people who built this place were artists."

Tristan opened his mouth and then closed it again.

"Well, I've been an idiot," he said. "Thank you, Amber. Thank you!"

Tristan couldn't settle to anything the next day. Amber had vanished once again, and no one else had returned from the test; when Alldusk and Merridy appeared for lunch, they announced grimly that the remaining students had barely made any progress. It was a relief when the afternoon drew to a close and Quinsley emerged from the kitchen to say it was time to collect the stragglers.

"We'll be having a bit of a feast tonight," he told Tristan, who was writing out a chemistry essay in the ballroom. "Should be a treat after this miserable ordeal, eh?"

Tristan nodded fervently. As Quinsley hurried up to the meadow, taking the stairs two at a time, Tristan closed his notebook and stuffed his books into his schoolbag. Then he went outside to wait for Quinsley to return with the helicopter.

The evening sky was clear and purple, framed by silky peaks still clinging to their coat of snow. It was fully dark by the time Quinsley returned, and Tristan heard the chop-chop-chop of the propeller long before he could distinguish the white body of the helicopter.

At last the helicopter settled onto the lawn, buffeting Tristan with a powerful gust of wind—he staggered, catching himself against the side of the building, and then hurried forward.

Quinsley jumped out of the cockpit and waved at

Tristan. "You'll have to help me with Leila," he called over the thrum of the propeller. Lowering his voice, he said, "She can barely walk, but she wouldn't let anyone support her. You might have an easier time persuading her."

Tristan nodded, standing back as Quinsley opened the hatch in the helicopter's belly. Leila was sitting just above the ladder, slumped against her backpack and clutching her knee. Though he couldn't be sure in the dark, it looked as if her jeans were ripped and her leg was grimy with blood.

"Leila!" Tristan said. "You look awful—why didn't you let them pick you up earlier?"

"Good to see you, too," Leila grumbled. Gritting her teeth, she turned and lowered herself awkwardly down the ladder. "I'm not *dying* or anything; don't look at me like that."

When she was almost to the ground, Tristan reached up and grabbed Leila's waist to steady her; he could feel her trembling as she set her feet awkwardly on the grass.

"I can walk, you know," she said brusquely as Tristan put an arm around her waist to hold her upright. Despite her protest, Leila was leaning heavily on his shoulder.

"I don't think so," Tristan said.

This time she didn't argue—without waiting for the other students to emerge from the helicopter, Tristan helped Leila hobble across the clearing and down the stairs to the ballroom.

"I'm surprised so few people made it back," Leila said, her tight shoulders relaxing as they passed through the invisible barrier and the warm air enveloped them. "I can't believe Zeke managed without a compass…"

Tristan snorted. "He's ridiculous. *I* didn't even make it back on my own."

"What do you mean?" Leila asked. When they reached the far side of the ballroom, she paused for a moment, resting her leg and clutching Tristan's shoulder for support.

"There was an avalanche," Tristan said darkly. "I was picked up before the first day was over." Sighing, he said, "I'll tell you about it later—we have to get you to the hospital room."

As they started walking again, Leila seemed to brighten. "I wasn't the worst, though. From what Rusty said in the helicopter, it sounds like he ran into Hayley on the second day." She laughed. "Even working together they went the wrong way."

At last they reached the hospital room, where Grindlethorn took over from Tristan and forced Leila to sit down on one of the hospital beds.

"Go on up without me," Leila said. "I'll be fine."

Hoping she was right, Tristan made his way up to the ballroom. When he joined Rusty at their usual table, Eli was telling him gleefully about a bear that had apparently attacked him.

"What happened to Leila?" Tristan interrupted as soon as Eli paused for breath. "She didn't tell me what happened to her leg—how'd she hurt it?"

"Dunno," Rusty said. "She wasn't talking much when Quinsley brought us back."

"I wonder why," Tristan said sarcastically.

Grinning, Rusty turned his chair back to the table. "Aren't you going to ask how I did?" He started piling food onto his plate—Quinsley had prepared smoked chicken kabobs, eggplant parmesan, and an overflowing platter of fruit.

Tristan snorted. "Leila already told me you failed miserably."

"Yeah, but did she tell you about the ice storm?" Sitting forward eagerly in his chair, Rusty bit a piece of chicken off his skewer and said, "Me and Hayley got stuck in this massive ice storm. That's why we got lost—there were huge icicles pummeling us, and we had to run into this creepy old forest."

"Honestly?" Tristan said. "Yesterday Zeke was going on about a blizzard, but I swear the sky was clear the entire time."

Laughing, Rusty shook his head. "You sure you weren't in a different state, or something? What happened to you, anyway?"

Tristan told his story as quickly as possible, making it sound as though the avalanche hadn't happened on the very first day. Then he said, "I'm going to see how Leila's doing." He got up and pushed in his chair. "You should bring her a plate of food once you're done."

Without waiting for Rusty to agree to this, Tristan left the ballroom and hurried down the two flights of stairs to the hospital. Grindlethorn was just finishing his ministrations when Tristan arrived—Leila was sitting up in bed, her knee wrapped with bandages.

"I want to go downstairs now," she said when Tristan pushed open the door.

Grindlethorn shook his head. "You're not walking on that leg, Swanson."

Leila scowled and swung her legs carefully over the side of the bed. "Well, I'm not staying in the hospital room. I won't be able to sleep." Tristan thought she was worried that Zeke would tease her for it.

"Well, if you want to go anywhere, someone has to carry you," Grindlethorn said.

Leila rolled her eyes. "Tristan?"

He laughed. "I can't promise I won't drop you." Still, he crossed over to Leila's bedside and slid his arms under her, one behind her back and one beneath her legs. When he hoisted her off the mattress, he tried his best not to jostle her knee.

Leila clasped her arms behind his neck. "This is humiliating," she grumbled as Tristan walked carefully from the hospital room.

"Don't worry," Tristan said vaguely, trying to find the next step down. "The others aren't back from dinner yet."

"Oh, I'm starving," Leila moaned. "I didn't want to say anything to Grindlethorn—I was afraid he might give me an hour of punishment just to be difficult." Her hands tightened around Tristan's neck, her fingers digging into his collarbone.

Amber was in the bunkroom when Tristan kicked open the door; she looked up as Tristan carried Leila to her bed and set her down heavily on the mattress.

"Thanks, Triss," Leila said.

Taking a seat beside her, Tristan flexed his arms to work out the cramps.

A moment later the hall filled with the cheerful babble of voices. "I brought food," Rusty called from the doorway, noticing Leila. Letting the door fall shut, he carried over the heaping plate of chicken and eggplant, which he set on her lap. "Now you can tell us what happened to you." He joined Tristan at the end of Leila's bed.

Leila shrugged, glancing at Tristan and then at the others. Eli, Trey, and Hayley were all watching her with undisguised interest—curiosity aside, they loved hearing Leila's stories.

"Oh, all right," Leila said. She took a large bite of eggplant, sending the sweet scent of basil wafting through the musty bunkroom. Trey, Hayley, and Cailyn climbed into their bunks and sat watching her. Leila shoveled more eggplant into her mouth; only when the first slice was gone did she set down her fork and put the plate on the blankets beside her.

"I was stupid," she began in a low voice. "I figured out where I was at once, so I hiked more than halfway back that first day. When it started snowing, I sheltered in a cave for the night. Someone had been there before—there was a fire pit at the back of the cavern, with a pile of sticks already mounded in place."

Across the room, Evvie narrowed her eyes at Leila.

"I decided to go exploring that night," Leila continued. "I made myself a torch and went poking around at the far back of the cave. It turned out that the cave didn't end there—I found a passage leading away from the larger cavern, about the size of the tunnels here.

"That was when I heard a rumbling overhead. I looked up and saw that the ceiling was starting to crack apart, so I ran for it."

Pausing, Leila took one of the kabobs from her plate and slid a piece of chicken off the skewer with her teeth. No one moved—after a moment, Tristan punched her lightly in the shoulder. "Don't be annoying."

Leila laughed. "All right, then." She set aside the skewer. "There was a hideous creaking sound right overhead, and a huge rock crashed down on me, knocking me to the ground and pinning my leg down. I couldn't move. My leg was wrenched sideways, and I started bleeding all over. I tried to shove the rock off my leg, but it was too heavy. Suddenly the ceiling rumbled again—the whole cave started shaking so much that the boulder was dislodged, and I managed to yank my leg free. I grabbed my backpack and crawled for the entrance, my leg hurting so much I could hardly see. Just as I reached the snow outside, the entire roof collapsed behind me."

"Damn," Eli said, looking impressed in spite of himself.

Tristan couldn't believe how unlucky everyone had been. Rusty and Hayley had been caught in an ice storm, Zeke in a blizzard; Eli had been attacked by a bear; Leila had been in a cave-in; and Tristan himself had nearly been crushed by an avalanche. He didn't even know how the rest of Zeke's gang had fared.

"Well, your knee looks way better now," Rusty said cheerfully.

Leila studied it for a moment. "Yeah. Grindlethorn says I'll be able to walk just fine by tomorrow morning. He did some spell on it, so I think I just have to wait for the poultice to set." She looked around at their half of the room; everyone was still watching her intently. Leila laughed. "Tomorrow I'll tell you about the angry dwarves that chased me away from their cave."

"There are *dwarves* living in...wherever we are?"

"Rusty," Tristan and Leila said at the same time.

"Aw, I was joking," Rusty said, though he still looked surprised. "I was just humoring Leila."

"Sure," Tristan said.

Leila reached for her plate and continued picking at her dinner, and after a few minutes the other students started dispersing and getting ready for bed. As he thought back over the last few days, Tristan remembered something.

"There's something I've been meaning to tell you, Leila," he said in a low voice. "When I got back, the teachers had a huge argument about the test. A lot of them, including Merridy, thought it had been a stupid idea."

Leila nodded. "I don't think they're used to teaching anyone. It looks as though we're the first students that have come here, at least in a long time. What if this isn't usually a school?" She set aside her fork and looked unhappily at Tristan. "What if they just brought us here to train us for something?"

"That can't be right," Rusty said at once.

Tristan kicked his shoes across the floor. "If you're right, what are we being trained to do?"

"Aside from magic?" Leila shrugged. "I have no idea."

Chapter 9

Delairium

When classes resumed the following Monday, the students were suddenly overwhelmed by the work they'd neglected over the weekend. Tristan was so busy that he completely forgot he'd tried to run away. He didn't even have time to think about what Drakewell had said to him and Amber.

Grindlethorn spent the first medicine class calling up each of the students who'd been injured during the test. "Fairholm, you're first."

Tristan stood uncertainly and joined the professor at the front of the room. "Sit here," Grindlethorn said brusquely, pulling out the chair from behind his desk. "Fairholm's ankle was twisted badly when he returned, with several torn ligaments and a slight displacement of the bone. Can anyone guess how I mended it?"

Tristan sank onto the padded chair; catching Amber's eye, he grinned briefly. She was, of course, the one who'd healed his ankle. He could have sworn she returned the smile.

Finley Glenn, sitting in the back of the room, raised his arm. "Sir, you would've used a paste of either Goldthread or Twinleaf to reseal the muscle tissue."

Most of the class turned to look at Finley in surprise; flushing, he slumped down in his chair and tried unsuccessfully to hide behind his stack of textbooks.

"Precisely," Grindlethorn said. "In this case, there was no surface exposure of the wound, so I used only the powdered Twinleaf." He swept his gaze around the classroom and scowled. "Why aren't you taking notes?" he barked. "Start copying now—you have a quiz over this tomorrow."

Muttering to themselves, the students took out their notebooks and pens. Tristan returned to his usual seat and tried to remember what Finley had said. Grindlethorn could've used Twinleaf or Golden...what?

In Environmental Studies that afternoon, Merridy was distracted and jumpy. She announced that every one of the students had passed the practical exam, though she would give them a written test later that week to make up for her generosity.

At the end of the period, Merridy held Tristan and Leila back while the rest of the class filed out.

"Are you both doing better now?" she asked in a low voice. "Tristan, you can walk on your ankle without any trouble?"

Confused, Tristan nodded. "Yeah, I'm—it's all better."

Leila gave him a significant look. "I'm fine, too," she

said to Merridy. "Grindlethorn says the bandages can come off tomorrow."

Merridy let out her breath. "I apologize. Your tests were too dangerous—it was bad judgment on my part. It will not happen again."

"Um...thanks?" Tristan glanced at Leila, bewildered.

Leila nodded. "It's perfectly fine, Professor. Good afternoon." Grabbing Tristan's wrist, she dragged him from the room.

As Tristan and Leila hurried back to the bunkroom, Leila said, "You were right."

Tristan frowned, running his hand along the cold marble wall. "What was that about? Why was Merridy apologizing?"

"It's like you said earlier—the teachers don't really know what they're doing. I think Merridy, at least, has never taught this class before." She tossed her braid over her shoulder.

"So..."

Leila sighed. "Merridy must have known we'd be in danger during the test, but I don't think she bargained on anyone getting seriously injured."

"What does that mean for us?" Tristan asked, pausing outside the doors to the bunkroom.

Leila put a hand on the door. "It means we should keep an eye out for the real reason we're here," she said in a low voice. "And in the meantime, don't trust the teachers."

Halloween was on Friday, and in a fit of unexpected

generosity, the teachers cancelled classes for the last two days that week. On Thursday, most of the students spent the day in the ballroom trying to get through their homework. Finally growing sick of Zeke's attempts to steal her half-finished essay, Leila abandoned her books around lunchtime and went to help Quinsley in the kitchen. Tristan suspected she was also hoping to learn more about the teachers' argument.

At this point Tristan and Rusty went back down to the bunkroom, no longer motivated to get their work done. They spent the afternoon throwing uncapped pens at a target circle someone had drawn next to Damian's bed, trying to get the pens to leave a mark on the clean stone. With Merridy's test still on their minds, they started guessing what would happen if any of them failed their classes.

"We'd probably spend the rest of our lives working off punishment," Tristan said.

"I bet they'd just send us back to juvie," Rusty said.

"Or jail, if we're eighteen by then," Tristan reminded him.

"You think Zeke's gonna last three years here?"

Tristan scowled. "With his luck, he'll be the next headmaster." He hurled his pen harder than he'd intended and missed the target by several feet. "Maybe they'll just abandon us in the mountains and let us wander forever."

"I bet they'll feed us to their pet dragons," Rusty said, squinting at the target.

"Or those angry dwarves Leila told us about."

Rusty grinned. "I don't think they eat people."

Several hours later, Tristan and Rusty still hadn't decided what would actually happen if they didn't pass their classes, though their theories were growing wilder with each guess.

"Who's marrying a mermaid?" Leila asked when she returned from the kitchen.

Tristan lobbed all the pens he'd been holding at the wall—for the first time, one actually left a bright blue mark right in the center of the target. "What did you find out?"

Leila put her hands on her hips and frowned. "I was helping in the kitchen. What was I supposed to have found out?"

Tristan and Rusty looked at each other, smirking, and said nothing.

"All right," Leila said, rolling her eyes. "I did get Gerry to talk about the tunnels, but only a little. He said—"

Just then, the door to the bunkroom opened. Leila broke off as Evvie appeared, clutching something behind her back. With a furtive little smile, Evvie hurried over to her bunk and stuffed whatever she'd been carrying into her backpack. Then she cleared her throat and paced stiffly across the room to join Tristan, Leila, and Rusty.

"Hi," she said, glancing from the ground to the circle of darts and back. "I—um—know we haven't talked much, but I was thinking I should maybe—er—get to know you guys better."

At any other time Tristan would have welcomed the chance to talk to Evvie. Now, though, he was more interested in hearing what Leila had been about to say.

"We were just going up to dinner," he said curtly. "If you want to eat with us, we're leaving now."

"Oh, um, thanks," Evvie said.

I'm sorry, Tristan mouthed to Leila.

Leila sat in an incensed silence all through dinner, while Tristan stared guiltily at his plate.

Rusty seemed unperturbed. "How do you like school, Evvie?" he asked kindly.

Annoyingly, Evvie didn't object to Rusty's use of the nickname. "It's not as bad as I expected," she said shortly. "My foster parents have probably forgotten I exist by this point."

Her tone was bitter—Tristan's anger faded slightly as he realized she probably still felt like an outsider here. He had forgotten she was an orphan.

"Aw, I'm sorry," Rusty said. "I dunno whether my folks still think about me or not. They didn't care much when I was arrested." Though his tone was light, a shadow passed over his face. "'Course, it doesn't really matter. This has gotta be the first time I've been useful to anyone."

"Yes, we certainly are useful," Leila said darkly. "But I don't think I want to know what we're being used for."

To Tristan's dismay, Evvie followed them back downstairs after dinner. Tristan stopped outside the bunkroom and said, "I just remembered, I have to go get my…"

He was saved the necessity of inventing something he'd left behind when Leila said, "Come on, Rusty. We have to get your textbook before Alldusk goes to bed."

"What?" Rusty said, breaking off mid-sentence and frowning at Leila. "I don't—"

Leila kicked his foot.

"Goodnight, I guess," Evvie said to Rusty. Biting her lip, she turned and vanished into the bunkroom.

As soon as the door swung closed, Tristan, Leila, and Rusty hurried down the hall and back towards the stairs— several of the other students were returning from dinner now, so Tristan led Leila and Rusty up to the second floor, where the hallway to Alldusk's classroom created a dark corner that hid them from view.

"What're you on about?" Rusty said indignantly when they stopped at last.

Tristan glanced down the hallway. "Leila had something to tell us." He nodded to her. "What was it?"

Leila rolled her eyes. "If you boys hadn't been so eager to flirt with stupid girls, I would've been able to tell you at dinner."

"Hey!" Rusty said indignantly. "I was just trying to be nice to Evvie—I mean, no one really pays attention to her."

"That's her fault, not ours," Leila said, scowling. "We don't have to be friends with absolutely everyone!" She rounded on Tristan. "Besides, Tristan pays plenty of attention to *Evvie*."

"Not anymore," Tristan said irritably. "I just wanted to be nice, but everyone likes Rusty better than me. All Evvie can see is my—" he stopped short. Clenching his jaw, he slouched back against the marble wall.

Leila gave Tristan a curt nod and turned on Rusty again. "I'm just annoyed at you, okay?" she said coldly. "If you want us to be your friends, you can't just keep abandoning us whenever you get the chance."

"I didn't abandon you," Rusty said with a bemused frown. "Maybe we shouldn't be so exclusive. There are only fifteen of us here—if we make enemies too fast, there won't be anyone on our side."

Tristan scuffed his foot loudly on the marble floor, trying to break up the argument. "Who says we have to take sides?" he said. "It's not like—"

Leila cut him off. "I'm just fed up with Rusty hanging out with us only when there's no other choice."

"That's not true!" Rusty said. "You should try and make some more friends if you've got an issue with me."

Leila scowled, hands curling into fists by her side. "Don't you dare tell me what to do. I'd rather have a best friend I can trust than—"

"Who says I want to be your best friend?" Rusty said loudly, making a face. "Eli and Trey are a whole lot nicer than you."

"Guys," Tristan snapped. "Shut up." He had just noticed a shadow bobbing towards them along the marble wall. The shadow grew taller, until its owner emerged from around the corner.

"It's Drakewell," Tristan said sharply. "Quick—in here!" He grabbed the sleeves of Leila's and Rusty's shirts and dragged them through an open door.

The room was lit by the dim glow of one magical

lantern by the door, and as Tristan pulled the door shut behind him, he looked around and recognized it as Alldusk's classroom.

"Doesn't Alldusk usually lock this place?" Leila whispered.

"It doesn't matter," Tristan said. "Just tell us what you found out, Leila. It'd better be important, after that dumb argument."

Leila and Rusty shared an irritated look that meant neither one was about to forget their squabble.

After a moment, Leila took a seat on one of the sturdy desks, feet dangling off the ground, and began.

"Well, first I wanted to know how Alldusk and Merridy managed to keep track of us during the test. It has to be something magical they use, because I can't believe they'd resort to technology after banning cell phones and computers. I mean, they don't even have light bulbs in this place."

"But Quinsley wouldn't tell you?" Tristan guessed, taking a seat beside Leila on the desk.

She shook her head. "However, he did say the teachers were watching us from down in the tunnels. Those unlit passages, I mean." Leila swept her eyes around the room as though looking for one of the tunnel entrances. "It sounds as though there's something really important hidden beneath the school. Something that would explain why we're collecting all of this magic, and what we're being trained for."

Looking interested in spite of himself, Rusty ran a

finger around the rim of a glass beaker. "So why did they need a bunch of criminals? Why not use regular kids?"

Leila twirled her fat braid around one finger. "I don't know about that," she said. "Most us aren't real criminals, though, are we? We were just unlucky. And *Evvie* is just an orphan." She said the name as though it tasted sour.

"That's right," Rusty said, now tapping the glass with his thumb. "Even Damian and Zeke aren't anything like the guys I met in jail."

Tristan sighed, unwilling to point out that he was a murderer. "If you're right about that," he said, "it means we were brought here for a very specific reason."

"Okay, so what else did Quinsley say?" Rusty asked.

Leila considered for a moment before replying. "Nothing specific. He talked a bit more about the thing they were using to watch us—apparently you can use it to keep tabs on anyone you want, anywhere in the world except the Lair."

"Yeah, 'cause we're underground," Rusty said.

"I don't think that's the reason," Leila said, tilting her head and frowning at him.

In the silence that followed Leila's words, Tristan heard soft footsteps tapping along the hall just outside the classroom. "Quiet!" he hissed. "Rusty, get the lights."

Rusty blew on the single glowing lantern, and the room was plunged into darkness.

Outside, the footsteps slowed and then came to a halt—Tristan reached for Leila's arm and tried to drag her off the desk, thinking they could hide. She got quietly to her feet and followed him away from the door. Then—

CRASH!

One of them had knocked the glass beaker to the floor, and the sound of its shattering echoed around the high chamber.

The classroom door swung open, revealing a tall figure silhouetted against the light from the hallway. Tristan ducked, pulling Leila to the floor with him, as the figure made a sweeping motion with one arm and every light on the wall flickered on.

It was Merridy who glared at them from the doorway, not a trace of sympathy in her cold eyes.

"Explain," she said coldly. "What are you three doing in here?"

Tristan got to his feet. "We were looking for a book Rusty left here earlier," he said quickly.

"In the dark?"

Leila cleared her throat. "It's difficult to find the lights. They're…um…really small."

Merridy's eyes narrowed further. "After hearing so many excuses from you three about homework, I expected a better story. Four hours punishment each, and if I catch you sneaking around again it will be doubled."

"Sorry, Professor," Rusty said, hanging his head. "It won't—"

"Just go to your room," Merridy barked.

With a last glance at Merridy, Tristan hurried out of Alldusk's classroom, Leila and Rusty close behind. They nearly ran back to the bunkroom.

"Damn, that was close," Tristan muttered as they slipped through the door to join the other students.

"What do you mean, close?" Leila said angrily. "We got four hours of punishment each."

"Yeah, but it could've been Drakewell."

Whether because of the extra punishment they'd just received or because she was still angry at Rusty, Leila was in a bad mood for the rest of the evening. When Tristan joined her sitting cross-legged on the floor to start his homework, she turned to him with a scowl. "You know what I just realized?" she hissed. "If the teachers had any idea what they were doing, they would've put boys and girls in separate rooms."

"Maybe there wasn't enough space," Tristan said reasonably, though he agreed with her.

"Don't make me laugh." Leila threw open her textbook with unnecessary force and nearly tore a page in half. "If they've got enough money for a helicopter and an airplane *and* a bloody underground palace, they could've built a second bunkroom."

Tristan opened his own textbook to the table of contents. "I thought you didn't like any of the girls here very much."

Leila frowned. "They're better than Rusty and Zeke."

It was with great reluctance that Tristan and Rusty left the ballroom, which was now half-decorated for Halloween, in search of a teacher to work off their punishment with. Leila and Rusty must have been angrier at each other than

Tristan realized, because Rusty joined Eli and Trey for breakfast to avoid sitting with Leila. Leila spent the meal persuading Tristan to work off his punishment with Delair, who would surely know a lot about the tunnels.

"What's the point of a holiday if we have to spend it working?" Rusty said. He'd wanted to spend the day carving pumpkins with the other students. "Couldn't Merridy have waited till next week to punish us?"

"We'll probably be done by lunchtime," Tristan said. "Then you can try apologizing to Leila, and everyone will be happy."

"No way," Rusty said at once. They had reached the lowest hall of the school, where Delair's mine sat dark and forbidding across from his classroom. "It's her fault she won't be nice to people."

Tristan sighed and decided not to argue.

Delair's classroom was locked when Tristan tried the handle, so he and Rusty turned towards the rough mine tunnel. There was a lantern propped beside the entrance; when Tristan blew gently on the top, it flared to life, casting an inadequate glow into the gloom of the tunnel.

"Are you sure about this?" Rusty asked, peering down the tunnel. From here they could smell the heavy, dank air that drifted up from the mine.

Tristan snorted. "There aren't any trolls down there."

"Says who?" Rusty said. Then he grinned. "It'll be an adventure."

Holding the lantern high, Tristan led the way into the dark passage. The floor was uneven and littered with loose stones; Tristan stumbled almost at once, after which he took more care with where he placed each foot.

The tunnel quickly began sloping downwards, at the same time growing colder and mustier. Soon the passage took on the mildewed, closed-in feel of a real cave, nothing like the warm elegance of the Lair. Before long the light from the main hallway vanished, leaving everything gray and hazy. From the dim cast of the lantern, Tristan could see the occasional passage leading off the main tunnel; he was beginning to wonder whether they'd taken a wrong turn when he heard a distant thud.

He stopped at once, alert and listening, and Rusty collided with him from behind.

"Oof," Rusty said. "Don't do that!"

Tristan shook his head. "Listen. I think it's Delair."

They both stood still for a moment, until a resounding clang echoed nearby. Tristan flinched.

As they rounded the next corner, treading carefully now, Delair came into view. He was no more than a hunched shape at the end of the tunnel, illuminated in the soft glow of two lanterns. The bald teacher was standing beside an empty cart, and as Tristan and Rusty watched, he hefted a pickaxe over his shoulder and swung it at the tunnel wall with a clanging crash.

"Professor?" Rusty called out, jostling Tristan out of the way.

Delair jumped and dropped his pick; when he turned and saw Tristan and Rusty, though, his face spread in a broad grin.

"You're here to do punishment, eh?" He bent down and retrieved his pick. "Bad idea for you kids to come wandering down here alone. Still, I could certainly use the help."

Shuffling away from the far wall, he pushed his cart forward. As Delair moved aside, Tristan caught sight of an odd, splintered luminescence coming from the rock itself.

"It's *glowing*," Tristan said, elbowing Rusty out of the way so he could get a closer look.

The hazy silver glow was nearly as bright as the two lanterns on the wall, casting its cold sheen across Delair's bald pate.

"'Course it is," Delair said, thrusting a pick at Tristan.

Tristan barely caught it—the heavy wood handle slammed into his knee and he winced.

"It's a vein of the purest metal."

Rusty shook his head in disappointment. "I can't see anything glowing," he said. "It's the aura, isn't it?"

Delair handed Rusty a second pickaxe. "Indeed. Turn out that lamp, Fairholm. It'll look brighter in the dark."

As Tristan blew out his own lamp, Delair extinguished the two lights on the wall with a quick wave of his hand. In the absence of other light, the exposed vein shone brighter than ever, infusing everything with a ghostly brilliance. It was like an icy moonbeam sculpted from rock—Tristan shivered and clenched his fingers around the smooth handle of his pickaxe.

"Now can you see it?" Delair asked eagerly.

Tristan watched Rusty, whose face had taken on the

deathly pallor of a drowned person in the odd light. After squinting at the wall for a long time, Rusty said, "I think there's something…how bright is it supposed to be?" His gaze was fixed on the wrong section of the wall, so Tristan doubted very much that he could see anything.

"Just as with magic vapors, auras appear brighter to certain people," Delair said, nodding happily at Tristan. "No one knows why that is, but everyone can become better with practice."

"Wait a minute," Tristan said, suddenly feeling very stupid. "This is the stuff that's all over the walls of the Lair, isn't it? Those pictures are made out of this stuff."

Delair raised an eyebrow at Tristan. "Of course, of course. How on earth did you notice the patterns?"

Tristan shrugged, feeling extremely relieved. It wasn't just Amber who was sharing in his delusions; the glowing shapes were something real, something that all of the teachers knew about as well.

"How bright is it for you, Tristan?" Rusty asked worriedly, clearly not following the conversation.

Tristan returned his gaze to the wall. "It's nearly as good as the lights a moment ago," he said, trying not to brag.

"Impressive," Delair said, relighting the lamps with a flick of his fingers. "You're better than I am, it seems— without the torches, I can barely make out your shapes in the darkness. It took me many years before I could see the patterns on the walls."

Rusty stared at Tristan, mouth open slightly.

To distract Rusty, Tristan said quickly, "Was that magic, what you just did? Lighting the lamps without blowing on them, I mean."

"Of course," Delair said. "Now, if you'll get to work widening this tunnel, I can teach you a few things that I should've gone over in class."

Even now he rarely came to class more than twice a week.

"Don't worry about falling rocks—I've got a safety barrier in place. That's another thing you can do with magic, by the way."

Tristan hefted the pick onto his shoulder and frowned at the wall. Not at all sure what he was supposed to do, he took a step backwards and swung the curved end wildly at the stone. A few small rocks broke free and crumbled to the ground.

"Wait, what?" Rusty said. His pick dangled uselessly at his side. "Did you just say you used magic *without* those marbles?"

Delair grunted. "Don't aim straight at the wall, Fairholm," he said. "You have to single out a weakness first." He pointed to a craggy knob of rock before turning to Rusty. "Yes, Lennox, I can use magic without it first being concentrated. So could you, theoretically." Delair shouldered his pick and resumed hacking away at the end of the tunnel.

"Huh?" Rusty said, squinting at the wall.

"Drakewell doesn't want me to tell you this," Delair shouted over the sound of his own hammering, "at least not yet. So don't go talking about it with the other kids." He tossed a chunk of stone over his shoulder and resumed his attack on the wall. "The teachers decided you'd be less tempted to make trouble if you thought magic could only be done with the marbles."

"What's the point of the marbles, then?" Tristan asked quickly. This was what he really wanted to know, the answer to why they were here.

Delair paused, resting his pick against one knee. "The real answer to that question is something even I won't tell you just yet. However, there is a second reason for the marbles."

He set aside his pick and turned back to the wall. Now it looked as though he was shaping something with his hands, though he touched nothing but air.

"As you know, the magic vapor is created by destruction—when you collect the vapor, you are gathering the essence of destruction. Even when you don't use the congealed form of magic, you need to destroy something to make the power work. When you work magic without the marbles, you destroy your own strength."

Tristan stared at Delair, thinking hard. To his left, Rusty was tapping the handle of his pick on the wall with a vacant sort of rhythm.

"I'm sure you boys can see why this would be dangerous," Delair continued. "When you draw from your own strength, you quickly become exhausted—if the spell is allowed to go too far, you could damage yourself beyond repair. It takes many years to build up the sort of endurance necessary to perform even the most basic tasks without depleting your strength."

"But you can do it now?" Rusty said. The pickaxe slid out of his lax grip and clattered to the ground.

Amber could do magic without the marbles, Tristan remembered suddenly.

Delair stepped away from the end of the tunnel and wiped his hands on his pants. Then he reached forward and splayed his hands just inches from the wall. With a click, a piece of glowing ore shifted and dislodged itself from the wall. The ore tumbled away from the dull rocks, perfectly intact, and Delair caught it. Then he threw it into the empty cart.

"What is that glowing stuff?" Tristan asked. It had to be powerful, with such a bright aura. "What are you going to do with it?"

"Ah, I'm so glad you asked," Delair said, blowing rock dust off his moustache so the ends fluttered. "This happens to be an element that exists almost exclusively in the earth's core. I'm planning to call it Delairium."

Tristan laughed.

"In fact," Delair said, "this is one reason the school was built here in the first place—it's the only location in the world with such an impressive concentration of Delairium. As to what it's used for…" He lifted his pick again and chipped off a loose sheet of rock. "Delairium releases a great deal of magic when it's melted. Among other things."

By the end of the morning, Tristan's arms ached and a heavy layer of grime clung to his sweat-slicked skin.

"Thanks, professor," he said as he and Rusty finally set down their picks. "We'll probably come back next week."

Delair chuckled. "You're planning to earn more punishment?"

"Not planning," Rusty said. "It just kinda happens."

Tristan picked up the lantern he'd taken from the entrance to the mine. Waving to Delair, he and Rusty turned and trudged back up the way they'd come.

"Well, that wasn't a complete waste of time," Tristan said. He had enjoyed the physical labor more than he'd expected.

"Are you kidding?" Rusty said. "Delair's awesome! I didn't know magic was so cool."

Tristan laughed. The lights from Delair's lanterns had faded in the distance, leaving them stranded in the pale glow of their own lamp as it bobbed along the wall. "I thought you were sad we couldn't carve pumpkins."

Rusty shrugged. "There's still the feast tonight, isn't there?"

As they neared the main hall, Tristan felt the warm air swirling down to mingle with the musty chill of the mine. "After we shower, we've got to find Leila," he said.

Rusty sighed. "I don't think she wants me around."

Tristan punched Rusty's shoulder. "You can't just give up! Come on, just apologize."

"For what? I haven't done anything wrong!" Rusty kicked at a loose rock on the tunnel floor. "It's Leila's fault she won't be friendly to anyone."

With a sigh, Tristan dropped his lantern at the tunnel

entrance.

Halfway to the kitchen, Tristan and Rusty ran into Alldusk. The professor looked distraught, his black hair sticking out from his head in odd tufts. Alldusk nearly collided with Rusty—he stopped abruptly, reeling, and grabbed the wall to steady himself.

"Boys! Thank goodness," he panted.

"What's going—what's wrong?" Tristan asked quickly.

Alldusk shook his head, clutching at his side. "There's been another attack."

"Where?" Tristan dreaded the answer.

"In my classroom."

Chapter 10

Hoarded Magic

Rusty swore loudly.

Tristan closed his mouth, stunned. It had been mere coincidence that they'd trespassed in the classroom that same night, but why should Alldusk—or Merridy, who had caught them inside the room itself—believe that?

When Alldusk cleared his throat, Tristan flinched.

"Now, I don't want to jump to conclusions," Alldusk said darkly, "but from what Merridy tells me, you boys and Leila look as though you were involved." He ran a hand distractedly through his hair, smoothing down the stray clumps.

Tristan shook his head fervently. "No. We didn't do anything. I'm really sorry we went in your classroom last night, but it was unlocked." He hugged his arms across his chest. "I swear we didn't—"

"What?" Alldusk cut sharply across him. "What do you mean, it was unlocked? I know I bolted that door last night."

Tristan glanced at Rusty, hoping for support. "That's why we went in," he said in a rush. "We didn't mean to trespass—we just didn't want to be overheard, so we ducked through an open door. We didn't realize we were in your classroom until a minute later."

Alldusk muttered something under his breath, frowning. "And where were you this morning?"

"In Delair's mine." Tristan took a deep breath, trying to steady his voice. "We've been helping him for hours—ask him if you'd like, but we haven't been anywhere else all day."

Alldusk sighed and crossed his arms over his chest. "I'm going to believe you this time, Tristan." He glanced down the hallway. "I may be one of the few teachers who decide to trust you in this. The three of us—and Darla Merridy, of course—are the only ones who know about the attack at this point, which means we still have to inform the headmaster. When Drakewell hears, be careful what you tell him. I don't think you need to be reminded that the headmaster can be very dangerous when he's angry."

A nervous weight had settled in Tristan's stomach, and he swallowed.

With a pained smile, Alldusk clapped Rusty on the shoulder. "Go enjoy the feast, both of you. With any luck, Darla and I will be able to sort this out without dragging you boys in."

He turned and swept down the hallway.

Once Alldusk vanished around the corner, Tristan

kicked the wall with all his strength.

"Damn it," he spat. He swung his foot at the wall again. "Why are we such freaking idiots?"

"But we didn't do anything," Rusty said, chewing on his lip. "Drakewell can't get mad at us when we didn't do anything."

"Sure he can," Tristan said angrily. "No one trusts a couple bloody criminals." The whole stupid situation was his own fault.

He slammed his fist on the railing. Everything he tried to fix got completely screwed up.

For once, Rusty didn't have anything encouraging to say. "Should we go to the feast?" he asked weakly.

Tristan nodded, suddenly feeling drained. "We should get upstairs before Drakewell catches us lurking around."

When they reached the tall doors to the ballroom, Tristan stopped with one hand on the knob and took a deep breath, raking his hair back into place over his scars. Then he led the way in.

The ballroom was lively and infused with color— orange streamers dangled from the walls, tattered cobwebs clung to the tables and chandeliers, and eerie shadows flitted across the marble surfaces. Tristan stared blankly at the riot of color, unable to shake the coldness that had tightened around his lungs.

"Rusty!" Hayley called from one of the tables. "Come help us." A smile spread across her round face as she waved Rusty over. She and Cailyn were bent over a pair of enormous pumpkins, their hands orange and dripping with stringy goo.

"I've changed my mind," Tristan muttered. "I don't want to help with this mess. Let's just go to the kitchen."

Rusty's grin faded slightly. "Aw, you sure you don't want to decorate?"

Tristan nodded.

"You go ahead, then," Rusty said. "Leila doesn't want to see me anyway."

Lonely and miserable, Tristan turned away from the festivities and slouched out of the ballroom.

Even before he reached the kitchen, Tristan could smell the rich aromas wafting down the corridor. As he breathed in the smell of spiced pies and sizzling turkey, he almost expected to find his mom standing over the stove, humming along to the radio. Instead it was Leila who stirred a simmering pot of broth, face lost in the steam, while Quinsley chopped potatoes behind her.

"What's with the Thanksgiving food?" Tristan asked. He crossed the kitchen to join Leila by the stove. "Shouldn't we have little skeleton cupcakes or—"

Dropping her spoon, Leila elbowed him in the stomach. "Out of my way," she said playfully. "Gerry says we won't be celebrating Thanksgiving, so we have to enjoy this while we have the chance."

Tristan turned and frowned at Quinsley. "No Thanksgiving?"

Quinsley popped a chunk of raw potato into his mouth. "Canadians celebrate Thanksgiving in October, not November, so we've decided to compromise and combine it with Halloween." he said thickly.

"Oh!" Tristan said. "So that's where we are."

Quinsley chuckled. "Drakewell probably didn't want the teachers to mention that. No idea why, but there you go."

Leila nodded at Tristan, looking pleased; then she must have noticed something in his expression, because her smile faded. "What's wrong, Triss?"

As though to give them privacy, Quinsley crossed to the opposite side of the kitchen and began washing dishes with an excessive clatter. Lowering his voice, Tristan told Leila how he and Rusty had run into Alldusk after working off their punishment. When he got to the destruction of Alldusk's classroom, she cut across him.

"Alldusk said *what?*"

"Don't worry," Tristan said quickly. "Alldusk doesn't blame us for it. Course, Drakewell probably won't let us off so easily."

Leila started muttering furiously under her breath—a lot of it sounded like cursing. Leaving the soup to simmer, she turned to the counter and began mashing a bowl of potatoes with vehemence. "This is all that stupid Evvie's fault," she said at last. "Evvie and her stupid—wretched—interfering—" She punctuated each word with a thrust of her potato masher.

"What?" Tristan said, watching the potatoes turn to starchy bits under Leila's masher. "How is any of this her fault? We're the ones who went into Alldusk's room, aren't we? I'm the one who dragged you and Rusty there. Evvie had nothing to do with it."

Leila slammed the potato masher harder than ever against the counter. The bowl of potatoes spun away from her hand, teetering on the edge of the counter. Tristan grabbed it.

"Damn it! Drakewell's going to kill us." Leila flung her masher at the counter.

Quinsley turned at the clatter and studied Leila with a raised eyebrow. "I'm not even going to ask," he said, eyes flicking from Leila's disheveled braid to the glass bowl Tristan was setting back in place on the counter. "The feast is about to start, though, so you might want to get out there and enjoy yourselves."

It was a gentle nudge to get them out of the kitchen; scowling, Leila wiped off her hands.

"I'm not sitting with *them*," she said as soon as they stepped into the ballroom, pointing to the table where Rusty, Hayley, and Cailyn were clearing away pumpkin seeds and gooey orange innards.

"You can't ignore Rusty forever," Tristan said, though he was equally reluctant to join the cheery crowd. He and Leila made for the one empty table.

The feast was delicious, but Tristan was too worried to appreciate it. Delair had come up for the celebration, joining the other teachers at the largest round table, and even Quinsley took a seat beside Gracewright once he'd finished serving the sizzling turkey and rich gravy. There were still two empty chairs—Alldusk and Drakewell were absent. Tristan didn't want to think what this meant.

The ballroom was decorated beautifully. Eleven jack-o-lanterns leered at them from the edges of the raised platform, candlelight flickering behind their gaping eyes. The chandeliers had been dimmed, and the ballroom floor had been transformed into a nighttime graveyard scene. Headstones hulked above the polished floor, draped in dusty cobwebs and shrouded in curling brown leaves. The whole room smelled of pumpkins and pungent candle smoke.

"Maybe we should try to forget about Drakewell," Leila said gently. She had followed Tristan's gaze to the decorations. "We don't need to worry all the time."

Tristan snorted. "Don't be stupid; I don't think we worry nearly enough."

"Yeah, but it's Halloween," Leila said. She smeared gravy over her potatoes with a spoon and took a large bite.

Nodding absently, Tristan dug into his mound of stuffing.

As the heaping plates of food steadily diminished, Tristan grew sleepy and content. Eyes slitted, he watched the shadows of two bats darting across the ceiling.

Just as Quinsley reemerged from the kitchen, balancing two silver trays stacked with pumpkin pies, the doors to the ballroom crashed open.

Tristan jumped, though he wasn't at all surprised to see Drakewell striding towards the platform.

"Teachers," he snarled, sunken eyes flashing. "Your vigilance has failed."

The hall grew silent.

"There has been another attack, in the very heart of this school."

Gracewright muttered something to Quinsley, and Merridy grew pale.

Drakewell stood still for a tense moment, nothing more than a ghostly shadow amidst the gravestones. Eventually his gaze moved away from the teachers and lit upon Tristan and Leila. The corners of his mouth curled down.

"Fairholm. Swanson." Drakewell scanned the other students until he found Rusty. "Lennox. Come with me." His voice was tight with anger.

Rusty jumped to his feet and stared at Drakewell with a wild expression, like he'd just been stung by a wasp. Tristan and Leila followed him warily to the door.

The three of them could barely keep up with Drakewell's clipped pace as he strode down the hall. Instead of turning into his office, he continued to Brikkens' classroom. Once they were inside, he slammed the door behind him.

"Sit," he said coldly.

They sat.

Drakewell touched one hand to the hourglass at his neck and then slapped both palms on the table. "Explain yourselves!"

Rusty flinched, but Leila glared at Drakewell, matching the intensity of his hollow stare.

"You were discovered in Professor Alldusk's office, mere hours before the place was destroyed. Will you speak for yourselves, or should I lock you away at once?"

Tristan swallowed. "We didn't do it," he said, trying to keep the tremor from his voice. "I swear we had nothing to do with it."

"How convincing." Drakewell sneered at him. "That would explain why you broke into Professor Alldusk's classroom, of course."

Tristan and Leila glanced at each other, uncertain.

"We—" Rusty began. His voice cracked; Tristan and Leila looked at him in surprise. "That is, me and Leila were arguing. Tristan wanted us to shut up, and he said the teachers were gonna get mad at us for making so much noise. Alldusk's classroom was open, so we hid in there and kept yelling at each other."

"Yeah," Leila said, taking up from Rusty when he faltered. "Only Professor Merridy caught us then, and she sent us out. Nothing was wrong with the classroom when we left—ask Professor Merridy if you want the truth."

Drakewell's scowl deepened, though he seemed momentarily satisfied with their explanation. "I will say no more tonight. However, remember this—you students have no idea of the magnitude of our work here. If something happened to this school, even I cannot guess at the consequences."

He sighed, a sharp hiss. "Fairholm, you remember our conversation. I will add this—there is a place somewhere in these tunnels where we have been gathering magic for eventual use. If anything were to disturb this place— anything at all—the magic would combust with unimaginable force. The whole Lair would be destroyed. The vandal would kill us all.

"I would have preferred to keep this information private, but given that you are implicated in the crime, I must make the three of you aware of the severity of sabotaging our school. If you or any of your classmates know anything whatsoever about the perpetrator, you *must* come forward."

Drakewell hooked a clawed finger around his hourglass. "There are a series of dungeons below this school. If I should come to the conclusion that any one of you three is responsible for this—" He stared at each of them in turn, the muscles in his neck tightening. "Let's just say you would never see the sun again. Now get out of here."

Tristan, Leila, and Rusty sat frozen for a moment.

When Drakewell rose stiffly from the chair, Tristan scrambled to his feet and hurried out of the classroom. The three of them started running before they reached the end of the corridor, bounding down three flights of stairs to the bunkroom.

Inside, they collapsed onto the floor beside Tristan's bunk, breathing hard. Tristan's heart thudded painfully against his ribs.

Leila was the first one to speak. "Why us?" she said angrily. "Wretched teachers—they're such..."

"We haven't done anything," Rusty said earnestly. He shook his sloppy hair out of his face. "They can't get mad at us. It's not right."

"They don't really seem to care about what's right." Tristan shook his head. "Remember when Zeke got rewarded for cheating? If their precious school is in danger, I think they'll try and keep it safe no matter what."

"So you're saying we're screwed, no matter what we do?" Rusty was indignant.

"Probably," Tristan said. "Of course, we could always try and find out who's actually been attacking the school, so we have proof it wasn't us. I think that's the only way we'd be cleared."

"How're we supposed to do that?" Rusty said.

Tristan shrugged. "I guess we could watch the other kids and see if they do anything suspicious," he said. "Or we could poke around in the tunnels."

"No." Leila's voice was sharp. "That's exactly what got us into trouble—being in the wrong place. If we go exploring, we'll only put ourselves in more danger than ever."

"Yeah, but—" Tristan began.

"No. I'm not doing anything stupid."

Alldusk was bleary-eyed and disheveled when he greeted them on Monday.

"The classroom is a mess, as I'm sure you know," he said, ushering them in.

It was worse than Tristan had expected. Most of the lanterns had been ripped from the wall, leaving the room shadowed and gloomy. In some places the wall itself had been gouged away; Tristan was reminded forcibly of the time Zeke had blasted a hole in the bunkroom.

Where hundreds of jars of liquids, rocks, and odd plants had once been stacked, the shelves now lay bare. The floors and tables had been wiped clean, but this served only to draw attention to the emptiness.

"Sorry about all this," Alldusk said wearily as he took his place in the center of the room. "We obviously can't hold regular classes for the present; instead, we'll take the chance to study the chemical uses of magical ingredients."

"You mean we're making potions?" Eli said eagerly.

Alldusk frowned. "No. First of all, we don't have any ingredients to play around with, so we'll be *studying* the magic rather than working with it. Second, what we are primarily concerned with is dissecting plants and rocks into their magical elements. There will be no brewing of potions in this class." He took a stance at the back of the room, with nothing but the polished dark wall behind him. "Take out your notebooks and pens. I'm sorry, but this means copying down what I tell you."

With a collective sigh, the students reached under the desks for their books. When Tristan straightened, he saw a line of glowing green script written across the wall behind Alldusk. He blinked.

"That's awesome," Rusty said, staring at the glowing words. "Why don't the other teachers write like that?"

Alldusk chuckled, his expression lightening fractionally. "Glowing chalk is largely impractical. It requires that the room be poorly lit, which makes it difficult for students to take notes."

"There isn't a library in this school, is there?" Leila said in Tristan's ear.

He tore his gaze from the hypnotic green chalk. "What?"

She was looking left, at a pile of books that Alldusk had used to prop up a broken table. "Do you think all the teachers have private hoards of books? Because if they do, we should see about getting our hands on a few of them."

Tristan raised an eyebrow at her. "What happened to staying out of trouble?"

"This isn't trouble," Leila said. "It's *learning*." She grinned.

Chapter 11

The Lady with the Golden Hair

The first half of November came and went, time passing much slower than usual since there was no Thanksgiving break to look forward to. Though the skies were clear on most days, the sun never shone warmly enough to melt the ground layer of frost.

Two days before what was supposed to be Thanksgiving, Gracewright met the students outside of her greenhouse and redirected them to the longhouse on its left. They hadn't held class outside of the greenhouse in months—had there been another attack?

But the professor was bouncing happily on her toes as she shepherded the students into the longhouse, flyaway hair bobbing beneath her knitted hat.

"We just received our shipment of Prasidimums," she said cheerfully, pulling the door shut behind her. The Prasidimums were not immediately obvious; eventually Tristan noticed a pile of what looked like dried tulip bulbs.

"What the hell's a Prasidimum?" Damian asked,

scowling at the bulbs.

Gracewright dropped to her knees on the grass. "They're magical plants." She brushed the crumbling skin off the largest bulb. "Very rare, and very potent."

Finley Glenn raised his hand. "I thought no one else knew about magic," he said, shoving his glasses up his nose. "So where are the shipments coming from?"

"An astute remark," Gracewright said. "Not everyone trained at this school becomes a—a professor."

What did the teachers do when they had no students to instruct?

Dropping the bulb, Gracewright clapped her hands. "Back to the Prasidimums. Once fully grown, these plants become a protective barrier, a very special barrier that only allows certain people through. We will be growing the Prasidimums without magic—unless allowed to flower properly, these plants become an impenetrable wall."

"Wow, that's just fascinating," Zeke said, smirking.

Gracewright smiled patiently at Zeke. Then she started passing around bulbs and clay pots. "We'll tend to the Prasidimums at the start of class each day. It takes about twenty days for them to flower, at which point we'll replant them around the school."

Tristan took a seat on the grass and eyed the shriveled bulb. Leila joined him, dropping her book bag by her side. Rusty found a place at the opposite side of the circle—he and Leila still weren't talking.

"Hey, Leila," Zeke called softly, leaning forward to talk around Finley's broad chest. She looked up suspiciously.

"You know what this bulb looks like?" He held it up and squinted in her direction.

Tristan nudged Leila in the knee. "Ignore him," he said out of the corner of his mouth.

Leila threw her bulb at Zeke's head.

By the end of the hour, most of the students were covered in dirt, most of which had been thrown by Zeke or Leila. Gracewright let them out early to change before their next lesson—she hadn't minded the dirt fight, since the Prasidimums had ended up in pots in any case.

Tristan hung back as everyone filed out to the snowy lawn, hoping as always that Rusty and Leila would simply forgive each other. Evvie was one of the last to leave—she stopped to ask a question, but before Tristan heard what she said, Leila grabbed his arm and hurried him out of the door.

"Couldn't you just give Rusty another chance?" Tristan said, annoyed.

"No," Leila said flatly.

"I still don't know what the big deal was." Tristan glanced around to see if Evvie was following them, but she was still in the longhouse. "What if I just stopped talking to you? Then would you let Rusty apologize?" He glanced at Leila. "I think he might, if you gave him the chance."

"Please don't say that, Triss." Leila was frowning at the scuffed-up snow. "You know I wouldn't have any friends if you abandoned me."

Tristan let out a sharp breath. "Do you really think I'd do that? In case you haven't noticed, I'm too damn scared to talk to half of the kids here. And the teachers—it's their fault I thought I was going crazy or some—" Quickly he broke off what he'd been about to say.

Leila stopped walking suddenly.

Tristan slowed. He'd been thinking of Drakewell, and of the glowing walls that had scared him for so long, but hadn't intended to say the words aloud.

"What do you mean?" Leila whispered. Now it was Tristan who avoided her curious eyes; Leila took his hand and squeezed it gently. "What is it?"

"I didn't say anything," Tristan said shortly. Shaking Leila's hand away, he kicked a snowdrift and stalked off.

Tristan was in a bad mood for the rest of the day. He struggled through the night's homework in silence, ignoring Leila when she tried to talk to him. He didn't want her sympathy.

"Triss? I was going to look over your geology essay, remember?" Leila said after dinner. "Do you still want help?"

Tristan was silent.

"We could play cards; I know you and Rusty like doing that."

Tristan clenched his jaw, the page of text blurring in front of his eyes.

"I know you're mad at me," Leila persisted. "If you'll just tell me what's wrong, I could—"

"You know what?" Tristan said, finally giving in to anger. "When you and Rusty were still friends, you used to tell stories every night." He slammed his textbook closed.

"Entertain yourself for once, all right? I'm going for a walk." Jumping to his feet, he stormed out of the bunkroom.

Near the end of the hallway, Tristan paused, because something out-of-place had caught his eye. There was a white cloth napkin splayed at the entrance to the dark tunnel, with a smashed tuna sandwich spilling from its folds. It looked as though someone had dropped it.

Curious, Tristan approached the tunnel entrance for a closer look. Someone must have passed this way recently.

"Hello?" Tristan called softly, peering into the darkness beyond the marble floor. His voice was quickly swallowed up by the gloom.

There was no response.

For a moment Tristan hesitated, trying to guess what Leila would say if she saw him. He was being reckless. Then he shrugged away the worry and turned into the dark tunnel.

The light from the hall faded almost at once, so Tristan pressed one hand against the wall to feel his way forward. The stone was rough and cold beneath his fingers, and the tunnel smelled like a musty old cellar. He crept forward, wincing at the crunch of his feet on gravel, while the air grew colder and drier on his skin. He edged down the tunnel until he reached a place where it swerved sharply to the right. Afraid of losing his way, he stopped.

The air was heavy and silent—the sound of Tristan's breathing was smothered, as though the walls were closing in around him. Bright spots danced along the corners of his vision, but when he waved his hand before his eyes, he saw nothing at all. It was hard to breathe the dense air. As he stood there, swaying, Tristan felt as though he was suffocating.

Gasping, he turned and began stumbling back up the tunnel, one hand digging into the sharp contours of the wall. The air of the tunnel was too heavy—it was folding around him like water, crushing his lungs.

At last he came around a corner, and the light from the hallway filled the ragged edges of the tunnel.

Tristan slumped against the wall in relief. "I'm an idiot," he muttered, just to drown out the silence. He'd never been afraid of the dark before.

Sliding to the ground, Tristan crossed his arms over his knees and stared at the opposite wall. The uneven rocks dug into his back; he tried to ignore the discomfort, thinking instead of who had dropped the sandwich at the entrance to the tunnel. Whoever it was, Tristan wasn't going to leave the tunnel until the person returned.

Soon enough, he heard footsteps crunching towards the place where he sat, the pace quick enough to suggest familiarity with the tunnel. What if it was a teacher? Tristan drew his knees closer to his chest and held his breath. What excuse could he give?

The footsteps came closer and closer. Before he was ready, the person came around the corner, almost running, and crashed into Tristan.

She shrieked as she fell—her knee slammed into Tristan's shoulder, pinning him to the ground, and he yelled in pain.

"Sorry!" the girl cried out. As her weight lifted from Tristan's shoulder, he grunted and raised himself on one elbow. The voice was familiar.

"*Evvie?*" he said, staring.

Tucking a strand of wild hair behind one ear, Evvie clambered to her feet. Once she had regained her breath, she scowled and fisted her hands on her hips. She made no move to help him.

Tristan jumped up, bruised shoulder throbbing. "Sorry, I—" He cleared his throat. "What the hell are you doing down here?"

Evvie's frown deepened. "What are *you* doing here?"

Tristan smoothed his hair over his face, thinking fast. After a moment he settled on the truth. "I was trying to figure out who'd dropped their sandwich back there." He gestured towards the tunnel's entrance.

"Shoot," Evvie said. She bit her lip, no longer meeting Tristan's eyes.

"Now you have to tell me why you were down here."

Evvie's eyes narrowed. Then she turned abruptly and tried to hurry away.

Tristan grabbed her arm. "If you don't tell me what you've been doing in the tunnels, I'll report you." He jerked her around to face him. "See if I don't."

Evvie tried to yank her arm free. She wasn't strong enough, so after a moment she gave up and just glared. "I hate you, Tristan."

He sighed. "I won't tell anyone, okay? I promise."

"Not even Leila?"

Tristan cursed. "No. Not even Leila."

For a long moment, there was nothing but silence. Evvie glanced at Tristan's hand on her arm; he grew uncomfortably aware of the warmth of her skin, though he didn't dare release her.

At last Evvie spoke. "There are rooms down here, in the tunnels," she said bluntly. "I thought..." She swallowed. "Well, I found one that I thought we could use as a—a second bunkroom. So we don't have to stay with Zeke's gang, you know." She put one icy hand on her arm and tried to shove Tristan's fist away.

"You've found another room for us to stay in?" Tristan blinked. "That's amazing! Why is it supposed to be a secret?" His image of Evvie conspiring with the teachers deflated rapidly.

Evvie shifted her weight from one foot to another, and Tristan loosened his grip on her arm, afraid he was hurting her.

"I don't know. I guess you can tell people about it," she said. "Not yet, though—wait a bit. Please?"

Tristan nodded. "If you show me the room. Now, while no one's around."

Evvie glared at him. "You're up to something." She struggled once more against Tristan's grip.

This time he released her. "I'm just curious," he said, holding up both hands in a gesture of innocence. "Really, I promise I won't tell anyone."

Looking as though she wanted to punch him, Evvie

shoved past Tristan and vanished into the dark recesses of the tunnel.

"Hey!" Tristan called, hurrying after her. An instant later the light vanished, so he pressed his hand to the wall for guidance. "Don't run off."

Evvie's footsteps slowed, though she didn't answer. Tristan scrambled along the tunnel, irrationally afraid of losing Evvie. After just a few paces he reached the branch where he'd turned back earlier; it was much closer to the tunnel entrance than he'd realized. Feeling a bit foolish, he paused.

"Evvie? Which way now?"

This time she actually stopped walking. "Just keep going forward," she said briskly. "That tunnel doesn't lead anywhere."

Tristan extended one arm into the void before him. For a moment he teetered in place, afraid to move his feet, clawing his fingers through the black emptiness. Nothing.

He stretched his arm farther, doubling over. At last his knuckles scraped against cold, solid rock.

"Okay," he said, trying not to let his voice sag in relief. "Where now?"

Instead of replying, Evvie began walking again, her footsteps padding softly. The tunnel continued as before, though Tristan thought he could feel the ground arching away beneath his feet.

"We're almost there now," Evvie called eventually. She stopped walking, and Tristan heard a rasp of gravel as she turned, followed by the hollow creak of a door.

The dank, cloying scent of old wood reached Tristan's nostrils before his probing fingers found the door.

"Where are we?" he whispered.

Tristan heard a heavy exhalation, and a small lamp flared to life. Blinking, Tristan looked around.

The first thing he noticed was Evvie—the glow from the lamp cast a beautiful halo around her blond hair. From there the light extended weakly to the edges of the room, throwing everything into a sepia haze. The wide room was vaguely circular, its floor empty aside from a crumbling bookshelf.

"There's only the one light," Evvie said apologetically, glancing at the orb.

"It's great." Tristan grinned—his imagination was already filling the space with posters and bunk beds and polished tables. "Really, Evvie, this is amazing. You're—" As his thoughts caught up to him, his face burned. "Thank you."

When Tristan and Evvie returned to the bunkroom, the others were clustered on the floor, circled around Leila. She was telling a story. Across the wall, Damian's gang listened just as intently.

Leila paused when Tristan entered. "Hey, you," she said, smiling. "I'm nearly done with the story."

Nodding, Tristan crossed the room and dropped to the floor beside her. He couldn't recall why he'd been in a bad mood earlier.

Leila resumed her story. "The rich suitor crept in

through her window that night, sword in hand, and cut off a lock of her golden hair. The girl had only feigned sleep, so she watched the man as he clambered back down the vine. She knew then that the rich suitor wished only to possess her.

"In the morning, the poor suitor knocked at her door with a handful of roses. 'My lady,' he said, 'I am not worthy to be your master. I cannot try to win aught but your heart.' At these words, the girl knew that the poor suitor was the only one who truly loved her. Though his gifts had been simple, he cared enough to respect her freedom. The end."

Leila got to her knees as soon as she finished, not waiting to hear anyone's response. Rusty grinned at her, but she looked quickly away.

"What was the story about?" Tristan asked as Leila rummaged in her book bag.

Leila paused and looked at him carefully for a moment. "It's about a beautiful girl who everyone wants to marry. She'll only marry someone who really loves her, so she pretends that she's under a curse. Whoever cuts a lock of her golden hair will own her."

"So she'll marry the one who doesn't steal her hair, right?" Tristan said. He glanced at Evvie, who had been watching him from across the room. Evvie shot him a threatening look.

"I'm glad you're talking again," Leila said.

"Sorry."

Chapter 12

The Secret Underground Bedroom

Someone screamed.

Tristan bolted upright. Everything was dark. "Whassamatter?" he mumbled, throwing off his sheets.

The scream died abruptly, and then a girl's voice began shouting.

"I'm going to murder you, Zeke Elwood!"

It was Leila.

"Leila, what—"

She didn't notice Tristan. "You're a wretched, hateful...where's that bloody knife?"

Frightened, Tristan jumped down from his bed and dashed over to Leila's bunk. "What's happe—"

Tristan stopped abruptly. Rusty had blown one of the lamps to life, and by its glow Tristan could see exactly what was wrong. Leila's hair—her beautiful black hair, long and sleek and always trapped in a braid—was gone. The entire plait had been shorn off, leaving nothing in its place but ragged curls.

Tristan opened and closed his mouth, gaping.

"Get away from me, Tristan," Leila said in a low, threatening voice. Lurching to her feet, she grabbed a pencil from her bedside table and brandished it like a dagger. A moment later she was hurtling towards the dividing wall.

"Don't!"

Tristan dove after Leila. When they both went crashing to the floor, he wrapped his arms around Leila's shoulders to restrain her. "You—can't—do anything," Tristan grunted. Leila struggled and jabbed him in the chest with her elbow.

Several lights on the other side of the room were now glowing. Zeke and Damian stood beside their bunk, laughing so hard they weren't making any sound.

The other students from Tristan's side of the room were starting to gather behind Tristan and Leila, curious and almost protective. Then Rusty stalked over and stood above Tristan.

"Give me that." Rusty yanked the pencil out of Leila's hand. He tossed the pencil to the ground and strode forward, glaring at Zeke.

Zeke was still laughing. Tristan clenched his fists, chest tightening.

"What—d'you think—you're gonna do?" Zeke choked out, still laughing. He collapsed on his bed and pounded the mattress.

Without a word, Rusty drew back his fist and punched

Zeke full in the face.

There was a hideous crack.

Zeke howled.

As blood began to dribble down Zeke's upper lip, Damian's laughter died at once. Without pausing to wipe away the blood, Zeke lunged at Rusty, yelling. He slammed his fists into Rusty's his stomach and bashed his shoulder against Rusty's jaw—

Rusty roared in pain and lashed out at Zeke, pounding an elbow into Zeke's chest.

Then Damian threw himself into the fight—the three boys crashed to the floor, writhing and kicking in a furious tangle.

Tristan's hands were numb with fury. Grabbing the edge of a desk, he wrenched himself to his feet and threw himself at Damian.

As Rusty wriggled free of the tangle, Tristan's fist connected with Damian's ribs.

Leila hurtled into the fight right behind him. With a shrill curse, she rammed her knuckles into Zeke's eye.

Zeke screamed.

Taking advantage of Tristan's distraction, something slammed him in the stomach—he fell backwards, arms flailing, and cracked his head against the frame of Zeke's bunk. A spasm of pain ripped through him, blacking out his vision.

He couldn't think.

Dimly he noticed a hot trickle of blood seeping down his forehead; he tried to blink away the darkness, hoping the blood wasn't his own.

"STOP!"

The roar came from the doorway. Still dazed, Tristan tilted his head back to see who had shouted.

It was Drakewell.

The headmaster stood just inside the bunkroom, his sunken eyes flashing as he watched the brawl. Even half-conscious, Tristan was frightened.

Leila punched Zeke one last time before the five of them broke apart, crawling and stumbling away from one another. Wiping his forehead on his sleeve, Tristan struggled to his feet and nearly fell over again as the blood surged to his head. He clutched a bookshelf, waiting for his vision to clear.

Rusty and Zeke had definitely taken the worst beatings—blood was smeared across Rusty's battered chin, and Zeke squinted past a swelling black eye.

"Damn you," Zeke spat at Leila. He no longer looked handsome.

With a rueful smile, Leila stood and helped Rusty to his feet. "I forgive you now," she told him.

He grinned and licked blood off his lip.

Once Tristan, Leila, Rusty, Zeke, and Damian had changed out of their bloodied, torn pajamas, they were patched up under Grindlethorn's irritable care. Not one of them dared to speak.

Drakewell was waiting for them in the hallway, looking angrier than ever. Tristan shifted on his feet between Leila and Rusty, his head throbbing miserably.

"Despicable behavior," Drakewell spat. "Are you nothing more than criminals? Prove that you can do better. *Prove* that you are more than delinquents, or you will be treated as such."

Each of them received twenty hours of punishment, and they were immediately put to work cleaning every toilet in the school. Between feeling guilty and regretting that he hadn't been able to hit Damian more, Tristan wished there weren't so many bathrooms in the school.

Tristan and Leila started out by cleaning the boys' bathrooms. Since they were scrubbing the tiles on their knees, they had rolled up their jeans and kicked aside their shoes.

"This damn magic is completely useless," Tristan said, sloshing water irritably over a black scuff mark. "What's the point of it if we've still got to clean by hand?"

"Hmm," Leila said. She paused, dangling her scrubbing brush in the air. "Do you think my hair could be grown back magically?"

"Probably," Tristan said, not looking up, "though you look nice with it short, too." Actually, he thought she looked prettier with her hair curling around her face like this. "Are you going to ask someone to grow it for you?"

Leila shook her head. "I'll keep it like this. I just wanted to know I had a choice."

For the first time in nearly a month, Tristan, Leila, and Rusty sat together at dinner. Now that his head had stopped throbbing, Tristan was so cheerful that the three of them were on good terms again that he forgot to be angry at Damian and Zeke.

"We should do punishment with Alldusk tomorrow," Rusty said. "Helping him restock shelves sure beats scrubbing toilets."

Leila grinned. "And he'd probably let us off easy. He likes you, Triss—you're still the best at collecting magic."

"Amber's better," Tristan reminded her. Quinsley was coming around with plates of chocolate cake—Tristan, Leila, and Rusty each took a slice and dug in with relish.

Just as Tristan finished scraping the last dollop of frosting off his plate, Evvie appeared and drew a chair over to their table.

Ignoring Leila's scowl, Evvie said, "Tristan? I'm going to tell people about that room, okay?" She cast a nervous glance at the table where Zeke and Damian sat.

Tristan nodded. "That'd be amazing." Turning to Leila, he said, "I wanted to tell you about this yesterday, but it's Evvie's secret, and I promised her I wouldn't say anything…"

As Evvie began to describe the room in the tunnels, Leila's expression quickly turned from irritation to delight.

"It's perfect, right?" Tristan said once Evvie had finished. "Our entire half of the bunkroom could move down there—then we'd be safe from Zeke, and we could turn the room into a real home."

Rusty's eyes sparkled with enthusiasm, though he hesitated for a moment. "Didn't we say we'd try and stay out of trouble?" he said, chipped tooth showing as he bit his lip.

"Good point," Leila said. Glancing from Zeke to the teachers, she shrugged. "Still, I think Drakewell is the only one who would punish us if he found out. After last night, I'm willing to risk it."

"What if we're locked away forever?" Rusty asked, eyes widening. "We'd starve to death in those tunnels, and—"

"Come on; I'm sure he wasn't being serious," Tristan lied.

After a moment, Leila nodded. "I think we should do it. Telling that story last night was a stupid idea—I don't want to share a room with Zeke any longer. Are there beds in that room already?"

"There's nothing but a rotting old bookshelf," Tristan said with relief, "so we'll have to drag our mattresses down."

"We'll do it tomorrow, then." Leila frowned at Rusty. "Are you coming?"

A reluctant grin spread over Rusty's face. "Oh, all right," he said.

After dinner, Evvie and Tristan retraced their path through the tunnels, Leila and Rusty stumbling blindly behind them. Even as Tristan laughed at Rusty, who kept tripping, he felt a nagging shame for his own fear the night before.

When they finally stood in the empty room, blinking in the flare from the single lamp, Leila and Rusty beamed at him.

"This is brilliant," Leila said. She gave Tristan a brief hug from behind, ragged curls tickling his neck. "We need more lights."

"Delair would probably donate a few if we asked," Tristan said.

Leila nodded. She made a slow circuit of the room, appraising every contour of the walls. "We should come up with a list of everything we need—mattresses are a good start, but if we'll be spending more time here we'll want a table, a new bookshelf, and a rug if we can find one."

"Okay," Tristan said. He could already imagine what the room would look like, bright and cozy and full, once it was finished. "Let's see if we can get this whole place ready tomorrow."

He turned first to Evvie. "You're in charge of moving mattresses. We need to find out how many people there will be."

Evvie nodded. "If everyone on our side comes, that'll make eight of us."

"Nine," Tristan said immediately. "You forgot Amber." He hooked his thumbs into his pockets and moved on to Rusty. "Tomorrow you can go to Delair to work off more hours," he said. "Get as many of those magic lights as you can, and see if you can find brackets or something to attach them to the wall."

"Cool," Rusty said.

"Leila, do you think Quinsley would lend us some old furniture?"

"I'll ask," she said. "If he has anything, I'm sure he wouldn't mind. Also—Tristan, you should see if Alldusk still has that broken table from his classroom. The one he replaced, I mean."

"Good idea," Tristan said.

Rusty's grin was wider than ever. "This is gonna be awesome. Like we've really got a home here, or something."

Tristan nodded fervently.

The next day, Tristan enjoyed school as he never had before. It was wonderful to share this secret; for the first time since the crash, he felt as though he had regained a fraction of control over his life.

Tristan and Rusty sat next to Eli and Trey in Brikkens' first period class; while Brikkens blathered on about something called the Theory of Independent Movement, they explained the plan in an undertone.

"Are you in on it?" Rusty whispered once Tristan had finished.

"You kidding?" Eli said. "Hell, yeah!"

Trey, who rarely smiled, gave Rusty a brief grin.

A moment later Eli pretended to make a trip to the bathroom, and didn't return until class was over.

"Those mattresses are bloody heavy," he muttered to Trey, still flushed with exertion. "I got yours too, mate. Tristan wasn't lying about that room—it's brilliant."

"'Course it is," Rusty said, pounding Eli on the back.

Rusty was able to talk with Hayley and Cailyn during Grindlethorn's class, where they were learning emergency bandaging techniques; the two girls agreed to move out of the bunkroom almost as readily as Eli and Trey.

"I can't believe everyone is deciding so quickly," Tristan said as they walked up to lunch.

"I'm not the only one who has a problem with Zeke," Leila said. She reached up a hand to smooth back her hair and stopped short, fingers splayed across her bare neck. Her expression darkened. "Besides, everyone likes Rusty."

At lunch, Tristan joined Amber at her solitary table.

"You're not here just to talk, are you?" she said, setting aside her glass.

Tristan fidgeted, wishing he could tell Amber that she was mistaken. "Well, Evvie's found a new room for everyone on our side of the bunkroom to move to," he said. "Just to get away from Damian and Zeke, you know. So, if you want to come, Evvie's helping us move our mattresses down to the new room during classes today." Tristan took a bite of his grilled cheese sandwich and then set it aside, scrubbing the buttery grease from his fingers.

After a long silence, Amber nodded. "I would like that," she said. "For you to carry the mattress, I mean. Evangeline doesn't like me very much."

"I don't think she likes anyone," Tristan said quietly. "But that means you're coming?"

Amber nodded and then fell silent for a while. She tore a small strip of crust from her sandwich and nibbled at it, staring vacantly at Tristan's plate. Tristan had the uncomfortable feeling that she was disappointed with him.

"You used to talk to me," Amber said at last, so quietly that Tristan could have imagined it.

"Yeah, after I failed Quinsley's test," he muttered.

"And when we were punished for the lemon tree."

Amber smiled, her cheeks coloring daintily. "Thank you for inviting me to come to the new room." She finally looked up and met Tristan's eyes. "Anyone else would have forgotten me, I think."

She was right, of course. "You should eat with us sometimes," Tristan said. "I would like that."

Instead of replying, Amber closed her mouth in a thin line. Tristan hoped she wasn't angry with him. He finished his lunch in silence.

After lunch, Tristan went down and helped Evvie move the rest of the mattresses to the secret room. Though Evvie's palms were lashed with mottled lines from the mattress ropes, she didn't complain. She was clearly a bit disgruntled nonetheless.

Classes were almost over by the time they finished, so instead of returning to Environmental Studies, Tristan lugged everyone's belongings down to the secret room as well. Leila and Rusty caught up to him at the end of the hall.

"Where've you been?" Rusty asked.

"I've been carrying down the last of the mattresses," Tristan said. "And your books and things too. Come on."

After dropping everything in the secret room, Tristan, Leila, and Rusty decided to beg more supplies from the teachers. They returned to the main hall and separated—Rusty went down to the first floor to help Delair, Leila made for the kitchens, and Tristan stopped at Alldusk's classroom.

The dark stone door was ajar when Tristan approached, a crack of light spilling onto the marble tiling.

Tristan eased the door open. "Professor?"

Hearing no response, he pushed the door farther.

One step into the room, he froze.

Alldusk had his arms around someone, and it was a split second before Tristan recognized her as Merridy. Her hair was unbound for once, and it was much longer and fuller than he had imagined.

Tristan stumbled back a step. Were they together? When Alldusk saw Tristan, he released Merridy at once. She yelped and stumbled into a table, her glasses clattering to the ground.

"Tristan!" Alldusk said, startled. He fidgeting with his hands for a moment before shoving them into his pockets.

Cheeks flushed crimson, Merridy fumbled for her glasses. When she found them, she jammed them on and hurried out of the room, head down. She slammed the stone door on her way out—for a moment there was no sound but the dull reverberations of the crash.

Tristan swallowed. "I'm really sorry." Alldusk was his favorite teacher; Tristan felt awful for walking in on him like this. Alldusk's face was stony. "I won't say anything, I promise, I—"

Alldusk shook his head, expression lightening. "Don't worry." After a moment he took his hands out of his pockets and straightened one of the chairs. "You were hoping to work off punishment, I assume?"

"Professor, I—" Tristan cleared his throat. "How old

are you and Merridy?" The question slipped out almost accidentally.

Alldusk's mouth twitched. "Darla and I are thirty, Tristan," he said softly. "New students are selected every fifteen years, though Professor Drakewell is the only one remaining from his year."

"Why?"

Alldusk laughed quietly. "No one knows. And I wouldn't go asking questions, if I were you." He turned and made his way to the back of his room, where his office door stood open.

Tristan followed, still apprehensive.

"The headmaster keeps his job for a reason," Alldusk explained, "but even the older teachers won't say why."

For the next two hours, Tristan and Alldusk worked side by side, separating and labeling and grinding ingredients. Neither one spoke.

By dinnertime, Alldusk's mood seemed to have improved considerably. As they began to clean up their workspace, sweeping the plant dust into a metal trashcan and wiping the table with lemon-scented rags, Tristan remembered why he'd come here to begin with.

"Do you still have that broken table, the one you replaced?" he asked.

Alldusk turned away from Tristan, shaking his rag into the trashcan. "Darla mentioned this," he said carefully. "She said a few of you kids are planning to move to a new bedroom."

Tristan fumbled with his rag and knocked over an

empty jar.

"No, don't worry—I won't report you." When Alldusk looked back at Tristan, his face betrayed no trace of shame. "Actually, I think it's a brilliant idea. As I said before, I don't think you kids have nearly enough space here." He ran his fingers through his black hair. "The table is still broken, but you're welcome to have it."

"Why can't you fix it with magic?" Tristan asked. He folded his rag in half, the frayed edges coming together in an imperfect line.

Alldusk nudged the trashcan back into the corner with his foot. "This is Brikkens' subject, not mine. You should have learned that magic can only affect what happens in nature. The magic won't always seem natural, but you can't just toss common sense aside."

Tristan thought back to his earliest lessons with Brikkens, back when he'd still attempted to pay attention. "Can't you change the color of things?" he said.

"Yes," Alldusk said, "because color is simply the reflection of light." Gathering most of the jars in his arms, he retreated to his office. "I'll see you at dinner," he called over his shoulder. "Afterwards, you and your friends can see about moving that table."

When Tristan returned to the secret room after dinner, carrying the splintered table with Leila's help, he was surprised to find that the space was already cluttered with new furniture.

"Where'd all this come from?" he asked, setting down

his end of the table.

Leila dropped the other side of the table and wiped her sweaty hair from her forehead. "Gerry didn't even let me help him in the kitchen," she said, "so I've been moving shelves and chairs and things all afternoon. There are several rooms past the kitchen that are mostly empty, and apparently people have been stashing old books and furniture there for years."

Rusty joined them a moment later, with a sack full of magic lamps and nails. Leila was better at hammering them into the wall than Tristan or Rusty, so they mostly handed her nails and held the metal plates in place.

Eventually all sixteen lamps were fixed to the wall and glowing merrily. The room was completely transformed, as bright and cheerful as the ballroom upstairs.

Just then, footsteps in the tunnel signaled the arrival of Eli and Trey.

"Hey," Eli said, grinning. "This looks nice." He spun in a circle, looking around at the walls and the furniture. "The lights are crooked, though."

"It's Leila who put them up, not me," Rusty said.

Leila glared at them both.

As the others began to arrive, Tristan and Leila set to work clearing a space along the far wall, where they spread the nine mattresses side-by-side. The wall was curved, so the beds ended up in something of an arc. Rusty and Eli were supposed to be arranging furniture, but instead they dug through the stuffed drawers, scattering bits of paper and other debris across the floor. In what looked like an attempt to be helpful, Trey knelt beside the pile of litter and sorted through it, occasionally flattening a crumpled sheet of parchment to see what was written on it.

Tristan struggled to keep a straight face. The room was such a wonderful secret, as though the earth itself had folded its rich, cold layers around this one bright heart.

According to the small clock perched atop a burnished copper vase, it was past eleven by the time Hayley and Cailyn joined them.

"We should play cards," Rusty said, beaming at the girls.

Tristan had been shoving the enormous bookshelf to the back wall—he straightened, rubbing his bruised shoulder. "Sure."

Leila glanced up from the stack of books she was organizing. "Gerry has a magical fireplace we can bring down tomorrow, Tristan," she said vacantly.

"Great. Do you want to play cards?"

There weren't nearly enough seats for the eight of them—Hayley and Cailyn shared a wooden chair, Eli took the short bench, and Evvie sat awkwardly in the squashy armchair. Tristan, Leila, Rusty, and Trey stood.

"We'll play poker," Eli said, whipping his usual deck of cards from his back pocket. "There's plenty of junk here—we can bet with pens or something."

As Eli dealt the cards around, careful not to let anything slide to the caved-in center of the table, Leila described her plan for the room in a whisper.

"We should have the fireplace right across from the

door," she said in Tristan's ear. "Once we get more chairs, we can group them around the fire." She pointed to the space, which was currently empty aside from an overflowing trashcan. The center of the room would be a study space, she explained, with the bookshelves and the table and the less comfortable chairs. The half-circle of mattresses could stay where it was, lining the wall to the right of the door.

As he listened, Tristan picked up his hand of cards and sorted through them, cupping them in his palm so Leila couldn't cheat. After furtively examining the broken table from different angles, he had an idea for fixing it. It had been ages since he'd gotten the chance to mend something, and he was looking forward to the work.

"What do you get for winning?" Evvie asked, making a face at her cards.

Rusty grinned. "Maybe Leila can bake you something."

"No way," Leila said. "If you win, you can clean up these pens."

Amber wandered into the room just after midnight. She gave Tristan a distant smile before choosing a book from Leila's pile and settling down in the far corner to read.

"We should get to bed soon," Tristan said, stifling a yawn.

"You're only saying that because you're losing," Eli said. More than half of the pens were stacked by his elbow.

Hayley got to her feet. "We still need to put sheets back on the mattresses," she said. She had lost her entire pile of pens on the second round; for the past hour, she'd been watching and trying to help Cailyn. "No, you keep playing," she told Leila. "It'll only take a few minutes."

Now that she had the chair to herself, Cailyn curled her feet under her and propped her chin on her hands, watching with a sleepy, contented smile as Eli dealt the next round.

By the time the game was finished, Tristan's legs were stiff from standing. "Okay, new assignment," he said, shaking out his sore ankles. "Everyone has to bring down a chair by the end of this week, or you have to sweep the floor. Deal?"

"That's not much time," Cailyn said, blinking lazily. She looked ready to fall asleep at the table.

"You have tomorrow and Friday," Tristan said crossly. "You shouldn't complain—some of us still have fifteen hours to work off."

Leila yawned. "Tomorrow I—I'll find a rug somewhere." She didn't seem to be paying attention to the conversation.

Smiling sleepily, the others began getting ready for bed. Hayley had finished tucking sheets around all nine mattresses; Tristan looked around, wanting to thank her, but she'd already fallen asleep.

In the morning, everyone who'd slept in the secret room was exhausted but cheerful. Zeke's gang could only scowl at Tristan and Leila during breakfast, since the teachers were watching, though Tristan knew there'd be trouble later.

As the students made their way to Brikkens' class, Zeke grabbed Leila by the collar of her sweatshirt and thrust her against the wall, pinning her down. "Where did you and your buddies go last night, huh?" he said.

Leila had been expecting this—digging her nails into Zeke's palm, she wrenched her shirt from his grasp.

Tristan shoved Cassidy McKenna aside and rounded on Zeke. "Get away from her," he snapped. He didn't want to start another fight; he had enough hours to work off already.

Leila jammed her fist into Zeke's jaw and ducked under his arm. Rusty dove towards Zeke, but Tristan and Leila lunged at him and grabbed his shoulders.

"Snap out of it," Tristan said, yanking Rusty around to face him.

After a moment, Rusty lowered his fists and ran a hand through his hair, breathing hard. "Sorry," he said.

As Cassidy stalked past Tristan, she gave him an ugly look.

The first few chairs began showing up in the secret room that evening—Evvie brought a serviceable wood chair for the table, and Eli hauled down a squashy maroon armchair, which he sat in all evening just to lord it over the others. After dinner Leila started writing up a list of everything they still needed, while the others called out ideas.

"Chairs," Cailyn said, looking pointedly at Eli, who smirked at the people standing around him.

"I already have that," Leila said.

"We'll need a broom," Hayley said. She stepped closer to the bookshelf and wiped a finger along the top shelf. A ring of gray dust clung to her finger when she held it up. "And a bunch of rags, if we can find them."

Leila nodded and bent over the table to add those to her list. "Anything else?"

Tristan looked up, remembering suddenly. "We need one of those Prasidimums," he said. "Gracewright said they only let certain people through, so if we planted one in the doorway, none of Zeke's gang would be able to get in here."

"That would be perfect," Leila said. She added this to her list. "It'd keep the teachers away, too, if they tried to kick us out."

Rusty laughed. "We should give this place a code name. That way no one will know what we're talking about when we mention it."

"I don't think anyone's that stupid," Tristan said, though he agreed.

"It should be The Cave," Rusty said.

Leila tossed her pencil aside and crossed her arms. "That sounds dumb."

"But what if it stood for something else?" Eli said, sitting up straight and digging his fingers into the arms of his chair. "Like…the Cool Awesome Very…Eh…"

Leila snorted. "Any other ideas?"

"If we got more books, it could be called The Library," Hayley suggested.

"Or the magical bedroom," Cailyn said eagerly.

"That sounds dirty," Eli said.

Leila shook her head. "We're trying to keep it obscure, remember?"

"What about calling it the Subroom?" Trey said. Tristan and Leila turned and stared at him. "It can stand for the Secret Underground Bedroom."

Still looking faintly surprised, Leila nodded. "Okay. Good idea, Trey. Everyone like the Subroom?"

Hayley, Cailyn, and Rusty nodded.

When Tristan returned from his shower, most of the others were sitting awake in bed. Rusty yawned fiercely, though he looked determined to stay awake.

"Tell us a story, Leila," Hayley said from her mattress.

Tristan climbed into bed and pulled his blankets around his shoulders while Leila settled against the wall. "Want to hear about how this school was built?" She looked around as though seeking inspiration.

"Is it a real story?" Rusty asked, propping his head on his elbow.

Leila shook her head. "Though Gerry thinks there might be an actual record somewhere."

"Just checking." Rusty grinned.

Crossing her legs, Leila began. "Once, long ago, magicians were powerful kings of men. They could do absolutely everything with magic, and common men could not contend with their might.

"Then Christianity began to gain power. The Christians preached that magic was evil, and magicians and their allies would go straight to hell. Several magicians joined the church and swore off magic, hoping to escape eternal punishment, and with their help the magician kings were overthrown.

"The magicians who did not join the church became outcasts, performing cheap magic tricks for a living. As they used their powers less and less, their skills diminished, and many secrets were lost forever.

"Then, one day, a young man decided to create and rule a kingdom peopled entirely by magicians. He began rounding up the wandering magicians, who were glad to follow him. Once his followers numbered more than a hundred, he set off across the sea towards the barren mountains of Canada. There he found a repository of a rare element that fueled great amounts of power when melted down, and which he and his followers could use to replenish their dwindling supply of magic. The magicians enslaved the native peoples and began to mine the element.

"When most of the metal was gone, it left behind an enormous cavern. Here the young king began to construct the castle he'd envisioned, fashioning an underground stronghold that was every bit as elaborate as the magicians' palaces of old. The slaves continued to mine the element below the palace, creating a complex network of tunnels where he stored the gold and the magic that he gathered over the years.

"The king reigned for seventy years, but when he died he had not appointed an heir. For years after that, the magicians fought amongst themselves, until most had died or fled. The only magicians who remained in the end were scholars who had avoided the fighting. They decided to search for the lost knowledge of magic. The teachers here today are descendants of those original scholars, still searching for the power of the magician kings."

"So that's why they're so rich," Rusty mumbled. He yawned and pulled his blankets over his head.

Leila shook her head, smiling.

Chapter 13

The Prasidimums

Thanksgiving came, without any celebration whatsoever, though Quinsley baked a couple of pumpkin pies for Leila to bring down to the Subroom. By now the Subroom was easily the coziest place in the Lair—Quinsley had come down to install the magical fireplace Leila had promised, and its fire burned almost constantly to ward off the chill of the tunnels. While the room was still in disarray, Tristan went in search of a pair of metal sheets, which he drilled holes through and bolted to the table to realign the broken halves.

Zeke, Damian, and Cassidy kept trying to find the Subroom, standing by the entrance to the tunnels for hours on end in hopes that someone would come by. After a few nasty scuffles, Evvie showed the Subroom occupants a few secret entrances to the tunnels, by which they could bypass Zeke's gang entirely.

The final piece of the Subroom was set in place one Tuesday in early December, when Gracewright announced that the Prasidimums were about to bloom.

"It should happen any day now," Gracewright said brightly, stroking a fist-sized bud that topped one of the rather ugly vine-like plants. The Prasidimums were each about three feet tall by now, growing in a coarse, prickly tangle of gray stalks. "Since this is a matter of school safety, all teachers and students will be required to come to the greenhouse as soon as the Prasidimums bloom. Their flowers only last an hour or two."

"And why do we want to see a bunch of dumb flowers?" Damian said.

"Maybe they're carnivorous." Zeke pretended to take a bite out of the air.

Gracewright smiled at Zeke. "They're not carnivorous," she said. "As I told you before, the barrier plants only allow people they recognize to pass. And in order to be recognized, everyone will need to give a drop of fresh blood to each flower before they close."

"Oh, no," Evvie said quietly from behind Tristan.

"Aw," Zeke said. "Is poor little Evvie scared of nasty blood?"

Evvie blushed. "No," she said testily. She looked down at her folded hands as she said, "Professor, how—how fresh does the blood need to be?"

Frowning, Gracewright tipped her sunhat back from her face. "As long as you're there for the blooming, you should be just fine."

Tristan watched Evvie, puzzled—she twisted her hands in her lap until she noticed him and snapped, "What are you looking at?"

"What if no one gives the plants any blood?" Finley asked.

"Good question. The barrier will allow all living things through, which unfortunately includes rats and cockroaches and mosquitoes, but it will exclude everything else, like debris and rain and wind. You can still carry inanimate objects through, of course."

Instead of following the other students down to chemistry after class, Evvie turned away from the group and headed deeper into the Lair. Tristan dawdled in the hall, wondering if it would be worth missing class to follow her. Then Rusty grabbed his shoulder and dragged him to the stairs.

"What's wrong with you?" Rusty said, glancing down the hallway.

Tristan stumbled down two steps. "Nothing," he said, tightening his fingers on the cold metal railing.

Evvie didn't return until Merridy's class an hour later. Merridy was in a tetchy mood; by the end of the hour, she'd doled out punishments to more than half of the class.

When Evvie disappeared again for the duration of dinner, Tristan's suspicions grew. After eating, Tristan, Leila, and Rusty sat in sagging armchairs by the fire, struggling to balance a set of complicated chemical reactions that Alldusk had assigned.

Tristan kept glancing at the door, wondering where Evvie was; just as he let his textbook fall shut, the door to the Subroom creaked open.

It was Evvie—Tristan jumped to his feet and strode over to confront her.

"What's going on?" he said.

Though Tristan had spoken quietly, Evvie backed away, eyebrows arching in alarm. "What's wrong with you?" she hissed.

Tristan shook his head. "There's something going on," he said. Noticing that Eli and Cailyn were watching him with curiosity, he bent his head and lowered his voice. "There's a reason you're worried about the Prasidimums, isn't there? There's someone you want to get through the barriers, or someone you want to keep out, and you don't want the teachers to know."

Evvie chewed on her lip, eyes narrowed. The room had gone very quiet, nothing but the spattering crackle of the fire punctuating the stillness.

At last, Evvie licked her lips and took a step back. "Come here," she muttered. She wrenched open the door, and Tristan slipped into the black hallway behind her.

"Drakewell hates kids," Evvie said. Her voice was thin and disembodied in the darkness. "There's someone—someone hiding in the tunnels. If they don't give blood to the Prasidimums, they'll be trapped down here forever. But Drakewell can't know."

"Who's down there?" Tristan said quickly. "Is it a kid? Where did they come from?" He began imagining abandoned babies and meaty-armed thugs and scheming sorcerers.

"Stop it." Though Tristan couldn't make out Evvie's

outline in the blackness, he could envision her pinched scowl.

He sighed. "Okay, so why did you tell me? You want me to do something for you, right?" His voice was bitter.

For a moment Evvie was silent. Then she said, "I need a diversion. Something that will make all the teachers go down into the Lair."

"Even Gracewright?"

Evvie made a small noise of assent.

"Why didn't you ask Rusty instead? I thought you didn't trust me."

A few pebbles scrabbled across the floor as Evvie shuffled her feet. "I don't know. But you didn't tell anyone about the Subroom. I don't think you'll say anything about this."

She was right, and that small measure of trust was wonderful. "Okay," he said faintly. "I'll try."

"Thank you," Evvie said warmly.

Tristan smiled into the darkness. He was being an idiot, but Evvie's gratitude could make this all worthwhile.

When he returned to the warmth of the Subroom, Tristan ignored Leila's suspicious frown and started gathering up his textbooks and papers. His stomach was already twisting at the thought of the diversion; it was hours before he managed to fall asleep.

Tristan was wary of speaking to Leila the next day, afraid she would talk him out of helping Evvie. On the way to breakfast, he caught up with Eli and asked quietly what materials would create a lot of smoke when they burned.

Eli sniggered. "Don't they teach that at criminal school? 'How to be a delinquent, in four easy steps.' One: burn things. Two: attack people with knives. Three—"

"Seriously," Tristan snapped. "Do you know?"

Shrugging, Eli said, "Rubber's best. Leaves work too, though they don't light well if they're wet." He grinned. "What're you trying to burn down, huh?"

"Nothing," Tristan said. "You'll see, all right?" Giving Eli a brief smile of thanks, he turned and waited for Leila and Rusty to catch up.

Leila met him with a scowl. "I hate when you do that, Tristan," she said, hitching her bag up on her shoulder.

Tristan shuffled up the stairs, kicking his toes against each step. "I'm sorry, okay? You'll be glad I didn't drag you into this."

Leila's scowl deepened.

When Leila dumped her bag next to their table and dropped into the chair, she turned to glare at Tristan. "If you'd rather share secrets with darling *Evvie*, you can sit with her," she said under her breath.

Tristan rolled his eyes and sat down beside her. "Oh, come on, she's not even my friend," he whispered. "I'd do the same for anyone in the Subroom."

At a sudden clatter, Tristan and Leila both jumped—Rusty had dropped the metal lid of the coffee pot.

He replaced it sheepishly and poured himself a cup. "What's wrong with you guys?" he said. "Aren't you excited to see the Pretty-mums?"

"No," they said together.

Tristan left breakfast early, muttering an excuse about having forgotten his textbook in the greenhouse, and took the stairs two at a time up to the meadow.

Outside, the wind sank its icy teeth into his neck. Hugging his arms across his chest, Tristan hurried to the cover of the trees. Though it hadn't snowed recently, the meadow was still encrusted with patches of frozen snow; Tristan had to look beneath the waving pine boughs to find dry leaves.

Dropping to his knees, Tristan wrenched open his book bag and began shoving leaves into its empty depths. More than once, he stabbed his wind-chapped hands with a pine needle; he winced and shook off the sting, fingers growing heavier as the wind ate into his flesh. Handful after handful he crammed in, shoving the leaves down, smashing them into a dense bulk.

When the bag was so full it strained at the seams, Tristan jerked the sides together and got stiffly to his feet, surveying his work. Something dark was closing down on him. It was so easy to plan this—too easy. He shuddered. It was a thin line—such an insignificant thing—that separated criminals from everyone else.

Tristan slung his weightless book bag over one shoulder and dashed back to the Lair, slamming the door against the cold.

Brikkens and Gracewright were still in the ballroom, along with Cassidy and her tall friend Stacy Walden, when Tristan came nervously down the stairs. He kept his eyes fixed on the double doors at the far end of the room, pretending that there was nothing odd about his bulging bag.

As soon as the ballroom doors swung closed behind him, he broke into a run, bounding down the stairs and sprinting along the hall until he reached the second floor. He had no time to return to the Subroom, so he hurtled into the boys' bathroom and shoved his bag into the stall farthest from the door. Then he dashed back up to Brikkens' class.

Tristan was gasping for air, his hands aching as the numbness wore off, when he collapsed into his seat between Leila and Rusty.

"Oh, Triss," Leila said. She rubbed Tristan's shoulder as though trying to warm him, her expression a mixture of sympathy and irritation; only then did Tristan realize he was still shivering.

Tristan was tense and jumpy all through his morning classes. Leila shared her textbooks with him, but he couldn't concentrate on Grindlethorn's lesson and kept answering questions incorrectly.

They had barely sat down to lunch when Gracewright came bounding down the stairs to the ballroom, fruit-topped hat askew and hands smeared with dirt. "They're blooming!" she called, breathless from excitement.

Tristan clenched his hands under the table to keep them from shaking.

"Everyone come quick!" Gracewright paused at the foot of the stairs to catch her breath. "The Prasidimums are blooming!"

The teachers jumped to their feet, followed more hesitantly by the students. Above the scraping of chairs, Alldusk shouted, "Bring your coats, if you have them. The greenhouse isn't large enough for all of us."

"No, no time for that," Gracewright said. She turned and bobbed her head towards the ballroom doors. "Good morning, headmaster."

Tristan flinched. Then Leila was tugging on his wrist, dragging him to his feet and towards the stairs.

An icy draft met Tristan just past the invisible barrier on the stairs, and he shuddered, still chilled. The sun had come out, melting away the edges of the lingering ice patches, but tall mounds of snow still lurked in the shadows of the wooden structures.

Tristan was shivering worse than ever. Clenching his jaw, he stamped his feet to keep warm.

Gracewright and the other teachers were clustered around the greenhouse door on the far side of the clearing, and they widened their circle as the students joined them.

It took ages for Evvie to appear, long enough that Tristan began to worry she'd lied to him. Gracewright had already begun talking, describing what each person would need to do, when Evvie finally emerged from the forest. Finding Tristan's eyes on her, she nodded to him, pale and stiff-faced.

"Students first," Gracewright said when she'd finished her instructions. "Form a line, please—careful there, no pushing."

Tristan jostled his way forward until he reached the front of the line, where he stopped just behind Cassidy. She tossed her hair and glared at him. His teeth were still chattering.

"Hurry along," Gracewright greeted Tristan when he joined her in the greenhouse.

The windows were steamed over, rivulets of water running down the glass and pooling on the wooden sills. Tristan's cheeks tingled in the humid warmth, and he rubbed his hands together to thaw them.

"Now, all I need is a drop of blood for each flower," Gracewright said.

In his distraction, Tristan hadn't noticed the Prasidimums—looking past Gracewright, he was startled to see that the greenhouse was crowded with garish color. The Prasidimums were brilliant purple blooms, each flower so large that it was barely supported by the brittle, twining stems. The petals were wrapped in a cluster like a sprawling head of cabbage.

"Don't worry," Gracewright continued. "I dispose of the needles after each use, so there isn't any risk of contamination or—"

"Professor?" Tristan said, remembering suddenly. "Do you have an extra plant that we could—er—borrow?"

Gracewright nodded absently. "By 'we,' you mean yourself and the other students who have moved to a new bedroom, of course?"

Wary, Tristan shrugged.

"You do realize that the barrier will be permanent,"

Gracewright said. "That means none of the teachers will be able to enter the room once it's planted. Unless it's removed, which isn't the least bit practical."

Tristan wasn't sure how the barrier worked to begin with—did the vines simply grow too thick for anyone to pass through, or was there a magical transformation involved? "How do you get rid of the barrier, then?" he asked, eyeing the coarse gray stalks.

Gracewright laughed and straightened her precarious hat. "Dynamite is the most effective method." She pointed to the back of the greenhouse, at a row of Prasidimums that were crammed together on the workbench. "You kids can take the vine on the left. I'll help plant it when the time comes."

Taking Tristan's wrist, Gracewright gently pricked the tip of his index finger with what looked like an ordinary sewing needle. He barely felt the pinch of the needle, though blood welled on his skin a moment later. Reaching for the nearest flower, he brushed a streak of blood onto its brilliant petals.

"Very good," Gracewright said. A moment later, something that looked very much like a butterfly's tongue unfurled from the center of the flower and touched the smudge of blood.

"Damn," Tristan said. "Are those plants carnivorous?"

"Not exactly," Gracewright said, chuckling. "Venus flytraps don't have tongues, do they? Now, smear a little blood on the other flowers, so I can get the others through here in time."

"Thank you, Professor," Tristan said, his stomach churning a bit at the thought of what came next. He was reluctant to leave the steamy warmth of the greenhouse. As the chill air swept through him, the moisture that had clung to his hair and arms turned to ice. Without glancing at Leila, he hurried across the clearing towards the Lair.

Once inside the old wood structure, he started running, bounding down the stairs three at a time. Cassidy had returned to her usual table and begun eating lunch— she narrowed her eyes suspiciously at Tristan as he skidded past. He couldn't make an excuse, though, since he had only minutes until the other students would return.

Tristan flew down the stairs and dashed to the boys' bathroom, where he grabbed his precious bag of leaves. He slung it over his arm and broke into a run once again, scattering debris on the marble floor with each lurching step.

At the top floor, Tristan veered towards the kitchen. He should've gotten matches earlier—he was an idiot—

He scrabbled through the drawers beside the stove, hands shaking. Forks, knives, papers—he shoved it all aside, the silverware rattling in protest, and clawed at the back of the drawer. Nothing. The second drawer was crammed with papers, choked so full Tristan could barely get it open. He yanked it out, sending scraps of paper skidding across the tiles.

In the third drawer down, he finally found a box of matches. He shook it just to be sure it wasn't empty. Leaving the kitchen in a shambles, he wrenched open the door to the ballroom.

Cassidy flinched as the door clattered open. Pausing at the edge of the dining platform, Tristan said, "Cassidy? Don't say anything to the teachers." He clutched the bag of leaves to his chest, breathing hard. "Please."

Cassidy's eyes were still wide, her nostrils flared. "Why would I tell on you?" she said sarcastically.

Tristan didn't trust her, but he was already out of time.

Just past the invisible barrier on the stairs, he dropped his bag on the first dark step and began tearing handfuls of crumpled leaves from the densely packed mass inside. When it was empty, he pulled the box of matches from his coat pocket.

His hands were surprisingly steady as he slipped a match from the box and scraped it down the coarse edge.

As the match sparked into flame, Tristan froze, startled by its brightness. Already the flame was creeping close to his fingers—there was no more time for second-guessing.

He dropped the match.

The brittle leaves crackled into flame almost at once, curling in a small burst of heat and sending the fire dancing along the step. Now Tristan had to open the longhouse doors so the teachers would see the smoke.

But he couldn't wrench his eyes from the fire. The invisible barrier, usually indistinguishable in the darkness, cast an eerie shadow on the flames.

Then someone opened the doors for him, letting in a shaft of weak light. With a great effort, Tristan raised his head. The fire was already shedding great billows of pale smoke.

"Triss! What the hell are you doing?"

It was Leila. "It's a diversion," Tristan said grimly. His eyes were beginning to sting—rubbing away tears with the back of his wrist, he coughed.

"Don't just stand there, damn it," Leila said. She hurried down the stairs, arms raised against the smoke.

When she made to grab Tristan's arm, she skidded on a dry leaf and lost her footing. Hurtling forward, she crashed into Tristan and knocked him over. They both flew backwards—Tristan smashed his shin against the edge of a stair, and together they went careening down the steps.

Leila was shrieking, Tristan yelling as they crashed down stair after stair, slamming painfully against the marble.

At last they came to rest at the foot of the stairs.

Tristan let out a stream of curses as he untangled himself from Leila. Everything hurt like mad; bruises throbbed all down his legs, and his lungs were knitted tight from the smoke. He coughed and slumped against the wall, waiting for the dizzying blackness to recede.

"I'm sorry," Leila said weakly. Pressing her hands against the wall, she clambered unsteadily to her feet.

Tristan nodded and spat out a charred leaf. With all the noise they'd made, he hadn't needed the fire to draw everyone's attention. Miserably he accepted Leila's outstretched hand and allowed her to pull him to his feet.

It was eerie to stand there, surrounded by perfect silence, knowing that chaos and flames consumed the stairway just past the barrier. Leila put a hand on Tristan's shoulder, and he was grateful for the weight of her fingers.

Ages passed before any sign of the fire reached the muffled safety of the Lair. The silence stretched thinner and thinner. Tristan longed to dart up the stairs and slip through the barrier, just to see what was happening. For all he knew, though, the small blaze could have flared up and devoured the stairs in a towering inferno.

How much longer could they wait?

Finally something appeared at the top of the steps. It was a shoe, dusty with ash; at the same time, the oily reek of smoke wafted down the stairs. The foot belonged to Drakewell. Startled, Tristan grabbed Leila's arm and dragged her out of the stairwell.

"You have soot on your face," Leila whispered urgently. She scrubbed at his forehead with her thumb; when she nodded, satisfied, Tristan smoothed his hair back into place over his scars.

Drakewell was followed down the stairs by the other teachers and students. Gracewright did not appear.

Last of all, Evvie slunk down the stairs, wiping her muddy hands on her pants. Soot particles clung to her hair. When she found Tristan and mouthed *thank you*, he turned away, scowling.

Drakewell's eyes lit first on Cassidy, still sitting motionless at her table, before he found Tristan and Leila cowering by the wall.

"Fairholm!" he yelled. "You are an abomination to this school. Your cruel, violent tricks will destroy this place, I swear—" He grabbed the black hourglass as though to wrench it from his neck.

"Professor!" Delair said loudly. "Desist, please! You cannot accuse Fairholm without proof."

Nostrils flaring, Drakewell turned on Delair. "You have no authority over me, old man," he said coldly. He rounded on Tristan again, voice rising. "What do you have to say for yourself, Fairholm?"

Tristan gulped. He was no good at lying. "What happened?"

"What *happened*?" Drakewell shouted. "Don't give me that bilge." He took a step forward, hands curling into fists. "You burned the entire building down, Fairholm. Don't lie."

Tristan cursed inaudibly. He was a bloody idiot. He had never wanted this, never expected to cause real damage.

Just as Tristan was about to make a halfhearted excuse, Leila spoke. "Professor?" She stepped forward, hands twisting together behind her back. "Please—I was the one who started the fire. But I didn't mean it to destroy anything."

Drakewell's eyes widened, the shadows beneath his brows growing darker. "Swanson!" he barked. "Is this true?"

Panicked, Tristan said, "No, Professor, she's lying, I—"

Leila kicked him sharply in the ankle, and he broke off, wincing.

"This behavior is intolerable," Drakewell said harshly, his eyes darting between Tristan and Leila. "If you don't give me the truth *right now*, you're both going into the tunnels. People have died down there before—this wouldn't be the first time."

"Headmaster, be reasonable!" Quinsley barked.

"You know we need Tristan," Alldusk said. His usually mild voice had a sharp edge to it. "He and Amber are the only ones with a natural inclination for magic. You said yourself that Tristan may have to take your place someday, Headmaster."

As though emboldened by Alldusk's words, Merridy raised her hand timidly and said, "We should take a vote."

Drakewell turned on her. "Put your hand down, Merridy," he barked. "This is not a democracy."

"Who says it's not?" Quinsley said angrily, advancing on Drakewell.

With Drakewell's attention averted, Tristan took a step back and pressed his spine against the wall. He took Leila's hand and pulled her back as well, afraid she would try to interfere again.

"We all started from the same place," Quinsley continued, his voice rising. "We weren't meant to divide power like this. I'm not just a bloody *cook*." He smacked his fist against the wall.

"Who appointed you as headmaster, anyway?" This was from one of the students—it sounded like Damian.

"You remember why I took charge here," Drakewell said. He was no longer shouting—his voice had gone low and cold. "You know *damn* well why I had to take the job."

"That doesn't give you authority over every decision we make," Alldusk said. Though his voice remained even, there was a dangerous glint in his eyes. "We could send you away, if it came to that."

Drakewell gave a harsh laugh. "Who would take my job?"

The teachers looked at each other.

"I'm sure we could manage it," Alldusk said grimly.

"And where would you send me?" Drakewell said, his sunken eyes narrowing. "No one has ever left this place."

Tristan shivered violently. *No one has ever left this place.* He hadn't realized that Leila's hand was still in his, but she tightened her grip, reassuring him. *No one has ever left...*

"Someone *has* left," Quinsley whispered.

Drakewell whirled, his face suddenly drained of color. Without another word, he stormed away, slamming the ballroom door with a crash behind him. From the hallway, Tristan heard something like a muffled explosion ringing against the marble.

The teachers exchanged startled glances; Alldusk whispered something to Merridy, who straightened her glasses.

"Fairholm," Grindlethorn said after a moment, "the fire upstairs is not our biggest concern just now. If you confess responsibility, we'll give you hours to work off rather than locking you up."

Tristan nodded quickly. "I set the fire," he said. He wanted to tell the truth before Leila could intervene. "I didn't mean it to spread, though—I had no idea it would burn down the building. I'm really sorry."

"Ridiculous," Grindlethorn said coldly. "Fifty hours of punishment for inexcusable stupidity. You can start right away by helping us rebuild the entrance."

Alldusk stepped forward. "Classes this afternoon are cancelled," he said, speaking to all of the students. "After lunch, please return to your rooms and stay put."

"Professor, don't give Tristan so many hours," Leila begged. "It was my fault too."

"Do you want punishment as well?" Grindlethorn snapped. "Shut up and get out of here."

Chapter 14

Pinecones and Punishment

Tristan still had thirty hours of punishment when Friday evening came, so for the next week he was banned from meals and spent every minute of his free time outside, sawing boards and hauling wood to the clearing. With most of the teachers helping, the new school entrance sprang up in a matter of days, though Tristan wondered why no one tried to use magic to simplify the process. The pale, fresh boards of the new longhouse clashed with the weathered logs all around.

Since Tristan could no longer join the others at dinner, Leila brought meals for him in the Subroom, which he ate hunched over his homework. Each night he returned to the Subroom after dark, arms cramped and numb from exhaustion, only to head straight for his waiting pile of textbooks, essays, and worksheets. Towards the end of the week, he was so exhausted that Leila and Rusty had to drag him off the end of his mattress to wake him, and he stumbled drunkenly to class without breakfast.

On the second Sunday after the fire, Tristan still had nine hours left to work off and was ready to collapse.

Leila shook him awake at noon; smoothing his hair off his ear, she whispered, "Good morning, sleepyhead."

Groaning, Tristan rolled onto his back and rubbed his eyes. "Tell Grindlethorn I'm sick," he mumbled. "I'm too tired to work." Every muscle in his body ached.

"Quinsley says they're letting you off," Leila said. She tucked another strand of Tristan's hair into place—he knew his scars were showing, but he was too sleepy to care. "He says it's an early Christmas gift. Break starts on Wednesday, remember?"

Tristan sat up, surprised, and squinted around the Subroom. "Where is everyone?" By this point, he had been anticipating another fifty hours added to his punishment once he'd finished this round of work.

Leila sat back on her heels. "They're up in the kitchen. Gracewright planted our Prasidimum an hour ago, and Quinsley made brunch for us to celebrate."

Shaking his head, Tristan climbed out of bed and let his rumpled blankets fall into a heap on the mattress. "I can't believe I slept through that," he said. Though he was still groggy, he smiled as he pulled on his sweatshirt and socks over his pajamas. It was wonderful to be free at last.

Tristan had already forgotten about the Prasidimum by the time he was ready to leave the Subroom; when he passed through the seemingly empty doorway, he was surprised when the light vanished suddenly.

"Did you turn off the lights?" he asked Leila.

"No."

Tristan took a step backwards, and the lights reappeared. "It's just like the barrier on the stairs," he said in wonder. "That's a Prasidimum too, it has to be."

"Yeah," Leila said. "That's what we all thought. Come on."

Rusty was waiting in the kitchen when Tristan and Leila arrived, along with Eli, Trey, Hayley, and Cailyn. All five of them were wearing their pajamas.

"He's alive!" Eli said, waving to Tristan from where he stood by the counter.

Rusty grinned and pulled out the chair to his right. "Leila thought you'd never wake up," he said. "Nice to see you again, buddy."

Smoothing his hair over his face, Tristan sank gratefully into the chair beside Rusty. Leila took the other one, and then Quinsley passed around plates. As they began helping themselves to the food, Evvie and Amber arrived. Tristan avoided Evvie's curious eyes—she hadn't said anything to him since the day he'd started the fire for her, and he was more than a little upset by her lack of gratitude.

"Happy holidays," Quinsley said, beaming at everyone. "Dig in."

There were towering plates of chocolate-chip pancakes, Nutella-filled crepes, and sweet cinnamon French toast. Tristan stacked a little of everything onto his plate and doused it with warm maple syrup before digging in. He ate ravenously, spearing whole pancakes and shoveling them into his mouth. He felt like he hadn't eaten for weeks.

"We should decorate our room," Hayley said. She set aside her fork and poured eggnog for herself. "We can get a tree from the forest, even if we don't have ornaments."

"Let's—" Rusty began, his mouth bulging with food. He swallowed, blinking, and tried again. "Let's make popcorn balls and string cranberries, like when we were little."

"Ooh, and we can fold origami stars and birds," Cailyn said, beaming.

Tristan set down his fork and traced the rim of his mug. "I haven't had a tree since I was seven," he said. "That was before my mom left." When his mom had dangled popcorn balls from the pine's branches, Marcus had given it a name and treated it like a puppy.

The others were looking at him curiously; Tristan cleared his throat and took a gulp of his hot chocolate.

"A tree would be awesome," Eli said, grinning. "Tristan, you can chop one down for us—you've got lots of experience hauling wood around."

Tristan grimaced, and the others laughed.

Classes the next day were devoted to midterm exams. Tristan and the others had spent all of Sunday afternoon studying in the Subroom—Rusty called out questions, and whoever answered fastest won a chocolate truffle from the tin Quinsley had given them. Despite the last-minute studying, Tristan struggled with every exam the following day; if he passed any of them, it would be a miracle.

Once their midterms were finished, there was nothing

left to complete before the holiday break, so Tuesday's classes were easy and festive.

Most of the teachers went out of their way to make their last classes enjoyable. Just as with Halloween, Brikkens had taken it upon himself to decorate the Lair for Christmas; when they came to class that morning, they saw that he'd hung red and green baubles from the branches of his lemon tree.

Best of all, Brikkens gave an actual lesson in magic for the first time in months.

Reaching down with great difficulty, he lifted two heaping baskets of pinecones and slid them to the middle of the table. Fat cheeks ruddy from exertion, he announced that they would be attempting to change the color of the pinecones.

Though the others tried half-heartedly to change their pinecones, Tristan and Amber were the only ones who succeeded. Before long, everyone—Damian and Zeke included—was crowded around Tristan's end of the table, shouting out colors to Amber.

"Gold!" Eli said. "Make a gold one."

"Can you do patterns?" Zeke asked lazily.

Amber looked flustered by the attention; she tugged at her wispy hair and stared at the marble in her hand as though she didn't know what it was. She probably could do this spell without the marbles. After a long pause, she released the marble, and candy-cane stripes blossomed on the two pinecones closest to her hand.

"Oh, bravo, my dear," Brikkens said from behind the

cluster of students. "That's very good indeed, very nice." He cleared his throat. "Be careful, there, Fairholm."

"What about little hearts?" Zeke suggested. He sniggered at Tristan, whose pinecone had begun to smoke.

"That's not very seasonal," Leila said derisively, narrowing her eyes.

Tristan looked between them, and Zeke shrugged. "Stars, then, if that's what little miss grumpy-face wants."

With an unhappy glance at Tristan, Amber gave her next pinecone stars. Tristan swatted at his own pinecone, hastily smothering the tiny flame that had flared from its core. He seemed to have an affinity for fire as well as for magic, he thought sourly.

At the end of the lesson, Tristan stuffed his four splotchy pinecones into his pockets and watched as Rusty and the others fought over the pile that Amber had enchanted.

"You should teach the rest of us how to do that," Leila said.

Tristan snorted. "Yeah, because I'm such an expert. I might as well open a house-painting business right now."

"Good idea," Leila said, laughing.

"Hey," Rusty said, joining them in the doorway. "At least painting houses would be easier than building them."

Once Merridy's lesson was over, the holidays had truly begun. Tristan, Leila, and Rusty returned to the Subroom, where they sat lazily by the fire and shared a bowl of popcorn. Leila had somehow gotten ahold of one of Zeke's old quizzes, and she amused them by reading aloud his ridiculous answers.

Hayley and Cailyn joined them before long, each carrying armfuls of pine branches and red ribbon, which they deposited on the broken table.

"Don't worry—we'll sweep up the needles when we're finished," Hayley said as she and Cailyn began twisting the boughs into garlands and wreaths.

Soon after the two girls arrived, there came a loud thud from the doorway. Tristan whirled to see an enormous pine branch poking into the room; the branch was cut off very abruptly by the invisible barrier, so the part that showed appeared to hang in midair. Swaying alarmingly, the branch grew longer and longer until, with a swish of branches, an entire tree was thrust through the doorway.

"Look what we've got," Eli called as he appeared from behind the tree, Trey slipping through the barrier after him. Wiping his forehead, Trey hoisted the tree into his arms and carried it to the far corner of the room.

"Nice," Leila said. "It smells wonderful." The honey-vanilla scent of fresh pine sap had already swirled across the room.

Rusty got to his feet to help with the tree, which already had two thin boards nailed across the base of its trunk. "Is it snowing yet?" he asked.

"A bit," Eli said. "Where's Amber gone off to, with all those pinecones of hers?"

Tristan stretched out his legs and leaned back in his armchair. "No idea. The extra pinecones are there, though." He gestured to the far side of the room.

Amber reappeared in the ballroom for dinner, cheeks flushed and hair speckled with snow. Evvie was still missing; even after dinner, when they retreated to the Subroom and began settling in for the night, she did not reappear.

Once he'd showered and changed into his pajamas, Tristan decided he couldn't wait any longer. "If Evvie doesn't show up in another ten minutes, I'm going to go find her." He dropped to his knees on his mattress and pulled back the covers. "Unless someone else knows where she is."

Rusty shook his head.

"Will you quit it?" Leila said, shoving a stack of books against the foot of her bed with unnecessary vengeance.

"What?" Tristan said, though he knew where this was going.

Leila snorted. "You're only doing this because you think Evvie's *pretty*, Triss. I wish you'd stop worshipping her—she still hates you."

"I don't worship her," Tristan said, peeved. He punched his pillow flat along the wall, where it served as a back rest. "I'd do the same for any of you. Even Eli."

"Aw, thanks," Eli said sarcastically.

Leila shook her head at Tristan. "I doubt it." Stretching out on her stomach, she opened a book and held it close to her face, as though trying to block Tristan from view. "If I vanished, you wouldn't go tearing off to look for me like this."

"No," Tristan said mildly. "If you were missing, I

would've searched for you hours ago."

Before the ten minutes were up, Evvie tiptoed through the barrier and appeared abruptly in the doorway of the Subroom. Tristan had been pretending to read, but when he saw Evvie he sat up and threw off his covers.

"Where've you been?" he demanded. Now that she was here, and obviously unharmed, he was annoyed that she'd given him reason to worry.

Evvie crossed to her mattress, looking distraught. "I don't need a babysitter," she said. Then she appeared to reconsider. "Um?" she said, louder than before. It looked as though she was trying to make an announcement.

"What is it?" Tristan asked, trying not to sound too harsh. He got to his feet and approached her slowly.

"It's the teachers," Evvie said, her lips barely moving. "They're doing something horrible."

Tristan nodded grimly—he'd already guessed as much, given their repeated arguments on morality. "What are we supposed—"

"No," Evvie snapped, cutting him off. "This is different. They're doing something *tonight*, and people are going to get killed."

Tristan swore. He hadn't imagined this. The teachers couldn't be murderers—well, maybe Drakewell could, but the others? "How do you know?" he whispered. Everyone was watching Evvie now.

"S-someone told me." She swallowed visibly, her small eyes darting around the room.

"Are they going to kill us?" Hayley asked, clutching her

pillow to her chest.

"We're not the ones in trouble," Eli said. "Damn it! What the hell are we supposed to do?"

"Are you sure this is true?" Trey asked steadily. It was impossible to tell what he was thinking.

Evvie nodded.

Closing her book, Leila got to her feet. "Guys?" she said. "We should talk this out. Come on." She made her way tentatively over to the fire, where she curled up on the sofa, bare feet tucked between two cushions.

Tristan crossed the room and sat down beside her, with Rusty on his right. The others settled down around them, claiming the remaining armchairs or drawing over chairs from the table.

"Okay, Evvie," Leila said sharply. "Before we can discuss anything, we need more details. Who told you about…whatever the teachers are doing? Can we trust that person? And what is it the teachers are supposed to be doing, anyway? The fact that people are going to die doesn't mean much. Are the teachers just abandoning people who need their help, or are they actually slaughtering people?" Leila sat back, hugging her knees.

Evvie's distress was plain. "I don't know," she muttered at last. "I don't know any of it. And I can't tell you who said it—they made me promise not to tell."

Eli jumped to his feet, kicking his chair away. "What the hell?"

Trey grabbed the back of Eli's pajama shirt, holding him back. "Sit down," he said.

Breathing heavily, Eli took a step back, though he did not resume his seat.

Tristan leaned towards Evvie and whispered, "Is this about the person I helped you with?"

She shook her head.

The others were starting to mutter to each other; after a moment, Hayley's sullen voice rose above the murmur. "I want to go home," she said. She was clutching a blanket tight around her shoulders, her face pinched as though she struggled not to cry.

"You don't have a home to go to," Leila said. "None of us do, isn't that right?" She looked around the circle, waiting for someone to contradict her. "We're not just criminals; we're criminals with nowhere to go after Juvie. That's why they took us."

"Shut up, Leila," Eli spat. "No one cares."

They were sitting so close together on the couch that Leila's shoulder was pressed against Tristan's arm—he felt her shoulders tense, ready to have a go at Eli, but he punched her gently in the knee. "Stop that."

Again Trey yanked Eli back towards his seat; this time Eli turned and began shouting at Trey instead. Tristan shouted at them to calm down, but suddenly everyone was yelling.

Hayley burst into tears. "I wanna go home! I'll just run away. I can't do this anymore."

Cailyn tried to calm her down, but a moment later they were both shrieking at Leila. Rusty waved his arms in the air, calling for order; when no one paid him any attention, he turned to Evvie and demanded that she tell them everything she knew.

"Guys!" Tristan roared. "Quiet!" He was scared at what this could turn into.

No one heard. He jumped to his feet and shouted again. When they continued to ignore him, he grabbed a porcelain teacup from the table and hurled it to the ground. The teacup shattered, spewing shards across the floor, and the crash finally startled everyone into silence.

"Stop it, everyone!" His voice was loud in the sudden lull. "Yelling won't do us any good. It's the teachers we need to fight, not each other."

With matching sullen scowls, Leila and Eli resumed their seats.

Trey folded his arms over his chest. "I'm going to find a teacher," he said softly.

"No!" Evvie cried. "Don't go, you can't, you—"

Ignoring her, Trey crossed the room and vanished through the barrier.

A moment later everyone's eyes returned to Tristan. What was he supposed to tell them?

"Evvie, are you *completely certain* that the teachers are killing people?" he asked.

She nodded glumly.

"Someone we know, or strangers?"

"Strangers."

"And are they doing it to protect us, or because of some insane magical war?"

Evvie's lip was trembling. "The people are innocent.

They don't know anything about this."

"Right," Tristan said. "First of all—Hayley, we can't run away. I didn't tell you guys about this, but I tried to escape during Merridy's survival test. You guys know how well that worked. I was making good progress, heading south, when I got caught in an avalanche, and the next thing I knew I was back in Grindlethorn's hospital."

Hayley sniffed and wiped tears from her swollen eyes.

"Right now we're completely at the mercy of the teachers," Tristan continued. "We can't leave, we can't disobey them, and we can't complain. But this Subroom isn't just a place where we're safe from Zeke's gang—down here, we're safe from the teachers as well."

"Gracewright knew that," Leila said. "Gracewright knew what we were doing, but she still agreed to plant the Prasidimum here. Some of the teachers agree with you, Triss—they don't want us to be helpless."

Leila was right, but that was the strangest part of the whole thing. If the teachers were arguing amongst themselves, divided and unhappy, what held them together?

"We need to gather our own strength," Tristan said. "If we have power, enough to threaten the teachers, maybe we'll have a say in what happens to this place—to us." He glanced at Amber, who sat curled in one of the wooden chairs outside the circle.

"We need to find out what this magic is for. Once we know the secret of this place, we can decide who's right and who's wrong."

Eli slammed his fist on the arm of his chair. "And

what about the people they're going to kill?" he demanded.

Tristan shook his head and slumped back against the cushions. "I don't know. But what can we do?" He wanted to take Evvie by the shoulders and shake her until she gave the answers he wanted.

Some of Tristan's worry must have shown in his face, because Leila rested her cheek against his shoulder and whispered, "We'll figure it out. Don't worry."

After a long moment of silence, Rusty said, "What about Christmas?" His quiet voice sounded very childish.

Leila smiled sadly. "I haven't celebrated Christmas in years. Let's just try and enjoy ourselves, okay?" Tristan followed her gaze to the fireplace, where soft magical flames danced along a log. "Once the holiday is over, we can decide what to do."

Though Eli gave Leila an ugly look, and Evvie crossed her arms and pouted, no one said anything more. Already it seemed as though the room had split apart, reverting to the wary friendships from the beginning of the year. Hayley was no longer crying; she and Cailyn had drawn their chairs closer together and were whispering, casting pointed glances at the others. Leila and Rusty had subsided into an uncomfortable silence.

After a long time, Trey reappeared in the doorway. Evvie noticed him first and demanded to know what he'd told the professors.

"I couldn't find them," Trey said. At his quiet words, the muttering died immediately. "I looked in every classroom, and knocked on the doors to all their bedrooms, but they're gone. The whole Lair is empty."

Chapter 15

Christmas in the Lair

I n the morning, the Subroom was still as divided as before—Hayley and Cailyn were already gone when Tristan woke, while he and Eli deliberately avoided each other.

"What's wrong with everyone?" Rusty asked, trailing disconsolately behind Tristan and Leila on the way to breakfast.

"I don't know," Leila said. In the dark tunnel, her voice was bodiless. "I honestly don't know."

Tristan said nothing. He was just grateful that Leila and Rusty hadn't turned on him as well.

At breakfast that morning, Alldusk called out a greeting as Tristan took his seat. Tristan avoided Alldusk's gaze and didn't reply. When Quinsley came around with orange juice and scrambled eggs, Leila was the only one who thanked him.

"Tristan, could I have a word?" Alldusk said when Tristan made to leave the ballroom.

Tristan couldn't ignore a direct question. "See you," he mumbled to Leila and Rusty.

"Is everything all right?" Alldusk asked quietly.

Tristan stared fiercely at his black shoes.

"If there's anything that you've seen or heard, anything that you'd like to talk to me about..."

With a curt nod, Tristan turned and strode from the ballroom. Alldusk must have guessed why Tristan was upset; how could he justify murder? How could he show his face in the ballroom as though nothing had happened?

Despite everything, the next week was one of the happiest times Tristan could remember. The halls of the Lair grew brighter and more colorful by the day—the doors were festooned with wreaths, the plain marble surfaces draped with pine garlands, and half of the enchanted lights glowed green or red. The far side of the ballroom was dominated by an enormous Christmas tree, so tall that only the lowest third had been decorated. Even standing on a rickety old ladder, Quinsley couldn't reach any higher.

Tristan and the other kids from the Subroom watched the teachers with suspicion, but nothing in their behavior suggested anything new. Brikkens sang carols as he shuffled though the halls, his warbling baritone surprisingly sweet, and Gracewright took to wearing a Santa cap that she'd probably knitted for herself. Whatever Evvie said, Tristan couldn't bring himself to hate them.

Every day, the sugary aroma of hundreds of baking cookies wafted through the halls. Leila spent hours helping Quinsley with the sweets, and at one point she dragged

Tristan and Rusty up to the kitchen to decorate gingerbread cookies.

"I don't think he agrees with the other teachers," Leila said. "Come on, we really should trust him."

"You're not even taking this seriously," Tristan said.

When Leila gave him a hurt look, he sighed.

"Sorry." Glancing around the Subroom, he caught sight of Amber, who was curled up in a corner with a pile of books. "Amber, you should help us with the cookies." He felt sorry for her—she had been trapped inside after a blizzard had practically buried the Lair's entrance.

Amber looked up from her book, eyes wide. "I don't know how."

"Come on." Tristan held out his hand, grinning; after a moment she took it and allowed him to pull her to her feet. "It'll be fun."

She bit her lip to hide a smile.

Up in the kitchen, Quinsley was mixing up two enormous bowls of golden-brown dough; he was delighted to see Tristan, Rusty, and Amber, and he set them to work at once, rolling out the dough and pressing cookie-cutter shapes into it.

Before long, Tristan relaxed and forgot his anger. Quinsley wasn't responsible for what the other teachers had decided; he was just a cook, and it was easy to trust him.

Amber hadn't exaggerated when she'd said she didn't know how to bake cookies. She watched Tristan with wide-eyed curiosity as he lifted gooey stars and snowmen from the floured counter, and when he gave her the spatula, she couldn't lift the dough without squashing it.

"Maybe I should do that," Tristan said, grinning. "You press the shapes, and I'll lift them to the pan."

Moving aside, Amber handed Tristan the spatula.

"Can't you just do this with magic?" Tristan asked, pulling the pan closer. "Sometimes I can't tell where your magic ends and you begin."

Amber ducked her head. "Drawing on power is harder inside the Lair," she said. "I should leave; I'll only get in the way."

Tristan nudged her with his elbow. "I was only teasing," he said. "Do any of us look like we're experts at this?"

Though Amber was silent, her shy smile returned.

Decorating the cookies took all day. "We should take some down to the Subroom," Rusty said, when the last of the frosting had run out.

Tristan kicked him—even if Quinsley knew about the Subroom, they shouldn't refer to it so openly.

"Ow!" Rusty yelped. "Have you got a plate we could use, Quinsley?" His fingers were brilliant with frosting, which he'd been sampling as he worked.

"Of course." Wiping his hands on his apron, Quinsley lifted a large metal plate from the nearest cupboard.

Leila was helping stack bowls in the sink. "Open up, Triss," she said, grinning. When Tristan obeyed, she stuck a frosting-filled spoon into his mouth.

On the morning of Christmas Eve, the students in the

Subroom came to an unspoken understanding—for that day at least, they would act as though nothing divided them. This time Rusty wasn't ignored when he went around the room, wishing everyone a happy Christmas, and even Evvie greeted Tristan quite civilly.

Eli remarked that their little Christmas tree looked wonderful. Leila and Quinsley had boiled sugar and made hand-pulled candy canes the day before, which she'd hung from every pine branch. Though Rusty had been eating candy canes off the tree since they'd arrived, no one could see a difference.

That night there was a lavish feast in the ballroom; each table was lit with enchanted gold candles and piled high with food, from savory turkey and honeyed yams to steaming zucchini bread and potato-cheddar soup. The students from the Subroom drew their tables together, until all nine were able to sit as though at one table.

Even Drakewell and Delair joined the teachers for the occasion, so the teachers' table looked far more crowded than usual. For once, Drakewell's sunken eyes were fixed on his meal rather than scanning the room for students to punish.

"It's just like Christmas always was," Rusty said, beaming around the circle. "I'm an only child, but I've got tons and tons of cousins. We'd all get together for Christmas at my grandma's place, and all the kids would eat around one big table like this."

"My parents are Jewish," Trey said, "so I've never celebrated Christmas before."

Eli snorted. "I'd forgotten about that," he said. "Why didn't you mention it? The teachers would've done something different for you, I bet."

Trey shook his head. "I don't care. Either way, it's just pretending. We haven't got much use for prayers here, have we?"

They returned to the Subroom after dinner, cheerful and drowsy, and Tristan and Rusty helped Leila carry down two heaping plates of cookies and eggnog. Everyone brought their blankets and pillows over to the floor by the fire, where they sat close together with their backs against the couch and chairs.

"We should've gotten stockings," Hayley said, her wide eyes reflecting the firelight.

Rusty snorted. "You think Santa's gonna dig through a hundred feet of rock to get to our fireplace?"

It was Leila's turn to laugh. "How old are you, again, Rusty?" She reached for a gingerbread snowman and bit off its head.

Turning, she lifted her chipped glass of eggnog and said, "Let's have a toast to Evvie."

Surprised, Tristan licked fudge from his thumb and reached for his own glass.

Leila continued, "Whatever your motives for showing us this room, we'll always be grateful for it. This is more of a home than most of us have known in a long time."

"Hear, hear," Rusty said, clinking his glass with Leila's.

Evvie buried her face in her knees—her cheeks had gone bright red.

At last, when the cookies had been reduced to crumbs, everyone began stumbling to bed. Tristan drew the covers over his head and mumbled, "Merry Christmas, guys." He wasn't sure anyone heard.

In the morning, Tristan woke to excited voices.

"C'mon, guys, we've got presents!" Rusty called across the room. He, Eli, Trey, and Hayley were clustered around the stout Christmas tree, digging through a pile of boxes.

"Did you have to wake us up?" Leila grumbled, rolling out of bed and hugging her blanket to her shoulders.

Tristan rubbed his eyes and smoothed his hair into place. "Is there anything from our families?"

"Nah, it's just from teachers and kids," Rusty said. "They'd never let people send stuff here."

"I thought the teachers couldn't get down here," Eli said furiously. "What happened to the Prasidimum keeping people out?"

"Are they going to kill us?" Hayley asked shrilly.

"Calm down," Leila snapped. "Quinsley had me drag most of this stuff down here. We're still perfectly safe."

Once everyone had gathered around the tree, Rusty passed out presents. Everyone got a tin filled with chocolates and cookies from Leila, though Tristan's and Rusty's were rather larger than the others. From Rusty, Tristan got an odd lamp that looked somewhat like a flashlight; Amber gave him a glowing cube of Delairium that she'd probably shaped with magic. Cailyn had given each of them a decoration for the room, made from bits of nature—wreaths of braided branches, bouquets and framed pictures made from dried flowers, and polished wood bowls.

"Did you make all of these?" Evvie asked, holding up her new vase.

Cailyn nodded happily. "Gracewright helped, though."

"Damn," Eli said, impressed.

As he unwrapped present after present, Tristan began wishing he'd given something in return; he hadn't even wrapped gifts for Leila and Rusty. There were even a few nice gifts from the teachers mixed in with the rest: knitted scarves and hats from Gracewright, a set of plates and silverware from Quinsley, and new textbooks from Alldusk.

"This is dumb," Eli said, dropping his book by the fire. "If Alldusk wanted to give us more homework, he could've waited another bloody week."

"They don't look like textbooks," Leila said, opening her book to the title page. Most of the books were bound in ancient black leather; hers was larger than the others, and blue rather than black. "Hey, this is neat!" she said. "Listen—'Simple Spells, Delicious Dishes—A Magical Cookbook'!" She laughed and began flipping through the pages. "Now I just need to learn how to use magic."

"Nothing like a good cookbook for motivation," Tristan said, grinning. He looked down at his own book, which was titled *A Beginner's Guide to Magical Theory: The Complete Compendium*.

"Now we really do have a library," Leila said happily. "This is excellent!"

When Rusty tossed the final present to Leila, she pried

open the lid and made a noise of disgust.

"What's wrong?" Tristan asked.

Wordlessly she held up the contents of the small box. It was the long chunk of her black hair that Zeke had cut off, knotted around one of Amber's star-spangled pinecones.

"Who's it from?" Rusty asked, picking up the lid.

"Zeke, obviously," Leila snapped, "unless someone stole this back." She glared at Tristan. When no one said anything, she flung the pinecone and the hair into the fire, where they sparked and vanished from sight.

Glowering, Leila followed Tristan and the others up to breakfast, all of them still in their pajamas. In the ballroom, they found another pile of gifts under the enormous tree. Each student received a bundle of new clothes from Merridy and Brikkens, all varied and fitted correctly, unlike their plain uniforms. The students from the Subroom also received a great assortment of furnishings—rugs and quilts, giant pillows and cushions, and a pair of little tables.

At last everything had been opened and Quinsley came around with breakfast.

"Thanks for the dishes," Rusty told Quinsley. "They're great!"

Quinsley winked at him.

Leila kept glancing over at Zeke's table as she ate. "I just want to hit Zeke," she said, cutting into her pancake so furiously that the table shook.

"Aw, where's your Christmas spirit?" Rusty teased.

Tristan leaned forward, his elbows on the table. "I

think Zeke's gang should be included when we decide what to do about the teachers," he said in a low voice. "So don't pick a fight with Zeke, at least until break is over, okay?"

Leila rolled her eyes. "Good luck getting the others to agree to that."

It wasn't long before Leila got a chance to take her anger out on Zeke. After the students from the Subroom carried down their new clothes and furnishings, they pulled on their new hats and mittens, intending to enjoy the fresh layer of snow. Someone must have told Zeke's gang what they were planning, because as soon as Tristan and Leila reached the doorway leading out of the Lair, they were bombarded with snowballs.

"Ha!" Leila yelled. She ducked sideways and scooped up a fistful of snow. Tristan threw his arms up over his face and ran for cover, dodging behind a tree.

The new snow was wet and heavy, and Tristan's boots sank knee-deep in the drifts as he packed snowballs. Once his arms were full of snow, he dashed away from the tree and began hurling snowballs at Zeke's friends. He aimed at grim, hulking Ryan Riggs but missed; his next snowball walloped Damian on the back of the head.

"Damn you!" Damian shouted. Dropping the snowball he'd been shaping, Damian threw a long, crooked icicle at Tristan, who ran for cover.

From the shelter of the forest, Tristan noticed Amber watching him from a distance, hovering like a shadow between two dark pines.

"Come join us," Tristan called, though he knew Amber

would do nothing of the sort.

To his surprise, Amber called back, "You and the others are always fighting. You should come for a walk with me instead."

Shrugging, Tristan brushed snow from his gloves and tramped through the snow to where she stood. "It's probably a good thing you dragged me away from that," he said. "Leila and Zeke are going to murder each other."

Amber blinked at him. Then she turned and began walking away from the school, stepping carefully so that her feet didn't break though the surface of the snow. Tristan tried to do the same, but his feet kept sinking in—the snow's crust was brittle and thin.

Finally he gave up and asked, "Is that a spell, what you're doing?"

Slowing, Amber let her feet sink through the snow. "Not a *spell*, precisely," she said. "I am using magic, though."

"But you're not using a marble, are you?" Tristan said, more urgent now. "Delair said that skilled magicians can use magic straight from their own body's energy. Is that what you're doing?"

Amber shook her head. "You can only draw a small portion of energy from yourself without becoming exhausted," she said. "All things have an aura, though. With enough awareness and deliberate control, you can channel magic directly from your surroundings."

This surprised Tristan. "Why haven't the teachers told us that? The marbles take so much time to collect."

"I think they've forgotten how." Amber turned and studied Tristan, head cocked sideways. "Or perhaps they haven't yet discovered it."

Tristan was taken aback. "Who *are* you?" he asked.

This time Amber did not respond. He was afraid he'd upset her.

Hurriedly Tristan said, "Why are we the only ones who can use magic? I mean, the others can barely see auras."

"We know how to control our thoughts," Amber said. "I told you before that your aura is brighter than most people's." She reached out a hand to touch Tristan's cheek and stopped short. "It's because you have closer contact with magic."

"Yes, but why?"

Biting her lip, Amber ran her hand along the drooping needles of a pine bough. "We know how to shut out what we don't want to think about," she said. "We have learned to create barriers around our minds." She plucked a needle and twisted it between her fingers, no longer meeting Tristan's eyes. "You want to forget something. Your thoughts are controlled because of what you fear."

She had to be right. "Magic itself isn't evil, is it?" Tristan said. "It's just whatever the teachers are using it for that's wrong."

Amber was silent. She knelt in the snow and scooped up a handful of powder in her pale fingers. For a moment she let the snow rest there—then, in a heartbeat, it all melted and ran through her fingers. More magic, beautiful and utterly confusing.

Chapter 16

Intralocation

B ack in the Subroom, Leila was nursing a bruised cheek and Rusty held a handkerchief to a cut on his forehead.

"Where did you go?" Leila demanded when she saw Tristan. "We didn't stand a chance without you!"

"Good to know I'm valued around here," he said with a wry grin. Moving closer to Leila and Rusty, he muttered, "I was talking to Amber. She really understands magic—when we decide what to do about the teachers, we should listen to her."

Rusty folded his bloodied handkerchief in half and pressed it back to his forehead. "We should do that soon, shouldn't we?"

Pursing her lips, Leila nodded. "I really don't want to bring it up again, but I think we should decide what to do before classes start."

They got their chance to talk with Zeke's gang on New Year's Eve. It had snowed again overnight, but

Gracewright had trampled down a large circle in the meadow and built a roaring bonfire in the center.

"I have marshmallows and chocolate, if you kids want to make s'mores," she said as the students traipsed up from the Lair. "Happy New Year!" She dropped a huge box beside the fire and trudged back to her greenhouse.

"This is dumb," Damian said brusquely. "It's too cold to stay out here." He turned back toward the stairs.

"Roast us some marshmallows, Cookie," Zeke taunted Leila, who was already on her knees beside the box of ingredients.

Leila jumped to her feet. "Wait. We need to talk to you guys." Her eyes narrowed. "*All* of you."

Zeke stopped. Damian put a hand on Cassidy's shoulder and stomped back to the fire. "What the hell are you on about?"

Gloved hands on her hips, Leila stalked to the edge of the trampled circle. "Evvie has something she wants to tell you."

When Evvie backed away, her nostrils flaring, Leila sighed.

"Actually, we all have something to tell you. But first, you have to swear you won't say anything to the teachers.

Rusty knelt by the open box and began shoving marshmallows onto skewers. Hayley and Cailyn took the rods when he passed them around, though they didn't seem interested in the marshmallows.

"Why would we promise anything stupid like that?" Zeke asked. His eyes glittered with interest, though, and his friends were following him back to the fire. "Drakewell's my good buddy—I tell him everything." He smirked.

Damian grabbed a skewer from Trey and thrust the end into the flames. "All right, Evangeline, let's hear it."

Evvie flinched and dropped her scarf. Bending down to retrieve it, she said, "I can't—I mean, I don't know—"

With a sigh, Tristan stepped forward and took over. "The teachers are doing something we don't know about, right?" he said. "They brought us to this place because they want to use us for something special; we're all criminals with nowhere else to go, and they chose us because of that."

When Zeke opened his mouth to interrupt, Leila threw a snowball at his shoulder.

"Last week, just before Christmas, Evvie found out something about what the teachers are doing. Apparently their work is getting people killed." He swallowed and lowered his voice. "We don't know whether the teachers are going out and—and murdering people, or if it's sort of a side-effect of their magic. But either way, we thought you guys should know."

"Why couldn't Evangeline have told us herself?" Cassidy asked haughtily.

Tristan glared at her until she turned away. Even Zeke stopped smirking as he bent his head to confer with Damian and Cassidy.

"If you're right," Zeke said at last, "we should get the hell out of here." There was no trace of a smile on his handsome face; the absence was startling.

"We can't," Leila said seriously. "We've already tried that."

Slipping his still-frozen hands into his pockets, Tristan stepped forward again. "What we need to decide first is whether we're going to do anything," he said. "Whatever we try to do, it will be really difficult, seeing as we're completely isolated here."

At that, several people started talking simultaneously—when Eli said loudly that Tristan was an idiot to suggest that they even had a choice, Leila and Zeke protested. Damian started shouting over Eli, until Tristan couldn't make out what any of them were actually saying.

Eventually the yelling subsided, and they spent most of the next hour in a heated conversation. Amber, Trey, and Finley moved over towards the fire, looking as though they wanted to stay out of the argument, while Rusty kept roasting marshmallows and passing them around. The others accepted them gladly.

"Okay," Tristan said finally, loud enough that everyone turned. "The most important thing now is making sure we're not completely helpless. We all saw how upset the teachers got when the vandal attacked the school, so we know they're already worried. If we did the same sort of thing—if we started sabotaging a bit of whatever big-scale magic they're doing—we'd be the ones controlling them."

Leila was nodding, though Rusty looked a bit scared.

"Also, we should start collecting our own marbles," Tristan said. "I know most of us can't use them, but someday they might be useful. If we get enough magic of our own, the teachers will have to listen to us."

"So," Damian said forcefully, "you're still pretending you didn't actually wreck Alldusk's classroom?"

Tristan sighed. "I *was* the one who burned the Lair's entrance," he said reluctantly, "but it was an accident. I honestly had nothing to do with the other attack."

Damian spat onto the snow. "Sure."

By that point, Cailyn's hands had turned bright purple, so they broke their uneasy truce and went inside to warm up.

Classes resumed on the first Tuesday after the New Year. Before they'd gotten so much as a day to readjust to the schedule, Merridy announced that she would be giving them another practical exam that Friday.

"If we get the test out of the way immediately, it won't disrupt your other classes," she said sharply, speaking over the unhappy grumbling.

Tristan groaned. This was the last thing he wanted now, with so much on his mind already.

"Are you serious?" Damian said. "There's so much snow we can hardly get outside! We'll freeze to death."

Merridy rapped her desk and waited for the disgruntled chatter to subside. "Not if you pay close attention this week," she said. "By Friday, you should be more than adequately prepared for the weather."

Bending over, Merridy lifted something from her chair—it was a stack of new textbooks, each one older and heavier than the *Earth Science and Environmental Studies* volumes she'd handed out at the beginning of the year. The room was filled with renewed grumbling.

As she walked around the room handing out books, Merridy continued. "Due to your general lack of success with the test last semester, I've decided to shorten the required distance to three miles. Also—over the break, my fellow teachers and I realized that you have not been adequately exposed to magic, and have therefore learned very little about its practical use. As such, we have decided to restructure each of our courses to include the use of magic, which, I have been told, most of you have not yet attempted."

"Brilliant!" Rusty said under his breath.

Tristan nodded fervently.

Once Merridy had handed the last two books to Finley and Ryan, she returned to her desk. "We will spend the next three days learning magical survival techniques. And, since you all failed so miserably at reading maps," she said, lips twitching, "I will teach you to locate this school with a spell."

A few of the students laughed.

"Quiet." Merridy's smile vanished. "If you continue to interrupt my class, you will each get an hour."

They began at once with a spell called Intralocation, which Merridy claimed would render maps useless.

"Intra—within," she said briskly. "Intralocation is the process of finding places you have seen before and can visualize. Extralocation is its more complex counterpart, which allows you to locate places you've never seen. Open your textbooks to page thirty-eight, please, and read the theoretical description of the spell."

Eagerly Tristan pried open his new textbook, titled *Everyday Alchemy*, and read the passage.

"How old d'you think this thing is?" Rusty whispered. "Alchemy's from the middle ages, isn't it?"

"Maybe the author was trying to be clever," Leila whispered back. "Now shut up, I'm trying to read."

Tristan had to reread the passage several times before he thought he understood it. It sounded as though the spell involved holding up a marble and imagining where you wanted to go. That seemed easy enough.

"Any questions?" Merridy asked.

Hayley put her hand in the air. "I don't understand, Professor. What does the spell do?"

"It's quite simple," Merridy said. "Once your marble is enchanted, it will float in the direction you must go, remaining at a constant distance from your center of gravity. You merely follow it until the magic has run out, at which point you enchant a new marble. Any other questions?" She looked around. "Yes, Finley?"

Finley put his hand down and folded his arms on his desk. "I thought magic could only modify processes already existing in nature," he said. He sounded uncannily like Brikkens. "How is an instinctive knowledge of directions something that exists in nature?"

"Excellent point," Merridy said, looking impressed. "Magical theoreticians are still debating that question; only a small fraction of magic is understood at present.

However, the best explanation I can give is that the magic takes your own knowledge of two separate locations and links them together like magnets, using your understanding of a destination to draw you along the shortest line towards that point."

They spent the rest of the hour trying the spell. Merridy drew a circle on her chalkboard and said that the circle was their destination; if the Intralocation spell worked properly, the marbles would lead them directly to the chalkboard.

The desks were shoved to the side, and the classroom quickly became a confusion of movement. Tristan watched Amber for a moment; she managed the spell on her first try, of course. Her gold marble bobbed in front of her face while she drifted along behind it, until the marble struck the chalkboard and dissolved. When Merridy congratulated her, Amber returned to her seat and buried her face in her textbook, cheeks pink with embarrassment.

It was difficult to concentrate with so much going on around him. Rusty released marble after marble, hoping they would stay in the air, and cursed when they plummeted to the ground and dissolved. Leila kept flinching—after a moment Tristan realized that Zeke was pelting her with his marbles. Remembering the time when Zeke had blown up the wall, Tristan dragged her out of Zeke's range.

"You don't think anything bad will happen if the spell fails, do you?" Tristan asked.

Leila gestured to Rusty. "If he was going to set

something on fire, he'd have done so already." She grimaced as Rusty dropped his tenth marble. "Are you thinking of running away again?"

Tristan shook his head. "I—probably." Leila had guessed his thoughts. He didn't want to stay and deal with whatever the teachers would be doing; it would be so much easier to leave all of this behind.

Turning away from Leila, who frowned at him, Tristan closed his eyes. With the marble cupped in his hand, he tried to visualize the circle in the chalkboard. It took a long time before he could clear his mind, and longer still before the marble began to grow warm, but at last it was so hot he couldn't hold it.

Wincing, he dropped the marble and shook out his hand. Then he realized that the marble was still hanging in the air where he'd cupped it. When he took a tentative step forward, the marble floated with him, as though it was an extension of his body.

Five steps later, he reached the front of the classroom.

"Excellent work," Merridy said when Tristan's marble collided with the chalkboard. Then she looked at the rest of the students, who were growing rowdier by the minute. "I suppose the other teachers were right to worry," she said with a sigh.

Tristan glanced back at Leila, who was still frowning in his direction. "Don't try and talk me out of it. I have to try."

Leila nodded sadly.

By Friday, all of the students except Cailyn and Ryan Riggs had managed the Intralocation spell more or less accurately. When Rusty successfully enchanted his marble for the first time, causing it to hang in the air so close to his face that he went cross-eyed, he jumped up and down like a little kid. Even Leila was ecstatic when her spell worked.

"Wow," she said. "God, this is amazing! I can't believe...I mean, it's actually real! Wow."

Tristan laughed.

On Friday morning, the students brought their backpacks and supplies up to breakfast, where Merridy passed them each a large bag of marbles.

"You don't look so good," Leila said shrewdly. She was plainly hoping Tristan would give up his plan to run away.

Tristan groaned. "I'm just tired." He had lain awake last night, trying to imagine life without Leila and Rusty. "If I don't come back, tell the others that they can escape too, if they want."

Leila sighed. "I'll be praying you fail, of course."

At that moment, Merridy pushed back her chair and stood. "Everyone will be picked up at five o'clock this evening," she said, "though I would recommend hurrying—it should snow this afternoon."

Just as before, Quinsley packed the students into the helicopter and dropped them each off at separate locations.

"Be safe," Leila said, handing Tristan his backpack as he clambered out of the helicopter.

He smiled weakly.

As the helicopter took to the air, its propellers whirring so powerfully that the nearby trees bowed away from the wind, Tristan dug in his pocket for a marble. Standing knee-deep in a crisp snowdrift, he studied the marble. His feet were already turning to blocks of ice.

Then he closed his eyes and thought of home.

The spell was already becoming easy. Tristan could picture the house as though he'd been there yesterday— torn screen door sagging from its hinges, tiled floor tracked with mud and crumbled snow, fire flickering in the stone hearth...

No, that wasn't right. Tristan shook his head to clear it; the marble in his hand was already growing warm, but he'd done the spell wrong. His home didn't have a fireplace— the hearth he'd imagined was the one in the Subroom. Cursing softly, Tristan squeezed the marble in his fist and waited for it to cool before closing his eyes and trying the spell again.

This time he thought he'd done it right, so he released the marble and allowed it to hover in front of his face, the orb shifting slightly as he moved.

With a glance overhead at the snow-dusted pine boughs, he began trudging forward, snow crackling beneath his feet. Apart from the crunch of his footsteps, the woods were unerringly silent; Tristan began walking faster, allowing the downhill momentum to carry him forward. Still the marble kept pace with him, glinting dully in the sunlight.

The slope grew steeper, until Tristan was stumbling

forward, half-running. Several times he caught his toe on a branch or rock, invisible beneath the snow; unable to move his feet in time, he crashed forward, the powder cushioning his fall.

At last the ground flattened. Breathing hard, Tristan straightened and staggered through a gap between two sentinel trees. Then he realized he was back at the school.

"Damn!"

He dropped to his knees in the snow, hating the sight of the dark buildings.

Why hadn't the spell worked?

Tristan snatched the marble out of the air and slammed it to the ground, wondering if there was something wrong with him. How had he managed to forget his own home so quickly?

Merridy, alerted by his shout, appeared suddenly in the doorway to the greenhouse. "Tristan!" she said. "Well done, indeed." Though she looked slightly worried when she noticed his expression, she didn't comment. "You'll receive full marks, of course. If you would like, Professor Brikkens is waiting in the ballroom with hot chocolate."

Tristan nodded stiffly. "Thanks, Professor," he managed to say. Clenching his teeth, he got heavily to his feet and trudged over to the Lair's entrance.

Somehow Amber was already in the ballroom when Tristan came down the stairs. He didn't know how she'd gotten back so quickly. He joined her at one of the tables, scowling.

"You don't look happy," Amber commented, stirring

her hot chocolate with an air of distraction.

"Well, I'm not," Tristan grumbled. He poured himself a mug of hot chocolate and stared at its foamy surface, hardly seeing. The teachers were murderers. How could this be his home?

Amber took a brief sip from her mug and then set it aside, getting to her feet.

"Sorry," Tristan said, trying to lighten his expression. "Don't go—I'm mad at myself, not at you."

She turned to look at him, eyes wide. "You have a very interesting face," she said quietly.

Though Tristan could tell it wasn't an insult, he smoothed his hair self-consciously over his scars. "I'll look for you later, all right?" he said.

Amber nodded. "The woods are beautiful when it snows." At this strange remark, she turned and made her way towards the stairs, her steps so light she could have been floating.

If Quinsley and Alldusk hadn't been in the ballroom, Tristan would have abandoned his drink and stalked down to the Subroom; instead he finished the hot chocolate, gathering his wits.

Cailyn returned soon after Amber left, which surprised Tristan—she hadn't been able to use magic in class, so she must have found her way without the Intralocation spell. Cailyn was followed closely by Evvie and Eli, and each one joined Tristan at his table when they arrived.

Gulping down the last cold remnants of his drink, Tristan got to his feet and said he was going outside to wait for the others. Evvie, Cailyn, and Eli were silent; not for the first time, Tristan got the distinctive feeling that they didn't like him very much.

It was a relief to leave the Lair, though the air had already chilled considerably in the half hour that he'd been inside. Despite the gathering clouds, the mountains seemed to glow—their silver aura radiated off the peaks like a million fragments of light, stark against the softer aura of what Tristan thought was the forest itself.

Tristan drew his jacket closer around him and tucked his chin into the warm folds of the scarf Gracewright had given him, wishing Amber was there. The air seemed heavy with magic, permeating the trees and threading across the clearing, so strong that Tristan's muscles tingled with the sensation of power. It felt like a dream.

Zeke was the next to return. He headed straight into the Lair, not even noticing Tristan, who stood just beneath the trees. Leila bounded into the meadow soon afterwards, beaming when she saw Tristan. "You came back!" Slowing, she joined Tristan at the edge of the forest. "But what are you doing out here?"

Tristan felt like he'd been pulled from a trance. "Nothing," he said distractedly. "So you got the spell to work, then?"

Leila nodded happily. "It's amazing. Let's get inside— aren't you cold?"

"Wait," Tristan said. His spine was still prickling with magic; if he went inside now, he was afraid he might never be so keenly aware of the power again.

With a curious look at Tristan, Leila turned and followed his gaze to the mountain peaks, now shrouded in gray. Tristan's hands were stiff, so he rubbed them together to ease the biting chill. If only they could build a little fire in the clearing, he'd be able to sit out here for hours, just tracing the magic with his thoughts. It was like a sixth sense, an ethereal awareness.

When Leila touched his shoulder, Tristan shivered convulsively; he hadn't realized how cold his entire body had become. He flexed his stiff fingers, imagining the fire down in the Subroom.

With a sudden thrill of adrenaline, a burst of heat blossomed through his hands, as though he'd submerged them in hot water. Was he going crazy? No—the warmth held, thawing and loosening his fingers.

"What's wrong, Triss?" Leila demanded.

Tristan started and realized she'd been staring at him for the past minute. "Nothing's wrong," he said quickly. He reached for one of her chaffed white hands. "Do you feel that?"

"My god," she said, looking frightened. "Are you sick? You feel like…like *fire*." Giving Tristan a look that dared him to laugh, she reached for his other hand and brought his palms up to her cheeks.

Tristan swallowed. "I think I just did magic," he said warily. "And I don't even know how."

"Oh," Leila said, eyes widening. She released Tristan's hands. "Of course you did."

After a moment, the intense heat in Tristan's hands

began to fade. "But I didn't use a marble," he said. "I don't get it."

"Delair mentioned this," Leila said. "He said we can sometimes use power from our own bodies, right?"

Tristan nodded, and Leila turned to the Lair's entrance. This time he followed her without argument.

"Be careful, though," she said, stopping to kick snow off her boots. "I think it's dangerous to draw magic from yourself if you don't know how to control it."

She was right, though Tristan didn't want to admit it. As he drew the heavy wooden doors shut and followed Leila downstairs, he felt a sudden absence. The strands of free-flowing magic had been severed.

Chapter 17

The Ultimatum

On Monday, just as Merridy had warned, the teachers all began very suddenly to teach practical magic. Merridy, of course, had spent the past week on Intralocation, and the others followed her example.

Grindlethorn began his class by saying, "In order to stay on track this semester, you kids are going to have to work harder than ever. I would advise trying your best to avoid punishment." His beady eyes lit on Tristan. "Since the headmaster has asked that I teach healing spells in addition to what I planned, we will have to cover twice as much material."

When Grindlethorn began passing back a difficult quiz they'd taken the week before, Tristan was not alone in shifting his paper to hide a failing grade.

"Hey, Professor," Zeke said lazily. "Ever heard of something called extra credit?"

"That's enough, Elwood!" Grindlethorn rapped his

knuckles on his desk. "For those of you who did poorly on this quiz, review your notes and pay better attention in class next time. Your final exams this semester will determine how we organize your classes next year, so it is crucial that you perform well."

With a yawn, Zeke folded his quiz into a paper airplane. "Now I'm *really* scared."

Delair was actually in his classroom when the students filed in, which was surprising in itself; stranger still, he was in the process of stacking a pile of rocks on each desk.

"Ah, good to see you," he said, beaming at the students. His white moustache fluttered as he exhaled. "The headmaster wants me to cover practical magic, instead of just the theory of elementals. That means we're done with lectures!"

That hardly mattered, since Delair had almost never appeared for class last semester.

Delair explained that each of the rocks on their desks had a scrap of Delairium buried somewhere near the center, and their task was to extract the element in its entirety. He handed around a set of marbles with no further instructions; he seemed to enjoy watching the students struggle.

Even Tristan couldn't figure out how to go about separating the Delairium from the plain granite. When the period ended, Delair told them to look through their textbooks for the appropriate spell. "Bring back your pile of rocks tomorrow—those of you who haven't managed to separate the Delairium from the granite will have to write an essay on the matter."

Tristan groaned. Dumping the pile of rocks into his book bag, he followed the others up to lunch.

Alldusk began his class two hours later with the same announcement about practical magic, though he said, "I'm afraid we don't have enough time to concentrate much on spells. Our most important job is collecting the orbs; now that your other classes are using them as well, we need to work faster than ever." He sighed and glanced at the door. "However, I can still teach you how to start fires with magic. That should satisfy Professor Drakewell."

Although the lesson itself was interesting enough, Tristan was dismayed when Alldusk followed the other teachers' example and assigned more homework than ever.

That night, instead of sitting around and talking, the students in the Subroom settled unhappily into chairs around the room and began struggling through their homework. Even Trey, who was usually ahead on work, stayed up past midnight along with everyone else. First Tristan wrote the introductory paragraph for Grindlethorn's essay on treating hypothermia and frostbite; afterwards he began diagramming the structure of orchids for Gracewright.

The room was silent aside from the rustle of papers and the busy scratching of pens, an odd contrast to the rowdy bustle of the holidays. Occasionally someone would ask a question to the room at large, and Tristan flinched when a branch in the fire crackled loudly.

"How far are you?" Rusty asked Tristan, frowning,

when Evvie finally announced that she was too tired to do any more work.

"I'm nearly done with Grindlethorn's essay," Tristan said, rubbing his eyes and yawning. Thinking about hypothermia and frostbite had reminded him of the first time he'd tried to run away, which did nothing to improve his concentration.

Rusty groaned. "I haven't even started that; I've been trying to write that essay for Merridy." He tossed his papers to the table with a sigh.

"And don't forget the chart of magical theories for Brikkens," Leila said wearily.

Annoyed, Tristan shuffled his papers into something of a pile. He couldn't think straight.

"What're you doing about those rocks?" Rusty asked. Reaching for his book bag, he dumped six lumpy stones onto his knees. "D'you reckon Delair will care if we just smash them?"

Leila snorted. "Probably."

"I guess I'll do this tomorrow night," Tristan said, looking doubtfully at his pile of unfinished homework.

A book slammed behind Tristan, and he jumped. It was Evvie. She got to her feet and folded her arms across her chest, glowering at Tristan.

"When are we going to start doing something about the teachers?" she asked pointedly.

Tristan rolled his eyes. "Do I really have to do everything around here?" Still, he stood and called for attention.

"Sorry, guys," he said. "I know we have lots to worry about already, but we should start stealing marbles tomorrow. Otherwise Evvie might mutiny."

Evvie looked furious.

The next day, after a furtive discussion over breakfast, Tristan and his friends began stealing marbles and magical ingredients whenever they could, slipping them unobtrusively into pockets or bags.

Zeke's gang caught on quickly, and by that afternoon, Zeke and Damian were doing their part to further the resistance. During botany, Damian backed into a clay flowerpot in the greenhouse and knocked it to the floor. The flowerpot shattered, spewing dirt and tattered leaves across the floor; Gracewright gave him a half hour of punishment and spent the rest of the period yelling at him.

Damian fixed Tristan with a murderous look, as though he blamed Tristan for Gracewright's reaction.

During chemistry, Tristan distinctly saw Zeke pocketing handfuls of marbles, grinning as his jean pockets grew lumpier by the minute. Zeke probably didn't care about the teachers—he was likely just seeing how much havoc he could get away with.

Tristan and the others from the Subroom were less conspicuous about what they stole; it was only when they returned to their bedroom and deposited what they'd collected that Tristan realized how much they had amassed.

"This is great," Tristan said as he added his three marbles to a vase. "We'll need a new bowl or something by the end of the week."

Crossing to his side, Leila upended her book back onto the floor. A pile of metallic objects clattered onto the stone—after a moment Tristan realized that they were knives.

"Damn," Rusty said, impressed. "Where'd these come from, huh?" He selected a knife from the pile and absently tapped the flat edge on his palm.

"Lots of places," Leila said. "I'm trying not to get caught, unlike *Zeke*." She made a face. "Speaking of which, the teachers are going to notice if we keep taking this much stuff every day. We should regulate it—how about we can only take one marble a day, and only if no one could possibly notice its absence."

Tristan nodded and drew a blue-handled switchblade from the pile of knives. Flipping the blade closed with his thumb, he pocketed it.

By the end of the first week, the tall vase was overflowing with marbles. Before long, two more vases and a salad bowl joined their collection.

February began with another snowstorm and a steep drop in temperature; unable to hold classes in her drafty buildings upstairs, Gracewright carried down an armful of fresh cuttings and borrowed Brikkens' classroom for several days. Each subsequent morning, Brikkens spent the class period grumbling about the dirt and leaves that Gracewright had left on his enormous round table.

Their innocuous marble-hoarding had continued for a

month now, and it was during one of these indoor botany classes that the first student was caught.

"Christiansen," Gracewright barked. "Hayley Christian-sen!"

Hayley jumped so badly that her trowel went flying.

"What are you doing with those marbles?"

Hayley drew her hand out of her pocket and revealed two gold marbles. "Sorry, Professor," she said, wide-eyed. "I wasn't paying attention." Even Tristan was almost convinced of her innocence.

"Very well," Gracewright said. "But be careful when handling marbles in the future. I want no accidents."

Hayley bobbed her head dutifully.

Tristan thought Hayley had gotten away easily, but that evening she was distraught. Ignoring Cailyn and Trey, she marched around the Subroom with a broom, attacking invisible dust bunnies and muttering to herself.

Watching Hayley from his usual armchair, Tristan felt horribly guilty. He had been the one who ordered everyone to steal; it would be his fault if anything awful happened to his friends.

That night, Tristan couldn't sleep. He kept sinking into half-dreams, his mind pacing the Subroom like Hayley. Again and again he started awake and told himself that he was being stupid. Finally he gave up on sleep and clutched his blankets to his chest, listening to the seconds tick by as he waited for morning.

After he'd lain awake for hours, Tristan saw a flicker of movement across the room—someone was getting up from bed, their small frame silhouetted in the firelight. When the figure straightened, he realized it was Evvie. As Tristan watched, head barely lifted from his pillow, Evvie slipped on her unlaced shoes and tiptoed to the doorway. Why on earth was she sneaking out in the middle of the night? Maybe she had just gone to the bathroom.

Tristan curled his legs to his chest, watching the clock. Five minutes passed…fifteen minutes…surely Evvie hadn't simply been in the restroom this whole time, unless she was trying to drown herself in the shower…thirty minutes…

He nearly dozed off again, the flames blurring in his hazy vision. At last he heard the shuffling of careful footsteps as Evvie reappeared through the Prasidimum barrier. Tristan dropped his head quickly onto his pillow and pretended he was asleep. He heard a soft creaking of springs as Evvie lowered herself onto her mattress. What on earth had she been doing?

In the morning Tristan felt as though he hadn't slept at all. Leila practically had to drag him out of bed for breakfast.

"Did something happen last night?" Tristan asked groggily, fumbling with his shoelaces.

Leila frowned. "What do you mean? We were all up late working on homework; is that what you're talking about?"

"No, I mean about Evvie—she was gone…" Tristan yawned hugely.

"You're still half-asleep," Leila said, laughing. "Come on—we won't have time to eat if you don't hurry up."

As they stumbled up through the dark tunnels, Tristan explained what he'd meant about the previous night.

When they reached the main hallway, Leila said, "Are you sure you weren't dreaming?" She watched Tristan carefully.

He rubbed his eyes. "If I was, it was a pretty convincing dream. She was gone nearly an hour, and I was awake the whole time."

Nodding, Leila grabbed Tristan's elbow and began running along the hallway. "I want to see if something's up."

"Hey, slow down!" Tristan protested.

Up in the ballroom, everything was as usual. Tristan didn't know what he'd been expecting; Evvie just looked as tired and sullen as the others.

"What's up with you guys?" Rusty asked. He was determinedly spreading marmalade on a toasted bagel.

Tristan took a long draught of his coffee. "Nothing."

Before he'd finished eating, there was a commotion at the door, and Delair came skidding into the ballroom. He was wheezing and clutching at his stomach, sweat glistening on his bald pate.

"My tunnel!" he cried, staring wildly around the room. "Where's Drakewell? My tunnel—the mine—it's been destroyed!" He staggered to a halt at the edge of the dining platform, face crimson.

"The headmaster doesn't eat here," Grindlethorn said coldly. "Which you would know if you bothered to join us more often."

Bobbing his head at Grindlethorn, Delair scurried out of the ballroom.

"I knew it!" Tristan said. He realized too late that he'd nearly shouted.

Everyone turned to stare at him.

Gracewright got to her feet. "Did you just say you knew there'd been an attack?" she asked, alarmed. She was clearly still upset about the destruction of her greenhouse all those months ago. "Fairholm," she said sharply, "were you involved in this?"

"No, I didn't do it," Tristan said quickly. "I promise, I had no idea about anything, I didn't—"

"Indeed," Gracewright said. She excused herself and hurried from the ballroom. Tristan had a bad feeling that she'd gone to fetch Drakewell.

Leila nudged him and whispered, "Are you saying Evvie—"

Tristan slapped her in the shoulder harder than he'd intended. "Shut up!" He was furious with himself—the last thing Drakewell needed was another reason to suspect him of something.

Leila said nothing, though she rubbed her shoulder and glared at him.

Was it possible that Evvie had been the vandal all along?

With a frown, Rusty put his elbows up on the table and studied Tristan. "Okay, so what's this all about?" His bagel lay abandoned on his plate. "How come you knew about the attack?"

Tristan tightened his grip around his mug, cursing himself. At last he whispered, "I saw something last night. Ev—uh—someone left the room for a really long time, and I didn't know why."

Rusty's eyes widened. "You mean it's someone in the Subroom who's been wrecking this place?"

It was Leila's turn to punch Rusty in the arm. "Hush!"

"I don't know," Tristan said. "But don't go blabbing about it, okay? I'm in enough trouble al—"

The doors to the ballroom crashed open, and Tristan flinched. Drakewell was standing in the doorway.

As Drakewell's sunken eyes found Tristan, he sneered. "Fairholm," he barked. "To my office." He looked triumphant, which scared Tristan more than if he'd simply been angry.

With a pleading look at Leila, Tristan got to his feet.

"Just tell him what you saw," Leila whispered. "He might believe you."

Stomach churning, Tristan followed Drakewell out of the ballroom. The hallway seemed much darker and quieter than usual.

Tristan hadn't been inside Drakewell's office before. There was a plain wooden desk in the center, and bookshelves lining the walls, but aside from those the room was empty.

"Sit," Drakewell said coldly, settling into a high-backed chair behind the desk. With a nervous glance towards the door, Tristan took a seat opposite the headmaster.

"This is the third time you've been implicated in a

serious crime against this school," Drakewell said, still leering at Tristan. "One such event could be labeled a coincidence, but three?" He tugged at the hourglass around his neck, showing his teeth. "Any final requests before I lock you away in the tunnels?"

"No, Professor, please," Tristan said breathlessly, his chest tight. "I didn't do anything to the greenhouse or Alldusk's room or the mine, I promise. I'm just unlucky, I swear I wasn't doing anything wrong, I—"

"Enough," Drakewell said sharply. "Gather your belongings."

"No!" Tristan cried. "I didn't know there'd been an attack yesterday, I had no idea!"

Drakewell clenched his fist around the hourglass. "That's interesting," he said icily. "Professor Gracewright informs me that you said 'I knew it' when the announcement was made. Clearly you *did* have prior information about the attack."

Tristan shook his head wildly. "No, I didn't, I swear. I was afraid something had happened, but I didn't know what." He grasped the arms of his chair to steady himself. "If I'd wrecked the mine, I wouldn't have said anything, would I?" he said desperately.

Drakewell's hideous smile slid away. "Explain," he said, turning over the hourglass in his bony fingers.

For a moment Tristan was paralyzed, watching the viscous black liquid ooze through the neck of the hourglass.

"I heard something last night," he said carefully. "There were strange noises, like something was moving around. If there's something in this school that's been attacking rooms, that's probably what I heard. So it made sense that the—the *thing*—had gone and wrecked Delair's tunnel." He shoved his hands into his pockets, hoping Drakewell would believe the lie.

"A convincing story," Drakewell said coldly. "Fairholm, I'm going to make a deal with you. What it is that you desire most?"

"I want my brother back," Tristan said without thinking. When he realized what he'd said, his face grew hot.

Drakewell shook his head, nostrils flaring in anger. "I cannot raise the dead, idiot boy," he said. "However, you may prove too useful to be disposed of. This is your deal— if you can catch the vandal before the end of the semester, and prove his guilt, I will forgive you." His eyes narrowed. "Fail to do so, and Amber Ashton will be punished in your stead."

"What?" Tristan nearly shouted. "Professor, no, don't do anything to Amber, I…"

Drakewell was horrible, twisted, manipulative—if it had just been himself in danger, Tristan would've protected Evvie and lied for her, but now? Drakewell was forcing him to choose between Evvie and Amber.

"Don't do this, Professor, please, I can't—"

"Enough. Get out of my office."

Tristan fled. He was breathing hard when he joined Leila and Rusty in Brikkens' class.

"Are you cleared?" Leila asked, hardly bothering to

keep her voice down.

Tristan dropped his books and slumped into his chair. "What do you think?" He put his head down on his arms. How could Drakewell be so cruel? *Evvie or Amber?*

Leila poked him irritably. "You told him about Evvie, though, right?" she whispered. "He should be interrogating her, not you."

Head still pillowed on his arms, Tristan shook his head. An odd sound filled his ears, like the twittering of a sparrow.

Rusty paused the busy scratching of his pen and elbowed Tristan from the other side. "Wait, are you saying Drakewell thinks you're the vandal?"

"You really just figured that out?" Leila said.

"But Tristan didn't even go anywhere near that tunnel, right?"

Tristan lifted his head. "It's a reasonable guess, though," he said miserably. "I did burn that damn entrance, didn't I?" *Evvie or Amber?*

Brikkens cleared his throat pointedly and rapped his pudgy fist on the table. Tristan and Leila turned, realizing that he'd paused his lecture to glare at them.

"Sorry," Tristan muttered. He wished he could make himself disappear.

None of the teachers mentioned the attack after that day, and Drakewell alone seemed to hold Tristan accountable. Maybe, just maybe, the other teachers would speak for him…

Regardless, Drakewell's ultimatum continued to weigh

on Tristan. What if Evvie's disappearance that night had been mere coincidence; what if she hadn't done anything wrong? And what if she had?

Evvie or Amber?

Chapter 18

Valentine's Day

On the second Thursday of the month, Brikkens clambered to his feet at breakfast and announced that they would be celebrating Valentine's Day with a feast on Saturday.

Quinsley, who had been hovering near the kitchen door, stepped forward. "When Darla and Brinley were still in public school, their teachers had a tradition of delivering Valentine's notes throughout the day. If any of you kids would like to send valentines to one another, I'll be making cookies tonight."

"Ooh," Hayley said. She turned and looked around the room, as though hoping to find a good-looking boy she hadn't yet discovered. "Will there be roses too?"

Quinsley laughed. "Abilene?" he said, glancing at Gracewright.

"Yes, you can have roses," Gracewright said happily.

"So," Quinsley said, "if you'd like to send a valentine tomorrow, stop by the kitchen and tell me sometime this afternoon."

Tristan made a detour to the kitchen just before lunch.

"Hello, Tristan," Quinsley said when Tristan pushed open the door. "Nice seeing you here—I'm suddenly the most popular teacher in the school!"

Tristan laughed.

Quinsley wiped his hands on his apron. "Okay, so who do you want to send valentines to?" He flipped open a notebook and uncapped the pen. "I'm molding chocolate hearts now, if you want to add those as well."

"Do one for Amber and one for Evvie," Tristan said. Drakewell's ultimatum was still tormenting him. His very existence put both girls in danger; this was the least he could do to make up for it.

"Right-o," Quinsley said.

"And I guess one for Leila and Rusty as well. Give Rusty an extra chocolate and leave out the rose."

Quinsley chuckled and added a note to his list. "Have a good lunch, then."

"Thanks," Tristan said.

Evvie or Amber?

Enthusiastic as always, Brikkens had decorated his lemon tree with pink and red streamers. "Miss Christiansen gave me a brilliant idea at breakfast yesterday," Brikkens said, handing around a pile of marbles. "I've borrowed a whole bucket of flower seeds, and today you kids will try your hand at growing them!"

"Haven't we seen enough of plants in botany?" Damian grumbled. "We'll probably be doing the same thing in Gracewright's class."

Pretending that he hadn't heard Damian, Brikkens reached down and produced a teetering stack of clay flowerpots and two enormous blue buckets. "Take a pot, a handful of dirt, and a few seeds each," he said.

By the time the flowerpots and seeds made it around to Tristan, Amber's flowerpot was already bristling with green shoots. As he watched, the first of the stalks swelled into a delicate bud, which shivered and then flared open in a brilliant pinwheel of yellow.

"Oh, marvelous," Brikkens said, clapping his chubby hands like an excitable child. "The ballroom is going to look splendid this weekend!"

With a thumb, Tristan patted down a small hole in the dirt and poured in his seeds.

Rusty, meanwhile, was rummaging in his bag, one hand clenched by his side.

"Rusty!" Leila hissed, leaning over Tristan. "Don't steal the seeds, you idiot. What are we supposed to use them for?"

Flinching guiltily, Rusty returned the seeds to his flowerpot and tossed his book bag to the floor. "I was just trying to help," he muttered.

"Yeah, well, try harder next time," Leila said, rolling her eyes.

At the end of the class period, Quinsley stopped by to deliver the first set of valentines. As he finished handing around flowers and sweets, he lowered his voice and said, "My list of jobs gets longer by the day." He winked at Leila.

By this point most of the flowerpots boasted at least a few blooms, and Brikkens happily doled out extra credit based on how many flowers each of them had managed to grow.

Quinsley continued to deliver valentines through the rest of the day—Tristan received a cookie from Rusty and a bag of creamy chocolates that was probably from Leila. When Evvie and Amber opened his valentines, he wished he could tell them how awful he felt.

The next morning, when Tristan stumbled up to breakfast, he stopped in the ballroom doorway, startled. The floors were a riot of color—in addition to the fifteen flowerpots the students had planted in Brikkens' class, someone had brought in a set of planters that were crowded with tulips of every color, so many that the marble floor was carpeted with brilliant petals.

"Happy Valentine's Day!" Brikkens called.

Tristan shook his head and followed Leila to their usual table. He was already growing tired of the hearts and the pink everywhere.

"Just wait until the feast this afternoon," Leila said wryly. "I was helping Gerry with dessert last night—I don't think I've ever seen so much pink in my life." She looked as exasperated as Tristan felt.

After breakfast, Rusty suggested that they go sledding, and Zeke's gang decided to join them. Rusty had never been sledding before, and he was acting more childlike than usual in his excitement. Tristan didn't feel like spending hours out in the cold, not with so much he was already worried about, but Leila and Rusty persuaded him to join them.

"Gerry found a couple of real sleds," Leila said. "I have no idea what the teachers were doing with sleds, but apparently they were stashed in that old room with all the other junk."

"They used to be kids too," Rusty said. "Hey, Tristan, we're gonna sled down that big hill to the lake. The one we hiked up, remember? It'll be great!"

Tristan shrugged and pulled on his jacket. "I guess it'll be more fun than homework." And maybe it would keep him from dwelling on Drakewell's ultimatum. He grabbed his gloves before hurrying back up to the ballroom with the others.

The air outside was clear and icy; Tristan's eyes watered in the sharp breeze as he trudged along through the snow. This was the first time he had returned to the edge of the hill they'd climbed at the start of the year, and he was surprised at how small and distant the lake appeared from up here.

Leila grabbed the first sled. Waving to the others, she took a running start and went flying down the hill, yelling happily. Then Zeke yanked the second sled from Rusty's grasp and jumped onto it, shooting off before Tristan could even think to stop him.

"Uh-oh." Tristan took a half-step forward. Zeke meant trouble.

At the foot of the hill, Zeke tumbled out of his sled to stop. Then, abandoning the sled, he bounded forward and tackled Leila.

"Hey!" Tristan yelled.

They were too far away to hear Tristan's shout of warning. Cursing, he started running down the hill, skidding and tripping as his feet tore a path through the powdery snow. "Get off Leila, you bastard!"

Leila was shouting and flailing her fists at Zeke; after a moment they both crashed to the ground, struggling furiously.

With a groan and a crack that was loud even from a distance, the ice beneath them gave way. Water splashed up as the ice splintered, and they both sank into the dark lake, yelling hoarsely. They were near the shore, though, so they hit the lake bottom before they'd sunk past their shoulders.

As Tristan reached the foot of the hill, Zeke stumbled to his feet and extended a hand to Leila. His clothes were dripping, and his entire body shook.

Leila got to her feet without Zeke's help. Then she shoved him in the chest so hard that he fell back into the lake. White-faced and trembling, she edged towards the shore. "I'm going to murder you, Zeke, I swear," she spat, clutching her arms to her chest.

Tristan yanked off his jacket. "Here," he said, pulling it over Leila's shoulders. "Let's get you back to the Lair; can you make it up the hill?" He rubbed her shoulders to warm her, frightened by how purple her lips were becoming.

"I have to make it back, don't I?" Leila snapped. She pulled away from Tristan's hands and stomped towards the hill, chin tucked into the neck of Tristan's coat.

Behind them, Zeke stalked to the bank and shook out his hair. "I'll get the sleds," he said shortly, speaking to no one in particular.

"See you later," Tristan told Rusty once he and Leila reached the top of the hill. "I'll be waiting inside."

"Are you okay, Leila?" Rusty's eyes were wide.

Leila was now shuddering uncontrollably; she appeared beyond speech. Shaking her head, she staggered forward through the snow, Zeke trailing close behind.

Once Tristan saw Leila safely to the showers, he returned to the Subroom to start on his homework. Alone in the room, Tristan couldn't force himself to concentrate. For a while he paced from end to end, watching the fire cast leering shadows across the walls. He began thinking yet again of Drakewell's ruthless deal, counting the months until the semester ended. It was nowhere near enough time to learn the secrets of this school. And a hundred years wouldn't be enough for him to decide which of his friends to send to their doom.

Evvie or Amber?

Aiming a kick at the frayed rug, Tristan resumed his pacing.

As he made another circuit of the Subroom, Tristan spotted Evvie's backpack and clothes stacked neatly beside her mattress. He crossed towards the bed and crouched beside her open pack; maybe her belongings would give him a clue. He hadn't forgotten the diversion he'd created all those months ago, nor the reason that Evvie had begged for his help—she had been helping some strange person hide in the tunnels. Could that person be dangerous?

Maybe he had long since fled. Or maybe he was involved in the secret of the school.

Keeping one eye on the door, Tristan began removing books from Evvie's backpack, handling everything with extreme care. There were schoolbooks and notebooks, pencils and loose papers. He even found a plain sketchbook at one point. That must have been the one item from home she'd chosen to keep.

Tristan thought back to the beginning of the year, to the plane ride when he'd first met Evvie. She had looked so sad and vulnerable when she'd first stepped onto the plane. Of course, that had also been the day Evvie decided she hated him. Tristan didn't blame her—he was ugly and scarred and mean, and she was a pretty little orphan who had no business spending her time with criminals.

Tristan clawed his hair over his scars. "Damn you," he muttered, hurling the sketchbook across the room.

The rest of Evvie's belongings were no more promising than her schoolbooks. Tristan didn't really want to go through her clothes, but he shook out a sweater and rummaged through the empty pockets of her black uniform jacket.

"Did you drop this?" a soft voice called from the doorway.

Tristan jumped to his feet. "Who's—"

He relaxed as he recognized Amber, her cheeks red from the cold and her pale hair windswept. She was holding Evvie's sketchpad.

"Thanks," he said, crossing the room and taking the sketchbook from her. "Are the others coming back now?"

"Oh, I wouldn't know," Amber said. "I was alone in the woods, tracing a lost bird. Eagles have incredibly powerful auras, you know, so strong they can be *sensed* rather than seen."

Tristan felt a bit dazed. "And... er... why do eagles have such strong auras?"

Blinking, Amber lowered her eyes, suddenly shy again. "It's because of the way they fly," she whispered. "They feed on magic as they soar, on the pure elemental air." With great concentration, she unwound her scarf and folded it over her arm.

Shaking his head, Tristan made his way towards the fire, where he settled into his favorite armchair. He should be putting Evvie's schoolbooks back in order, but he was more interested in looking at her art. Running one finger along the top spiral of her sketchpad, he flipped open the cover.

At first Tristan was disappointed—the first page was blank aside from a very simplistic sketch of a leaf. He had expected something more exciting from someone who had chosen a sketchpad as her sole possession. Tristan turned the page.

Most of the sketches were of leaves or trees or small insects, though in the later pages Tristan found crude drawings of everyone in the Subroom except Amber. Tristan recognized himself immediately as the sketch with a grotesquely gutted face. Evvie's representation of Rusty was more accurate than the others, and she had added a small heart beside his cheek—gritting his teeth, Tristan tightened his grip on the sketchpad until the pages crumpled slightly.

She's stupid, Tristan thought savagely. *Rusty's an overenthusiastic fool.*

No, that's rubbish, he told himself angrily. Rusty was a much better person than Tristan.

Clenching the arm of his chair, Tristan started flipping pages again, faster than before. There was Drakewell, and Alldusk in his tailcoat with long vampire fangs added, and Merridy, and...

Tristan stopped. Here was a drawing of two children, a boy and girl he'd never seen before. Though he couldn't tell from the sketch, they looked younger than five. Were they Evvie's siblings?

Marcus.

Tristan's hands went stiff and the sketchbook slid to the floor. In that unguarded moment, he was hit again with the memory, so vivid that he could feel the hot blood trickling down his face, and he doubled over from the shattering impact.... *I trust you...*

"What's wrong? Tristan?"

Something touched his shoulder, and he jerked away. A cool hand smoothed back his hair—Amber was there, kneeling before him, and the sketchpad was once again resting on his knees.

"I'm all right," Tristan said shakily. Taking a deep breath, he spread his fingers and then curled them into fists.

"What happened?" Amber asked. Combing her pale fingers through Tristan's hair, she rose and perched on the arm of his chair.

If anyone else had asked, Tristan would have brushed aside the question. "It's the memories," he said, pressing his forehead into his hands. "I can't tell where they end and the magic begins."

"I know," Amber whispered.

It was a long time before Leila returned from her shower, and longer still before the others came trudging in from outside, their boots and gloves caked with snow.

"I'm starving," Rusty said, shaking ice from his scarf as he crossed to the fire. "Is the feast gonna start soon?"

Leila didn't bother to answer him; she was still sulking. "I don't think I'll ever be warm again," she grumbled. Though she was wearing two sweaters and a scarf, her lips were faintly blue.

"Cheer up," Rusty said. "You've still got all your fingers, haven't you? We'll get you some hot tea and hot soup for lunch."

"And some goddamned hot-pink cookies," Tristan said, grinning ruefully.

Leila snorted.

Watching Evvie that evening, Tristan was irrationally jealous. The fact that she liked Rusty didn't make his choice any easier, but Rusty ought to know the truth. If Evvie really was the vandal, she had been deceiving them all.

After the Valentine's feast, no one was in the mood for

homework. Hayley started folding origami hearts from her notebook paper, her eyes on Eli and Trey, who were playing a furious game of cards that involved a great deal of slapping and cursing.

Tristan just sat and stared at the fire, his stomach aching from too many pink cookies. By midnight, he had resolved to learn the truth about Evvie's secret. If she went wandering in the tunnels again, he would follow her.

Evvie or Amber? He wished this holiday didn't exist.

Chapter 19

The Secret of the Tunnels

Though Drakewell still gave Tristan dirty looks whenever they saw each other, the headmaster made no further mention of his ultimatum. Weeks passed with no attacks, until Tristan dared to hope the trespasser had decided to leave. Maybe it wasn't Evvie, after all, and Tristan wouldn't have to choose one of his friends to destroy.

What with magical tasks for homework on top of the written workload, the students had no free time to speak of. Tristan grew accustomed to seeing his friends sitting in silent, strained concentration, clearly trying to work a tricky piece of magic. Despite being overwhelmed with homework, the students in the Subroom continued to steal marbles; their pile in the corner was quickly becoming a formidable hoard.

Unfortunately, they still had no idea what the teachers were doing, or, indeed, what they could do with their own growing stack of marbles. As far as anyone knew, the marbles could only be used one at a time, and a single marble didn't contain enough magic to be particularly powerful or threatening.

The beginning of April passed, and then Easter, and suddenly the end of the year was looming.

"Are you going to tell Drakewell about Evvie?" Leila whispered. Merridy had spent the past half hour lecturing them about the importance of their upcoming finals.

"I'm not saying anything until I'm positive," Tristan replied, keeping his eyes fixed on Merridy. "Imagine what Drakewell would do to Evvie if she really was the vandal." He didn't want Leila to realize how sick he felt just thinking about the end of the year.

The truth was that he'd been watching Evvie carefully for the past several weeks; twice he'd attempted to follow her into the tunnels, though both times he had quickly lost her.

Class was over, so Tristan and Leila got to their feet and made their way towards the door. "I wish you would make more of an effort," Leila said, frowning at Tristan. "Do you *want* to be locked at the end of the year?"

Tristan sighed. "That's not the problem." *Evvie or Amber?* He knew who Leila would choose, and it didn't help. "Besides, it's hard figuring stuff out about Evvie. If you come up with a way to stalk someone in the dark, let me know." Annoyed, he readjusted his book bag and started walking faster.

"Hey, what're you guys talking about?" Rusty asked happily, squeezing past Finley and Ryan to join Tristan.

"Stalking people," Leila said at once.

They had to pause in their conversation then, since Evvie was walking directly behind them; once they reached the empty Subroom they resumed speaking in whispers.

"Okay, you've gotta tell me what's going on now," Rusty said.

Leila settled onto the sofa and began digging through her bag. "We've talked about this before," she said shortly. "Tristan has to find the vandal, remember?"

"Oh, yeah," Rusty said, "or else bad stuff will happen, right?"

Slouching back in his chair, Tristan smoothed his hair over his face. "It's hopeless. I wish I could just give up."

"Brilliant plan," Leila said sarcastically. "Come on, Triss, you have to let us help you."

"I'd love it if you could help me," Tristan said, exasperated. "But unless you know how to find something that can't be f—"

He sat up suddenly. "That's it!" Why hadn't he thought of it before? "I can use Intralocation—or Extralocation, or whatever the hell you'd call the spell—to track Evvie!"

Leila nodded slowly. "That could work. You'd have to be careful not to run into any teachers, though, because it would look awfully suspicious if they caught you roaming the tunnels in the dark."

Rusty was bouncing up and down in his chair; Tristan was tempted to smack him with his textbook. "This is so exciting! Besides, why would the teachers be in the tunnels? Let us come explore with you!"

"I'll be following Evvie, not exploring," Tristan said impatiently. "And I don't even know if the spell will work."

At Leila's urging, Tristan began attempting the spell that night. When Eli and Trey returned to the Subroom and began working on homework, Tristan, Leila, and Rusty gathered handfuls of marbles and went in search of somewhere to practice.

"I just need to hide in a place you wouldn't think of looking," Leila said. "Too bad it's dark outside."

Tristan laughed. "You want me to follow a ridiculous marble all around the Lair? That'll look even more suspicious than wandering in the tunnels. Besides, what if we run into Drakewell?"

"Just say you're playing hide-and-seek," Leila said, giggling.

Rusty decided to follow Tristan while Leila went off to hide, and they spent the next several hours working on the spell. It took more concentration than regular Intralocation, especially once Leila started moving around just to complicate things. Tristan kept dropping marbles and losing his grip on the spell halfway to wherever Leila was waiting, though he was much better than Rusty, who was too distracted to even get a marble to hang in the air.

As Tristan and Rusty sneaked past Drakewell's office at one point, Tristan heard Drakewell muttering in a low monotone; he shivered, wondering if Drakewell was working some awful spell. When Rusty acted as though he wanted to stop and listen to Drakewell, Tristan grabbed him by the sleeve and hurried him away.

Once Tristan was able to find Leila consistently, she chose more and more difficult hiding places, squeezing herself into supply cabinets or lurking in the tunnels just beyond the reach of the hallway lights. She even hid in the girls' bathroom one time; unwilling to follow her in there, Tristan snatched his marble from the air and called to her from the hall.

"That's not fair," Tristan said, punching Leila gently in the shoulder when she emerged.

Leila grinned. "Scaredy-cat! No one else was even in there." She smoothed down her rumpled hair, which had grown nearly long enough to pull into a ponytail.

By midnight, the three of them were giddy from exhaustion, and Tristan had mastered the spell.

"Do you realize we still have two papers to write for tomorrow?" Leila said, giggling.

Tristan cursed good-naturedly.

"They're not due until after lunch," Rusty said. "We've got plenty of time."

Trey and Hayley were still awake in the Subroom, hunched over their papers and scribbling furiously, and they gave Tristan, Leila, and Rusty odd looks when the three of them filed in, though thankfully neither asked questions.

"'Night," Tristan said, yawning. He collapsed into his bed with most of his clothes still on, and was asleep long before Leila returned from her shower.

After that night Tristan began stuffing his pockets with

marbles before he left the Subroom each morning, so he was ready just in case Evvie disappeared into the tunnels again. He got his first chance to follow her just a week later.

The students were heading downstairs after class, Tristan, Leila, and Rusty at the rear of the group, when Tristan saw Evvie slip away and take the stairs down to Delair's hallway.

"Did you see that?" Leila whispered.

Tristan nodded. "See you guys later." He reached in his pocket for a marble. Leila took his book bag from him and slung it over her shoulder.

"Good luck!" Rusty said.

Tristan sprinted down the stairs, pausing at the bottom to look for Evvie; she was hurrying down the corridor ahead of him. Glancing back, she turned left and disappeared into Delair's mine shaft.

He started running again, this time careful to tread quietly. The rubble in Delair's once-destroyed mine shaft had been swept away, and the tunnel looked as empty and dark as ever. At the entrance to the tunnel, Tristan stopped and set the marble to hover at arm's length from his face. He could already smell the dank, musty air from the mine, though Evvie's footsteps had faded in the distance.

One eye on the marble's faint golden glow, Tristan started forward into the darkness. He put a hand on the wall, trailing his fingers over the rock to be sure he was going in a straight line. For a short distance the glow from the hall outlined the jagged walls and uneven floor, and before the light had faded entirely, the marble turned sharply right, hovering at the entrance of an unfamiliar short-ceilinged passage.

Tristan hesitated. What if he got lost down here? Or what if the ceiling caved in?

It's just a new tunnel, he told himself sternly. Besides, if he got lost, the teachers would probably come after him within hours.

Taking a deep breath, Tristan started forward again. Now he could see nothing but the golden shimmer just ahead; he was afraid to blink, though his eyes began to ache from staring too intensely at the single point of light. He quickened his pace.

The marble led Tristan deeper and deeper into the earth, turning and winding through side corridors and rooms with rotting wood doors. He hadn't seen or heard Evvie for ages; his heart pounded faster as he wondered if he had messed up the spell. His heels began to ache and his eyes stung from trying to see things that weren't there.

Shivering, Tristan folded his arms to conserve the last of his warmth. It was just the nature of darkness to stretch and warp time until nothing existed beyond that single dizzying point of light.

At long last, the gold marble stopped moving. When Tristan took another step forward, the glowing orb remained motionless; he went cross-eyed trying to watch it. He trailed his fingers along the wall until he felt the wood surface of a door, smooth and sturdy like the one leading to the Subroom. He found the cold metal handle and pulled open the door, holding his breath as it creaked softly back.

As soon as the door was open, Tristan's marble bobbed forward once again. Then it vanished, its light extinguished.

"Damn," Tristan muttered. Reaching into his pocket, he pulled out a second marble and concentrated on Evvie until it hung suspended before his face. Again he cursed—almost as soon as he had released the marble, it too had vanished. He fumbled for a third.

Then he thought of something. Carefully now, he reached out a hand and tried to feel his way through the empty doorway. His fingers slammed into something solid, and he ran his hand across the odd, smooth surface, satisfied. The doorway was guarded by a Prasidimum. This had to be where Evvie kept returning.

Tristan took a few hurried steps backward until his two marbles reappeared on the outside of the barrier. He snatched them from the air and dropped them into his coat pocket, hoping he hadn't alerted Evvie to his presence. Then he crouched down across from the door, staring at the curtain of impenetrable darkness as he waited.

Tristan had no way of telling the time, so he measured spans by how long he could stand to remain in one position. After what seemed like a long time, his knees and heels began to ache from crouching; getting to his feet, he stretched out his arms and shook his stiff legs to loosen them. He considered enchanting another marble just for something to look at, though eventually he picked out a faint streak of light on the wall.

Surprised, Tristan stepped forward and pressed his

fingers to the delicate line, hoping he wasn't hallucinating. Soon he realized that it was a vein of Delairium, thin and meandering as a thread. While the delicately glowing ore wasn't bright enough to shed light on the surrounding walls, it gave his straining eyes something to focus on. Unlike the phantom shapes that had terrified him at the beginning of the year, this Delairium was comforting and oddly familiar. Yawning, Tristan touched the scars that crisscrossed the left side of his face. He could get used to the darkness.

Too soon his legs grew stiff once again; stamping his feet a few times, Tristan slouched back to the floor, this time sitting with his back against the icy stone. He was getting hungry now, and he wondered how much time had passed since he'd left Leila and Rusty. Maybe dinner had already started.

Eventually he gave up his vigil. With another yawn, he got to his feet and enchanted a new marble to lead him back towards Delair's mine. Next time he would have to move faster.

Tristan was nearly running by the time a soft glow came into view. At the familiar sight of Delair's mine tunnel, he stopped and sagged against the wall, gasping for air. Raking his hair back into place, he returned the marble to his pocket. He'd never seen anything as beautiful as the cheerfully glowing lamps that lined the hallway.

Dinner had started, just as Tristan had guessed, so he stopped in the bathroom to splash water on his face before making his way upstairs to rejoin Leila and Rusty.

"Well?" Leila said eagerly when Tristan sat down. "How was it?"

Tristan was starving, and his hands were still half numb, so he grabbed a hot baked potato and bit into it whole before answering. "I found where Evvie's been going," he said quietly once he managed to swallow. "I followed her for ages, until I got to a room with a Prasidimum in the doorway. I couldn't get past the barrier, but that's where she's hiding her secret, whatever it is. I waited forever, but she never showed up again."

Leila nodded, frowning. "But why does she need to hide something? And what does that have to do with the school's secret?"

"Oh, shoot, I can't believe I didn't tell you this," Tristan said. He took another huge bite of his potato before setting it aside. "Remember the diversion?" he asked softly.

"You mean that ridiculous fire?" Leila said, leaning forward.

Tristan nodded. "Well, like I said, Evvie asked me to distract everyone while we were setting up the Prasidimums. I didn't tell you this, but she said there's someone hiding down in the tunnels. She needed the diversion so she could get that person's blood for the barriers, because otherwise they'd be trapped down there."

Rusty's eyes widened. "How come you didn't say something before now?"

"Sorry," Tristan said. He slit open the remaining half of his potato and spooned sour cream into the center. "Like I said, I forgot." The teachers' argument that day and his subsequent fifty hours of punishment had driven the matter completely from his mind.

Leila stirred her soup absently. "That's really interesting," she said. "I don't suppose...no. I guess we don't know any more than we did before." She was staring at the teachers' table with great concentration, though she didn't appear to be looking at anything in particular.

"You're the one who always figures things out," Tristan said, nudging Leila. "Are you sure you don't have any ideas?"

Still twirling her spoon distractedly, Leila turned her gaze to Tristan. "I don't know," she said. "Isn't this exactly what the teachers were afraid of, though? Someone hiding out in the tunnels, I mean. That's why they made the big fuss about planting Prasidimums everywhere."

Tristan nodded.

"Well," she said, "what if the person that Evvie's hiding is the vandal?"

Tristan bit his lip and nodded slowly. "I'd thought of that," he said unhappily. "But that would still make Evvie responsible for the attacks." If he turned himself in as the vandal, would Drakewell leave Evvie and Amber alone? It was an idea.

Leila said, "Tomorrow we should go exploring a bit, down the tunnel you followed." She glanced up at the teachers' table. "I doubt you'll be able to find the same room again, but at least we can't get lost."

Though he was terribly behind on homework again, Tristan agreed. The following day, as soon as classes were over, he fetched a lantern from the Subroom and joined Leila and Rusty in Delair's hallway. "Ready?"

They nodded.

The tunnels looked much smaller and rougher with their walls illuminated by the lantern; Tristan hardly recognized the first dark opening he'd turned down yesterday. Lifting the lantern above his head, he beckoned Leila and Rusty to follow him.

"We should look in all the rooms we find," Leila whispered. "Maybe we'll find something interesting."

"Or they might just be full of old junk, like the Subroom was," Tristan said. "Besides, I didn't find any doors yesterday, except a couple that I had to go through to follow Evvie."

"Yeah, but you didn't have any light," Leila said. "Look, I see one right ahead." She put a hand on Tristan's shoulder and pointed down the dim tunnel.

Tristan sighed—she was right.

"What if it's locked?" Rusty asked. He nudged Leila aside and grabbed for the doorknob. Tristan and Leila didn't need to say anything, because Rusty had already shoved the door open, answering his own question.

The three of them crowded forward and peered into the dark room. Tristan could make out the outline of a lopsided pyramid, and as he edged forward, the pyramid began to sparkle in the lamp's soft magical glow.

"Bloody hell, is that *gold*?" Rusty gaped at the pile.

Tristan nodded. "Sure looks like it." The pyramid looked as though it was comprised of thousands upon thousands of gold coins; when Tristan knelt beside it, he realized that the gold had simply been melted into slightly irregular discs, blank-faced and gleaming. Tristan picked up a coin, cold and smooth between his fingers, and polished one side on his shirt. He could see a tiny glowing dot on the disk where the lamplight was reflected in the metal.

"No wonder the teachers are so rich," Leila said. "I bet they've been mining this for years, along with the Delairium." She dropped to her knees besides Tristan, running one hand down the side of the gold pyramid. Clattering and chinking, a handful of gold disks slid down and landed beside Tristan's knee. "I wonder why no one bothered to lock it up." Leila scooped up a handful of gold discs and stared at them. Then she slipped the entire handful into her pocket.

"Hey!" Rusty said. "How come you're stealing those?"

Leila raised her eyebrows. "Why shouldn't I? What do you call what we've been doing with those marbles for the past three months?" She shook her head at him and added a few more gold discs to her other pocket. "It'll give us more power over the teachers," she said in annoyance, when Rusty continued to look offended. "It's not like I have anything to spend these on."

"Good idea," Tristan said. He set down the lantern and shoved a few gold discs into the pockets of his jeans and coat. Then he laughed. "Hey, you and Eli can use these as poker chips."

Rusty snorted. "Okay, okay, I guess it's all right."

Eventually they left the room with the gold and

continued on down the tunnel, stopping at each door they came across (there were quite a few, just as Leila had predicted); most were empty, or cluttered with ancient junk. Soon Rusty started complaining that he was hungry, and Tristan's stomach began to growl as well.

"Just a bit farther," Leila said. "It probably isn't even dinnertime yet." Impatient, she took the lantern from Tristan and led the way forward. Tristan dragged his feet, imagining a heaping bowl of mashed potatoes drowned in rich gravy.

Leila stopped in front of the next door and rattled the handle. "I think this one is locked," she said with interest. Tristan frowned as the taste of gravy faded from his mouth.

"Are you sure it's not just stuck closed?" he said irritably.

Rusty pushed Leila aside so he could get a closer look. "Naw, there's a big iron bolt."

"Let me see that," Tristan said, grabbing the lantern. He'd forgotten that this was one of the lanterns that turned on and off at a single tap; when he fumbled with it, he accidentally tapped the metal plate and extinguished the magic light. The tunnel was plunged into darkness.

"Argh!" Rusty cried, flailing his arms around. Leila yelped—he had smacked her in the stomach.

"Sorry, I didn't—" Tristan stopped. The tunnel wasn't completely black, because there was a strange glowing circle of light on the bolted door in front of him. It was Delairium, of course, but what startled him was the picture it made.

"Triss, what's wrong?" Leila hissed. "Turn the light back on!"

"Wait." Tristan leaned closer to the door, and from close up the spidery lines within the circle were unmistakable. It was the image of a globe. This was the room Drakewell had warned him about, the room that Tristan was supposed to keep absolutely secret and stay far away from.

"Oh, come on," Leila finally snapped. Reaching out, she found Tristan's arm and snatched back the lantern. She tapped the metal plate and flooded the tunnel once more with light. "Why the hell are we standing in the dark?"

Tristan was still staring at the door. The Delairium was so faint that it had vanished when the light came on, but he could picture exactly where the outline of the globe was traced into the smooth wood.

They should never have come here. If Drakewell realized that Tristan had disobeyed his direct orders, he would be livid.

"What're you looking at?" Rusty asked, bending forward and squinting at the door.

Tristan straightened. "Nothing. Let's get out of here."

"You know something about this door," Leila accused. She frowned and raised the lantern. "This has to be something important, don't you think? I mean, the teachers didn't even bother to lock up that massive pile of gold, but this…"

"You reckon this is it?" Rusty said, eyes wide. "The secret of this school, I mean."

"Guys," Tristan said nervously, "we really should get out of here." His eyes were playing tricks on him; he could have sworn he'd just seen the flicker of approaching lamplight in the tunnel behind him, but it vanished as soon as he'd looked closer. Leila had to be right about this room.

After a long, disgruntled silence, Rusty said, "Okay, so can we eat now?"

Leila snorted. "Yes, Rusty. Let's go."

When they reached Delair's mine tunnel, Tristan was about to slump against the wall in relief when he saw a wavering light.

"Delair's here," he whispered, throwing out a hand to stop Rusty. "We've got to be careful—we're in huge trouble if he finds us snooping."

"Aw, Delair's not gonna report us." Rusty tried to push Tristan's arm out of his way.

Leila shook her head sharply and grabbed Rusty's shoulder. "Tristan's in enough trouble with the teachers already." With her other hand, she tapped the lantern against Tristan's shoulder to extinguish the light.

"You guys are no fun," Rusty said. "All right, I'll be quiet." When Leila released him, he rubbed at his shoulder where she'd held it.

Tristan craned his neck to see where the light was coming from, and after a moment he saw that it was spilling from an open doorway almost directly across from where the three of them stood. There were voices coming from the room, quiet and urgent.

"Now," Leila whispered, touching Tristan's shoulder,

"let's get out of—"

CRASH!

Rusty had tripped over a metal bucket filled with rocks; it toppled onto its side with a thunderous clatter, making their efforts at creeping around pointless.

"Rusty!" Tristan and Leila said together.

"Run!" Rusty shouted, his voice cracking.

"No, we haven't got time," Leila said desperately. "Hurry, let's hide in here, so he doesn't know we've been down the other tunnel…"

They darted towards a room on their left—it was scarcely larger than a toilet stall, though they managed to cram into the corner, pressing their backs to the wall. Tristan could feel Leila's ragged breathing on his neck.

A second later Delair's voice said, "There was a light in the hall, just a moment ago."

"Damn!" Leila whispered.

Crunching footsteps and lamplight approached; Tristan heard a soft scraping as the metal bucket was set upright again, followed immediately by a new voice.

"I have to leave. Good evening." The voice was female, though Tristan couldn't tell who it belonged to.

As the light bobbed closer still, Tristan put his arms around Leila's waist and pulled her back, forcing the three of them to fit into the impossibly small corner. Holding his breath, Tristan dug his shoulders into the stone wall.

Then a bright light shone directly on their faces. "I should have known it would be you, Fairholm," Delair said, chuckling. "You have quite a knack for showing up where you don't belong. Come on out; the only punishment you'll receive tonight is a lecture."

Laughing nervously, Tristan unwound his arms from Leila's waist and stepped forward.

As Leila relit their lantern, Delair led them along the tunnel until they reached the main hallway.

"So you're not gonna report us?" Rusty asked. When Delair shook his head, Rusty muttered, "Told you so," to Leila.

"Now for the lecture," Delair said, stopping at the mouth of his tunnel. "Fairholm, I'm sure you realize how much danger you are in, which would explain why you hid—sloppily, I might add." He winked and cleared his throat. "Drakewell is no longer willing to forgive you; I'm sure he made that inescapably clear earlier this semester. And if he caught you and your friends sneaking around the tunnels, I have no doubt he would expel all three of you without waiting for the other teachers to give their opinions. You would be sent straight back to Juvie. Is that clear?"

Tristan glanced unhappily at Leila and Rusty. Expulsion would be nothing compared to what Drakewell had threatened to do to Amber, but if he had known that Leila and Rusty were in danger of getting kicked out, he wouldn't have allowed them to follow him into the tunnels.

"Yes, it's clear, Professor," Leila said, scowling.

Delair nodded. "Don't plan on being this lucky again, kids. See you in class tomorrow."

Apologizing once again, Tristan, Leila, and Rusty

hurried away.

"Can we get food now?" Rusty said as soon as they reached the end of the hall.

Tristan ignored him. "You guys are not exploring with me again," he said tersely, crossing his arms.

"Oh, Triss, don't—"

"No," he said, in a tone that didn't allow for argument.

The end of the year was now racing towards him so quickly that there was something he couldn't put off any longer. He needed to speak to the two people he was putting in danger: Evvie and Amber.

Tristan found a chance to talk with Amber the very next day. After Merridy's class let out he gave his bag to Leila, who complained and asked him what he was up to; eventually she promised to take his books down to the Subroom and bother him for an explanation later. Then he followed Amber up to the meadow, where she made for the trees as usual.

"Amber?" he called uncertainly. He didn't want to frighten her away before he had a chance to ask his question, so he stopped on the new grass just outside the Lair's entrance.

At Tristan's voice, Amber froze and turned cautiously. When she recognized him, some of the fear left her eyes. "Oh, Tristan. Why are you here?"

"I had a question—no, there's something I have to tell you," Tristan said. The air was light and warm despite the breeze, so he rolled the sleeves of his blue shirt past his elbows as he crossed the clearing to join her. "Can I walk with you?"

Amber beamed at him in response.

When they had wandered far enough into the trees that Tristan could no longer see the clearing over his shoulder, he crossed his arms and began. "Remember what Drakewell told us at the beginning of the year, about that room where the secret of the school was supposed to be hidden?"

"Of course." Amber stopped to pluck a jay's feather from the ground. "He described the door to us—the door with the globe of Delairium."

Tristan nodded. "I know we were supposed to stay away from it no matter what, but—well, I sort of stumbled across it last night."

"And you think Drakewell knows?" Amber shook her head. "It's not possible for him to read your thoughts, though perhaps there is another way for him to find out. But you're afraid of what he might do to you?" Slowing, she slipped the blue feather behind her ear, where it stood out like a streak of fire against her pale hair.

"Yeah, and—since he told both of us, I don't want him to blame you as well." Tristan stopped and took a deep breath. He hadn't been sure whether he wanted to say this next bit; Amber might understand, though, and she deserved to know the truth.

Giving Tristan a half-smile, Amber sank fluidly to the ground, where she sat cross-legged with her hands splayed over the budding grass. Tristan dropped to his knees beside her.

"Drakewell thinks I know who the vandal is," he began carefully. "And I do have a...a suspicion. But I'm afraid of what would happen to that person if I accused them." He glanced up and met Amber's intense gaze, though a moment later he dropped his eyes guiltily to the roots of a nearby tree. "A few months ago, Drakewell said I had to tell him what I knew about the vandal by the end of the year, or he would—he said he'd punish you in my place."

For a long moment Amber was silent. Her expression hardly changed, though Tristan saw a slight crease in her brow that meant she was thinking intently. She should be furious at him.

At last she met Tristan's nervous gaze, her lips twitching in a wry smile. "Thank you for telling me," she said. "I can't guess who you think the vandal might be, though I am certain he or she is important to you. However, I have been keeping a few secrets from you as well."

Tristan laughed. "You're nothing but secrets," he said. "It doesn't matter that you haven't told me a few of them, does it?"

Amber shook her head. "This is important. You see, Drakewell spoke to me in private as well, perhaps the very same day he drew you aside. I don't think he believed I knew anything about the vandal, but he made the same threat to me." She smoothed her wispy hair and smiled at Tristan. "If each of us is too valuable to be destroyed, but

Drakewell intends to punish whoever fails to learn the truth, then it seems our best course of action would be to do nothing."

"Drakewell was tricking us, then!" Tristan wanted to laugh aloud. "Maybe he wanted to test us or something." At last he was freed from the miserable guilt that had gnawed at him all spring. "This is wonderful! Come on, let's walk some more." Jumping to his feet, Tristan took Amber's hand and pulled her up. Though she looked bemused by his enthusiasm, she returned his smile.

For a long time they strolled through the awakening forest, following pale green dapples of light that filtered down through the budding aspen leaves. Squirrels and birds darted across their path, and once they even stumbled upon a white-spotted fawn that stared at them for several long minutes before bounding away.

"You see why I love the forest?" Amber asked shyly as they began to make their way back to the school. Her turquoise eyes were lit up with happiness, and she looked ready to float away into the trees.

Tristan grinned at her. "I'm beginning to understand." He had already loved the wilderness around the school, but it was amazing to see the effect it had on Amber.

When they reached the Lair, the sun had just sunk below the distant ridge, and the other students were beginning to gather in the ballroom for dinner. Tristan was still smiling to himself when he joined Leila and Rusty at their usual table.

"What have you been doing?" Leila asked suspiciously.

"Nothing, I—" Tristan broke off, because Evvie had just entered the ballroom. At the sight of Evvie, his bubble of happiness imploded—if Evvie was the vandal, then she was still endangering everyone at the school, and he, Tristan, would still be responsible for anything bad that happened if he failed to report her.

He had to learn the truth before Evvie got the chance to do anything awful.

"What were you going to say?" Leila asked, frowning.

"Nothing."

Chapter 20

Unexcused Absences

I t was another week before Tristan found a chance to speak with Evvie. Finals were nearly upon them—it was early May, and there were only three weeks remaining in the school year. Tristan was distracted from his preoccupation with the vandal by an ever-growing pile of homework.

After Grindlethorn, Merridy, and Brikkens had each spent a lesson going over the format of their exams, Damian interrupted Alldusk's lecture to complain loudly about finals.

"What's the point of exams?" he asked heatedly. "It's not like we'll be applying for colleges, so why the hell should we study? Are we going to be stuck doing punishments for the rest of our lives?"

Alldusk gave Damian a thin-lipped smile. "There are other reasons to perform well aside from the fear of punishment."

"Sure," Zeke said sarcastically.

"Though I wouldn't rule out punishment as a motivation," Alldusk said sternly. "More importantly, some of you will be given the option to return home for the summer, but this privilege will be revoked if you fail too many classes."

"Go home?" Rusty yelped.

"What the—?" Eli said. "You kept that quiet!"

Tristan said nothing. He had already known they would be going home for the summer, since Alldusk had mentioned it in passing months ago, but the significance of it had not registered at the time.

"You're lying," Damian said. "You're just going to send us straight back to Juvie, right?"

Alldusk held up his hands for silence. "Drakewell will speak with each of you in the next week to discuss your options. A few of you still have remaining time to serve, so you won't have the option to return. And anyone who wishes may choose to remain here over the summer."

It was the very next day when Drakewell called Tristan to his office to discuss the summer with him.

"You will be allowed to return home," Drakewell said, peering at a set of notes. "However, if the trespasser is not apprehended before the end of the year, I may rethink that decision."

Tristan swallowed.

The week before finals, everyone began studying for exams in earnest. The ballroom became the main hang-out for students, both from the Subroom and the bunkroom—a bookshelf with textbooks and reference volumes had appeared along the back wall, and the tables were piled with pens and extra paper. Quinsley kept the students well supplied with treats, appearing every hour or so with cookies and hot chocolate for anyone studying there.

Leila had borrowed the *Beginner's Guide to Magical Theory* from Tristan, and she was now attempting to read it cover-to-cover before exams began. "I'll feel more comfortable taking the tests if I'm not just memorizing random facts," she explained patiently. "Besides, I might learn something useful." She gave Tristan a significant look. "For instance, you still haven't told me what was so important about that locked door we found."

Tristan rolled his eyes.

Unhelpfully, the teachers seemed to think this was a good time to assign every homework project they hadn't gotten around to yet. Even chubby little Finley Glenn, who always finished his homework on time and knew the answers in class, was seen scribbling away in the ballroom long past midnight. Cailyn was struggling in most of her classes, so Rusty, Trey, and Hayley tutored her whenever one of them had a free moment.

When the students weren't studying in the ballroom, they were hiking extensively to collect magical herbs for Gracewright; examining and recording every variety of rock and mineral that Delair brought to class; and demonstrating to Grindlethorn the proper methods of treating various injuries by bandaging their own limbs.

"They're going to kill us," Rusty grumbled one

morning, staring listlessly at his empty plate. Even his unshakeable cheerfulness had been dampened considerably by their workload.

Tristan had barely slept the night before. Rubbing his tired eyes, he slumped back in his chair.

"I learned something last night," Leila said, dropping a large pancake onto Tristan's plate. She waited for a moment, clearly hoping for a response. Tristan merely yawned, staring blearily at the pancake, and after a moment Leila sighed and continued.

"Well, that book of yours says it *is* possible to do magic with lots and lots of marbles working together, but you need a conduit for any large-scale spells."

This sounded important, though Tristan could not think why. Lots of marbles working together, he thought slowly. We have lots of marbles in the Subroom. The school has lots of marbles somewhere…

"So you mean all those marbles we've collected are useless?" Rusty asked sullenly.

"We can still use them as leverage," Leila said, "but yeah, we can't do much actual magic with them."

"Wait," Tristan said. Something had just fallen into place. He couldn't believe it had taken him this long to figure it out. "Drakewell told us there's a place in this school where lots of marbles are stashed, right?"

Rusty and Leila looked at each other and nodded.

Tristan stared at the wall, thinking hard. "And the pile of marbles is dangerous to destroy. But…there has to be a conduit somewhere, too. That's what Drakewell meant."

Tristan was talking half to himself now. "I bet the marbles have to be close to the conduit, and the conduit has to be the room with the globe. So—" He broke off, unwilling to voice what he'd just realized.

The locked room with the Delairium globe on the door was very close to the room Evvie kept returning to. That couldn't be an accident. Which meant Evvie, or the unknown person hiding in the tunnels, had to be targeting that locked room. And an explosion there would kill everyone in the Lair.

Tristan jumped to his feet. "I have to talk to Evvie." He scanned the ballroom. "Crap, where is she?"

"Tristan!" Leila grabbed his wrist. "We have class in five minutes. You can't go running off."

Cursing, Tristan kicked his book bag. Then he sank slowly back into his chair.

The day felt like the longest Tristan could remember. Ominously, Evvie did not appear for Brikkens' class or even for lunch.

"Come on, Leila, let me go after her, I've got plenty of time," Tristan said when they reached the ballroom. "I've got the marbles with me; I just have to run down and—"

Leila grabbed his shoulder. "Not now," she whispered, pointing towards the doorway.

Blinking sleepily, Tristan turned and saw Drakewell stalk into the ballroom. Hayley, who was standing directly in the headmaster's path, gave a squeak and dove out of the way.

"Quiet," Drakewell said unnecessarily. "I only require a

moment of your time."

Hayley huddled by the wall, unmoving.

"Your teachers should be handing out an exam schedule sometime this afternoon," Drakewell said in a bored tone. "As summer break is fast approaching, those students who have decided they wish to remain here over the summer should come speak to me." He narrowed his eyes suddenly. "Where is Miss Rosewell?"

With a groaning of wood, Brikkens shifted in his seat. "Oh, dear," he said. "Miss Rosewell was absent from my class this morning, and I must say she missed quite an important lesson. Such a pity, isn't it?"

For some reason, Drakewell glared at Alldusk. "Notify me the moment she reappears," he said. "Better yet, send her to my office."

Turning, he swept out of the ballroom.

"We should start on that assignment of Grindlethorn's," Leila said briskly, breaking the silence that Drakewell had left in his wake. Tristan had the shrewd idea that she was trying to distract him from Evvie.

"I don't have time for that," Tristan said under his breath. "Seriously, Leila, I've got to go after her."

"Wait until classes are over," she whispered.

Oblivious to Tristan's distress, Rusty had started tying a length of gauze around his wrist and labeling it. When the doors to the ballroom crashed open once again, Tristan flinched, spilling his cranberry juice all over Rusty's bandage.

"Argh, I'm bleeding!" Rusty said.

It was not Drakewell who stood in the doorway this time but Alldusk.

"Has anyone seen Darla today?" he asked with a frown. "She was supposed to meet me just now, but I can't find her."

Tristan jumped to his feet. "I'll see you guys later," he said. "Sorry about the cranberry juice."

He broke into a run as he left the ballroom, nearly colliding with Alldusk in the doorway. "Sorry," he called over his shoulder.

Reaching the stairs, Tristan grabbed the rail and jumped the last four steps. With stiff fingers he dug in the front pocket of his jeans for marbles; he found three, which he grasped tightly as he ran. They felt like good-luck talismans.

He didn't see anyone on the stairs, though that was lucky since he was making quite a racket skidding along the marble floors. By the time he reached Delair's mine tunnel, he was panting and clutching at his chest. Tristan hardly needed the marbles to find Evvie; by this point he could navigate these tunnels by touch. He didn't want to make any mistakes, though, so he performed the spell as usual. When the marble began drifting lazily towards the depths of Delair's mine, Tristan set his mouth in a grim line.

"Okay, Evvie," he muttered. "Let's see what you've been doing down here." Taking a deep breath, he started off into the blackness.

The distance to Evvie's room seemed longer than usual, and Tristan's anticipation grew with each step. Was

Evvie the vandal? He should have told someone sooner, before it was too late. Or was she just helping hide the vandal? Did she know the school's secret?

And above all, why was someone trying to destroy the Lair? Did the teachers have dangerous enemies, or was the vandal just a rogue lunatic?

As the tunnel wound deeper into the earth, Tristan grew cold, sweat turning to ice on his neck. He set his jaw and tried to ignore the seeping chill.

The spidery globe of Delairium seemed to shine brighter than ever from the door of the locked room; Tristan stopped beside the door for a moment and pressed his ear to the crack, listening. He heard nothing but his own unsteady breathing. Letting out a deep breath, he unclenched his fists. Whatever Evvie or the vandal had planned, it wasn't happening yet. Somewhat reassured, he picked up his pace and hurried on to the room guarded by the Prasidimum.

At the familiar door, Tristan pocketed the marble and leaned back against the wall to wait. Already his frantic anticipation was beginning to drain away; he was no longer sure that Evvie hadn't simply gone for a walk in the forest. She could be working off punishment with Merridy, or maybe she was sick. Wishing the Prasidimum didn't cut off all sound from inside the room, Tristan folded his arms and scowled at the darkness. In the ballroom far above, Leila and Rusty had likely just finished showing their labeled bandages to Grindlethorn. They would be climbing the stairs to Botany now, rejoicing in the sun and the brilliantly blue sky.

Tristan shivered.

Unlike before, Tristan had barely settled in to wait for Evvie when the door creaked open. He gave a start and nearly fell over. Holding his breath, he fumbled for a new marble and set it to track Evvie again. As the person began walking forward, footsteps crunching softly, the marble stayed motionless in front of the door—unless Tristan had messed up the spell, this person was someone new, not Evvie at all. There was a brief silence as the stranger stopped to light a lamp; in the sudden glow, Tristan recognized Merridy's tight bun and narrow shoulders.

For a moment he stood frozen, one hand stretched towards his floating marble. He couldn't decide whether to follow Merridy or wait for Evvie. Either way, what could the two of them possibly be doing down here?

As the bobbing light disappeared around the corner, Tristan made up his mind to wait for Evvie. He could always set his marble to track Merridy if Evvie took too long to appear.

Soon the door opened a second time. Evvie crept forward, raising a softly glowing lamp. Holding his breath, Tristan pressed his back to the wall. Evvie was looking behind her, watching something at waist height that was invisible behind the Prasidimum barrier.

A moment later two children followed Evvie into the tunnel. They were very small, and they were holding hands. The little boy had his thumb in his mouth.

Startled, Tristan lowered his hand and took a step

backwards.

Evvie whirled; she'd heard his tentative footstep. "Tristan!" she yelled. "You—god, Tristan, you ruin *everything*! I should've—gah!" She made a fist and shook it at his nose.

Tristan raised his hands quickly and backed away. "Evvie, I'm not trying to hurt you or—or your kids."

Evvie glared at him.

"Just explain what you've been up to. You've been avoiding me for weeks now, and Drakewell thinks I'm the vandal, and I was *this close* to turning you in."

"You *what*?"

"Tell me what the hell you're doing," Tristan said, looking from the little dark-haired boy to the blonde girl at his side. They were probably only four or five. He had the strangest feeling he'd seen them before, though he'd had no idea they existed.

"Why on earth would I tell you anything?" Evvie asked shrilly. "You just said you'd report me, or—"

"Drakewell hates me," Tristan said flatly. "I was only going to report you because I thought you were the vandal, and I think the vandal is about to try destroying this place."

Evvie shifted uncomfortably, and Tristan's suspicions returned.

"You don't know who the vandal is, do you?" he asked sharply. "Because whoever it is, they might kill everyone in the Lair if they're not careful."

"We go now?" the little girl asked, grabbing Evvie's sleeve with one small hand.

Evvie bent down and put a hand on the girl's cheek. "Really soon. Don't worry, we'll still have time. I'll get you away safely, I promise."

"Why is it all dark?" the boy asked, tugging on the girl's hand.

"Mommy said it's a dragon cave."

Suddenly Tristan remembered—he had seen these children in Evvie's sketchbook. The drawing had made him think of Marcus.

"Why are the kids in danger?" Tristan asked Evvie. "Just tell me what's going on."

Evvie sighed and handed her lamp to the girl, whose eyes widened in delight.

"I'll tell you if you shut up."

Tristan pressed his lips together and nodded.

"Well," Evvie said, "I found these kids hiding in a cave on my way back from Merridy's first test, months and months ago. They lived in a tiny village up near here, but there was an avalanche, and a lot of the houses were crushed." Evvie lowered her voice. "I think their parents were killed, but the kids went looking for them up in the cave. It's how they survived."

Tristan thought back to that first test. Evvie had been one of the only students to find her way back unaided…and she'd gone missing the night she'd returned. "You said you were going to bed early," he said slowly, "and I followed you…but you weren't in the room. Were you down here, finding somewhere to hide the children?"

Evvie nodded sharply. "Drakewell hates children,

remember? If you say a word to him, he'll—"

The girl nudged Evvie's side with her blonde head. "I count to two hundred now," she said.

"Already?" Evvie said, her face darkening. "We don't have much time. Come on; we've got to leave now."

She took the girl's tiny hand in hers and picked up the boy, who nestled his head against her shoulder.

Evvie had already taken two steps away from Tristan when she stopped. Without turning, she said, "You—er— might want to get out of this place too. You're right about the vandal."

"Are you serious?" Tristan said flatly. "You're saying I should just abandon everyone and save my own neck?"

This time Evvie turned. "Trust me, this place isn't good. The teachers—they've been doing something horrible. The attacker is doing the right thing." Her eyes were scared, but her mouth was set in a thin line.

The little boy lifted his head from Evvie's shoulder and stared at Tristan.

"Damn you, Evvie!" Tristan shouted. "I'm not going to turn traitor on my friends! They're the only family I've got."

Swallowing visibly, Evvie turned and began hurrying away, nearly dragging the girl along at her heels.

"I don't care about your stupid morals," Tristan yelled after her. "I'm not letting everyone die!" He cursed loudly and snatched a marble as though readying to throw it at Evvie. Then she vanished around the corner, her light flickering away into darkness.

Tristan lowered his fist, breathing hard. He was no closer to finding the vandal than before, though he knew what he had to do next. There wasn't time to find everyone and convince them to leave the school. With a final glance at the Prasidimum-guarded doorway, he turned and broke into a run, following the threads of Delairium along the wall as he raced towards the room with the globe.

His feet pounded along the rough stone. Would it be too late? How the hell was he supposed to get into the locked room? And when he did, what would he find?

Suddenly a wall loomed in front of him; Tristan threw his hands out to stop himself. Legs tingling, he leaned against the rock and tried to catch his breath. For a frantic moment he thought he'd come the wrong way. Then he looked over his shoulder.

There was the door, barely two paces behind him. The Delairium globe was as bright as ever. He didn't know how he had missed it.

Chest tight, Tristan crept forward and pressed his ear to the door. He clutched a marble in his pocket, the cold orb digging into his palm.

For a long time there was silence.

The globe on the door glowed steadily, stark and thin in the blackness. Eventually Tristan's racing heart slowed and he began to grow cold once again.

At last there came a muffled scraping, magnified oddly in the space behind the door; it had to be a large chamber. The scrape was followed by a hollow clang so loud that Tristan didn't need his ear to the door to hear it properly.

He jumped back, staring wildly down the hall. The vandal was already at work, perhaps minutes away from killing everyone in the Lair.

And Tristan was absolutely alone.

CRASH!

Tristan jumped, nearly dropping his marble. Something large had smashed to the ground inside the room, or maybe a piece of the wall had been blasted away. How much time did he have? His heartbeat sounded like the ticking of a bomb.

For a moment Tristan couldn't decide what to do; he bounced on the balls of his feet, tensed and ready to run. Then, with a curse, he lurched forward and slammed his fists against the door. "Someone come!" he called in desperation, though he knew there was no one around to hear. "Help!"

His voice was drowned by a new series of crashes from the room, loud as an avalanche. *Why didn't I tell the others to get out?* It had been reckless of him to think he could stop the attacker alone.

Again Tristan slammed his fists on the door, this time throwing the weight of his shoulder against the wood as well. As he was about to hurl himself a third time against the glowing outline of Asia, something grabbed his shoulder.

"Argh!" Tristan whirled, ready to strike at whoever had assaulted him.

It was Leila.

"Damn it!" he yelled. "What are you doing here, you

idiot?" When he wrenched Leila's hand from his shoulder and took a step back, he realized that Rusty was there as well, lurking in the shadows behind Leila.

"Don't lecture us," Leila said in a hurried whisper. "We know that's the vandal in there. Do you really think we'd let you do this on your own?"

Tristan cursed and kicked at the wall.

"So, how are you planning to get in there?" Rusty asked cheerfully. Leila's lantern cast a strange glow on his face.

Tristan rounded on him. "Guys, this is serious! Someone dangerous is in that room, and I'm pretty sure they're a few seconds away from blowing up the Lair!"

"Triss, calm down," Leila snapped. "You're the only one of us who can actually do magic, but you're completely useless if you can't concentrate."

Irritated, Tristan drew in a deep breath. At another loud crash he winced, though he quickly steadied himself and turned back to Leila and Rusty.

"Okay," he said. "I'm going to try unlocking this door by magic. You guys should leave. Run as fast as you can; maybe you'll have time to warn the others."

Leila and Rusty shared a glance. "No, we're gonna stay."

"There isn't enough time," Leila whispered.

"Fine!" Tristan shouted. "Then get the hell out of my way!"

There was another crash, louder than before, followed by a rushing sound like wind.

Fighting his anger, Tristan dug for another marble. It couldn't be too hard to unlock the door; if he concentrated enough heat on the lock, it should melt away. He was just having trouble concentrating.

Shaking his head irritably, Tristan closed his eyes and imagined the first heavy bolt falling open. He would focus on each of the three locks separately, moving cautiously so the magic couldn't slip out of control. This first lock was easy—once he broke through the padlock, the bolt would slide free.

Please work.

Tristan tightened his grip around the marble. Where was Evvie now, and how did she plan to sneak past the teachers? Did she know a secret entrance to the Lair?

You're not concentrating, whispered a voice at the back of his head.

"I can't do this," Tristan muttered, mostly to himself.

Neither Leila nor Rusty spoke. They were watching him with nervous trust, eyes gleaming in the lantern's glow. It was their faith in him that spurred Tristan to try again. Frustrated, he pressed a fist to his forehead and closed his eyes, focusing every stray thought on the padlock.

As reluctant as a spark in snow, the marble began to warm. Tristan let out a careful breath and released the marble. Eyes closed, he waited. He heard nothing but the continued crashes and scrapes echoing from within the room, so he opened his eyes.

The lock was glowing red. To his amazement, the padlock appeared to be lengthening, all the while glowing brighter and brighter—suddenly it dropped free of the door, landing at his feet in a red-hot glob. It had melted away.

Tristan almost laughed in relief. Rusty began to speak, but thankfully Leila clapped a hand over his mouth. Tristan couldn't afford to lose his concentration.

The next lock was set in the door handle; instead of trying to melt it away, he would have to focus on twisting through the gears. Tristan found another marble and closed his eyes, wishing he knew more about locks. If Eli were here, he'd probably be able to pick it without magic. Tristan was just guessing when he imagined the lock's innards like a cavernous metal labyrinth, the rigid walls ready to slide apart if he exerted pressure in the right place.

Tristan dropped the second marble, which was already so hot that it seared his palm. He waited two nervous heartbeats before opening his eyes.

KABOOM!

The wall exploded in a great fiery ball of light. Rocks flew from the wall, shattering and bursting in midair. The door splintered in half with a heaving crack. The glowing Delairium globe split along the western coast of Africa.

Tristan stumbled backwards, throwing his hands over his head—his foot caught on a shard of rock and he crashed to the ground, stones slamming into him.

Scrambling to his knees, Tristan tried to crawl away, but his right arm was smashed nearly senseless by a careening boulder. Leila and Rusty were screaming at him, their words lost in the tumult. Tristan barely made it two feet.

With a rumble and a creak, a piece of the ceiling shifted and gave way. Tristan looked up just in time to see a rain of fist-sized boulders plunging towards his head. The darkness roared, and then everything faded. Tristan barely felt the impact.

Chapter 21

The Map Room

When Tristan struggled awake, everything began hurting at once. His head was close to splitting in two, and a splinter of fire was wedged along his spine. Shuddering, he bit his tongue so hard he tasted blood. As he managed to focus his wavering vision, he realized that he was still lying in the tunnel, surrounded by pale, blurred faces.

"Hold still," said a clipped voice somewhere near his left shoulder. It was Alldusk. A moment later the professor brought something cold to Tristan's lips. "Drink this. It'll help."

Gagging slightly, Tristan let his mouth fall open and gulped at the liquid that Alldusk tipped carefully down his throat. As he moved his face, he noticed that something had dried in a stiff line down his jaw.

"Can you hear me, Triss?" Leila's voice whispered. Shifting, Tristan saw that Leila knelt beside his head, clasping his left hand with both of hers. He hadn't even felt her touch. Rusty stood nearby, watching nervously.

"Why'd you come down here?" Tristan asked Alldusk, his voice slurring slightly. "You're s'posed to be outside. It's not safe."

"I should think not," Alldusk said with a frown. "But the tunnel roof was stabilized by magic. It should not have come down."

Tristan struggled to sit up. "My—" he choked on a mouthful of dust "—my fault. I tried to break through the door. Vandal's in there." He gestured weakly at the splintered doorway.

Already the medicine was easing Tristan's pain, and as his thoughts cleared, his panic mounted. In the time he'd been unconscious, the vandal had likely blasted the room to pieces. Any moment now, the whole Lair would blow up.

Alldusk straightened and tucked away the flask of white liquid. His knuckles were very white.

"Has anyone seen Darla?" he asked shakily.

Tristan almost shook his head. "Wait—I did see her earlier. Down in the tunnels. She came out of a dark room, and I hid in the shadows and let her go."

Alldusk barely let Tristan finish his sentence. He dove towards the splintered door and began heaving shards of wood out of the doorway. Tristan ducked as the piece of wood with Australia's outline came hurtling towards his nose, and Rusty did a funny hop to the side to avoid being impaled by Japan. Alldusk continued to dig deeper and deeper, hurtling stone and wood like he'd gone crazy, until there was enough space for him to shove his way through.

As the last rocks clattered to the floor, the room beyond exhaled a wave of musty, acrid rock dust. Tristan coughed again. When he recovered, wiping his mouth on his sleeve, he got a brief glimpse of a cavernous, well-lit chamber. Then Alldusk threw himself into the opening and shouldered past the broken door.

"What're we supposed to do, huh?" Rusty asked, bending over to examine a splinter of wood. "I thought having a teacher here would be helpful and all."

When Alldusk toppled into the room, leaving the doorway gaping, the tunnel was washed with light. Blinking, Tristan took a deep breath. The particles of rock dust were already beginning to settle, clinging to his skin and caking the roof of his mouth.

He'd made his decision when he had spoken to Evvie—no matter what immoral mission the teachers were trying to carry out, he had to stop the vandal if it cost him his life. If his friends died, he would have nothing left. There was no safe home, no loving family, waiting for him outside the walls of the Lair.

Easing his hand out of Leila's grasp, Tristan staggered to his feet. A new bolt of pain shot through him, and he leaned against the wall until his lightheadedness passed. "Please stay here," he said, looking from Leila to Rusty. "You guys aren't any good at magic; you'll just be in my way."

"Thanks," Leila said sarcastically. She and Rusty followed Tristan through the broken doorway and into the bright room beyond. He sighed; he hadn't expected anything different. But when he turned and got his first good look at the secret room, he forgot Leila and Rusty entirely.

The room shone as though baking in the lazy afternoon sun. Shielding his eyes with one hand, Tristan squinted to the far wall. The chamber was large, far larger than anything he had imagined. Even though they were deep underground, this room had to be fully half the size of the ballroom, with hundreds of lanterns glowing across its high rounded ceiling. The center of the room was dominated by an enormous sphere, twice as tall as Tristan, its lower half sunk into the ground.

For a moment Tristan stared at the sphere, uncomprehending. Then he recognized it with a start. It was an enormous three-dimensional copy of the globe on the door, the continents shaped from polished stone.

Once Tristan's eyes had adjusted to the light, he was able to look past the shimmering globe to the wreckage strewn about the walls. It looked as though there had once been a series of stone tables circling the room; nothing remained now but dust and rough boulders.

In a far corner, surrounded by gray rubble, Alldusk was embracing Merridy with something like desperation. For some reason Merridy was not returning Alldusk's embrace; she stood with her arms stiffly at her sides, looking over Alldusk's shoulder.

"Where's the vandal?" Tristan asked quietly, looking around. He could see no one in the room apart from his friends and the two teachers.

Then he realized the truth.

When the greenhouse had been attacked last semester, and Tristan had spied on the teachers' discussion afterwards, Merridy had been the first to suggest that they should blame a student.

Merridy had gone into Alldusk's office on the night of the second attack.

And Merridy had been helping Evvie take care of the children, so she had warned Evvie to get them to safety before she blew up the school.

Merridy was the vandal.

"Professor Alldusk," Tristan said, his voice rising. "There's no one else in here. Merridy—"

"Have you seen Evangeline?" Merridy asked sharply.

Alldusk took Merridy by the shoulders and held her away from him. "What's wrong?"

"*Have you seen Evangeline?*" Merridy repeated urgently.

"Yes, she was supposed to be in class," Alldusk said, "but I saw her up in the ballroom. There were two children with her."

Merridy nodded and took a step away from Alldusk, clasping a hand on the front of her jacket. "Then it is time. I apologize for this, Brinley." Her voice wavered, though her eyes remained hard. "I have always—" she hiccupped "—always loved you."

Tristan thrust one hand into a pocket and closed his fingers around the cold orbs he'd stashed there. Merridy's expression was dangerous. Clenching his teeth against the ache in his shoulder, Tristan began sidling around the globe, edging away from the door. Within moments he could no longer see Alldusk or Merridy. He took three more cautious steps sideways, until Rusty and Leila were out of sight as well, and then began backing up.

A dull *thud* echoed from the opposite side of the room. Tristan couldn't see what was happening, so he took another hurried step back. There was an unpleasant thunk, and Leila shrieked.

"You're crazy!" she yelled at Merridy.

Tristan guessed that Merridy was throwing shards of rock at Leila and Rusty; at least she hadn't started hurling spells.

"Darla!" Alldusk shouted, and Tristan heard a series of frantic scrapes and thuds.

He took two more steps backward, trying not to limp, until he felt the stone wall pressing against his back. From here he could see the blackened doorway on his left and Merridy and Alldusk on his right. Merridy's bun had come loose, and she clawed at Alldusk's eyes with her bony fingers.

Alldusk looked as though he was afraid to hurt Merridy. Instead of hitting her back, he grabbed her wrists and held her struggling fingers away from his face. Panting, he dragged her to her knees before releasing her.

Merridy was back on her feet in seconds. This time she reached in her pocket for a handful of marbles and turned on Tristan. She was still holding a jagged shard of rock in her left hand like a dagger.

When she saw that Tristan had crossed to the other

side of the globe, her eyes widened. She lunged forward, looking deranged. "Tristan Fairholm, get out of my way!"

Something about the way she spoke made Tristan turn. He realized suddenly that he'd been leaning against a stone door, a second entrance set firmly into the wall. *That's where the magic is stored.* Tristan was sure of it. And now that Evvie was safely outside, Tristan was the only one standing between Merridy and her goal.

Merridy advanced on him, raising her handful of marbles. With no spell in mind, Tristan drew the fistful of marbles from his pocket and copied Merridy's gesture.

"Darla!" Alldusk yelled. "Darla, don't hurt Tristan!"

Merridy ignored Alldusk. Tristan flexed his arm, ready to hurl his magic at her, but she stopped several paces away from him and closed her eyes. Again the dust drifted to the floor, leaving behind a sweeter smell of minerals. Tristan's hand stiffened.

No one seemed to breathe. Merridy's hand twitched almost imperceptibly, and Tristan did not realize at first that she had released a marble.

Then the ground in front of Merridy exploded with a sound like fireworks. Chunks of rock split free and hurtled through the air, dust whirling up from the floor. Pebbles and boulders slammed against the globe's polished surface and bounced off, careening towards Tristan.

Tristan jumped away from the stone door, a sliver of rock missing his forehead by inches. He threw his hands over his head, shielding his face from a rain of pebbles.

Still standing by the door, Leila and Rusty had escaped

the blast, though the ceiling of the room was beginning to shift. It looked as though it could not withstand another explosion. A large slab of rock heaved and strained at its fetters, letting loose a stream of pebbles.

"Watch out!" Tristan yelled. The loose stone was close to the door, right above Leila and Rusty. He bounded towards them, but he was not nearly close enough.

Just as the stone began to crack free, a wave of dense air crashed through the room, ringing in Tristan's ears like a silent thunderclap.

Everything went still.

The entire room might have been plunged underwater. The ceiling stilled and seemed to solidify once again, while the shards of rock still flying through the air slowed and dropped harmlessly to the ground.

The blast had come from the doorway. Hugging the wall, Tristan turned to see who had cast the spell. There stood Drakewell, face dark with fury, hands outstretched. Tristan backed away from the headmaster, fearing another attack, but Drakewell slumped against the wall, his face crumpling. Tristan remembered Delair's words—it was dangerous, very dangerous, to use magic without marbles, because it drained your body's energy. Drakewell had nearly crippled himself to keep everyone safe.

As Drakewell staggered forward, hand outstretched towards the enormous globe, Tristan realized that the headmaster had been accompanied by the most unlikely person imaginable. Slowly, nervously, Zeke stepped into the room.

"What have you done to the Map Room?" Drakewell asked faintly, failing at his usual icy tone.

The Map Room. That's very fitting.

Leila's eyes widened. "Oh my god, where's Merridy?"

Tristan whirled. The stone door behind him was now cracked open—in the momentary confusion, Merridy had slipped through.

Drawing a sharp breath, Tristan threw himself at the door and wrenched it open. He was still clutching his handful of marbles as though they would shield him from harm. One step past the door, Tristan tripped, his feet sliding out from beneath him. With a painful jolt, he crashed down two stairs. His hands flew open as he caught himself, and he dropped his fistful of marbles. As he jolted to a halt, the marbles continued to clatter down deeper and deeper, echoing eerily.

Heart pounding in his throat, Tristan staggered to his feet. From the light of the Map Room, he could see where he stood: on the third step of a narrow staircase spiraling down into darkness.

The stone door ground shut behind him, smothering the light. Tristan groped for the metal rail and eased his way down the stairs, stagnant air filling his lungs. Every second could be his last. He felt very naked without his handful of marbles.

A small metallic clink echoed from the depths of the room, followed by a blossom of light. Merridy's pale, determined face was thrown into relief by the lantern she held.

"You will not stop me, you know," she said steadily.

Tristan took a wary step forward. He had nearly reached the base of the stairs. "I thought you were training us to take your place. Why do you suddenly want to kill us instead?"

Merridy shook her head. "I had no more choice than you when I first came here. But this school is an evil place. Drakewell is a murderer, and the others are his accomplices."

She lifted her lantern so it cast light on the rest of the room. Behind her, a deep rift in the floor glittered softly. Tristan blinked. The pit was filled with thousands upon thousands of marbles.

"When this place is gone, it will be as though the school never existed. And you will thank me for it." Merridy's voice had grown stronger.

"I'll be dead," Tristan said flatly. "And so will Leila and Rusty and Amber. Alldusk too." He took another step down, his anger building. "I thought you loved Alldusk."

Merridy lowered her eyes. "That is why I must do this." Her hand shook slightly, sending rippling shadows across the wall, as she turned to the pool of marbles.

Tristan's head pounded. He wanted to attack Merridy, to throw her to the ground. Leila and Rusty were so close, so vulnerable. Even without the handful of marbles, Tristan could feel a dense, furious cloud of magic building within him, rippling with electricity. He raised an arm. *Too dangerous*, a small part of him whispered. He ignored the voice.

Recklessly, Tristan wrenched a tangle of raging magic from inside him. Then he brought his arm down and hurled the power at Merridy.

For a moment nothing happened. Merridy was about to fling her marble into the basin of accumulated magic— her shoulders tightened...

With a roar, an enormous ball of fire exploded to life over the pit of marbles.

Merridy screamed.

Crackling and spitting, the fireball hurtled forward. It slammed against the wall, flared white, and spun back at Merridy. As it flew, it shed a trail of flames.

The flames lashed out hungrily at Merridy, who spun out of the way just in time. Her sleeve caught fire; shrieking, she waved her arm in the air and dashed towards the spiral stairs.

Tristan lurched to the stairs and scrambled up just behind Merridy, fleeing his own fireball. Just as he reached the top, the fire snarled and flared blue and then spluttered out. Though the flames were still seared in Tristan's vision, nothing remained of the fire but the smell of charred fabric.

At the top of the stairs, Tristan threw open the door and doubled over coughing. The smoke raked at his lungs, and he squinted fiercely.

The Map Room was silent. Merridy had come to a halt beside the globe, and the others were frozen in place. Tristan wondered what they had heard.

Suddenly a white-hot pain lanced through Tristan's head. He swayed, dizzy and sick, and clutched at the wall.

Blearily he saw Leila and Rusty rushing to his side, and he nearly toppled forward when Leila grabbed his elbow to support him. Half-blind, he scratched at his face, fighting the pain, trying to rip its claws from his skull. The raw power was consuming him, crushing him, destroying him.

He wasn't strong enough for this.

Garbled voices drifted from the doorway; Tristan heard them as though listening with his head underwater. It was a moment before he could recognize words.

"—you had planned this from the start?" said Drakewell's muffled voice. "After working with us and living with us for fifteen years, you set out to destroy us?"

"Of course not," Merridy said shrilly. "But I began to change my mind when I spoke to you earlier this year. About myself and Alldusk, remember? You said you would kill any children of mine before they lived a day."

Tristan blinked hazily, trying to regain his footing.

From the other side of the globe, Alldusk groaned. "Darla, why didn't you talk to me? We could've found another way, we could've—"

"No," Merridy said coldly. "I can't believe I never questioned any of this before. But when Evangeline returned with two children nearly killed in Drakewell's avalanche—an avalanche that even you agreed had gone too far!—I knew I could no longer support such an evil, twisted cause."

Tristan rubbed at his sightless eyes until the wavering room came back into view. Something overhead was groaning and growling hungrily—cracks appeared along the length of the ceiling, and the rocks began to sag.

"Run!" Alldusk yelled, bounding towards the door.

Tristan tried to push Leila and Rusty away, hoping they would get out of the room while they still had a chance, but he was so weak they didn't seem to notice. For some reason Zeke had joined them near the globe.

Now the cracks on the ceiling had threaded over to the place where Tristan stood; the high stone vault snapped and began trickling dust.

Gasping, Tristan gripped Rusty's arm and staggered towards the door, tripping with each step. Merridy took one last look at Alldusk and fled through the splintered doorway. Drakewell lunged for her, but he was still too weak, and he fell to his knees.

Rusty reached the safety of the doorway and followed Drakewell and Alldusk into the dark tunnel.

"Triss!" Leila shrieked, yanking at his arm. "Hurry!"

Looking up, Tristan saw that a jagged slab of rock directly overhead was straining to break free. "I can't," he said, choking. "Go, I—"

Leila gave him a mighty shove forward. Tristan stumbled and collapsed; his shoulder slammed into the ground and was wrenched sideways. He moaned and shifted just in time to see the ceiling directly over Leila give way.

At the last second, Zeke dove on top of Leila, forcing them both to the ground. With a roar like thunder, the ceiling crashed down on top of them.

Chapter 22

The Natural Order

Triss?" Someone ran a gentle hand down Tristan's cheek, followed by a warm rag. Tristan stirred and opened his eyes, feeling very stiff and disoriented. To his surprise, the pain he remembered was almost gone.

"Where's Merridy?" he asked at once. His mouth was cottony and dry. Before he could ask for water, though, a glass was brought to his lips. Gulping gratefully at the cold water, Tristan looked sideways and realized that it was Leila standing beside his bed.

"Merridy got away, didn't she?" he said. "I couldn't control that fireball; I should've tried something less dramatic, maybe that would've—"

Leila pressed the glass back to his lips, cutting him off. "Oh, hush. Alldusk was talking to me while you were unconscious, and he said Merridy would have blown up the school if not for you. Honestly, the first thing you think of is apologizing…" Leila shook her head and wiped Tristan's forehead with the rag once more.

With a deep sigh, Tristan sat up and looked around. He was in Grindlethorn's hospital room; on a bed nearby lay Zeke, fast asleep. Tristan wasn't sure yet how he felt about everything that had transpired in the Map Room.

"Are you all right?" Tristan asked Leila, swinging his legs over the side of the bed. The last time he'd seen her, she had been crushed beneath a mountain of rocks.

Leila nodded. "I only got bruised a bit," she said quietly. "Zeke saved me—he took the worst of the impact."

Tristan blinked. He remembered seeing Zeke dive for Leila, but the whole scene had been a bit fuzzy. "Why'd he do that?" he whispered.

"No idea."

"What was he doing down there, anyway?"

Leila bit her lip. "I think he followed Alldusk, and Drakewell found him lurking in the hallway outside the Map Room."

They were silent for a moment. Tristan still felt a bit lightheaded.

"I bet Drakewell's furious at me," he remarked.

Leila shrugged. "He really can't blame you for anything except trespassing in the tunnels, and we would all be dead if you'd followed his orders." She reached for Tristan's hand and pulled him to his feet. "Come on; Rusty's waiting for us in the ballroom."

Zeke was the only one absent from dinner when Tristan and Leila arrived. A few of the teachers applauded when they noticed Tristan, though Drakewell and Alldusk remained grimly silent.

Tristan kept his eyes down as he crossed to his usual table. The teachers had a right to be furious with him; he had overstepped his boundaries in a dangerous way down in the Map Room.

"You okay?" Rusty asked when Tristan and Leila took their seats.

Tristan nodded, scanning the room for Evvie. Had she left with the twins and Merridy, or was she—Tristan did a double take when he saw Evvie at her table, pale and nervous-looking but definitely still there. It came as an even greater surprise when, noticing his gaze, she gave him a faint smile.

"What's happened?" Eli demanded, getting to his feet and edging towards Tristan. "People have been vanishing all day, now you three are all bloodied up, and the teachers haven't said any—"

"Settle down," Drakewell said coldly. As he addressed the room, his features regained their usual hard cast; he no longer appeared tired or weak. Eli slunk back to his seat, looking disgruntled.

Once the students had muttered themselves into silence, Drakewell cleared his throat and began.

"This afternoon, we discovered who was responsible for the destruction of Professor Alldusk's office, Professor Gracewright's greenhouse, and Professor Delair's mine."

Damian and Cassidy glanced angrily at Tristan.

"Regrettably, the vandal was revealed to be none other than Darla Merridy, who has fled the school."

Hayley and Cailyn exchanged shocked glances, and Eli

swore under his breath. Evvie twisted her hands in her lap, lips pursed.

"Tristan Fairholm, Leila Swanson, Rusty Lennox, and Brinley Alldusk were injured in their attempts to apprehend the vandal, and Zeke Elwood is likewise recovering in the hospital room."

Tristan looked up, startled. He couldn't believe the headmaster was going to let him off this easily.

"Is Zeke going to be okay?" Damian asked.

When Grindlethorn nodded, Damian's permanent scowl seemed to lessen somewhat.

"Now," Drakewell continued with a heavy voice, "it is time you learned why you were brought to this school. When you know the truth, you will understand why we kept it from you until now."

At this, every one of the students sat up straighter.

"You see, we are not teaching you magic merely to send you home, more intelligent than before. We are not hoping to enrich your minds or spread the knowledge of magic. Magic is dangerous; once you learn its secrets you must remain here."

"Then what's the point?" Damian asked peevishly.

Drakewell fixed his hollow eyes on Damian. "The reason you were recruited—the reason this stronghold exists—is because of something called 'the natural order.' The term refers to the balance of all dualities: civilization and nature, light and dark, life and death.

"The magicians who built this Lair chose the location for its inaccessibility. Magicians knew the value of wild places long before most humans, because magic is derived primarily from nature. With that understanding in mind, these magicians created a place where magic could be concentrated and used for greater purposes. Here they planned to maintain the ever-teetering duality of civilization and nature. Here they set the power of nature against humanity."

Leila's mouth opened in surprise. "Do you mean—"

Drakewell touched the black hourglass around his neck. "We have a room deep beneath these floors where we have stored up hundreds of thousands of magic orbs. This room—the Map Room—gives us the power to cause natural disasters. Using its magic, we can stir up hurricanes and tornadoes, send tremors through the earth, or trigger avalanches."

No one spoke. Tristan felt a strange pressure building against his eardrums. To hear Drakewell saying something like that, speaking so calmly—it was insane.

"The magicians who were here before us sent the shock wave that caused the Great San Francisco Earthquake, and started the drought that let the Dust Bowl ravage the plains."

"You're joking," Damian said finally, his voice hard.

Drakewell just stared at Damian for a long time; eventually Damian blinked and looked away, muttering something inaudible.

A hazy darkness was gathering at the corners of Tristan's eyes. He breathed in deeply through his nose, trying not to pass out. *The world's gone mad*, he thought with frightening calm. Just for good measure, he bit the inside of his cheek hard. *Definitely not dreaming.*

"That seems wrong," Rusty said anxiously.

Tristan was surprised that he managed to speak at all.

"I mean, killing all those people just for the sake of some idea about order…"

Tristan swallowed the blood that was now welling on the inside of his cheek. He wanted to nod in agreement with Rusty, to beg the teachers for an excuse—anything, anything at all—that would justify what they were doing here.

"We're not the only ones trying to manipulate this balance," Alldusk said. His voice was very calm, though his face remained ashen. When he got to his feet, Tristan noticed that his left arm was in a sling.

"There are others out there,' he continued, "people with no knowledge of magic, who are trying to outsmart nature and tip the balance in their favor. Look at genetic engineers—those scientists are playing with the very foundations of life. And what reason do they have to do this?"

Alldusk paused and met Rusty's indignant stare, though he did not seem to expect an answer.

"They want wealth. Long life. Health. Power. They're messing with the natural order because they're selfish. The human race is selfish." Alldusk shook his head. "We have a much harder task here—siding *with* nature *against* our own race. We maintain the order that is chaos, simply because we must."

Another long silence followed Alldusk's words.

Slowly, reluctantly, Tristan's thoughts were beginning to catch up with him. Right or wrong, his teachers—and hundreds of intelligent magicians before them—had been ravaging the earth with disasters for centuries. What he wouldn't give right now to forget everything Drakewell had just said...

Someone was speaking again, and Tristan realized he had been lost for several minutes. *Later*, he told himself. *I'll think about everything later.* He took another deep breath.

"—because the world holds itself together with magic," Drakewell was explaining impatiently. "Allow that to vanish, and the world will simply crumble. There will be nothing left but dust. In a way, we are preventing the complete annihilation of humanity by helping maintain the balance."

"What about the disasters that happened before this place existed?" Leila's expression was inscrutable.

"There have always been magicians playing around with the weather," Drakewell said. "The majority of them were causing plagues, floods, droughts, and the like for selfish reasons—war, riches, or mere curiosity. This establishment is the first place where those same powers have been directed towards creating and maintaining balance."

This time no one dared to voice any further misgivings. Tristan had managed to block out most of his thoughts, though one remained clear. If any single person could be allowed to decide the fate of so many, that person should rightfully be an angel or a demigod. And the teachers were far from either.

Drakewell let the silence linger, one thumb hooked through the hourglass chain circling his neck. At last he folded his arms over his chest and said, "If you have any further questions, go to one of your teachers. We will try to answer as best we can."

The side door opened as though on cue, and Quinsley leaned around the corner with a hopeful grin. "Dinnertime, headmaster?"

Drakewell gave a curt nod and spun on his heel. He was nearly at the ballroom doors when he stopped and turned. "Fairholm!" he barked. "Come here."

Tristan started.

"Go on," Leila whispered, prodding him in the side. "You have to tell him that you're innocent; he can't lock you up, not without setting half the school against him."

Still dazed, Tristan stumbled to his feet and walked stiffly towards Drakewell.

"I'm sorry, Professor," he said, refusing to meet Drakewell's eyes. "I thought Ev—Evangeline had something to do with the attacks all along, but I didn't say anything. I was afraid you'd hurt her. Please, if you have to punish me, leave Amber alone. She hasn't done anything wrong."

Drakewell straightened. "Quiet, Fairholm," he said tiredly. "It would be absurd to blame you for any of this."

Tristan blinked in surprise.

"No, I merely wished to say that you and Amber

Ashton will have a very special job next year. When summer is over, you two will begin overseeing my work in the Map Room."

Suddenly Tristan understood. This was why the other teachers seemed to fear Drakewell, why he insisted they could not do without him. He worked the Map Room. He was the one actually creating the disasters.

"Professor, did you know from the start that I would be good with magic?"

Drakewell's eyes glinted with malicious humor. "Oh, yes. Strange, isn't it, to feel an earthquake in North Dakota?"

Tristan went cold. Before he could ask another question, though, Drakewell spoke once more.

"Just so you know, your mother would be overjoyed to have you home for the summer. She was furious to hear she was denied visitation rights at the detention center."

This time when Tristan opened his mouth in horrified protest, Drakewell turned and closed the ballroom doors firmly in his face.

Tristan just stood there, frozen, rage boiling within him. He wanted to chase after Drakewell, to attack him with his bare hands, but his legs had turned to jelly. At last he turned, dizzy and nauseous, and made his way back to the table.

He was more unsettled than ever. The person he had been a year ago would have put a bullet in Drakewell's head, never mind the consequences. He was still half-tempted to run after the headmaster and strangle him.

"Tristan?" Leila's voice cut into his thoughts, and he struggled to focus on her freckled nose. "You're not in trouble, are you?"

Tristan shook his head numbly. "No. No, Drakewell doesn't blame me at all."

With a joyful yelp, Leila flung her arms around Tristan. He cringed and nearly lost his balance. His head was still spinning.

Despite everything, final exams began the following day as planned. Tristan was determined not to think about the Map Room until he had time alone, so he threw himself into last-minute studying. The other students were avoiding the topic just as doggedly, though Tristan often caught sideways glances from people like Cailyn and Eli. Over the next few days, he found himself feeling unexpectedly fond of every student in the Lair—well, except perhaps Damian. They were in this together.

Zeke was back at breakfast that morning, managing to look haughty and self-confident even on crutches. One of his legs was fully encased in a white cast, and his face was covered in gauze pads and medical tape.

As soon as Leila saw Zeke, she rose and crossed to his table. Hands on her hips, she said, "Why did you save me?" Her voice carried easily to Tristan and Rusty, as did Zeke's reply.

"Your face is ugly enough without getting all smashed up."

Leila's back was to Tristan, so he couldn't see her face.

"I could steal your crutches, you know."

Zeke ignored her threat. "I, on the other hand, have such a handsome face that the scars just make me look fierce." He bared his teeth at her and then grinned.

"All I can see are bandages," Leila said. "Those are *really* fierce, you know. Awfully attractive, too."

Zeke just laughed.

Shaking her head, Leila rejoined Tristan and Rusty.

Their final exams were no more difficult than Tristan had feared. The practical tests for Brikkens, Alldusk, and Delair involved performing simple spells, all of which seemed inconsequential in comparison with the magic Tristan had unleashed in the Map Room. Gracewright and Grindlethorn's tests were more difficult, and Tristan was sure he'd forgotten or confused most of his terms; the best thing he could say about those tests was that they were over.

Alldusk had been gloomy and quiet ever since Merridy's betrayal. Had he forgiven Merridy, or was he still furious?

Once exams were over, there was a single week remaining before the students went home. The weather was beautiful, so Tristan and his friends spent most of each day outside, swimming in the icy lake, exploring the woods, and telling stories around a bonfire in the clearing.

One evening, as everyone was heading up for dinner, Evvie stopped Tristan and asked to speak to him. When the Subroom was empty aside from the two of them, she said, "I wanted to—er—to thank you."

"For what?" Tristan was startled.

"You let me go," Evvie said. "You could've brought me to Drakewell; you could've told him about the twins and about how I've been sneaking around all these months. But you didn't."

Tristan just blinked, confused but gratified. Had she known all along that he'd been covering for her?

"Oh, and thank you for that diversion."

Tristan made a face at her. "Very funny." He hadn't forgotten the fifty hours of punishment he'd spent rebuilding the entryway. "By the way, what about Merridy? Is she safe? Are the kids okay?"

Evvie nodded. "They're heading for Darla's sister's house. Darla wanted to leave a message for Alldusk, I think, but she didn't have time."

"Alldusk is upset enough already," Tristan said. He dug his toe under the corner of a rug. "You go up without me. I'll come in a moment."

Evvie turned and made her way to the door; she had put one foot through the Prasidimum barrier when Tristan said, "By the way, do you still hate me?"

Evvie smiled at him. "We'll see." Then she vanished through the barrier.

Feeling somewhat happier than before, Tristan sank into his favorite armchair and stared at the shadowed hearth. Maybe it was better that he knew the truth. Sitting at home, he was useless against disasters; he was one person, one lone body, standing against all the fickle whims of nature. Here, knowing what was behind everything, he had a chance to finally understand.

Tristan sighed and slumped deeper into the chair. With knowledge came sadness, but also power—he would learn what he could, waiting and watching, and maybe someday he could change things. Either way, he should try to be happy here. This was his home.

With a glance at the row of messy mattresses shoved against the Subroom wall, Tristan got to his feet and made his way up to the ballroom where his friends were waiting.

The day before they would fly home, Leila packed a picnic lunch and joined Tristan and Rusty outside. They walked for a ways, enjoying the warmth of the late spring, until they passed the edge of the trees and came to a narrow meadow that hugged the mountain slope.

"Amber told me about this place," Tristan said. The meadow was brilliant green and peppered with delicate alpine blossoms.

"I'll have to thank her," Leila said. She spread out a blanket and set the bag of food in the center. Then she sat cross-legged and leaned back, staring up at the sky.

Rusty dropped to his knees beside her. "I'm gonna miss you guys so much. What d'you think you'll be doing here, Leila?"

She would be staying at the Lair over the summer, along with six other students.

"No idea," she said. "They'll probably have us cleaning and fixing up the Map Room."

"What do we have for lunch?" Tristan asked, taking a

seat. He didn't want to talk about the summer; he was getting nervous about seeing his mom again. In her position, Tristan wasn't sure he would forgive himself.

Leila drew out three rolled napkins. "You're as bad as Rusty," she said. "Quinsley made burritos, and I brought extra guacamole."

"Excellent." Rusty reached for one.

At the edge of the clearing, a pair of foxes scampered out of the trees and bounded through the swaying grasses. Tristan unwrapped his burrito and took a bite, refusing to think about anything else. The burrito was still warm, sharp with cilantro and onions; he leaned back on one hand and took another bite, listening to the distant trill of birdsong.

"I asked Quinsley, you know," Leila said distractedly. "About how this school was really founded."

"You mean it's not that story about the magician princes building a kingdom?" Rusty was grinning.

Leila sat up straighter. "This place was created by a group of European magicians who came to the Americas in the early seventeenth century. Like Drakewell said, their magic was powered by nature, and at this point Europe was getting so crowded that the magicians could only do simple spells. When they saw the native populations here being ravaged by disease and war, the magicians were afraid that the Americas would soon become just like Europe. That was why they built the Map Room, and why they started worrying about their 'natural order.'"

"I liked your version better," Tristan said. "More mysterious." He took another bite of his burrito.

Rusty sighed happily. "Too bad we can't spend all our time like this." He plucked a stray grain of rice from his shirt and flicked it away. "I wish we could send letters this summer."

Tristan snorted. "*We* can send each other letters, genius. It's just Leila who can't get mail." At the thought of his mother's house, Tristan felt another wave of apprehension.

Leila shrugged. "I've got something better for you guys. You won't miss getting letters, I promise."

"What is it?" Tristan asked eagerly, peering into the picnic bag. Ever since the fight in the Map Room two weeks ago, Leila had spent her evenings scribbling away at something in a notebook. Tristan hoped this was what she referred to.

"Hey!" Leila tugged the bag closed. "You'll just have to wait and see."

After eating their fill of watermelon slices and gooey, fudgy brownies, Tristan, Leila, and Rusty lay back on the blanket with their heads together, staring up at the frail white clouds.

"This place is just so beautiful," Leila sighed. She touched Tristan's hand with one finger and then clasped her hands over her stomach. "Even if we weren't forced to stay here, I think I'd want to live up in these mountains forever. I wish I could paint, or something like that. There's something really romantic about painting the mountains."

Tristan laughed. "Maybe that's what you can do this summer. Then we'll have something to decorate the

Subroom with once we're back."

"Yeah, that'd be awesome!"

Leila snorted. "Unlikely. I'm about as artistic as a worm."

"I've met some awfully artistic worms," Rusty said, his mouth twitching.

At last the sun dropped towards the jagged ridge and the air began to cool; reluctantly they gathered the remains of their lunch and headed back to the Lair.

It took Tristan less than five minutes to pack the entirety of his belongings into his backpack. He was leaving most of his books and school supplies in the Subroom. As he was shaking out his blankets just to be sure he hadn't forgotten anything, something fell free and clattered on the ground. Kneeling, Tristan picked up the broken watch he'd brought from home all those months ago. He had been a different person then, shattered and empty after Marcus's death. Now he had friends and a place, however disturbing, where he truly belonged. He no longer recognized the specter from juvie.

With a sigh he pocketed the watch.

Everyone hiked down to the runway when it was time for the plane to leave—all of the teachers came, and Leila and the six remaining students joined them as well.

"Okay, these are for you guys," Leila said, pulling two notebooks from her bag. "Don't read them until you get home. And don't get too excited; they aren't much."

Tristan hugged her fiercely. "Thank you so much. I'll

miss you."

"We'll be back before you realize we're gone," said Rusty, hugging Leila as well. "Don't let the others bother you." He nodded at Eli, Amber, Cailyn, Damian, Finley, and Ryan, who would be staying with her over the summer. If Tristan had to guess, he would say Damian and Ryan hadn't been given a choice.

"Ha," Leila said. "Don't worry about me."

On the tiny plane, Tristan and Rusty fought over the window seat; Rusty won, so Tristan had to stand up to wave goodbye to Leila.

Evvie was the first to be dropped off, followed by Tristan. When Tristan made his way to the front of the plane, grinning at everyone, Quinsley opened the door to the cockpit and pressed a wad of cash into his hand. "It's for a taxi," he said. "See you in August!"

Tristan nodded blankly and climbed down the ladder to the deserted runway. He stood motionless, watching as the plane reversed and then sped into the air once again. He felt very small and out-of-place. For a long time he could not bring himself to move, watching the sky as though searching for something he could not quite put his finger on. This place was so empty, so barren, and Tristan felt as if every ounce of vitality had been dredged from him. He could have collapsed on the spot.

Ages passed before Tristan realized what had unsettled him.

The bleak concrete expanse was devoid of magic.

Though he had not noticed it while living in the rugged

mountains, Tristan had become so aware of the auras permeating the forest that he had come to rely on the presence of magic. It filled him, heightening his senses and expanding his awareness of the world.

Here he could feel nothing, and the absence was jarring.

Summoning the last of his energy, Tristan stumbled to the airport entrance in search of a taxi. While he rode into town, past busy intersections and rows of matching houses, he tried to adjust to the uncomfortable lack of magic. There was no wilderness here, nothing to sustain the fragile power.

Now Tristan knew exactly why Drakewell had allowed him to return home for the summer. After his complete immersion in the world of magic, he could hardly recognize this city. It was ugly and empty, and Tristan wanted nothing to do with it.

Already he wished he could return to the Lair.

Before he knew it, Tristan was veering down a vaguely familiar tree-lined street; his mom's house was at the end, completely dwarfed by the mansions looming on either side. Her front lawn was already brown and withered.

"You can let me off here," he told the driver, handing over the cash from Quinsley. "Keep the change." Then he slung his backpack over one shoulder and strode up the path to his mom's front door.

He had to knock several times before she answered. At last he heard footsteps clicking towards the door, and it swung open. There was his mom, thinner and sterner than he remembered, but unmistakably familiar.

For a split second, Tristan wondered if his mother would recognize him. His hair was long, half of his face was torn up with scars, and he probably looked a lot more serious than before. Then his mother gasped.

"Oh my god." Eyes widening, she grabbed Tristan's arm and pulled him into a clumsy embrace, where she started sobbing onto his shoulder. "Tristan, my Tristan. Where have you been?"

Tristan's eyes stung, and he patted her awkwardly on the back. Had she forgotten what he'd done? At last he was able to lead her inside, closing the door behind him. "Are you okay, Mom?" He guided her to a kitchen stool.

Hiccupping softly, she nodded. "Oh, my baby. I can't believe you've come home."

"It's just for the summer," Tristan warned her, but she didn't seem to hear.

It was a long time before his mom calmed down enough to show Tristan where he would be staying. He would sleep in the basement, in the room he and Marcus had shared when they'd stayed with her in the past.

"It's such a mess, I know; I'll clean it out just as soon as—"

"It's fine, Mom. Really. Don't worry." Tristan set down his backpack and moved a dusty box off the bed. "You go back to whatever you were doing; I'll be up in a moment." Right now he wanted to be alone, to have space to think. He was so confused and overwhelmed that he hardly knew what to say.

Nodding, his mom hugged him once again and dabbed at her eyes. "I'll make your favorite lasagna for dinner tonight, okay? We'll have a feast, you and I."

Tristan swallowed hard.

Once his mom had left, Tristan closed the door to the tiny, drab basement and sat down on the old bed. Pulling open his backpack, he drew out the notebook Leila had given him and opened it to the first page. The familiar handwriting was like a draught of cold water to soothe his nerves.

It began with a letter. As he flipped through the pages, he realized that there was a different letter for every few days of the summer. Kicking off his shoes, he crossed his legs and began to read.

Dear Tristan,

I wrote these letters just so you'd remember that I'll be thinking of you all through this long summer. You're only allowed to read one a day, so no looking ahead. I hope you enjoy yourself; I can only imagine how weird it must feel to return home after everything that's happened to us.

When I think of you, I'll picture the crazy magician who grew a tree in the middle of our classroom and blew up the door of the Map Room. If I really miss you, though, I'll just think about how much fun we had decorating Christmas cookies and roasting marshmallows.

Tomorrow I'll bake you a batch of chocolate chip cookies and eat them all myself. Then you'll wish you hadn't abandoned me here. Just kidding.

Anyway, I can't wait for August. Have a wonderful summer.

Love,
Leila

Smiling, Tristan lay back on his bed and hugged the notebook to his chest. The Lair was still there, hundreds of miles away. Here he was a criminal; there he was a *magician*. It felt strange thinking of himself that way, but he had proved himself, and next year Drakewell would teach him the secrets of the Map Room.

Besides, Leila and Rusty and Amber and all of the others understood exactly how he felt. No matter what this summer brought, he had a family waiting for him on the other side.

The end

About the Author

R.J. Vickers is the author of the Natural Order series, as well as *Beauty's Songbook*, a Beauty and the Beast retelling, and *College Can Wait!*, a gap year guidebook for reluctant students.

When she's not writing, you can find her hiking, traveling, taking photos, and crocheting.

Though she grew up in Colorado, she now lives with her husband in New Zealand.

You can find her online at rjvickers.com.

Also by R.J. Vickers

The Natural Order series

The Natural Order
Rogue Magic
Lost Magic
The Final Order

The Kinship Thrones world

The Fall of Lostport
Hunter's Legend

Standalone Works

Beauty's Songbook
College Can Wait!

Made in the USA
San Bernardino, CA
23 November 2019

60351695R00239